Kaylyn's Story
Book 1:
Dragon's Guardian

Kristin Stecklein

Southern Prairie Library System
421 N. Hudson St.
Altus, OK 73521

ISBN: 1535133600
ISBN-13:9781535133609

CONTENTS

ACKNOWLEDGMENTS

My thanks and appreciation goes to:

My family – For reading the continual support and helping me to find new fans.

Angela – For always keeping it interesting and fun.

My friends and fans – For choosing my books when I know there are millions more out there. Thank you for your feedback and excitement. I always love hearing about how you're impatiently waiting for the next.

Chapter 1

"Behave, Kaylyn," I muttered to myself, stalking across the rocky ground. I kicked a stone moodily, glaring at the scenery I would have otherwise appreciated. I was at the edge of the Esperion Mountains, the mountain range that ran from the north part of Centralia to the western deserts. I'd followed the mountain range in the distance until the dirt had started to turn to rock, then followed the shadows westward. The sun was starting to sink behind the mountains, turning the sky a glorious series of colors that I wasn't in the mood to enjoy.

"Act like a lady, Kaylyn." I continued to mutter blackly. "You need to catch a husband someday. You don't want to be an old maid, do you?" I kicked another stone. "As if turning thirteen makes me an old maid."

The horse whickered behind me. I glared at it a moment, in case it was mocking me, then went back to grab a torch, items for making a fire, and a sack of soft powder from the carriage the horse had pulled. Inside was a trunk of clothes, a pack with a dwindling food supply, and various items I hadn't wanted to leave behind. The horse's food was on top of the carriage.

"So what if I've never had a suitor? They'd rather have my sisters anyway. Maybe I *don't* want to get married. I apparently wouldn't make a good wife anyway." I slammed the end of the torch into the soft ground, then proceeded to light a fire, grimly satisfied. Here was something that my sisters and my mother couldn't manage to do. I could at least do something as simple as lighting a fire far better than they ever could. And since it was the end of February, I'd need that skill to keep warm.

The fire lit, I opened the sack of green-colored powder and sprinkled some of the power onto the fire. The delight of watching the flames turn green, grow stronger with the momentary flare then fade back to the warm colors of a fire never ceased to interest me. Amina, my only friend, had spent four hours with me, playing with green powder, watching the different shades it turned as more or less of the powder was dropped in. The only real danger was making sure the flames didn't grow so high they caught my clothing on fire. That was less of a worry for me because my sleeves only just covered my shoulders. If anyone else had seen me, I'd have been in trouble. The top was obviously too small for me, because any appearance of shoulders was scandalous. The flames couldn't have caught my hair, which I'd cut half an hour away from home. My black hair now swung just above my shoulders. My hair hadn't been that short since I'd been a child. If my mother ever saw me, she'd hide me away until my hair reached an acceptable length again.

"I guess I'm hopeless," I said, feeling more peaceful as I watched the flames turn an emerald shade. "Which is why I'm never going back. You won't miss me anyway." I gave a mocking curtsey to an invisible gentleman. "Oh, yes, I think all women have a duty to bear eight children," I said with syrupy sweetness. "And that women shouldn't risk waiting to marry in case they turn eighteen and become spinsters. Hah!" I made a derisive noise. "I'd rather be a spinster." I stuck my hand in the bag to grab more powder. "And I will never marry for money."

I'd played with the green powder for maybe five minutes when a roar startled me. The sound was so huge and so foreign it could only have been one thing.

"Dragon," I breathed, scrambling to my feet. Although dragons lived in the Esperion Mountains, people rarely saw them. Those that did encounter a dragon almost always came away with a story of their near death. I didn't care how dangerous it was; I had to see a dragon.

There came another roar, and this time I could clearly understand the anger in the sound. I was more careful as I climbed up the rocky ledge to peer curiously over the edge, then froze in horror.

3

There was a huge, white dragon on the ground, one wing furled, the other looking as if it had been stepped on by some huge being. The dragon was curled, hissing in defiance, roaring in pain and anger at the dozens of brown wyverns overhead. Some had landed, but those were more endangered. All dragons could blow flame and the long neck allowed them to twist it in any direction. I watched the dragon send flame at an overeager wyvern in front, and the creature shrieked, trying to escape its death without success. For all that wyverns looked like dragons, they were far stupider. They were also smaller, so the dragon had the advantage of bulk. Wyverns were roughly the size of a horse and their tails were short and stubby. Adult dragons were usually more than three times their size with long tails like their necks. However, the number of wyverns gave them the advantage; they were winning.

I wanted to help, but hesitated. I couldn't fight this many wyverns. I wasn't sure I could manage one wyvern, but the dragon was outnumbered. The wyverns were screeching what I could only describe as a victory cry as they swooped down again and again to lash out at the dragon who was unable to fly to escape them. I wasn't big enough or good enough to handle all of these beasts, but I could make them think I could. Wyverns were easily confused. They'd attacked near my home often enough that I knew their biggest weakness…fire.

I raced back to grab the torch, the sack, and my bow and quiver of arrows. Using the green powder, I sprinkled a little on each arrow, then dipped the arrowhead into the torch a second before firing. As the arrows went through the air, they burst into green flame, growing larger before plunging into my target. I didn't always hit the wyverns, but I made sure I would never hit the dragon. Those that had landed took flight, searching for their new attacker. And suddenly I realized that they would be coming after me.

I screamed in terror as one of them came for me. I instinctively scrambled for the torch, dropping everything as I dove to avoid the swipe by the wyvern. It swooped overhead, screeching angrily, unwilling to risk the searing burn of fire. Grabbing for my bow, I knocked it over the edge of the cliff and watched it plummet to the ground with dismay.

I felt something that I could only describe as a sigh in my mind, as if the world had given up that I was good for anything.

"Oh, shut up!" I shouted, and grabbed the sack, plunging my hand in and throwing a handful of powder at the torch. The flames flared and turned bright green as the mass of powder hit it, and the wyvern that had dived down for me swerved, panicked at the sight of an unnaturally colored fire, and slammed into the ground farther away.

Interest was now in my mind, interest that wasn't mine. Fear didn't allow me to think about that oddity. I grabbed my quiver and slung it on my back before I picked up my torch and scrambled down. Two more flares of green powder kept the wyverns off me until I managed to get to my bow. I shot another arrow lit with green fire at the wyverns above me, then raced towards the safety of the dragon, stopping momentarily to send another arrow towards the wyverns. I was fumbling to string the next arrow as much as my hands shook, but the bright flare of green flame was enough to keep them away. I just hoped the dragon didn't decide I was an enemy too and engulf me in flame next.

The dragon adjusted around something as I got closer. *"You shoot badly."*

My arm jerked on this shot, sending it miraculously into a wyvern. The dragon had spoken in my mind, and the sensation was shocking. A flood of information suddenly followed those words. The dragon was a female. She was angry. She didn't like me. She respected my bravery. She had something she had to protect. And there was a feeling of despair I didn't understand.

She spoke again, her voice critical and dry. *"You do better when you are supposed to do worse."*

"You're welcome," I retorted, voice shaking and ruining any attempt at bravery I'd shown. "Can you flame?" I fumbled for the sack of powder.

"Throw the bag."

5

I hadn't meant to use the entire bag, but I obeyed and threw it up in the air towards the most wyverns. The dragon tipped her head back and sent a stream of flame in the air. The bag caught fire and exploded into green flame, catching most of the wyverns as the powder spread and flamed. Those that survived scattered. Those that didn't fell to the ground as burning heaps. The area was suddenly silent except for the crackle of flames.

I sank to my knees, shaky. My body trembled with adrenaline and fear. "Are you okay? Are you...oh, geez," I whispered. There was a large gash across her chest, the softer skin not covered by scales, and blood, it could only be blood even though it was black, was dripping down over her scales. I could now hear that she wasn't breathing well. "I...I..." I knelt helplessly. "Is there anything I can do?"

The dragon stared me down. To my astonishment, I saw her eyes changing color; flickering, deepening, the eyes always on me. I'd heard stories about dragons' eyes changing, but always that they went their deepest red just before flaming. I watched for red cautiously.

"Human, if I asked you for something, would you do it? Something that would ensure the life of another?"

I nodded slowly, wondering what it was.

"Do you have someone you can trust? Someone who can help you?"

I thought of my brother. "Maybe. I don't know what I'm doing so I don't know..."

"I have an egg," she said bluntly. *"And I am going to die."*

My mind immediately tried to reject that thought. Dragons didn't just *die*. I couldn't name three instances I'd heard of a dragon being killed, not that could be proved anyway. But with her injuries, I knew nothing else could survive. And I suddenly understood the feeling of despair. She knew what was coming. I swallowed hard. "Where do you want me to take the egg? Where would I find other dragons?"

"Not other dragons." Her gaze never left mine. *"You must raise my young one."*

6

"Me?" I squeaked. "You want *me* to raise a dragon? I can't! No one knows anything about dragons! And I don't know what to feed it or…"

"I will tell you. I will only be able to tell you once. Then you must take my egg and go." She shifted, showing the shimmering, pale egg.

"It's nearly as tall as I am," I said despairingly.

"You must find a way. The wyverns will be back."

"Don't you have a…a husband or something? Someone I can go find?"

"My mate is dead," she answered. *"And any dragon would kill you on sight."* She let out a groan, a deep sound that frightened me. *"You are young, are you not? For a human?"*

I nodded, heart in my throat. "Thirteen. I just turned thirteen day before yesterday."

"Young. But old enough. I have heard stories of girls marrying at your age."

"Yes, but not many, and it's not really that way anymore. We marry at fifteen now, and sometimes at fourteen."

"Such a difference," the dragon said in amusement.

"Most don't marry until they're sixteen," I continued, hoping she'd understand. "I won't be a good caretaker for your baby. Surely there's some way to help you."

"There is not. You let fear stop you from seeing the truth. Without a parent, my baby will die. It is less than a week from hatching. Do you have a way to take my egg somewhere safe?"

I thought of the carriage over the hill. "Yes," I whispered.

Her tail curved around, pushed me closer so that I was trapped under the gaze of those soul-searching eyes. *"Will you swear to me now that you will take care of my hatchling? Will you swear to protect it from your kind and raise it?"*

My eyes filled with tears. This great creature knew she was going to die and she was focused only on saving her egg. "Yes. I swear. I swear I'll take care of him. Her. Whatever it is. I'll take care of it the best I can."

7

She let out a great cough, curled tighter around the egg a moment, then relaxed. *"Get what you have brought. I will help you as much as I can."*

I raced away, up the rocky outcrop to the carriage. The horse needed a little coaxing and a lot of pushing to get him to the dragon. I'd covered his eyes so he couldn't see, but what he could smell didn't encourage him to move. He tried to rear up twice and I fought to keep him steady, talking soothingly and trying to keep him calm. The dragon simply watched until I got the horse and the little carriage around near the egg. She managed to get a paw under the egg, and together we pushed it inside. I wasn't sure how I'd get it out, but decided that would be much later.

"The egg must be warm," the dragon said. *"Not hot, but warm. You must speak to it constantly. It does not know you. If it does not recognize your voice, it will harm you. It does not recognize you as a friend, or a caretaker. I have tried to tell it that you will protect it, but I cannot be sure it will not harm you."*

"Is it rational?" I asked, thinking of human children.

"It is. Dragons are born smarter than humans. It will know how to speak as I speak. It will know and remember whatever it hears through its shell. It will know that you are not a dragon and so you must be careful."

I nodded.

"It will be hungry. Hatching is the best time to gain its trust. You must show you can care for it. Have food ready when the hatching begins. It must be able to get to the food on its own. Feed it meat, small pieces so it does not choke. Liquids. Milk with honey. You must never feed it cooked meat."

"Won't raw meat make it sick?"

"Semi-cooked. Never fully cooked. Dragons must eat raw meat. You must cook it a little for the first month. Then lessen it. By the second month, it should only eat raw meat. It will not be able to flame until after the first year. You must teach it how to fly. You must oil it or the skin will crack and bleed and the scales will fall off. If the scales are discolored, it is a sign of sickness. Some human medicines will work. Some will poison it. Always test it before."

"How?"

"Use a scale holding a little blood; mix the medicines with the blood and put it on the scales. If either is discolored, it is not safe for dragons. Clean the dragon often. Dirty dragons will become sick and lose scales."

I listened to everything she told me, trying desperately to commit this to memory. I asked questions and listened for almost an hour. Finally, her eyes closed wearily. *"That is all I can do. Take my egg. Go."*

I didn't know this dragon, but I didn't want to leave it out here. "Is there anything I can do? Some way to help you?"

"No, human."

"Please, give me something to try." I stepped towards her.

She let out a growl, her eyes snapping open. I saw they were bright red. *"Go, human. Now."*

I backed away quickly, tears stinging my eyes. "My name is Kaylyn, not human."

"Kaylyn? It is a silly human name."

"Well, it's the name of the human who's going to be raising your son or daughter, so get used to it." I wiped my eyes. "What should I name the baby?"

"It is your choice. It must be like dragon names."

"I don't know any dragon names."

"Two parts. Skywind. Crystalwing. Blackfury." Her eyes closed again. *"If you look, you will find names of dragons. Humans keep records of dragons because they fear us. Now go."*

I obeyed this time, knowing she'd never let me get close. I turned the horse and walked it away from the dragon.

As I reached the top of the hill, her voice, fainter, resounded in my mind. *"Tell my hatchling I was Rosewing, and my mate was Courageheart."*

"I will," I thought back, not knowing if she would hear me like this. There wasn't a reply.

From inside the carriage, from the egg, there came a sound. Fear. Curiosity. It made me think of a child calling for its mother.

"Everything will be okay," I told it, tears stinging my eyes again. "I know I'm not much, but I'll take care of you now." Behind me, the sun slowly set, casting us into darkness.

Chapter 2

I traveled slowly so as not to disturb the egg, speaking to it the entire way, long into the night. I headed for the only place I knew to go; the School for Officers and Gentlemen. My brother went to school there and was a corporal in Centralia's army. By the time I finally reached the School's grounds, my throat was hoarse, I desperately wanted water. and I was wickedly tired. The tension didn't help. I had no idea what to say if anyone caught me.

The gate bearing Centralia's old standard of four symbols on a red and blue shield was unlocked. It wasn't supposed to be, but I opened it and led the horse and carriage inside. From there, I quickly reached the area where the recruits enrolled here slept, and called up in a whisper-shout. "Warren! *Warren!*"

A face quickly appeared at the window. "Mary Beth?" a boy whispered eagerly. "You were supposed to be here hours ago!"

My eyes narrowed. "I'm *not* one of your floozies! Where's Warren?"

The boy squinted at me. "Aw, it's *you*," he complained.

Before I woke anyone up by shouting at the boy, my brother, always a light sleeper, popped up at the window. "Kaylyn, what are you doing here?" he hissed. "We've been looking for you for two days!"

"Warren, I need help!"

"Great," I caught him muttering. "What have you done this time?"

"Warren, *please*," I begged.

He dragged his fingers through his black hair. "I'll get caught if I come down there."

"I bet you wouldn't have worried about that with Mary Beth!" I hissed up. "Or another one of your painted women."

11

"Hey, Mary Beth's not like that!" the boy defended.

"She's not a call girl," Warren hissed back at me. "She's a good girl!"

"I bet *Mother* would approve! After all, she taught me and my sisters that *good* girls showed up at a *boy's* school in the middle of the night!"

"You're here now, aren't you?" Warren pointed out.

"Because I need help! Warren, this is *important*!"

He made a sound of frustration. I waited. Not only would no one care once they figured out what I had, but he'd risk worse than punishment for me.

He heaved a loud sigh that echoed off the stone. "Stay there!" he ordered in a whisper. "I'll be right down."

I didn't stay. I guided the tired horse to the entrance and spoke to the egg. "My brother's coming," I told it. "My brother, Warren. He'll help us. He'll know what to do."

The door creaked softly open and Warren came sneaking out. "Kaylyn, where have you been?" he hissed. "Your sisters have been worried *sick*..."

"I went to the mountains," I whispered. "And I saw this dragon being attacked by wyverns and so..."

"You saw a dragon?" Curiosity overrode Warren's anger a moment. His brown eyes, the same color as mine, were bright with excitement, erasing the tired lines. "What did it look like?"

"She was hurt really badly." Tears came to my eyes again. "I think she's dead by now, Warren."

"She? How do you know it was a she?"

"I helped chase the wyverns off. She had an egg, and she made me promise to take care of it. So I have this dragon egg that's going to hatch soon, and I don't know what to do with it."

Warren was absolutely silent, gaping at me. Then he shook his head. "Kaylyn, what have you gotten into this time?" He felt my forehead. "I *told* you Amina wasn't someone to hang out with. What did she get into?"

"No, Warren!" I yanked his hand away and dragged him over to the carriage, pointing. "It's a dragon egg," I whispered. "And I'm supposed to raise the dragon inside it. What do I do?"

Warren stood still a moment, then hesitantly reached out and touched the egg, running his fingers over the shell lightly. From inside came a growling sound and the egg rocked. Warren yanked his hand back. "It's really a dragon egg," he whispered in awe.

"I *told* you it was!"

He didn't move a moment, then he shook his head. "Stay here," he ordered. "I'll be right back." And he took off into the darkness.

"I'm sorry," I told the dragon inside. "I didn't know you could tell if others touched the shell. I didn't know he would. If we're going to get you out of the carriage, they're going to have to touch your egg. We can't move you any other way. I promise they'll be careful. I promise they won't hurt you."

A strange sound came from the egg, but was momentary and no other sounds came.

My brother came back quickly with someone else. I recognized him, despite the fact he wasn't wearing anything to display his status as a noble or as second in command at the School. "Lieutenant Marcell, I need someplace warm for my dragon egg," I said, hoping I sounded forceful and not desperate and tired.

Lieutenant Marcell was a calm man, and I'd rarely seen him anything but calm. At the sight of the dragon egg he came to a halt, then slowly walked around the carriage, studying the egg inside. He'd taken the time to dress and wore a white tunic, brown pants, and boots. When he reached for the egg, I cried, "Don't!" I immediately flushed as he paused. "I...I'm sorry, sir, but it doesn't like its egg being touched."

He pulled his hand back and turned to face me. "How did you get this egg, Miss Madara?"

"The mother was dying and gave it to me."

"You didn't steal it?"

"I wouldn't steal an egg!" I protested. "And I'm not stupid enough to steal from a dragon! Rosewing *gave* the egg to me and told me I had to be its mother!"

"Calm down, Miss Madara; I had to check. Corporal, go raise the captain. He'll need to know about this."

I shivered. The night had gotten cold. Instinctively, I reached for the egg, feeling it. It was cooler than before. "I need to get the egg someplace warm," I said again as my brother took off again. "Please, Lieutenant. Rosewing said it had to be kept warm."

"Of course. Let's start with the stables. Your horse is tired. We'll move the egg from there when we get the chance." He took the reins and guided the horse forward. I walked beside the carriage to the stables. It was slightly warmer inside. As Lieutenant Marcell unhitched the horse and led it to an open stall, I slid inside the carriage. "We're in a stable right now," I told the egg. "Where the horses stay."

"Can the dragon hear you?" Lieutenant Marcell asked as he latched the door to the stall.

"Yes, sir. The mother said so. She said I had to talk to it so the hatchling would know me."

"Hatchling? She called it that?"

I nodded.

"And she said the dragon was about to hatch?"

"Less than a week."

"Where did you find this dragon?"

"In the mountains, sir. Being attacked by wyverns."

"And she gave you the egg?"

"She said she was dying. She was hurt really badly. Her blood was…black, like a wyvern's."

Lieutenant Marcell offered his hand. "You're hurt," he said gently. "Let me look at those injuries."

"Injuries?" Puzzled, I looked at my arms. There were red splotches that I was only now beginning to realize hurt. I'd been so intent on making the horse walk, and walk in the direction I wanted, and I'd been so tired that I hadn't noticed. "Oh."

He gently took one hand and helped me down from the carriage as if I were a lady coming to a ball. "Burns?"

"I…I guess so. It's probably from the green powder. It turns flame green."

"Marvelous stuff," he said, seating me a few steps away from the carriage and starting to inspect my arms. "Although it's all we can do to keep the recruits from going through barrels of it. How did you get burned by the green powder?"

"I threw it in the air and Rosewing set it on fire. It got rid of the wyverns."

"I'm certain it did."

"Lieutenant!" My brother came back, panting. "Captain says he wants all of us in his office."

I shook my head. "No. I won't go. The egg is cold and I have to stay with it."

"Kaylyn, now isn't the time for one of your stubborn fits," Warren hissed.

"I'm not going anywhere without this egg!" I shouted at him. "It's my responsibility! I won't leave it for *anybody*!"

Lieutenant Marcell made a quieting gesture. "Corporal, rouse three men to help us move the egg. We should be able to get it in the great hall. We can build a fire there. Will that do?" he asked me.

I nodded.

The egg let out a growling sound and rocked in the carriage.

I hurried over to it. "Look, I told you we'd have to have help to move you," I told it. "You're practically as tall as a human already! Dragons can move you easily, but we can't. And you can't stay in this carriage. We're going to get you someplace warm. Please, dragon, just work with me here. I'm doing the best I can."

There was a shifting sound inside the egg, but all was quiet.

"Corporal," Lieutenant Marcell said, light brown eyes on the egg and me.

"Yes, sir."

15

I gave every argument I could to the egg, but the dragon inside was still unhappy. The three servants who'd been roused looked awed and a little afraid. We pulled the carriage inside the great hall, and then to a smaller room. A fire had already been built, and together we all worked to get the egg out safely. The dragon made a growling sound and wouldn't be soothed until we set the egg down on a nest of blankets. Everyone drew back and I knelt in front of it, apologizing and saying we wouldn't touch the egg again. "You can stay here until you hatch," I told it. "We won't move you."

"Lieutenant Marcell. Corporal Madara." The captain, his eyes tired and showing we'd woken him from sleep, stood behind the carriage. "Would either of you care to explain to me why there's a carriage in the great hall?"

"We had to move the dragon egg to a warm place, sir," Lieutenant Marcell explained. "Take the carriage to the stables," he ordered the three men.

As the carriage was removed, Captain Durai came in. His skin was a very pale brown, with brown eyes that slanted slightly and black hair that was cut military short. Unlike Lieutenant Marcell, he was dressed in sleep clothes and a robe. He observed the egg a moment, his expression revealing nothing. "Where did we get a dragon egg?"

"My sister, sir," Warren offered, at rigid attention in front of the man in charge of the entire School. "She requests a safe haven here."

"At ease, Corporal," Captain Durai said without taking his eyes off the egg. "Your sister's name?"

"Kaylyn Madara, sir."

"Miss Kaylyn, I would like to hear the story of how you got this egg." He looked out the door at the servants lingering, trying to find the source of the commotion so early in the morning. "I believe we'll need some water and some food."

They hurried to work and Captain Durai closed the door. "Have a seat," he told everyone, and took a chair of his own. "Miss Kaylyn," he prompted.

Hesitantly, I told the whole story. I wasn't interrupted. When I got to the part about Rosewing, my eyes teared up again. "She wouldn't let me help her," I choked out. "She's just *lying* there, maybe dead. And if the wyverns come back, she won't be able to defend herself."

"She's a dragon, sis; she can defend herself with flame if nothing else," Warren tried to soothe me.

"She couldn't *before*! She certainly can't now that she's been *bleeding* for hours! She wouldn't pass off her egg to a human if she thought she was going to live. Dragons *hate* humans. Everyone knows that."

"And when was this encounter?" Captain Durai asked, directing me back to my tale.

"I met Rosewing a little before sunset."

"Where, exactly?"

"The Esperion Mountains." I was starting to want nothing more than sleep. "The distance of walking for almost eight hours."

Lieutenant Marcell looked quietly impressed. My brother glared at me. I glared back, daring him to say anything about where I'd been. He didn't, but he wanted to.

"You walked since sunset yesterday?" Captain Durai repeated.

"No, sir, about an hour afterwards. Rosewing taught me how to hatch and raise the dragon, and then we started walking."

"How did you know where to go?"

"I've been to the School before, sir."

"I doubt you've been to the School from the Esperion Mountains," Lieutenant Marcell said gently. "And the sun was likely gone before you got very far. Did you ever get lost?"

"No. I used the constellations. The North Star. Warren taught me." I could almost feel myself wilting. I'd never gone for so long without sleep.

"You took a direct route here then?"

I nodded. Then I realized why they were asking. "Are you going to look for Rosewing?"

"If we can."

17

I knew they weren't going to help Rosewing. "I'm not lying." Instead of sounding confident or strong, I sounded pitifully resentful and petulant.

"There are others who will need some kind of proof," Lieutenant Marcell explained. He rose. "You're tired. Captain, I'll see if I can ascertain a more certain location, then we can let her rest."

"I have people that need to be contacted. You'll lead the group to find this dragon. Miss Kaylyn, provided you have told the truth, you have a safe haven as requested." Captain Durai stood and crossed to the door. Outside, the servants stood, holding trays and looking nervous about entering. "I'll take one of those to my office," he said. "Another inside." He gestured and headed up the stairs. The first servant sprang eagerly after him, leaving the second to cautiously approach, nervously staring at the dragon egg.

With Warren's help, I managed to describe the area where I'd been between mouthfuls of delicious-smelling food. Warren had spent a great deal of his childhood exploring and knew where everything was. Lieutenant Marcell said Warren would accompany them on the trip to find Rosewing and let himself out with the coordinates written down on a map.

"What were you doing there, Kaylyn?" my brother demanded, now openly furious.

"You know exactly what I was doing there," I shot back, too tired to fight well.

"Running away from home? That's mature."

"I don't want to be mature!" I shouted at him. "I *hate* it at home! *You* got to run off to be an officer, but *I* don't get to leave until somebody decides they want to marry me! I don't *want* to marry, and I *won't* stay in that house until that happens! All Mother does is lecture me and all my sisters do is whine about all the balls and stupid functions that they can't attend because they don't know anyone of higher status well enough!" I mocked in their whining tone. "And they'll *never* marry well! *You* came home for three days last time you had a break and couldn't get away fast enough! What am *I* supposed to do?"

18

Warren colored slightly. "I'm an adult, Kaylyn."

"You're sixteen. That's only considered adulthood if you're a woman and married. I'm not going back home."

He looked frustrated. "What am I supposed to do with you?"

Tears filled my eyes. It was the one phrase I'd heard for most of my life, meaning I didn't belong and nobody knew where I had to be to make sure no one had to put up with me and my antics.

"That wasn't...I didn't mean that," he said helplessly.

"I'm just tired. I've walked for eight hours and my arms hurt and my feet hurt and I want to sleep." My voice was watery and wavered.

He looked guilty for causing tears. Dad had always been the one to deal with me. Since he'd died, Warren hadn't been home much and he didn't know how to fix things. It was easier to revert back to training, so that's what he did. "I'll see if I can find a room."

"I want to stay here."

"Kaylyn..."

"I want to stay here!" I shouted at him.

"All right! I'll tell Lieutenant Marcell you want to stay here! Just get some sleep, all right? You look terrible." He backed towards the door.

"I don't care." I was back to being petulant as I shoved myself out of the chair and stalked wearily over to the gleaming egg where I curled up on the nest of blankets that had been arranged around it.

There was a sound from the egg I could only describe as irritation.

"If you want me to move, dragon, then you can hatch and throw me out. Otherwise, I'm going to sleep here and you're going to deal with it."

There was a soft hiss, but I felt it was more defiance than real anger. I bunched up some blankets to form a kind of pillow, then I let myself fall asleep.

I slept with the egg as much a defense as anything. Trouble was growing for this egg and me, and I knew I was at the mercy of whoever was in charge. I wasn't powerful enough to demand anything. I didn't have money to bribe with, power to wield, or a family name to hide behind. I was a very minor noble, barely worthy of the title of noble. I wasn't enough of a noble to gain the rank of 'lady'. My mother had been Mrs. Madara when she'd married, and unless I married higher in the social chain, that's what my title would be as well. I was afraid if I ever left the egg that I wouldn't be allowed to see it again, or that it would be gone when I came back. Everyone would want the dragon egg, or be afraid of it.

I awoke to find someone had covered me with another blanket and a tray of food was sitting on the floor. My stomach growled with hunger. The food was still warm, and I wasted no time in eating it. Lieutenant Marcell came in as I was finishing up.

"You're back already?" I asked. His dark brown hair was long enough to look windblown and there was a considerable amount of dust on his boots and up his pants.

"It takes less time on horseback and during daylight. We found what was left of Rosewing," Lieutenant Marcell said as he took a seat in the chair in front of me. "The other dragons had gotten there first. They burn their dead," he explained. "All the wyverns you accounted for were still around."

"I told you I wasn't lying."

"There's no doubt of your story now. The generals are on their way from Vicoma."

I felt a wave of worry. "I don't want them here. They'll take it."

"There's no knowing what they'll do."

"They're going to take it. I know they are. Can't you make them stay away? At least until it hatches?"

"They'll be here tonight or tomorrow morning. I can keep them out until tomorrow, but not after that. What happens then is out of my hands."

I bit my lip. "Do you think there's any way to make them leave us alone?"

"It would depend on your ability to convince the generals you're capable of providing what they're looking for."

I let out a groan of despair. "Like they'd *ever* pick me for anything."

"You never know," he consoled me.

I looked at him, squinching my eyes in displeasure. "Would *you* pick me for anything?"

He gave a half-smile. "Perhaps not at first glance, but I'm learning about you. You have the stubborn determination to walk for hours, through the night, and the bravery to fight wyverns to help a dragon, not knowing if she would welcome your help. It's very obvious that you're trustworthy by the way you've held to your promise to Rosewing, and you're smart enough to find a way to find help and be able to use military skills your brother taught you. I see potential in you."

"They won't. They'll see that I'm a girl and that's it."

"Don't be so quick to judge," he admonished me. "You don't know what they'll do."

"If they wanted women to do things, they'd make it happen. But it's not happening because they don't want it to happen. They're the reason women aren't allowed to do anything. We're barely allowed to speak for ourselves." That came out sullen. I hated needing a man around to get anything done.

"Changes aren't quick. You wouldn't want them to be, or they wouldn't last. Progress is being made. It's tough when a country changes. There are plenty of other countries far more conservative than we are."

I rolled my eyes at that.

"After all," he continued, "without a ruling royal family, a lot of things had to adjust. Change is happening, whether they like it or not."

I looked at the egg. "Maybe not enough," I whispered.

Chapter 3

True to his word, Lieutenant Marcell kept the generals out. I talked to the egg, telling it everything I could about the people coming. It was as much because Rosewing had told me to speak to the egg as it was a way to get my worries out. I tried to come up with ideas to make the generals leave us alone, but all of them were childish fantasy and I knew it.

The intrusion came the next morning. I was pacing in front of the fireplace, nervously tugging at the borrowed dress I wore. As the door opened, I whirled, braced defensively. There were five of them, dressed in full uniform, as if they were going to impress the egg. I resisted telling them the dragon couldn't see us.

Only three of them looked at me; the rest of them were staring at the egg. Of the three that looked at me, it was brief and it was clear they found me lacking. Captain Durai was there, along with Lieutenant Marcell and my brother. Warren looked awed by the amount of powerful people in the room and eager to please. The military men with the generals at least attempted to look professional as they took their place along the wall and were much more subtle about staring at the egg.

The fat general, short, round, and his bulk straining his blue and red Centralian uniform, was the first to puff forward. Just as I was about to state he couldn't touch the egg, Lieutenant Marcell caught my eye and shook his head slightly. I wanted to protest, but held my tongue, unsure if he'd already told them not to touch the egg, or simply giving way.

The fat, little man circled the egg once. "Quite a find," he said. "Yes, quite a find. A dragon *egg*!"

"With less than a week until it hatches," another commented. "And this girl found it?" He turned his appraising gaze to me, looking down his long nose. "Are we certain she didn't steal it? The last thing we need is a dragon coming after us for egg-stealing."

Lieutenant Marcell quickly answered before I screamed the answer, and a few insults as well. "The mother is dead. We checked Kaylyn's story. If the dragons knew about the egg, they haven't shown any signs of looking for it."

"I don't believe this girl is bright enough to steal a dragon egg," I heard someone say.

I stiffened with the insult. "I'm not stupid enough to steal one," I snapped out.

All gazes now turned to me. I glared at them all.

"You are of a noble rank, are you not, *Miss* Madara?" Emphasis was put on the title.

I colored slightly. "Yes, I am."

"You're little more than a child!" a grandfatherly-looking general exclaimed.

"I'm *not* a child." It was said through gritted teeth. Warren gave me an imploring look, begging me not to act like I usually did.

"Where's your brother?" The fat general turned around, seeking the male in charge of my future.

Warren stepped forward. "Here, sir!"

"How old are you, Corporal?"

"Sixteen, sir!"

He glanced at me. "And you must be younger than he is. Are you the youngest?"

"She's the youngest of my triplet sisters, sir," Warren answered quickly, knowing my temper was on a short leash.

"You see?" he asked the others, as if the minutes between my birth and my sisters' caused a great lack of knowledge. "She's just a child! And left with the responsibility of a dragon egg? A great weapon?"

"I am *not* a child." It wasn't quite a shout, but it wasn't quiet either. "And the egg is *mine*. It's not a weapon."

I was given a patronizing smile. "Miss Kaylyn, you don't know what it could be." Greed was written all over his face.

"I know what it's *not*, and I know it's not *yours*."

"There is a question of ownership, Maddox," someone murmured to the fat, little general.

"Easily fixed, Olina. Corporal Madara." General Maddox gestured to my brother.

Warren looked nervous. "Yes, sir?"

"Who is head of the household?"

"I am, sir. My father died."

"So you retain control over your sister?"

Horrified, I was momentarily speechless. Warren had the power to take my dragon.

Warren sent me an apologetic look. "Yes, sir."

"Warren!" I begged.

"Do you believe your sister is fit to care for a dragon?" General Maddox asked.

Warren hesitated.

"Warren!" It was a plea and an accusation.

"Kaylyn, it's a *dragon*," Warren implored. "What am I supposed to do?"

"I made a *promise*! I know what I'm doing!"

"Young lady, you have no idea what you're doing," General Maddox told me. "Sergeant…I'm sorry, *Corporal* Madara, do you believe your sister is fit to care for a dragon?" he asked again.

I could see my brother wavering. Promotion was what the generals were offering, and he wanted it.

I felt my eyes narrow. "*Dad* would *never* have hesitated," I hissed.

Warren flushed guiltily.

"Young lady, that is underhanded," another general chided me.

"You just threw promotion at his feet!" I bellowed at him. "Why not make him a captain next? Or would that be too *underhanded*? I thought they taught *responsibility*, and *morals*, and *trust* here. Or is that only when *you're* not around to *buy* loyalty?"

Warren stared at the floor as General Maddox puffed up.

"Miss Madara, hold your tongue," he barked.

"No! I won't let you take this dragon egg!"

"That is not your choice, Corporal." The general's tone was no longer kind. "Answer my question."

My brother wouldn't look up from the floor. "General Maddox, sir, I was trained that my first priority is to my family. I was also trained to trust my judgment, and the judgment of others. No one has ever said dragons have poor judgment, and my sister is not a liar. If she said that a dragon trusted her with a dragon egg, then it's the truth. If a dragon trusted my sister with an egg, that dragon's judgment is that my sister is qualified to care for the hatchling. And if that is so, then it is my duty to assist my sister in whatever she may need to raise this dragon. Sir."

I felt like cheering.

Several eyes narrowed. "I see." General Olina's voice was chilly. "You are dismissed."

"Corporal, wait outside until further notice," Lieutenant Marcell ordered.

Warren flashed me a resigned look, bowed, then left, the door closing softly behind him.

"Your brother may have given in, but you have yet to meet our approval," General Maddox snarled.

"I'm the wrong gender to meet your approval," I said bitterly. "It's *my* egg."

"Do you have the resources to take care of this dragon? Food? Water? Shelter? If you were removed from this facility, could you, or your brother, provide for a growing dragon?" At my hesitation, he gave a smile of victory. "I thought not, *Miss* Madara."

"So we aren't rich," I snapped out. "I'll take it back to the dragons after it hatches."

"Then why didn't you before? Did you not tell Captain Durai that the dragons would kill you on sight? If so, then clearly you cannot take the dragon back."

"What do *you* care?" I demanded. "We're only *minor* nobles." I knew resentment was obvious. "Barely above sinking into the grime of working class, right?"

Several faces looked pained. The letter that a servant had shared with the entire country hadn't reflected well on the ruling generals, most of whom had come from wealthy, higher-class noble lines. Once the word had spread on what the generals had written to each other, a strike from the working class and a few of the very minor nobles had put everything on hold. Concessions had been made in order to keep peace and stop revolt among the poorer but skilled people needed for the wealthy to have what they wanted.

"That was…misinterpreted," another general offered.

"'Those who enroll in the School for Officers and Gentlemen should be kept where they belong. Only those with the advanced education money can buy deserve to attain higher rankings in the military system, lest we offend those powerful enough to do us damage'," I quoted, watching more of them wince.

"The point is that you aren't prepared enough…"

"Wealthy enough," I interjected stonily.

"…to be able to care for this dragon. And such a magnificent creature should not be left to starve or be mishandled by a willful, young girl." General Maddox glared at me. "A girl who, I'm told, has run away from home and clearly ignores the rules of convention." His eyes fixed pointedly on my hair a moment. "You have shown no ability to care for this dragon egg."

I let the comment about the length of my hair pass. "You haven't shown the ability to care for anything except yourself!"

"Remove her," he ordered to the men behind me. "We'll take the egg."

"No!" I threw myself forward, but was held back by the men with him who had suddenly grabbed me. "No, you can't!"

He ignored me. "Something this powerful in the hands of a girl will end only in disaster. It's better if those who know what they're doing is in charge of it. Captain Durai, the egg will come with us."

"You don't have a clue what you're doing!" I shouted at him. "None of you do! You don't know the first thing about caring for a dragon!"

"And you do?" Derision was clear on his face.

"I've spoken with a dragon mother. She taught me how to care for a hatchling."

Had he not been a general, I guessed he would have rolled his eyes. "How old are you?" It was nearly dripping with condescension.

"Thirteen." It was shot out as a challenge.

General Maddox shook his head. "You're far too young to handle this kind of responsibility. We can find someone older with more experience."

"Girls my age marry and have children!" I shouted at him.

He looked irritated. "Remove her," he ordered again.

Panicked, I blurted out my one defense as they started to pull me to the door. "If that dragon hatches and I'm not here, it'll kill you!"

The men dragging me paused.

I spoke quickly, knowing this was my one shot. "The dragon only knows my voice. The mother wasn't sure it would take to *me* in such a short time. It doesn't trust you, and if it doesn't trust you it'll kill you. You *can't* take it!"

"You see, Maddox?" General Olina asked. "It's dangerous. We can't use it as a weapon. It'll only turn on us. We need to destroy it."

"Before it hatches," another added.

"But the possibilities, Hesperian! Think of the possibilities!"

"I am, Maddox. I'm thinking of the possibilities that this creature will not be under control. That once it hatches, its cries will eventually bring down the wrath of its kind. This creature, I'm certain, will bite the hand that feeds it, and anything else it can reach."

I struggled to get free while the generals debated among themselves. I got nowhere, and in the end, General Maddox nodded, reluctantly agreeing. "If it won't take to us, we have no other choice."

"You *can't* kill it!" I screamed. "It's a *baby*! It hasn't even hatched yet!"

They ignored me. Women didn't deserve their attention, only men, and only men of any social rank would matter to them. If I'd been a boy, they might have listened to me. I struggled harder, fighting to free myself, hoping there was something I could do.

"Stop it." The man on the right murmured the command quietly to me. Both his hands were clenched to my arm to keep it in his grip. "It won't do any good. I don't want to hurt you. We have our orders."

"But I *promised*," I pleaded.

He shook his head slightly.

While the generals discussed the best ways to kill a dragon, I slumped, sniffling hard. Both men glanced at me, looking pained.

"Miss, please don't cry," the man pleaded softly.

"You're nothing but filthy murderers," I said, my voice wavering. "All of you."

He sighed, relaxing his grip a little more. I didn't move, desperately calculating. If they were afraid of dragons, I only had one chance. I continued to sniffle, keeping myself on the verge of tears. Finally, it was decided they'd shoot the egg, and see what happened. As the two men ordered to shoot moved into position, I ripped my right arm free and scratched with my fingers at the other, drawing blood on his neck. As he flinched, I yanked free, throwing myself forward, pressing flat against the egg, one arrow a mere step from my back.

"If you harm this baby, I'll tell the dragons." My eyes were squeezed shut and tears were swimming behind my eyelids. "I'll go to the mountains, and I'll find them, and I'll tell them each and every one of your names and what you did and they'll come destroy you. They won't rest until all of you are dead, and they'll kill any human they see. You may not want to listen to me because I'm a female and have little status, but dragons don't care about status. They'll care that I saved one of their own and then you killed it."

"Kaylyn, you don't know how this dragon is going to act," Lieutenant Marcell said gently. "You said yourself it may very well hurt you."

"I gave my word! My word may not hold as much weight as yours, but a dragon asked for my promise and I gave it! I'll die before I let any of you make me break my word. Now get out!"

"Why you impudent…" a general began indignantly.

"Get *out!*" I screamed at him.

A hand clamped on my arm, jerking me around. "Now listen here, you guttersnipe," General Maddox snarled.

From the egg came a furious hiss and a rocking that drew everyone's attention.

"I don't think the dragon likes you threatening his caretaker," Lieutenant Marcell said mildly. "If it can hear everything we say, this is perhaps not the best way to gain a dragon's trust." His voice held a thread of censure. "And were her brother in the room, he could call for satisfaction for laying a hand on his sister."

I jerked my arm free from the general's loose grip. Lieutenant Marcell had just given me my answer; the mother's right of protection. "Captain Durai, you promised me a safe haven. Doesn't that promise extend to those beneath me? If I'd brought my child, wouldn't it have the same promise?"

"It would," Captain Durai answered.

"This dragon is under my protection, the same as a child. If you gave me a safe haven, then you gave this dragon a safe haven. Until we've done something to negate that, would you *please* make everyone leave us alone?" I begged with my eyes. "Mother and child are supposed to be tranquil and have a happy atmosphere with no stress during the last month of childbearing. Can we at least have the few days left to be tranquil?"

There were mutterings, but as there were many fathers, fathers-to-be, and grandfathers, this latest decision on having a happy, healthy child wasn't something any of them could argue against. Many women were ordered to sit and be pampered during the entire time of pregnancy so that the child would turn out well and the mother wouldn't miscarry. Transferring this policy to a dragon hatching was a little fuzzy, but they weren't doctors and no one knew enough about dragons to refute it. And since the dragon could clearly hear us, there wasn't a question that this hadn't been a tranquil time for the baby.

"I'm afraid, Generals, that she has a point. Perhaps if we give her and the hatchling time and peace we can decide what to do once the dragon has hatched." Captain Durai's voice was slightly apologetic.

There were mutterings, unhappy dislike, but they cleared out. I rested my cheek against the egg, whispering over and over that it was going to be fine. The egg was silent.

A hand rested gently on my shoulder and I flinched, looking up at Lieutenant Marcell. "If you need anything, let me know," he said kindly.

I turned away, huddling against the egg. "You don't care. You were going to let them kill it."

"I can't overrule them. I'm bound by the rules of society, Kaylyn," he said quietly. "If there's anything I *can* do, all you have to do is ask. I promise I will make sure it's done." He lightly touched my skin where General Maddox had grabbed me. Thankfully the burns had healed enough that it didn't hurt much, but there were red marks from where the guards had held me that were likely going to turn into bruises. "I'll send your brother back shortly with medicine. And next time, a fist will work better than a scratch, though I'll ensure they don't lay a hand on you again."

I felt all anger disappearing. He didn't approve of what they'd done, and he had tried to stand for me. And I was going to need a stronger ally than Warren if I was going to last. "When the baby hatches, he's going to need food. Meat, semi-cooked. Still a little raw. Milk and honey."

"I'll tell the cooks to have it ready. Any kind of meat?"

"I think so. Rosewing didn't say."

"Is the dragon a boy?" he asked, referring to my slip of calling the dragon 'he'.

"I don't know. Rosewing didn't know. I just have this sense it's a boy." I stroked my fingers over the shell. "Thank you, Lieutenant."

"Just Dillon, Kaylyn. I don't think we need formalities anymore."

I nodded. "Thank you, Dillon. Thank you for standing up for me."

He waved that aside, as if there was something normal about what he'd done. "You're the only person I know who's had a conversation with a dragon. To have the guts to fight over a dozen wyverns is incredible. To gain a dragon's approval is unique. You're going to be something special, Kaylyn, and I foretell great things from you."

I blushed. "I'm the youngest of triplets. I'm the same as two other people. Nothing special's going to happen to me."

"I think it's already happened. You just need a little help getting where you need to go." He winked at me. "And if the stories I heard from your brother are true, you aren't anything like your sisters."

I blushed deeper. "I'm really not a troublemaker."

"You're thirteen. Everyone gets in trouble at thirteen." He patted my shoulder, then went to answer the timid knock at the door. "Corporal."

My brother looked defeated. "May I talk to my sister, sir?"

"Of course. When you're finished, I'd like to see you in my office."

The moment the door was closed, I raced to my brother, holding tightly. "Thank you," I whispered.

"I'm not very good at being Dad, am I?" he asked.

"No. But you're my brother. You're not supposed to be. And you were the best brother ever today." I looked up at him. "Are you going to get in trouble?"

"I don't see how I wouldn't." He gave a heavy smile. "But I guess Dad would be proud of me."

"He would. And I'm proud of you too."

Chapter 4

Warren would have been in disgrace and kicked out of the School if the generals had gotten their way. They didn't take defeat from a girl well, and apparently there was no breaking the mother's right of protection or the safe haven. Lieutenant Marcell had stated there were no grounds for punishing Warren, and reassigned him with me. Warren was in charge of making sure I didn't break any rules that would allow Captain Durai to revoke my protection. I knew how much I owed Dillon for what he was doing, and I wasn't sure how I would ever repay him.

"David heard General Maddox say it!" Warren's friend told us. "He said for sticking up for your sister, he could forget ever making captaincy!"

"But he's been picked to take over the School for years!" Warren objected in a whisper. "Everyone knows it! It's only dependent on when Captain Durai retires!"

"Not anymore. General Maddox said Captain Durai had been ordered not to promote Lieutenant Marcell."

"I really hate him," I muttered.

"Captain Durai?" Warren asked.

"Maddox. Fat, slimy, little worm."

Both recruits looked appalled. "You can't say that!" the boy stammered. "He's a general! We're supposed to respect our elders!"

"I'll respect him when he can respect somebody besides himself."

They both shook their heads and turned back to each other. "How's Lieutenant Marcell taking it?" Warren demanded.

"Nobody would know if I hadn't heard. He doesn't act like anything's changed."

"I heard Lady Marcell was furious with the generals," Warren whispered. "I guess it's because of that."

"Is he going to be okay?" I asked worriedly. "Can the generals do anything else to him?"

Both of them shook their heads. "If they were going to do worse, they'd have done it already," Warren informed me.

"Not making captain is insult enough," the other boy added. "Especially when he was supposed to be Captain of the School." He peeked out the door. "I have to go," he said. "Before someone comes looking for me."

"I have to stand outside," Warren said to me. "Do you need anything?"

I shook my head. Warren stepped outside, leaving me to contemplate this turn of events. I hadn't considered that someone else might get in trouble. I understood that Warren worshipped the ground Dillon walked on, since he'd protected Warren, but I couldn't understand why Dillon would work so hard for me and my family. He was a powerful noble, with everything my family lacked. We didn't have anything to offer, and now he was suffering for defending me. It was so rare that someone like him would make a stand for someone outside his sphere, and a female at that.

I was rolling a metal ball across the floor, from hand to hand, because the dragon hatchling seemed to like it. He made a singing sound that just felt happy to my mind, and so I continued to roll it while I thought. There was a dress folded next to my pallet on the floor that needed to be repaired, but I was avoiding that chore. I figured entertaining a dragon was enough.

I looked up as Dillon came in. "Aren't you busy?" I asked, letting the metal ball roll to a halt.

"Not too busy to check up on you and the hatchling. How are you?"

I studied him as he moved to sit beside me. "You're in trouble, aren't you?"

The smile became wry as he leaned against the wall. "I guess everyone's heard if you've heard."

"Did they dishonorably expel you?"

"No. They just won't promote me again. Being a lieutenant isn't all bad. It's more of an honor than a lot of people gain. And it's dishonorably discharge, by the way," he added.

"But you were supposed to take Captain Durai's place one day. And I messed it up, didn't I?"

"No, *I* made a decision, and I will live with the consequences of that decision."

"I hate Maddox," I grumbled.

Dillon tossed the metal ball in the air a few times. "Maddox is angry and letting greed blind him. That's all. Maybe when he and the others calm down, they'll see things aren't as bad as they believe."

"After they dishonorably discharge you and kick you out of the School?"

"They won't do that. Captain Durai won't, anyway."

I couldn't understand how he took this so calmly. It made me feel worse, because ultimately it was my doing. I slouched down and crossed my arms, grumbling. "It's not fair."

"Kaylyn, I thought you knew by now that life wasn't fair."

"I know it. I don't have to like it. Everyone at the School loves you. And you ought to be a general because you have more sense than any of them." I sent a scowl to the door.

"It's all right, Kaylyn," he said patiently. "It's nothing to get upset over."

"Yes, it is," I countered. "You stuck your neck out for me, and Warren. And the hatchling," I added, pointing to the egg. "And I know this is usually a men's thing, but I owe you for everything you've done for me and my family. I don't know if it's worth anything to you, but I'm in your debt."

Dillon studied me for a minute, then clasped my hand. "It means more, coming from you, than it has coming from others. I'll remember, and I'll remember that you'll be willing to honor it if the time comes that I call in that debt." He handed the metal ball back to me. "Your brother says that sound is driving him crazy." He gestured to the ball.

"The dragon loves it." I started rolling on the ground, and the hatchling let out a singing sound at the same pitch as the metal ball, only prettier. When I stopped rolling the ball, it stopped the sound.

Lieutenant Marcell looked fascinated. "May I?" he asked.

I handed the ball back to him, watched him tie a string to it, then start rolling it around on the floor, directed by the string. The dragon started humming again.

Lieutenant Marcell was grinning when he stopped. "I could do that for hours."

I couldn't help but like him. "You aren't like most nobles," I blurted out.

"Why's that?" he asked.

"Because you think rolling a ball on the floor is fun. Because you didn't let my brother get expelled. Because you stuck up for me, and I'm nobody."

He took my hand in his. "No," he said quietly. "You are a female, and you are a minor noble. Those two facts are simply two descriptions for you. Those are not the only things that determine who you are in life. If you recall what Warren said, I remember him saying that dragons aren't known for having poor judgment. A dragon looked at you, read you, and saw something in you she could trust. She didn't see that you were a female, and she didn't see that you were a minor noble. She saw a person brave enough, strong enough, and worthy enough to provide for her hatchling. If she hadn't seen that in you, she would have asked for something else, or she wouldn't have asked at all." Then he kissed the back of my hand in a gesture of respect.

I was honored, pleased, and baffled simultaneously at his words. "But you're a ranking officer and a powerful noble," I protested.

He raised his eyebrows at me. "Does that make me any more of a person?"

"It usually does to your sphere."

Dillon gave a smile. "Perhaps I know a little more than most people in my sphere." He let go of my hand as a knock came at the door. There was a brief murmured conversation, then Dillon looked at me, hand resting on the door. "Do you need anything?"

"Another pillow would be nice. Maybe something to do?"

"I'll see what I can do," he promised, then he left.

I was left alone until Warren entered half an hour later. "If you don't stop banging that metal ball around…" he warned.

"The hatchling likes it," I defended.

"It's driving me crazy. If you want something to do, then I have plenty." He set down a dress, a skirt, three colors of thread, and two needles.

"Warren!" I protested. "You know I hate sewing!"

"You need more clothes than you brought. Alter them to fit you. I asked the Matron General…"

"Who's that?" I interrupted.

"The matron over the female servants. I asked her to fit three blouses for you, so expect her to find you. And be nice, Kaylyn."

"I hate sewing." I felt like sulking. "This wasn't what I had in mind when I told Dillon I wanted something to do."

"Lieutenant Marcell told me to find something because I knew you."

"I'm telling Dillon to find someone else next time."

"*Lieutenant Marcell* trusted me with this," Warren said with emphasis.

"He said I could call him Dillon, so I'm going to, *Corporal Madara*," I imitated, crossing my arms.

Warren shook his head. "You're going to get him in more trouble," he warned.

"He didn't seem to think so. He's…different. He's not like most nobles."

Warren nodded in understanding, his attention diverted briefly. "He wants to make this a place where status matters less. A place where people have to earn their way up no matter who they are."

"Why does he care?" I asked.

He shrugged. "I don't know. I'm just glad he does."

36

"Do you think there's a chance the generals will forgive him?"

"Why do you care?"

"Because it's not fair. I don't want to have ruined his career."

Warren shrugged once. "It's not fair," he agreed. "And I don't know if the generals will forgive him. I hope so. Mostly I just want the generals to leave before they block me from promoting too."

"What are the generals doing anyway?"

"I don't know. They're waiting for someone, I think."

"Do you know who?"

"No one does. But I don't think it's going to do any of us any good."

The mysterious visitor that the generals were waiting for showed up that afternoon, an hour before dinner. I was talking to the egg, trying to describe what Centralia was like while I sewed. I'd been bored enough to give in to sewing when Dillon entered. "Kaylyn, there's someone outside who'd like to see you," he said, apology clear.

"Can't it wait?" I didn't think there was a person in the world who would be someone I wanted to see right now.

"It's someone who says he can help you."

"I'll be right back," I whispered to the egg.

Outside was a man. I knew he was a powerful man because all the generals were treating him with avid respect and he wore silk monogrammed with what I figured out after a moment was supposed to be a dragon. The stitched dragon looked positively evil. The man wasn't much taller than I was, and had considerable bulk. His head was completely bald and his eyes were a dull, light blue. He looked down his long nose at me. "Is this the girl?"

I curtseyed silently.

"My dear, do you know who I am?" he asked kindly.

I shook my head.

"This is Doctor McDragon," General Maddox said with pride. "The only man who's gained research on dragons."

"I've been living in the wilderness for years, studying them," Doctor McDragon said. "And I've come to offer my services."

Everyone was watching me, waiting for my grateful thanks. I couldn't imagine how he had that much weight if he lived in the wilderness.

"I've spoken with a dragon, sir. She taught me everything she thought I'd need to know," I said, thinking I deserved a reward for being polite after the way I'd been treated.

"There's more to know about dragons than can be taught in an hour," he said gently. "Do you know how dragons sleep? How often they eat? What's good for them? Do you know what kind of dragon you have?"

"There's more than one kind of dragon, sir?" I asked, cautiously hoping he could help.

"There is. There are five kinds of dragons." He held up his hand imperiously and two rings flashed in the light. "There are bronze dragons. Their scales are actually made of bronze. They are the most powerful and most dominant of dragons, and also the wealthiest. They add their bronze scales to their hoard of treasure. There are white dragons. These are the shyer dragons and their color ranges from the purest white to grey. The black dragons are the cruelest and most dangerous."

General Maddox nodded enthusiastically in agreement. "A black dragon named Ironclaw nearly ripped my arm off and killed me," he said seriously.

Doctor McDragon's tone was all sympathy. "You were lucky to get away with your life, General. Next are the green dragons. They're the most peaceful of dragons. But be warned that no dragon is very peaceful or kind. And last are the blue dragons. They can live in the water."

I found this fascinating. "Does the egg color make a difference?"

"Of course it does! The color of the egg will tell the color of the dragon! What color is the egg?"

"White. Pearly white."

"Then that's the color your dragon will be."

A white dragon. I pictured Rosewing. She'd been a white dragon. It made sense.

A niggling little thought protested at the back of my brain. I didn't know how, but something told me it wasn't a white dragon. The image I always got in my brain was a black dragon. It wasn't helped by my difficulties in picturing a bronze egg, or a green or blue egg. Eggs just weren't in the rainbow of colors dragons were.

"And what have you named this dragon?" Doctor McDragon asked, turning my attention back to him.

"Named? Oh, I…I haven't yet. Rosewing hadn't. I thought I should wait until it hatched. Since we don't know if it's a girl or a boy," I added.

"White dragons are exclusively female," he said gravely. "And bronze dragons are exclusively male. The rest are mixed. That dragon in there is going to be a female, white dragon."

Everyone looked at me for my reaction. I frowned. I was almost positive it wasn't a girl.

"You can't change a baby's gender, dear girl," Doctor McDragon said gently. "A child is what it is."

"I don't care what he looks like," I said bluntly. "I just don't think it's going to be how you say. I have this sense that it's a boy."

There were snorts that made my face flush. "She thinks she knows more than the Doctor," one of the generals scoffed.

I felt my face redden further. "I haven't studied dragons for years, but I met one and I spoke to her and she didn't try to hurt me, which is more than any of you can say," I snapped to the ground. "It's not a girl, and it's not a white dragon. I don't know how I know; I just *know*."

"When the dragon hatches, we'll see," Doctor McDragon said, waving his hand as if to smooth it all over. "I will tell you what you need to know about the hatching of this egg. It will take hours. The dragon will have to fight its way out of the shell. When it breaks free, you must feed it immediately. It will be weak, unable to walk."

That went against what the mother had told me. I hid my suspicions and just listened, but with a seed of doubt firmly planted.

"You must feed it liquids at first. No solids. Just like every other animal, it will be too weak at first. After the first month, you can slowly start weaning it on fully-cooked meat."

I interrupted here. "Rosewing said never to feed him fully-cooked meat. Dragons are supposed to eat raw meat."

"Dear girl, dragons never eat raw meat. They cook anything they eat with flame. They have the ability to produce flame from the day they come out of the shell."

"Dragons can't flame until after the first year," I immediately disagreed.

He looked exasperated. "Dear girl, I am an expert in this field."

"Yeah? Well, Rosewing is a *dragon*, and I think that qualifies her far more than it does you," I said hotly.

"Then her injuries took a toll on her mind. She was confused. Or perhaps you didn't hear correctly."

"She spoke in my mind. Everything she said was perfectly clear."

"She spoke in your *mind*, you say?" General Maddox was intrigued. "That's just what the vicious Ironclaw did to me!"

"It is the preferred method of speaking among dragons." Doctor McDragon was in his element. "Also, my dear girl, you should know to never give a dragon water. Giving a dragon water will put out its flame."

I was tired of being called 'dear girl'. Everything he said countermanded what Rosewing had told me. "But other liquids won't?" I snapped. "That makes no sense. What do they drink if not water?"

"Dragons don't need anything to drink after the first month." He held up a hand imperiously again. "Before we go further, we should name the dragon. It's important to welcome the hatchling into the world with a name."

"Something to do with white?" suggested General Olina. I noted that with disgust since he'd wanted to kill my dragon.

"Yes, but also something feminine." He went quiet, closed his eyes, and put an intense look of concentration on his face. We waited. The generals looked expectant and as excited as a child waiting for his favorite toy. I wondered if he even knew how to properly name a dragon.

His pale blue eyes opened and he smiled. "Crystalscales."

There was a murmur of approval.

I wasn't impressed. "I need to stay in there with him."

"Her, my dear girl. It's a girl."

I didn't answer.

The generals praised Doctor McDragon on his clever name and brilliance while I headed back for the room. I paused next to Dillon. "Can you get me a list of all dragon names we have?" I whispered.

He nodded. "I'll see what I can do."

"Thanks." I closed the door and crossed over to the egg. "Well, there's an idiot out there who thinks he knows more about dragons than dragons do," I informed the egg. "He says because your egg is white you'll be a white dragon, and that you'll be a girl because white dragons are always girls. I just don't feel that's what you are. I don't care what you look like, but I can't see you like Doctor McIdiot says you're going to be."

There was a sound, a croak I couldn't identify. I seated myself and tried to go back to my sewing. When Dillon entered, I was glaring at the material I'd thrown across the room, my hand wrapped in my skirt.

"I'm guessing it isn't going well," Dillon said with humor.

"I hate sewing," I informed him. "And I've jabbed my hand fourteen times. It *hurts*."

Dillon set the sheets of paper down in front of me, then went to retrieve the material. I moved so he could settle down beside me, watching in disbelief as he started sewing. "The trick with this is not to grab too much material on the big stitch," he explained.

"How do you know how to sew? Men don't sew. That's a woman's task and no man I knew would do it, except for the tailor."

"Those who go more than two years in the officer side of the School learn this. Soldiers need to know how to care for their own things, and that includes making repairs to their weapons and their clothing. There are a few who balk, there always are, but they all learn it. Before I met my wife, I had to fix all my clothes myself because I couldn't afford a tailor." He passed it back to me. "Take it slow. How are your burns?"

I unwrapped my hand from my skirt. I'd jabbed the needle into the burn on the side of my hand. He took my hand and inspected it.

"I think they're healing okay. I've never been burned before. They itch sometimes."

"We can get you something for that." He released my hand and watched me start to sew. "There. That's fine. Just take it slow."

"This is so boring," I grumbled.

"I never minded. You can still talk and think about other things. For instance, have you thought of a name for this dragon?" He gestured to the egg.

"I don't know if I should pick one. I have ten options of how he's coming out."

"Five if you're sure it's a boy."

I flushed. "I know I said it, but I don't know if I'm right. It could be a girl. It could be white."

There was a sound from the egg that I could only describe as annoyance.

Dillon smiled. "I'm guessing he isn't."

"It's more than that. I want this name to be *right*. I could name him Happyflower, but it wouldn't be him. I'm hoping that once I see him I'll be able to find a name that suits him."

"That's very responsible of you, and very mature. You're already avoiding the worst mistake I think parents make."

"What's that?" I asked curiously.

"Forcing their child to be something besides who they are. We have dozens of recruits who are here because their mother or father decided they were going to grow up to be one of the generals who lead the country. Those recruits are miserable most of the time.

I was one of the lucky ones. What I wanted was the same as what my family wanted. You're going to let this dragon be who he is."

I thought of my family. "I hate having to be what others want all the time. Why would I make someone else live through that?"

"You'd be surprised." He watched me jab my hand for the fifteenth time and suppressed a laugh. "I'm just going to guess this is an example of our discussion?"

"'Ladies sew'," I mimicked in my mother's voice. "'Men want a wife who can uphold her responsibilities.' Why do any of you ever *care* if women can sew? Especially the wealthy ones who can hire a tailor?"

"I can't say. I only cared because my wife did the repairs on my clothing."

"If I *ever* marry, my husband can repair his own clothing or pay a tailor to do it." I reached the end of the material with relief and quickly tied the string off. Having broken numerous threads in my life, I was very good at finishing off a string, or what was left of it.

We both inspected the material as I held it up. It was acceptable. The dress wasn't anything to boast about, but it was decent.

"I think that looks good," Dillon complemented.

"I think my mother would have a fit if she saw this."

He chuckled. "Have you written to your mother?"

I dropped the material to my lap, looking away. "My mother isn't interested in hearing from me."

"She is your mother."

"She prefers my sisters. Once Dad died, she didn't know what to do with me. She's probably glad I'm gone." The truth hurt. I'd never gotten along well with my mother.

Dillon gentled his tone. "No matter what, it wouldn't hurt to at least write. Tell her you're safe. Let her know Warren will take care of you."

"Everyone knows where I am, don't they? I mean, there's a dragon egg here." It had brought the generals. I assumed everyone else knew as well.

"Why do you think the recruits are so upset?" he inquired with a slight smile. "The School is on lockdown. No one's allowed out or in, no mail's allowed out, and no girls are allowed either."

"I guess Mary Beth doesn't get to visit," I said, smirking.

He chuckled. "Mary Beth still visits, does she?"

"You know her?"

"Recruits aren't as sneaky as they think they are. When I was a recruit, it was Ellen. I had my girl already, so I didn't visit with Ellen."

"She's a painted woman. And you let her come?"

"Of course not. But recruits are inventive. The servant girls have the Matron General who's tougher than our drill sergeants, and I suspect she wakes up every half hour to count the girls. We have a harder time locking down dormitories of young men who miss their sweethearts. If we catch the girls, we send them home. Usually publicly. We hope it embarrasses them so they don't try again. Mary Beth is unfazed." He picked up the needle and placed it inside the spool to hold it there. "Write a letter to your mother."

"It doesn't matter, does it? She won't get it."

"I think I can make an exception for you. I let Warren mail his letter so your mother would know you weren't missing somewhere. Everyone else is going to have to suffer until that dragon hatches and we figure out what to do with both of you. It should be soon, right?"

"I was told less than a week, and it's been almost four days." I glanced at the egg. I wanted it to hatch soon. At least out of the shell it would be able to defend itself a little.

"When it does happen, Warren knows to lock up and let me know. You'll have privacy for this hatching. We wouldn't want someone creating problems and getting bitten. And although a few of the recruits are sure they'll die of curiosity, I've ordered that no one assist. Unless you need help."

I shook my head. "Thank you."

"You're having a child. This should be a joyful time." He grinned at me as he headed for the door. "With as little stress as possible. I just visit every now and again to make sure you're as content as can be."

"I think visiting me is more of a stress relief for you than me."

"Trust me, you're much better off in here. I wish I could claim right of motherhood right now."

"I'm sorry."

He gave a half-smile that I knew was tinged with some regret for himself. As much as he tried to downplay it, we both knew his life dreams were most likely gone. "I know. But we'll get through it somehow. Maybe this is for the best."

"It's not," I whispered softly once the door had closed. "And if I can, I'll find a way to repay you and make you a captain again."

The baby dragon inside the egg trilled once. I didn't know if it was agreement or if it was mocking me too.

Chapter 5

I may have been done talking with Doctor McDragon, but others were not. I was informed the generals were in conference with him almost constantly, questioning him about what would be best for this hatchling. I was just hoping the dragon would hatch before the doctor told them some lie that would make them believe I wasn't necessary.

My disgust for Doctor McDragon was apparently singular. Everyone else was in awe and whispers about what he said over everything from dragons to pillows were the only things in discussion. I told Warren I didn't care what he said and finished my sewing alone in the one place where I could feel secure about my knowledge. I told myself again and again I had to be right. Doctor McDragon may have been a highly respected authority, but he was no dragon mother. Dying or not, I would do what she said.

"Sis, we're coming in!" Warren called.

"We?"

Struggling under the weight of a large wooden beam, Warren and two other recruits made their way slowly in.

"What are you doing?" I demanded, standing in front of the egg protectively.

"It's a beam," my brother said. "Doctor McDragon says dragons sleep hanging upside down, like bats. So we're going to bring this beam in here so it has something to hang from while it sleeps."

"How is it supposed to get up there if it can't fly?" I asked.

Warren and the others paused. "I didn't think of that," he said at last.

"Warren, that man doesn't know *anything* about dragons. Just put the beam somewhere and leave us alone."

"But he's Doctor Mc*Dragon*. He lived in the wilderness for years and studied dragons. He's written books! He's the only expert on dragons."

"Now there are two," I said. "Me. And I don't trust him."

"Kaylyn, you're…"

"I'm what?" I challenged. "A girl? A child? I may not be Doctor McDragon, but I'm not wrong. Set the beam down and go away. I don't want to hear anything more about Doctor McIdiot or his made-up stories about dragons!"

"She's just grumpy because she's tired," I heard Warren whisper under his breath as he set the beam against one wall.

"She's always grumpy," one of his friends muttered back.

I glared at the fireplace until they left. I was tired, but I tried to stay up and fight it. Eventually, after nearly falling asleep twice, I curled up on my pallet, hugging the pillow tightly as I quickly sank into exhausted slumber.

I was jerked awake by a furious rocking. To my astonished eyes, I saw a tiny crack appear in the egg. There was a trilling sound filled with determination, and then what sounded like someone driving an iron spike into an immovable wall.

I dashed towards the door and yanked it open. "Warren!" I said breathlessly. "Warren, it's hatching! I think it's hatching!"

Warren nearly fell over, then quickly caught himself. "Hatching? Are you sure?"

I glanced behind me. "Fairly certain."

Warren pushed me back inside. "Food will be here shortly. I'll let Lieutenant Marcell know." Then he closed the door and locked it.

It was mesmerizing to watch. The dragon growled as it fought with the shell. I realized the baby was using a horn when it broke through, a piece flying to the wall. Eyes wide, I backed up a little further. Doctor McDragon had said this would take hours. I couldn't see how. The door was unlocked briefly for the giant tray of food to be pushed inside, then the door was closed and relocked. I locked it from my side as well, then turned back to watching the dragon destroy the shell.

It was black, and I couldn't help the tiny shot of satisfaction in the back of my brain. The scales were jet black in contrast to the white opalescence of the egg shell. Its claws and the horn on its head, the baby horn that would fall off after a year, were ivory colored, offsetting the black. As it climbed out, what remained of the shell fell to the stone floor.

The dragon looked at me first, eyes slits of grey mingled with another color.

"I'm Kaylyn," I said cautiously.

"Kaylyn." Like his mother, I felt a presence in my mind, curious, suspicious, and hungry. He was starving, and I felt it as assuredly as I felt his knowledge of what he was; a male, black dragon who felt threatened. Voices outside the door became suddenly louder, and his head whipped towards the door. He hissed his defiance, the wings I hadn't noticed before raising from his body in a gesture of warning. They were black as well, and I could see the joints that allowed him to control the wings with finite precision. He hissed at the door again.

I scooted the bowl forward a little, turning his attention. "I have food," I said.

"I am hungry." He sounded hungry.

"I have more if you want it. Come eat."

He wasted no time in coming for the food. He snapped up the meat hungrily, drinking the liquid dry. He demanded more to drink with commanding noises and I gave it to him, occasionally tossing in another bite of meat. As he ate, he relaxed a little more. His eyes darted occasionally to the door, as if someone out there would come steal his food, but they slowly calmed from a dark, stormy grey to a darker blue.

When the bowl had been emptied the second time, he sat back and regarded me. I stared back, unsure of what to do. Inside, I was in awe of him. He was beautiful. I itched to touch his scales, to feel them and see how they seemed to shine. I ended up tucking my hands behind my back so I wouldn't anger him and risk getting my fingers bitten off.

"I guess you need a name," I said at last. I had some ideas from the list Dillon had given me. "Maybe...Blackstar. Or Emberonyx. Or Nightwing." I studied him thoughtfully. "You have a temper. Something to do with fire. Firestorm. Blackfire. Nightfire." That had a certain ring to it and I nodded slowly, saying it again. "Nightfire."

He made a soft humming noise, one of approval. *"Nightfire,"* he repeated. *"You are Kaylyn."*

I nodded silently.

He seemed to go through some internal debate, his eyes changing colors, flashing. I didn't know what to do. Rosewing had only told me what to do up to this point. She hadn't told me about anything further. If this dragon was as smart as Rosewing had hinted at, I hoped he'd know what to do. I wondered if I'd done enough to have him choose me as his mother.

Nightfire seemed to come to some decision, and paced forward on all four feet. I held very still. He walked to me, rose on his back legs, hesitated a moment, then touched his muzzle to my forehead.

The thoughts in my head swirled. I could almost see a line joining from his mind to mine. Mindlink, I suddenly understood. Dragons called it a mindlink. My thoughts could flow to him, and his thoughts to me through this new pathway. More than just thoughts, I realized with a jolt, but emotions. I felt his uncertainty for this world he didn't understand, the danger he felt from the people outside, but I also felt the simple belief that I would protect him. He didn't think of me as a mother, but as a partner who would take care of him when he needed it; a guardian.

"I will," I promised silently. *"I'll take care of you and protect you as best I can."*

"They do not like you," he warned. *"They will not let you."*

"I was right and they were wrong. And Dillon will help us. He helped us before."

"I heard. I remember." There was something in his tone that made me think of fire.

"You can't flame, right?" I asked.

"No. Or I would use it on all of them."

I decided I'd found the only other being in existence who could possibly be more hotheaded and less politically correct than me. I had an idea of what my brother felt like. "Maybe you shouldn't," I suggested. "That'll just make them mad."

"I do not care. I am a dragon."

"Well *I* care, and if they don't hurt you for it, they'll hurt me. So play nice."

I felt his dislike for that course of action, but he nodded his head once. I took it as a good sign and lifted the board out of the way to unlock the door. "Warren!" I called. "You can unlock the door now!"

There was the sound of the door unlocking on the other side.

"Bring her out, my dear," Doctor McDragon called. "Have you told her what her name is yet?"

I opened the door and walked out first. Doctor McDragon's smile froze on his face as he took my dragon in.

"*His* name is Nightfire," I informed them all.

Nightfire sat next to me, observing all the people and sensing their emotions. "Who is the fool who calls himself a doctor of dragons?" he demanded.

"The fat one looking about to faint," I told him silently, enjoying his expression.

Nightfire's gaze zeroed in on Doctor McDragon.

It was General Maddox who stated the obvious. "That's not a white dragon."

"He's not a girl either," I said, feeling triumphant.

Doctor McDragon cleared his throat once. "On rare occasions, black dragons are hatched from a white shell. It's so rare I've only seen it once..."

"Dragons do not allow humans near hatching sites," Nightfire said with utter certainty.

"I wasn't *at* the site, per say. I was farther back."

"Dragons would know. I hear the horses in the stable. You could not be close enough to see."

"His hatching didn't take hours either," I informed the rest of the room.

Nightfire observed the increasingly anxious fraud dispassionately. "You know nothing of dragons."

Doctor McDragon was sweating, I was intrigued to see, lines of sweat rolling from the top of his bald head down his cheeks. "You're just a hatchling. You don't know…"

"I can hear through the shell. I learn what I hear. I know who wanted to kill me." His dark gaze moved to Generals Olina and Maddox. "I know there are male white dragons. I know there is a female bronze dragon who hatched not long ago. I know that bronze dragons are not made of bronze metal." Scorn dripped from his words. "And dragons do not wish to hoard treasure. Treasure is a human desire. Dragons want nothing of your shiny trash."

I felt myself smirking. "Guess I was right after all."

"But all your research," General Maddox protested.

"He made it all up," I stated. "Every last bit of it."

"I did nothing of the kind!" Doctor McDragon said, striving to appear imperious.

"You lie," Nightfire said.

"I…the insult!"

"Dragons know. Do not doubt the word of a dragon." There was a threat there.

Doctor McDragon hadn't quite given up yet. "I have spent *years* living in the wilderness, hiking up and down the Esperion Mountains…"

"Alone?" I asked, interrupting. "Or with servants?"

"Alone, of course. Nobody comes with me."

"Then you must have magic," I said frankly. "Because you didn't climb any mountains like *that*. You look as if you've sat in your noble manor and spent the day eating. And nobody with hands like yours does hard labor."

His nerve was failing him. I was sure it didn't help that Nightfire was glaring unwaveringly at him. "I don't know what you mean."

51

"Your hands," I said, pointing to them. "White. Soft. Not a mark on them. Look at Lieutenant Marcell's." I pointed and Dillon obligingly offered his hands, palm up. "Calluses. Scars. You can't live alone and not have to work hard. Where did you get food? Did you hunt? Who skinned the meat? Who carried everything you'd need to study and live in the mountains? Who built your fires? Pitched a tent?" I crossed my arm. "You're a fraud," I said emphatically. "Admit it. And if you call me 'dear girl' one more time, I'll ask Nightfire to bite you."

"I am not…"

Nightfire opened his mouth and hissed, showing gleaming teeth. Doctor McDragon stumbled backwards fearfully. "Yes, I made it up," he blurted out. "I made it all up. Nobody knows anything about dragons; who would know if I was lying?"

The generals, especially General Maddox and General Hesperian, looked like children who'd just had their favorite toy taken away. "You made it up? All of it?" Maddox repeated. "But you're Doctor McDragon!"

Dillon interjected then. "Kaylyn, why don't you and Nightfire follow me? I have a place for you to stay." His look suggested I not protest.

I would have anyway but Nightfire sat back, observing him. "You are Dillon," he stated with certainty.

Dillon bowed respectfully. "I am. If you would please follow me."

I held my question until the door closed and then I blurted out, "Why? I want to hear him say it!"

"You heard him say enough. I don't want anyone accusing you and Nightfire of intimidating or threatening a false confession out of him. You're right, he made up everything, but you can scare him into admitting it and he can claim he lied to protect himself."

"He makes sense for a human," Nightfire told me. I sensed that thought had only been to me.

"So I don't make sense?" I asked.

He didn't answer. *"Where are we going?"*

"I don't know. Where are we going?" I asked.

"Primarily, away from the generals and doctor."

"Can't we watch Doctor McDragon fall apart?" I pleaded. "I was right! All the generals told me I was stupid and wrong, and I can show them I wasn't!"

"Which is exactly why we're going elsewhere. You've proven your point. If you stay there and mock them, you'll ruin any respect you might have gained."

I sighed in disappointment. "All right. Can I at least have them apologize to me?"

He chuckled. "Doubtful. But they will certainly be less inclined to disagree with you." He pushed open the main doors. "Go explore. Walk it off. When you come back, we'll have more food prepared."

Nightfire liked that idea. "I will be hungry," he stated.

"You just *ate*!" I protested.

His voice was offended. "I am no bigger than a *human*." He sneered the word and gave me a condescending glance out of light green eyes. "I will need to eat much to grow."

"You'll grow fat is what you'll do," I informed him.

He flipped his tail to convey annoyance and trundled off down the path, looking curiously at this thing, then that, already forgetting me.

"Aren't you going too?" Dillon asked me.

I didn't know whether to feel hurt, abandoned, or angry. "Why? He obviously doesn't want me to go. He doesn't even *like* me. And I didn't do anything to deserve that." I sat down on the stone steps and glared moodily at the ground. "Ungrateful dragon."

Nightfire paused in his walking, and I felt hesitation and some repentance, and what I thought might be guilt. "You may come."

I didn't leap to my feet. My pride had been hurt and I wasn't ready to give in so quickly. "Don't bother on *my* account, your highness. Let me know whenever you need feeding next and I will be sure to attend to your needs."

Through the emotional link, I sensed him searching for what I felt. In response, I felt an apology for hurting my feelings and a patience that I'd seen on adults' faces; a kind of patience gained by age and wisdom that he already had. *"I am sorry,"* he thought to me, and I sensed again that I was the only one getting these thoughts. *"Please come with me. I do not mind your company."*

I was appeased enough that I gained my feet. "Can we go outside the gates?"

"Best if you don't. No one else knows there's a dragon here. I will go inform the recruits so they know. Let me know if you need anything at all."

"He is not bad for a human," Nightfire told me.

"What am I then?" I demanded.

"Mine." And with that one word statement, he trundled further down the path.

I paused, considering it, questioning what that meant, then decided it was as appropriate as anything.

Despite the fact that Nightfire was smaller than I was, I was fairly certain he'd eaten twice what I could. I couldn't imagine how he could stomach that much, feeling a little sick myself. For some reason, I felt as if I'd eaten too much when I hadn't eaten anything. Finally, Nightfire explained what the mindlink did. He'd overeaten, but I felt just as miserable as he did. He informed me it worked the other way, so anything I felt he would feel too.

The recruits all crowded around windows to stare at us. Nightfire sprawled out on the grass while I sat nearby, studying him. His eyes were halfway open, tracking movement of a butterfly. I'd explained what it was to him. To my fascination, I saw his eyes changing colors. "Can all dragons' eyes change colors?" I asked him.

"Yes."

"Do they always mean the same thing?"

"Of course."

"All I've heard is that dragons' eyes turn their deepest red right before they flame. No one knows what the rest of the colors mean."

"Humans only know what they wish to know."

"Hey," I protested. "It's not like you're willing to share anything."

"Why would dragons want to share when you only want to kill us?" he demanded, eyes flickering a light pink color that I guessed to be annoyance.

"We aren't *all* like that. I'm not. Dillon's not. Not everyone's as stupid as the generals." I shook my head. "Nobles."

"Do all humans rank themselves according to how much shiny, human trash they have?"

"Pretty much."

He snorted in contempt, his eyes flashing light green again.

"I don't like it either, but I can't see it changing any day soon."

"Erm. Milady?"

Since no one else was around, I looked for the speaker. A nervous servant girl stood at the top of the steps, ready to flee inside. "Milady, Lieutenant Marcell wishes to speak to you," she called.

"Where is he?" I asked.

"His office." She curtseyed quickly and, with her message delivered, fled back inside.

"Humans are easily frightened," Nightfire commented.

"She probably thinks you want to eat her."

"Humans taste terrible."

"How do you know?" I asked curiously.

"All dragons know."

I didn't question further. "Good to hear." I gained my feet. "Are you staying?"

"I am too full to move."

"You don't get to overeat again," I ordered him. "This is awful."

He closed his eyes as if to ignore me, but I muttered, "I told you so," as I headed inside.

Dillon was waiting in his office. "How's Nightfire?"

"He overate."

"The servants are afraid of him."

55

"He says humans taste terrible. I don't think he's going to eat anyone." I seated myself in a chair. "Why did you call me?"

"To tell you the decisions made by the generals that concern you and Nightfire."

"What happened with Doctor McDragon?" I protested.

"He left in disgrace. Further punishment is pending. Everyone knows he lied and he fully admitted his dishonesty. At the very least, he's lost credibility to his reputation. And as for you, you've been moved to the military."

"What does that mean?" I asked.

"It means you're under military jurisdiction now."

"Nightfire is *not* a weapon," I said angrily.

Dillon shrugged. "They can always dream. Either way, it means you have a place to stay. You and Nightfire can stay here as long as you want."

"You mean, we *have* to stay here."

"Think of it as less of a restriction and more of a gift. You won't have to go home. You can stay here with Warren, and the generals left an hour ago."

I perked up at this. "They did?" I was nearly overjoyed. "They really left?"

"They don't normally spend much time here. They signed the documents stating that Nightfire is under your guardianship, making you in charge of him on paper, and you are under military establishment now."

"Where? Army?"

"Not defined. They're thinking a special branch. All I know is you're under my rule now."

"I thought I was under your rule before."

"Now you're under my rule as a recruit, so all military rules and School for Officers and Gentleman rules now apply to you." He placed a sizable book in my hand. "Some light reading. The Code of Conduct for Officers and Gentlemen. Every recruit is required to read it."

I eyed it doubtfully. "Would I be an officer, or a gentleman?" I asked dryly.

He grinned. "Military makes you an officer."

"So I can gain a rank?"

He shrugged. "Again, there isn't a lot we're sure of. We'll see how things work. You don't have any commitments yet because we have no idea what kind of commitment a dragon takes. Once we have an idea of what you need, and what your dragon needs, we'll find a place for you." He tapped the book in my hand. "Have that read by the end of the week, and you'll be tested on it."

I stared at the book, then I stared at him. "Tested? On this?" I repeated, aghast.

"Welcome to the military, Kaylyn," he said with an evil smile. "I suggest you get reading."

Chapter 6

I read the book three times by the end of the week. I was determined not to fail my first test here. One of the frowning instructors stood over me while I took it, which made me nervous as I struggled to think. With Nightfire's help to occasionally remind me of the beginning of a specific passage, I passed the test easily. To make sure I would have passed anyway, I counted the questions that Nightfire had helped me on, and still ended up a handful of points above passing. This didn't make anyone happier, except my brother and me. Nightfire didn't care about what he deemed 'useless human laws'.

Although almost everyone was awed and spent all their free time and conversations talking about Nightfire and trying to watch him, they were still fearful of him. No one ventured near him if I wasn't around, and even then they didn't venture close. Nightfire didn't mind it. The side effect was that almost everyone avoided me like the plague. I didn't normally mind that, it was only when people avoided me as if I actually had the plague that got to me. I didn't like how people would go out of their way to avoid interacting with me, especially the younger, newer recruits.

My brother and his close friends would occasionally eat with me and would help with any questions I had. They helped roll in the four barrels of oil after I'd used six different kinds to determine a plant-based oil was what Nightfire preferred and was the best in easing the effects of dry skin and a baby dragon's growing needs. The oil prevented cracking, eased itching, and was supposed to help prevent infection. Nightfire had already gotten one after we used too much of the wrong oil. We'd discovered it when my side itched unbearably and his black scales had turned purple and white and started to fall off on his side. I'd panicked and Dillon had been the one to assure me that Nightfire was not about to die. After switching to another oil, the infection had gone away.

Being left alone meant I spent a lot of time with Nightfire when he wasn't sleeping. He had thousands of questions, and I answered them all as best I could. At night, he'd climb into the little place the recruits had set up for him. Dillon had the foresight to find a place Nightfire would be pleased about staying in and the recruits had built a temporary, stable-like building for Nightfire to stay in. It was built right below where my room was, so I could look down to him. Occasionally I'd climbed through the window and down to him when he'd called to me. It was much quicker and much less annoying than running down the hallway and down the stairs to the hallway that led outside, past all the people who would avoid me or give me strange looks. I heard mutterings that the School would be destroyed if I wasn't here to control the black dragon, but I could never figure out who said it.

The time I didn't spend with Nightfire either made me angry or bored me. I had little interest in the library and I was constantly being turned away from one room or another. When I demanded to know why, I was politely informed that this was a place to train male officers and gentlemen, and I was neither. Dillon had finally intervened after I'd berated the third man that day, much to the delight of the servants nearby and the embarrassment of my brother.

"Kaylyn, do you even *want* to learn tactics?" Dillon asked.

"What if I did?" I was fuming. "I'm military, right? Then why won't you allow me to *be* military? According to all your instructors, since I'm a female, I'm apparently an idiot incapable of knowing much more than my name! If the enemy attacks one day, what are you going to do with me? Do I stand in the back and wave a little handkerchief at them like some useless child as they march off into the sunset?"

"It's a little soon to speculate on that," Dillon said gently. "If you wanted to learn, I'll ask for you. The professors don't know where you're supposed to be."

"Would you please tell *me* where I'm supposed to be? I'm tired of doing nothing! I can only oil Nightfire so many times a day! I understand nobody wants me here, but I don't really want to be here either! This is the one place where you all think women should be silent and spend their time primping or sewing." My lip curled in disgust.

"Have you tried the library?"

"They all stare at me. I was led over to the tiny section on sewing and embroidery and expected to stay there. I was informed I wasn't *allowed* to touch any of the history books or much of anything else."

"The weapons room?"

"'This is not a place for a female'," I imitated in the self-righteous tone that had accompanied the statement. "'And I'm afraid you will only distract my recruits.' I'm not *good* enough to learn on my own. I don't know what I don't know."

"The great hall?"

"There isn't anything to do there either except have people stare at me and whisper."

He sighed. "What about the kitchens?"

"I was never taught to cook and no one in there has the time or patience to teach me anything. Half of the people in there are afraid to come near me anyway." I glared at the ground, feeling miserable. "I really hate this place. I'm just a nuisance in the way. Again."

He rested his hand on my shoulder. "Let's see if we can find someplace for you to be," he said quietly.

I was in better spirits after I watched Dillon inform the master scribe I was allowed to read whatever I wanted to read. The man tried to argue, but Dillon won. As soon as Dillon gave me his nod, I immediately pulled three books and two old scrolls off the shelf and left with them, ignoring the scribe's outraged squawk.

"You will have to check those out, like anyone else," Dillon said when he found me later.

Nightfire and I were already studying the scrolls. "I was here," I said, pointing to where I'd met Rosewing. "And all the dragons are supposed to live up here, in the Esperion Mountains." I was already opening another book, letting Nightfire study the scroll. "So long as he doesn't try to forbid me taking something," I told Dillon.

"You're allowed to check out anything in there. All the scribes have been informed of that. They ask that you be careful with them."

"I'm not going to destroy these and neither is Nightfire." I leaned against Nightfire's side and started to read. "The Esperion Mountains were so named after the explorer, Lord James Esperion, who was a first cousin to the royal line."

"Why does that matter?" Nightfire inquired.

"It means he got his royal cousin to give him money so he could go explore," I said matter-of-factly.

Dillon grinned. "It's a little more delicate than that."

I made a noise of skepticism.

"Not that much more," he conceded. "But a little more." He sat in the chair by the door. "Were the books for you or Nightfire?"

"Nightfire." I nodded to the black dragon. "He's smarter than everyone here. His memory is incredible. He can name everyone in this place, their full title and their nickname, and I mean *everyone*. We sat outside yesterday and he named everyone who passed by. But he has all these questions that I can't answer. He can hear the lessons inside sometimes, if they have an open window, but he doesn't understand it all. Besides, this is better than doing nothing, which is all I'm allowed to do."

"We'll find something for you to do," he promised. "I'll speak to Captain Durai."

"Captain Durai said I couldn't take anything until this set of classes had finished. And none of the instructors want to deal with me so I can't get any private lessons." I flipped a page moodily back and forth. "As if I needed reminding that nobody wants me."

"That isn't true. I'm afraid you're in a place where most people tend to cling to old traditions."

"You mean the ones where women could barely write their name because nobody thought we were smart enough to learn?"

"Not that old. But the military has a hard time seeing women as equals, especially in matters of war. It'll get better," he promised.

"Yeah, right," I muttered. I wasn't sure he believed it either.

"Humans are strange," Nightfire commented.

Dillon left me reading to Nightfire. I read to him for the rest of the day, until my throat was long past dry and my voice was hoarse. Since I was interested in the book, I carried it with me to dinner and settled myself at the end of a table to read. Warren and his friends were halfway down the long, scarred, oak table.

"Look here. The girl found a book," someone's voice mocked behind me.

I stopped reading, but never took my eyes off the pages in front of me.

"What's the girl reading?" A hand grabbed the edge of the book.

I slammed my hand on top of it, glaring up at the face of a tall boy, slightly bulky, with a lineage as long as his nose and golden hair. "Hands off."

"That's Lord Kipper to you," he informed me regally. "And I can do what I want."

He tried again, and I held tighter to the book. "Not here you can't," I said grimly. "Get your hands off."

"Back off, Kip," my brother called, voice tense. "Leave her alone."

Lord Kipper ignored him and settled across from me. "What is this? History? Isn't that too much for your tiny, little brain?" he taunted me. "Shouldn't you be sewing something?"

I itched to pick up the book and slam it into his face. He wouldn't be so arrogant with a broken nose. Remembering the rules, I pulled the book a little closer to me and kept my eyes firmly fixed on the word 'Centralia'.

Lord Kipper elegantly rolled back the silken cuffs on his sleeves. His family had wealth, and he was showing it. His clothes and shoes were expensive. What I guessed to be an heirloom ring on his middle finger showed he was the firstborn and would likely inherit everything. He couldn't be more than sixteen, and already he had all the arrogance that his lineage provided. "This table is a little wobbly, isn't it?" he inquired as he bounced the wooden table once.

I let out a gasp as I grabbed for the water glass wobbling dangerously close to the book. Pretending not to notice what he was doing, he bounced it again. "I'll have to mention it to the servants," he said, giving an innocent smile. "Unless you would take care of it for me."

I wasn't doing anything for him. "If it bothers you, you take care of it," I said tartly, holding onto the glass.

He shrugged easily, his eyes on me as one of the servant girls poured him a glass of water. He didn't thank her. She remained invisible to him as she moved quietly to another table.

His attention was finally distracted by one of his friends, and I pulled the book a little closer to me, knowing in a moment I'd have to put it away before he ruined it and got me into trouble for it. I marked the page carefully; then as I started to close it, he turned, bouncing the table again, his brown eyes mocking me. I decided I wasn't going to put up with it.

As he bounced the table yet again, I reached for my glass, deliberately knocking it into his, and both of them spilled across the table and into his lap. He leapt up, swearing. I jumped to my feet too, the book held protectively. "I'm *so* sorry, Lord Kipper," I said sweetly. "I guess you're right. The table *is* awfully wobbly."

He glared at me as he wiped at his clothing. If it hadn't been water, his outfit would have been ruined. As it was, he had to leave or endure wet clothing through dinner. "You common, little..." he started to hiss.

"Recruit Kipper!" Captain Durai's voice rang across the room. "What are the rules about swearing as stated in the Code of Conduct for Officers and Gentlemen?"

He faced front, coming to attention. "Swearing is not deemed appropriate for settings where gentlemanly behavior is required, sir," he stated.

"And the punishment?"

His features tightened minutely. "At least one hour of work where you see fit, sir, since you caught me."

I saw Captain Durai glance momentarily at me. I still held the book protectively to my chest. "Since it appears some of the dining equipment is not to your standards, you will have an hour to correct it. The kitchen staff will provide you the tools after dinner is over."

"Yes, sir." Recruit Kipper bowed a little stiffly, which could have been due to the wet clothing, then walked away from the spilled water, silently fuming.

"I'll help," I offered as one of the servant girls came over with a cloth to dry. I set the book down on a dry spot, righted the glasses, then wiped off the table while the girl took care of the water on the bench and the floor. She whispered a soft thanks before reclaiming the cloth and moving back to the kitchens.

I picked up the book and saw a shifting on the bench. Warren gestured impatiently. "Sit here," he ordered as he took a seat at the end of his friends, pointing to the spot beside him. "Before you get yourself in more trouble."

"I'm not in trouble," I informed him, seating myself next to him.

"Kip isn't going to like you," he warned me.

"Warren, *nobody* here likes me." I cracked the book open. "I have a question."

He looked a touch resigned. "What?"

I ignored his tone. "What's a...turn-i-ket?"

"Tourniquet," he confirmed. "And I'm not sure. Why?"

"Because it says something about it in this book, and I don't know what it is."

Warren turned to his friends. "Hey, what's a tourniquet do?" he asked.

"I don't even know what that is," said the person directly across from him.

"Doesn't it have something to do with horses?" one asked.

"No, it's something for medicine," another decreed.

"We don't know," Warren interpreted. "But I can ask in class tomorrow."

"Thanks." I closed the book and set it next to me on the bench as servants brought food to our table.

The next day, Warren informed me at tourniquet was a piece of cloth that restricted blood flow. "If you cut your arm here," he said, pointing to my elbow, "then you tie something tight above it, and then less blood escapes."

"Thanks. I have another word." I closed my eyes, trying to remember. "Cariole. It has something to do with transportation."

"I know that one." This was Canesfield, an old friend of Warren's who tolerated me. "My grandfather used to own one. It was an old carriage, a small one that had a cloth covering so people could take it down if they wanted."

"What about appatis?"

"How do you find these words?" Warren asked.

"I read," I informed him.

"I thought you didn't find reading that much fun."

"What *else* am I to do?" I demanded.

Warren quickly let that slide. "I'll ask."

For a week I asked questions to Warren and his friends and they brought the answers back to me during meals. During the week, we learned an appatis was a treaty that protected a village that surrendered from looting and abuse if they paid the ransom to the occupying force. We also learned that gules was a red color on a coat of arms, a kunnin was a wooden throwing stick we thought was used for hunting, and a yett was a type of wrought-iron gate that opened and closed like a set of doors rather than raising or lowering like a portcullis. Warren didn't seem to mind asking his professors these questions, although I wasn't sure that the instructors knew why he was asking.

One night, hours after the warning for lights out had been called, Nightfire called me. *"I want to walk,"* he informed me.

I got up. I'd been lying sleepless for hours. *"I'll walk with you. Give me a few minutes."*

65

Nightfire waited patiently while I slipped my shoes on and a dress, and then locked my door, climbing out the window. He assisted me with the last few steps, then we started walking.

The grounds for the School were large and well-maintained. It took a large crew of groundskeepers to keep it looking military pristine. Nightfire and I walked from the dormitories to the north gate, the gate that led to the forest and the Esperion Mountains, then around to the east gate, which was one of the two main gates. The east gate led to the nearest town, Caspane, and the south gate was the direction in which all the important places were, such as the capitol, the university, and the quickest road to what was quickly becoming the highest acclaimed school of learning for women; the Academy for Fine Ladies. It was a place where women were trained to be good people of society, good wives, but it was also one of the few places were women were taught past what was offered in the local schools everyone was required to attend for six years. I guessed it was something like the School for Officers and Gentlemen for women.

As we started to approach the east gate, we heard it quietly rattling. Confused, the gate was supposed to be locked, I moved closer to the wall. Nightfire stopped moving and became nearly invisible in the blackness as I crept silently forward.

A girl, a few years older than me, quietly closed the gate behind her. Her hair was straight and smooth, a dark, deep brown that looked almost black in the darkness. As she turned, I stepped out of the shadow and she spotted me. She paused for a moment, looking almost disappointed rather than frightened at getting caught. She wasn't a servant. No servant I'd seen wore a dress so scandalously short or cut so low. I could see the woman's knees and could almost see her shoulders while her cleavage left very little to the imagination.

I narrowed my eyes. "Who are you?"

The woman flipped her hair out of her face. "No need to get jealous, sweetheart," she crooned. "I'm not after your honey." She held out a hand elegantly to show me her gold bracelet glittering to show she had wealth. "My name's Mary Beth."

I crossed my arms. "You aren't allowed here."

She chuckled and dropped her hand. "Honey, you aren't either."

"I live here. You don't."

"You live here?" She sneered a little now. "A servant girl. Sweetie, my father employs dozens of your kind. You can take your grievances elsewhere or I'll make sure you're fired."

A soft growl sounded behind me, and I heard Nightfire's soft footsteps.

"My name is Kaylyn Madara," I stated. "Not sweetie. And I'm not a servant either."

Her eyes widened. "You're the girl with the dragon!" And her eyes nearly popped out of her head as she finally saw Nightfire. He stood right behind me.

"And you need to leave." I pointed.

She quickly slipped the bracelet off her wrist. "Honey, look, it's no big deal. I haven't been able to visit in a while. Everyone was kept out because of your dragon. Look, just take this, and I'll be gone in an hour or so." She offered the sparkling piece of jewelry to me.

I snatched it, then threw it at her feet. "You're nothing more than a floozy. Get out."

She gasped at the insult. "I'm a noble!"

"Then you're a *rich* floozy. Either way, you need to leave right now, and don't come back. I don't want to see you as long as I'm here."

Nightfire growled softly again. "Leave, human," he warned her. "I will not be so forgiving a second time."

Mary Beth let out another gasp, this time of fear, and ran. I glared until she left, then hugged Nightfire's neck. "That was great," I told him.

"She is a weak human. Greedy. I do not like her."

"I don't either. Snobby, spoiled little brat. 'My father employs dozens of your kind'," I mimicked. I scooped up the bracelet that Mary Beth had forgotten. "I guess Dillon can deal with this tomorrow," I said.

"What is this?" Dillon asked when I deposited it on his desk the next morning.

"It used to be Mary Beth's bracelet. I guess it still is. She forgot it."

"She *forgot* it?" He inspected it, whistling softly. "Daddy's little girl, all right."

"She won't be back," I said, unconcerned. "I don't know what to do with it."

He looked at me, shook his head, fighting a smile. "You weren't up past curfew, were you?"

"Up and out. Couldn't sleep. Nightfire needed to walk. He says nobody stares at night."

"I could give you punishment for that. Do you know the standard punishment for being up and out past curfew?"

"Five laps around the grounds and one hour of punishment work in the stables. And it would be a further hour if I didn't know the punishment."

He gave a rueful smile. "I guess there wouldn't be much point in punishing you, would there? Warren warned me you were a handful." He went back to the bracelet, inspecting it a moment, then laying it on the desk. "The recruits will be disappointed."

"The servants won't. She threatened to get them fired; that's how she kept getting through."

"Is it?"

I nodded. "Mattes is in love with her, so he unlocks the gate. The other servants won't say anything so they can keep their jobs."

"I'll see that this gets returned to Mary Beth."

"Lady Mary Beth. She's a noble."

He smiled. "I'll see it gets returned to Lady Mary Beth, and warned about the consequences of blackmail. I'm sure your threat was good, but I think I'll reinforce it. Are you getting along with the servants, then?"

"They keep calling me Lady Kaylyn for some reason and won't talk much. Especially once Nightfire's around. Why do they think I'm a high-ranking noble?" I asked, perplexed.

"Your family was granted a title."

I was astonished. "We have a title?"

"Yes, you do."

"Why?"

"Because the generals saw fit to give you one. I believe services offered to Centralia were one of the reasons."

"You mean I found a dragon egg." My tone went sour. "Great. Now I'm a *noble*."

"You were a noble before."

"Not one that mattered." I muttered under my breath a moment. "I bet Warren's thrilled. And my sisters."

"Not you?"

"It doesn't matter. Nothing's changed, is it?" I straightened. "Anyway, there's Mary Beth's bracelet. I'm going to go read with Nightfire."

"What are you on now?"

"I'm reading history, but Nightfire's on the tactics book."

He chuckled. "Find something for the headache."

Nightfire was lounging half in, half out of his makeshift home, eyes closed, basking in the sun. I could sense he was awake and waiting for me. "Tactics?" I asked with some resignation.

I felt the affirmation in my mind and acquiesced, retrieving the book and settling myself against his neck.

I read through the book painstakingly, struggling to get all the words right that I still didn't completely understand, wondering in the back of my mind how any of this made sense. Nightfire just listened, eyes closed, absorbing it all in.

"Do you hear her?" The sneer in the voice caused me to look up, already preparing for a fight. It was a stocky boy, standing with a pack of his classmates. "She thinks she can understand tactics." His friends scoffed and laughed with him.

Temper boiled. I wanted to hit him. He'd never touch me, not with Nightfire at my back.

"There is another way." Nightfire was all for fighting back, but he knew how to do it smarter. *"Hurt his pride, not his face, and he will not forget it."*

I got up and walked over to him. "You don't think we understand tactics?" I inquired, knowing my eyes were glittering.

"Not a chance," he said. "Your dragon isn't smart enough; and you?" He gave a derisive laugh. "You couldn't understand anything in the library."

I flipped open the first page, held it up to his face so he could see the words and the cover was to me. "Let me know when I miss a word," I said. And with Nightfire supplying me the words, I recited the entire first page and half of the second from Nightfire's memory. They'd all crowded around the book in the beginning, but now they were silent, uneasily shifting as I read off the page word by word, paragraph by paragraph, my gaze moving from face to face.

"What do you think now, Lord Magnus Leolin? Or should I call you Leo like your buddies?" I inquired, watching him flinch back. I turned my gaze to the boy next to him. "You? Maynard Lennox?"

He flushed, ducked his head.

"Did you know that, or did your dragon?" one ventured forth nervously.

I snapped the book shut in front of Magnus's nose. "Wouldn't you like to know? If you don't mind, we have studying to do." I strutted a little as I resumed my place next to Nightfire and cracked the book open to our previous spot and started reading again.

When the area had deserted, everyone in class, I lowered the book. "Do you know what any of this means?" I asked. "Because I haven't understood a word of it yet."

"I understand."

I grunted and gulped water to ease my dry throat. "At least *one* of us does."

"Someone is still watching us."

"Who?" I looked around.

"I cannot tell. His thoughts are quiet. I only know that he is there." A moment later, while I uselessly tried to find this person,

he said, *"The person is gone."* He nudged the book in my hands. *"Read."*

With a sigh, I went back to reading.

We took a break an hour before dinner and Nightfire returned to his home to nap, falling asleep quickly. I started to walk, knowing his sleepiness would make me drowsy if I didn't move around or move farther away. I was halfway down the path between the main building and the east gate when a familiar voice called to me.

"Kaylyn!" a voice sang.

My head jerked up from studying the frog in the grass. "Amina!" I cried, delighted as I raced down the path to her.

Amina grinned at me when I reached her, showing her slightly crooked teeth, tossing her brown hair over her shoulder. "Of all places, Kaylyn, you come here! I thought we swore off rules and responsibility."

I shrugged, slightly embarrassed. "Well, I didn't really have much of a choice."

"Can I see this dragon of yours?"

"He's napping, and he doesn't like being disturbed when he's asleep."

"He's asleep? Good! Let's go! I have more green powder." Her brown eyes sparkled with devilment as she grabbed my hand. "Let's go light it all on fire! And then we can go exploring in the forest!"

As much fun as that sounded, I hung back. "Amina, I can't," I said with apology. "I'm supposed to stay here."

"So what? No rules, no responsibility, Kaylyn! We can do whatever we want!"

"I can't anymore. I have to stay with Nightfire."

"You just said he's napping."

"I'm responsible for him. I can't just leave."

Her brown eyes went flat. "I thought we swore never to say that," she hissed. "We aren't *responsible* for anything! Until we marry, we don't *have* to do anything but what we want! You promised me that you were willing to break the rules."

"I promised I'd take care of Nightfire. I can't just go off and leave him."

She snatched her hand away, temper there. "You're a fraud, Kaylyn. You aren't a true rebel. You aren't anything."

"I didn't *have* any responsibility before," I hissed back, trying to hide the hurt. "There wasn't anything at home that *mattered*. This matters. Nightfire matters. I won't break my promise to him or his mother. Please, Amina. Just stay here and…"

"No." Anger was plain. "You aren't a real friend. A real friend wouldn't break their promises. You *promised* me that friends came before rules!"

"I guess I found a better friend," I snapped.

She sucked in a breath sharply, hurt briefly hitting, then anger. "Fine, Kaylyn! Then take your new friend and *stay* here! I *never* want to see you again!" She turned around a stomped off.

"Same goes!" I screamed before running inside and slamming the door shut. Upstairs, alone, I wept because I didn't have any friends. All I had was Nightfire, and he wasn't Amina.

Chapter 7

I didn't go to dinner. I'd already had an encounter with Warren, he'd heard Amina had visited, and I wasn't hungry. I was wallowing in self-pity when Dillon knocked lightly on my door. "I heard you've had a rough day," he said with some sympathy.

I nodded, hugging my pillow tighter.

He gave a half-smile. "It's the first time I've had to do this with a female. Walk with me, Kaylyn. I need to give you a talk about the realities of life and growing up."

"Did I break a rule?"

"You aren't in trouble. I just want to talk."

I replaced my pillow on the bed and got to my feet. Dillon led me outside, but didn't speak until we'd reached the north wall. "A friend visited today," he prompted.

"She's not a friend anymore. She's mean. And self-centered. And I hate her."

"I think you miss her too," he suggested gently as we walked around the edge of the grounds, following the walls.

I wouldn't admit to that. "I told her I had to stay here. I told her I couldn't leave Nightfire alone. He's my responsibility. And Amina said if I wouldn't break the rules for her then I wasn't really a friend."

"Do you believe that?"

"I don't know."

He was silent for a moment. "Do you think that if you'd broken the rules that you'd still be friends?"

"Yes. We'd be exploring the forest and playing with green powder right now."

"And what about when you came back? What would happen then?"

"I'd be in trouble," I admitted. "Warren would be upset with me. He'd have been worried. Nightfire might be upset. You'd give me punishment."

"All true. Today you had a choice to either go with Amina and take the consequences, or stay here and take the consequences. As hard as it is to accept right now, you made the right choice. You've proven you're capable of being responsible."

I sniffed and kicked a rock, watching it bounce across the path. "Responsibility stinks."

"A hard lesson, but it means you're becoming an adult." The approval in his voice helped to take some of the sting over my lost friendship.

"You're nicer than Warren. All he said was, 'I told you so'."

"I take it Warren didn't approve of Amina?"

"Nobody did. But she was my friend. Or I thought she was. I guess I can't pick good friends either." I got angry so I wouldn't cry. "She shouldn't have asked. If *she* were a friend, she wouldn't have asked."

"You're thirteen, Kaylyn," he said gently. "You don't see how things change as you grow up. People grow in different directions. Amina was, like you, looking for a way to rebel. You've moved out of where she is, and she hasn't. You'll find different people to call friends, permanent people."

"I wanted Amina to be permanent."

"I know. And maybe she'll grow in the same direction you have."

I looked up at him, reading his expression. "You don't think so, do you?" I asked with very little hope.

"You're being required to grow up very quickly, with a lot expected of you. Amina, I would guess, isn't."

I shrugged miserably, knowing he was right. Amina had nothing but marriage expected out of her. She could do more if she wanted, because she was of higher rank, high enough that marrying someone to attain the title of 'lady' wasn't as preposterous as it was for me. She had more money to spend, more chances to find something to occupy her time. She could afford painting lessons, music lessons, learn to speak another language, all those things that I could never afford.

"Is it not possible that the people here could become permanent friends?" he asked quietly.

"It is for you. Captain Durai doesn't know what to do with me. None of the instructors want to put up with me. All the recruits except for a handful avoid me. Servants don't really speak to me. Nobody wants me here. Even Warren wants me to go elsewhere. He just wants to be a recruit. He doesn't want to be the head of the family."

"It's a tough responsibility, caring for someone else. Especially when you don't know how."

I could easily draw the parallel. Warren and me. Me and Nightfire. I kicked another rock and didn't say anything.

"As a friend, Kaylyn, I'm sorry about Amina," he said quietly. "I'm sorry you lost a friend today. I'm sorry things aren't getting better."

"It's better than home." It was only better because I had a little freedom. Nobody criticized me every day here, but that was the only other small perk to being here with a dragon. I desperately wanted to run away again, take Nightfire and go anywhere else.

"You would tell me before things became unbearable, wouldn't you?" Dillon asked. It was almost as if he could read what I was thinking.

"I'm not a whiner."

"I don't want you miserable. You've run off once, and I'm fairly certain you'd run off again if you wanted to. Don't let it get that far. You can always talk to me."

"I know."

"Do you?"

"Yes. I promise, I know."

Dillon left after I made my promises. I didn't think it could get worse. I told myself I could stick it out. I was wrong.

My 'stick it out' attitude disappeared the next day. Nightfire had given me an idea when he said he could hear classes through open windows. I'd been climbing on the roof for a few days to listen, just because it gave me something to do. I'd discovered Warren's history class and had settled down to listen to the lecture when Warren asked the teacher about a word I had found yesterday.

"Where do you find these words, Madara?" the man asked with humor.

"In books, sir."

"Why the sudden curiosity?"

"I like to know what things mean."

"You mean your sister wants to know," a voice muttered not too softly.

"What was that, Kipper?"

I winced, remembering Lord Kipper. He hadn't bothered me since I'd spilled water on him.

"I said it's not him, Mr. Quallis. It's his sister. She's finding all the words and having her brother ask."

The instructor no longer sounded amused. "Madara, is this true?" he demanded.

"Yes, sir." Warren sounded slightly nervous.

"I'm disappointed in you, Madara. Does your sister not have enough to do?"

"She just wants to learn, sir," Warren excused.

"If she wants to learn, there are plenty of things more suited to her gender and sensibility. You should not encourage her in unfeminine habits. A girl needs a firm hand, Madara, and since she's been allowed more than she should, it's your duty to rein her in. A woman's sole duty is to marry and raise the children. The sooner that she's married, the better."

My gasp of outrage had been loud enough for those inside to hear. What had followed had been a screaming and shouting match between myself and Quallis that had brought Captain Durai, Dillon, and Nightfire, as well as most of the people in the School since a good deal of the shouting between us had been while I was on the roof. Dillon's firm order had brought me inside the classroom through the window where my brother looked as if he wanted to sink through the floor. Everyone else had been dismissed.

"For pity's sake, Kaylyn," Warren begged softly as Captain Durai and Dillon listened to complaints about my existence. "Did you have to make such a scene?"

"How would you feel if you heard someone say that all a man is good for is marriage and Mother should be reining you in?" I hissed at him.

"The entire *School* was outside listening to you scream at him!"

"Then he shouldn't have said that in front of all those people. Or did you not mind the fact he was telling you how to manage our family?"

"No, I didn't like it, but I know better than to make a scene like you did. Mr. Quallis deserves our respect."

"He doesn't deserve any respect!"

"Do you hear her?" Quallis demanded of Dillon and Captain Durai, his face flushed with anger still. "She's a little hellion and she doesn't belong here!"

The hellion comment would have had me screaming a reply at him, but Dillon spoke first. "Kaylyn," he warned before I could make a sound.

I hesitated a moment, anger battling with control, but started to object.

"Lady Madara, you will have your time to speak." Dillon's tone was firm, telling me I would regret speaking. "But it isn't now."

I clenched my jaw shut and felt furious tears start to build.

"Your concerns have been noted," Captain Durai stated. "But as we reminded everyone, Lady Madara is military, and this is the only training facility in Centralia."

"We have camps elsewhere. Send her to some military outpost where she can do less damage. All the…" Quallis suddenly let out a yelp and nearly fell over. Nightfire had climbed on the roof and stuck his head in. His eyes were red with anger and he hissed once.

I raced over to Nightfire and wrapped my arms around his neck. It made me feel better that he was on my side. He'd decided that I was the one human who was acceptable. He liked Dillon and even Warren, but he was ready to defend me to any of them. Gently, he lowered his head a little and rested it against my cheek in comfort.

"What is she telling it?" the professor demanded nervously.

"Nightfire's not an *it*, you arrogant *noble*," I said with anger, remaining where I was.

"She uses that dragon to get her way," Quallis accused.

"I think it's time Lady Kaylyn had a chance to speak for herself." Dillon's expression, when I looked at him, suggested I be a little more polite. "Why were you on the roof?"

"Because nobody here will teach me and I don't have anything to do! I'm not an idiot, and I'm *not* a hellion! Nobody would have known I was there if he hadn't told the entire class that Warren couldn't manage his family and all I'm good for is becoming somebody's wife!"

Nightfire growled softly, and I felt the vibrations down to my toes.

"Oh, stop it. You aren't helping." But there was no heart in my order.

"A woman's duty is to marry and raise children," Quallis said, trying to sound imperious.

"You said it was my *only* duty, and that the sooner I was married, the better."

"You are too young to be here. You're barely more than a child."

"You thought I was old enough to *marry*!"

"I think this would be better conducted separately," Captain Durai stated, interrupting the argument. "Corporal Madara, do you have anything you want to add?"

By Warren's silence, I guessed he didn't.

"Lieutenant, I'll leave Lady Kaylyn and Nightfire with you."

The professor and my brother both left, following after Captain Durai. Once the door closed, Dillon spoke briskly. "Kaylyn, front and center, please."

I let go of Nightfire and stood in front of Dillon, staring at his shoes so I wouldn't cry. "I…"

"No. I want to talk first, and then you can speak." He waited a moment, then spoke. "I realize you're having problems here. I realize that there are feelings of inequality towards females here and that you're having to deal with it. I actually think that climbing on the roof to listen to lessons was rather ingenious. I can support you through all that, up to the point where you stood on the roof in public and shouted at a professor, who has worked here for years, like an unmannered child. You don't have to agree with his beliefs, you have the right to be offended, and he was out of line for saying what he did in front of a public setting. None of that excuses your actions. He will be held responsible for his actions, and you will be held responsible for yours."

I started to object and he held up a hand. I fell silent again, hurt.

"Do you suppose that your actions hold any more honor and should gain any more respect than his?" he asked. "You are military and you have our reputation to uphold, as well as your own. You have brought no honor to the Madara family today. Frankly, Kaylyn, I had thought better of you. You have shown no signs of maturity and no reason why you should be trusted with any responsibility. You are no longer a child, and that means you no longer get to act without thought. A lady, an adult, should think about her actions, consider the consequences, and realize that sometimes the best course of action is not the first instinct. You should remember that there are those who are looking for an excuse to remove Nightfire from your care, and this display today wasn't something that would make them change their minds." He waited a moment to let everything sink in. "Do you have something you want to say?"

I didn't even hesitate. "I *hate* this place and I wish I'd *never* come!" Then I burst into tears and threw myself in a chair. "I'm tired of everyone hating me!"

Nightfire couldn't reach where I was, but he sent comforting emotions to me; concern, caring. The soft humming, meant to soothe, reached my ears.

Dillon gave me a handkerchief, voice a little less hard. "Kaylyn, just because you're in trouble doesn't mean I hate you."

"It doesn't matter! I don't think I can stand another *week* here much less the rest of my life! I don't even know if I'm *ever* getting out of this awful place! I'd rather be *anywhere* but here!"

He breathed out a sigh. "You said it wasn't that awful yesterday."

"I changed my mind. That chauvinistic idiot said I didn't belong here, and he was right."

Dillon didn't say anything, proving I was correct. Everyone knew this wasn't where I belonged. I didn't know where it was I belonged, and it appeared he didn't either.

"You're confined to quarters until dusk tomorrow," Dillon said without anger. "Meals will be brought to you. You may leave only to care for Nightfire, and then you will return to your quarters or risk further punishment."

As far as punishments went, it could have been worse. It was awful enough as it was, but nothing that I hadn't already been doing. I thrust out my hand clenching the handkerchief to give it back. "I'm going."

He took the cloth, then gently wiped away the stray tear before releasing me. "Things are in motion, Kaylyn. We'll find you a better place soon. I promise." He flicked his gaze to Nightfire, nodding once. "Dismissed."

I instantly moved to Nightfire, burying my face in his neck. I didn't have to say anything. Nightfire already knew what I thought, and I felt his agreement. If it hadn't been for Dillon, I'd have left one night with Nightfire to go anywhere but here. "I think I have to go be in trouble," I said to Nightfire's neck. "Sit in my room in isolation and reflect."

"It will not be long," Nightfire comforted me. *"You can still read."*

I gave a little smile. "There is that." I sniffed once, then started to climb out the window.

I walked across the roofs to the building across from Nightfire's hut, and then I climbed down to take the stairs up to my room. Once inside, with the door locked behind me, I cracked open the heavy tactics book, sitting by the window. "In battle, one must consider the advantages of horses," I read while Nightfire curled up below.

The punishment of confinement was bearable. It helped that it rained for most of the morning. I watched it fall, playing with the raindrops sometimes while the recruits and servants dashed to and fro. I didn't bother going to dinner, even though my punishment was over.

Three more days passed slowly. The professors, despite the heat, kept the windows closed so I couldn't hear their lessons. Dillon invited me up to his office to help with paperwork in order to break the monotony, but I knew he could tell how restless I was becoming. I was starting to feel caged in, and Nightfire was the same. All Dillon would say was that things were in motion and I should bear it a little longer.

I'd returned the books to the library and was pacing across the cobblestones and back to hear the echo of my footsteps. Everyone was in class or training, and the servants were busy with the preparations for dinner and cleaning up after lunch. Nightfire had settled down on a roof for a nap when I heard someone else's footsteps mingling with mine. Curious, I looked around for the other person.

A man, dressed in sturdy, green and brown clothes and wearing a knife at his waist, approached and bowed to me. "Lady Madara." His voice was a light tenor, not a deep bass like my father's had been. There also no arrogance and nothing that suggested this man was a noble, but he wielded power through calm control and self-confidence. His dignity seemed to require respect. He made me think of a king, a kind one from the few storybooks I'd read.

"Oh." Nervous, I curtseyed back. "I'm not a Lady, sir."

"As the first human to ever establish a relationship with a dragon, you've moved up the ranks of society." His blue eyes smiled. "My name is Raz Greenclaw. I wondered if I could have a moment to speak with you."

"I do not trust him." I could feel Nightfire's suspicion.

"You don't trust anybody," I replied. Aloud, I said, "We can't go far. Nightfire is supposed to be napping."

"We don't have to go far." He clasped his tanned, callused hands behind his back and studied me. "Have you thought about how you're going to live?" he asked, going straight to the point.

"What do you mean?" I asked.

"I'm sure raising a dragon is difficult. Probably more difficult with people trying to interfere. Have you thought of where you and Nightfire might live?"

I shrugged. "I don't know where we'd go. I'm under military jurisdiction so I can't leave without their say-so."

"I have already spoken to Captain Durai. If you found a suitable place, he would be more than willing to relocate you and give you funds to support yourself and Nightfire."

"I'm sure he'd be thrilled to be rid of me," I said bitterly, looking at the ground. Inside, I was upset. I knew I was causing problems, but it still hurt that nobody wanted me.

"They are fools," Nightfire informed me.

"A girl from a barely-noble family isn't something anyone wants," I said aloud.

"I don't believe that's the case," Raz said. "In fact, there's a group of people who would like to help you."

I looked up at him. "Who?"

"The Eagles."

My eyes widened. "The…the Eagles?" It was an awed whisper, mingled with a touch of hope.

He smiled. "Yes. There is a place you and Nightfire might be content to live at, and I have volunteered to train you."

"Train me? In what?"

"You're under military jurisdiction," he reminded me. "Whether you two like it or not, you're going to be used as a

82

weapon. And for you to protect your dragon, you're going to need to learn to fight. I'm offering to teach you everything you need to know. Hopefully you'll be trained well enough that you can use what you've learned to protect yourself."

"I am supposed to protect you." Nightfire was suspicious and jealous.

"And I'm supposed to protect you. Even your mother said I was awful at archery, which is pretty much all I can do. It would get you out of the School, away from all the people. This is a huge honor, Nightfire. The Eagles...they're Centralia's heroes."

Nightfire rose and padded down to sit beside me, regarding Raz through narrowed eyes.

Raz bowed, his golden-brown hair turning shades in the sun. "It's my honor to meet you."

"Of course it is."

"Nightfire!" I felt my face flushing in embarrassment.

"Would you be interested in what I offered?" Raz asked him, unoffended.

"We can fend for ourselves."

"Perhaps. But there's a lot both of you can learn. And politically, you can't fend for yourselves. Perhaps, out of the public eye, you can be forgotten for a little while."

Nightfire was silent, but I knew he was warming up to the idea. He hated all the people here and the way we were treated.

"Maybe it would be a better home for us," I said silently. *"It would at least be less populated. And the Eagles are the best at what they do. It would give us something to do. Something to work for."*

Nightfire rested his nose against my side, seeking comfort. *"We will be together?"*

"Of course." To Raz, I asked, "We will be together, won't we?"

"Of course. There's a bond between the two of you. It would be foolish to try and break it or cause strain by keeping you apart."

I rubbed Nightfire's nose. *"He's smarter than most of the generals. Are we going?"*

"Yes. We will go."

"Nightfire and I would love to come. When do we leave?"

Raz smiled. "Tomorrow morning. That will give you time to pack. I'll inform Captain Durai of your decision." Then he bowed to us. "Call for me if you wish to speak to me. Otherwise, I will see you tomorrow morning, at dawn."

I started at him as he left, my mind trying to take it all in. In a matter of a few minutes, I'd been given a new home. "We're really leaving," I said finally. "We're getting out of here."

"It cannot be too soon," Nightfire grumbled. *"So many humans make my skin itch."*

"We don't make your skin itch," I replied. "Aren't you going to miss this place at all?"

He snorted.

I smiled. "Me neither."

Chapter 8

I was in the middle of packing when Dillon knocked on the door. "So you're leaving us."

"It's for the best. You know Nightfire and I don't fit here." I stuffed the books into the trunk, struggling to close the lid.

"I hope you won't forget us," Dillon said, coming in to help. He lifted the lid, pulled two of the books out, then helped me latch the trunk. "I know you haven't had the best time here, but I'd like to hear from you now and again."

"I'll write once I know where we're going." I felt like skipping as I dashed around the room. "I have to write to Warren anyway." I smacked my forehead. "Warren doesn't know! I haven't told him yet! What time is it?"

"Dinner. I noticed you didn't show up and guessed what you were doing." He sent me a smile. "I'll see you off tomorrow morning if I can."

"You'll be glad to be rid of me. I'm sure the entire School will throw a party." I struggled to reach the shoe stuck under my bed. I managed to grab it and towed it out, stuffing it in a sack. "It'll have to be less exciting without me here to cause problems."

Dillon was suppressing a smile. "Where's the other shoe?"

"I don't know. I think I've packed it already." I stared at the sacks stuffed full of my things. "It might be in that one." I pointed to an overflowing sack.

"I'll send one of the ladies to help you repack. And it may be calmer here, but I know some of us will miss you."

I stared around the room. "Was I going to do something?" I asked, trying to remember what it was I had forgotten.

"You were going to tell Warren you're leaving."

I smacked my forehead again. "Right! Dinner!" I dashed out the door and down the hall to Dillon's quiet chuckle.

I raced into the great hall where everyone was eating. "Warren!" I called.

He waved to me and I ran to him. "I'm leaving," I said breathlessly. "Someone's come and they're going to train me elsewhere."

Worried, he rose to face me. "You're leaving?"

"At dawn tomorrow." I could barely contain my glee.

"Are you sure about this? It's really sudden, Kaylyn."

"This is an honor, Warren. Dillon and Captain Durai have already approved it. I've packed almost everything. I just wanted to let you know because I probably won't see you tomorrow."

Warren hesitated, torn between wanting to ask more questions as my brother, and following Dillon, who we both trusted. In the end, he gave in. "If you're sure. I'll see you tonight before lights out."

"All right." I sent him a beaming smile, then dashed back out. It was finally hitting me. I was going to be free of this place and its people. I wouldn't have to be stared at anymore.

"*Freedom!*" My scream of pure excitement and joy echoed down the stone hallways. I didn't care who heard me. Wherever I was going had to be better than this.

Warren showed up minutes before the curfew. A motherly servant woman had already helped me unpack and then repack, chiding me good-naturedly over my organizational skills. Everything was folded neatly and organized so that all my shoes were together and we were certain nothing had been forgotten. I was laying out my outfit for tomorrow when Warren knocked on the door, staring absently at the room now bare of anything marking it as mine except for the luggage at the foot of the bed. "All packed?"

"All packed."

"Do you have any more room for this?" he offered a piece of leather rolled up and tied at both ends. I unrolled it and saw a series of gleaming tools.

"Dad's carving tools," he said quietly. "You always carved. You should have these. I'm no good with them, and Mother and our sisters aren't ever going to do anything with them."

I rolled the leather back up and slid it inside the custom-made bag with my last name sewn on in black letters. "Thank you." I held the tools tightly to my chest, fighting the momentary sadness.

"Yeah, I miss him too sometimes," Warren said softly. "Success and safety, Kaylyn. To you and Nightfire." Then he hugged me tightly before dashing down the hall to the called warning of lights out.

I hadn't been sure I would be able to sleep for excitement, but I slept deeply and awoke at Nightfire's call. It took a few minutes to dress and brush my hair, then I lifted the two bags of clothing and heaved them through the window to the ground below.

"Do you need help?"

I poked my head out the window to see Raz Greenclaw standing in front of my bags, a grin on his face. "I can help carry, if you like."

"I only have two more. I'll be down in just a minute."

"Take your time. We have to be properly seen off anyway."

By the time I hauled my final two bags down the stairs with me, a servant carrying the trunk, Raz had already loaded my baggage inside the carriage, and someone had loaded three barrels of oil, a barrel of salted fish, feed for the horses, and the cleaning tools I used on Nightfire. Raz took one bag, then the other, and closed them inside the carriage with my trunk. "Good morning." He bowed to me.

"Stop that," I said, wary. "I'm not noble enough for that."

He merely smiled. "You are a Lady."

"I'm thirteen. Stop bowing to me, all right? It's weird. Is there food?"

"Provided by the kitchens." He handed me a canteen. "The food is in the driver's seat, where we'll be sitting."

"Where are we going?"

"South."

"South where?"

"To a meeting place, and then on to where you'll live."

"What's it like? Are there a lot of people there? Is it big?" I asked eagerly.

"There aren't a lot of people there, and it is big."

"How big? Bigger than the School?"

"I don't see the point in comparing apples to pears. It doesn't seem fair to either one. I'll let you make your own judgments."

"I see you're ready." Dillon came out with Captain Durai. "The guards will be notified of your arrival by the time you get there," he said to Raz.

Raz nodded.

Dillon looked at me, and his face softened a touch. "Kaylyn, I want to hear from you," he said, attempting to sound stern.

I threw my arms around him in a hug. I was going to miss him. He'd been fatherly, and as much of a friend as I'd ever had here. "I'll write," I promised.

Dillon returned the hug, then released me, pushing me gently towards the carriage.

"If you are through, are we going to leave now?" Nightfire asked impatiently from the top of the carriage.

"Don't act superior," I told him. "You'll miss him too."

Raz climbed up in the carriage, then offered his hand to help me up. "Ready?" he asked. At my nod, he set the horses in motion, and we rolled through the south gate towards my new home.

The ride was silent for the first half hour. Nightfire dozed and I ate breakfast. Raz declined and focused on guiding the horses.

"So are you an Eagle?" I asked finally once I'd finished eating. "I wanted to ask before, but I thought I shouldn't since nobody's supposed to know."

He glanced at me. "Are you expecting an honest answer?"

"You said the Eagles are training me. Doesn't that mean I have to know who they are?" I demanded. "Or get to know something about them?"

I could see the hint of a smile. "Will you promise that you won't tell anyone what my answer is?"

I was delighted. "So you *are* an Eagle! You wouldn't care otherwise."

"I could be making you promise and saying no, just to be cruel."

"You will not." Nightfire joined the conversation. "You are an Eagle."

"Dragons know when you're lying," I said helpfully. "They read emotions."

A smile flickered on his face. "I'll have to remember that."

Nightfire was annoyed. "Silly humans play silly human games. Dragons do not play silly games."

"How would you know?" I demanded. "You haven't seen any other dragons."

He blew a breath at me and closed his eyes again.

"Temperamental, isn't he?" Raz commented as I fought to get my hair out of my face.

"Always. And I'm warning you that people say I'm just like him."

"Who said that?"

"The recruits at the School."

"Apples to pears, Kaylyn."

"What does that mean?" I pushed my hair out of my face again.

"There's no point in comparing you to Nightfire. You're two different beings with two separate personalities. One is not better or worse than the other."

I started to scratch an itch on my neck that wouldn't be appeased, then turned and glared at Nightfire. "You didn't tell me you needed oiling," I accused.

"I wanted to leave. I can wait."

"Last time we waited, you got an infection and I nearly scratched my skin off. Raz, can you stop for a minute, please?" I asked. "I have to take care of Nightfire."

Raz pulled the carriage to a stop. "Do you need help?"

"No. Just a few minutes." I climbed down, pulled the lid off one barrel, dipped my hand in, then stood on the back to reach Nightfire's neck, which he stretched out accordingly. His skin was already starting to get rough and crack in one spot. "Where else?" I asked.

He stretched out his right wing and I oiled the edges of it, then wiped the rest on his jaw. "Done," I said.

Raz was on the ground and watching as I dug in the carriage for a cloth to clean my hand. "Full moon tonight," he commented.

I glanced out the window. I could see it in the sky, a white orb visible even in daylight. "Is it important?" I asked.

"Eagles meet every full moon."

"Every Eagle?"

"No. But every time there's a full moon, Eagles get together."

"Oh." I considered him for a minute as I wiped off my hand. "You're not very old, are you?"

Although that hadn't really been a polite question, or phrasing of it, Raz just laughed. "I'm older than you." He closed the carriage door and assisted me back up in the front of the carriage, setting the horses in motion again.

"How old are you?" I persisted.

"Nineteen."

Nightfire had his doubts. "A human child seeks to train a human child?"

"Just how young can you be in the Eagles?" I protested.

"The Eagles don't take people by age, they take people by skill. I think the youngest Eagle we had was your age." He nudged my foot with his. "And she was the best on the staff we ever had." He settled back in the seat. "As for my being a human child, I realize I'm not as old as most trainers inside the School, but I know what I'm doing. If you have doubts about my skill, there will be plenty of other Eagles to choose from. You can pick one of them to train you." It was said in a very mild tone, as if being insulted in such a way wouldn't bother him.

"I feel your pride, human," Nightfire informed him. "I care not for your pride. I care for Kaylyn."

"I'm thirteen!" I said, outraged. "And you're two months old! I don't need you protecting me!"

"I know more. I will not let a human waste our time because he wishes to prove something."

"You're being ungrateful," I protested. *"He's getting us away from the School, isn't he? How would you feel if Doctor McDragon showed up to tell you how you were supposed to act?"*

"Doctor McDragon is a fool," Nightfire stated, not keeping with the private conversation. "I do not care what a human has done for us if it is not for us he has done it."

Raz's eyes were lit with curiosity despite the conversation. "So you really can speak with your mind?" he asked, intrigued.

"It is not your concern, human," Nightfire said, his mental voice a low growl.

"Nightfire!" I pleaded. "He's not doing any harm! He's just curious!"

"Others were just curious."

"All right," Raz said, interrupting the argument. "If you don't want to tell me, I won't ask. And Nightfire, I don't have something to prove. If I did, I have an apprentice to find and train."

"Kaylyn could not become your apprentice?" Nightfire demanded, now insulted on my behalf.

"Eagles are supposed to hide, to blend in. I could choose her, but it was suggested that I find another since she is currently tied to a dragon. She is powerful in her own right because of that tie."

"She will always be tied to me." It was as much of a boast as I'd heard from Nightfire, but it was also a challenge.

"Then there's no need to make her an Eagle," Raz said, maintaining his composure. I found that impressive. Most people knew better than to yell at a dragon, but they looked like they wanted to after this much time speaking with Nightfire. "She can be as proficient as she wants. She doesn't really have a standard to be measured against. If she wants to be as good as an Eagle," he flashed a grin at me, "then she's in the right position to have that chance."

I flushed, tucking my hair behind my ear. "I'm no good at fighting."

"You aren't now," he corrected. "That can be fixed. And if the stories I hear are true, you fought off wyverns to save Nightfire."

"It was mostly Rosewing. She even said I was horrible at archery. I had this sack of green powder. It causes flame to grow and turn green."

"I see. Smart," he commented. "I've seen this powder. Did you turn your candle flame green?"

I immediately felt a little more at ease because he had clearly done the same. Here was someone who didn't think playing was a bad thing. "A lot," I confessed.

"Spent more money on that green powder than I should have," he said reflectively. "But I had great fun with it."

I giggled, catching Nightfire's mental huff.

"Would you like something for your hair?" Raz ask as I pushed it out of my face for the umpteenth time.

I felt myself blushing. "It wouldn't stay. It's not long enough." After I'd had my fight with Amina, I'd cut it shorter. My mother would have fainted had she known exactly how short my hair was.

He gave me a considering glance. "I think it suits you."

I wouldn't have been more shocked if he'd said he had four wives. "You...you what?" I stammered, flabbergasted.

"It suits you," he repeated. "Although if you'll let it grow just a little longer, we'll be able to keep it out of your face."

I opened my mouth to reply, then realized I had nothing to say to that and turned my attention to my feet, feeling myself go warm with embarrassed pleasure. I'd expected contempt, or derision, or even ridicule. Raz wasn't like others. He was more like Dillon.

"Is this human love that you feel?" Nightfire asked, curious and a touch suspicious.

"No," I answered firmly. *"I like him as a friend, not for courting."*

Nightfire approved of that. He was possessive and wasn't ready to share me.

"I might want to marry someday," I pointed out, although it wasn't a strong possibility or one I was seriously considering.

"Someday is not today. And I do not trust him."

"Why?"

"Because he is a human."

I rolled my eyes at that.

"What was that for?" Raz asked, catching the eye roll.

"Nightfire. He doesn't think much of humanity. Considering who he's met, I don't blame him either. Surely the Eagles will improve his opinion," I said, glancing back at him.

"What makes the Eagles so special?" Nightfire demanded of us both. "They are human as well."

"Eagles hold themselves to a higher standard." This was from Raz, who clearly thought I deserved to know something after all. "We're the defenders of Centralia. When war threatens, we're there to defend."

"Why is that different from the Army?" Nightfire asked, genuinely curious. "Does the Army not do the same?"

"The Army is under government rule," I said quickly. "Eagles aren't."

Raz nodded. "We aren't directed by others. While the Army can be used for other purposes, keeping the peace, or attacking another country, the Eagles can't. We're solely for defense, keeping the enemy from crossing our borders."

"Have we ever attacked another country?" I asked. "I can't remember if anyone ever said."

"We haven't. We have won territory from the Silons during wars, but Centralia has never attacked first. However, if that were to change, the Army would be called up and they would be bound to follow orders. The Eagles are not."

Nightfire was skeptical about this arrangement. "Are Eagles not loyal then if they are not bound to serve?"

"We are bound to serve, but we take a different oath." Raz seemed lost in thought as he spoke. "The Army swears to serve and protect. Eagles, among our oath, promise to defend. We have our own oath that we honor just as deeply as fealty to a king. We hold each other accountable. When war comes, the Eagles send out a call to mobilize. Whoever doesn't come has the other Eagles to answer to. If we break a law of our own, then our own people hand out our justice. We also make sure that the Eagles stay in existence by picking protégés. I was chosen by another Eagle for my talent and my values to become an Eagle. Once I became an Eagle, I was given this." He tapped the pendant he wore around his neck. "And I will find my own protégé and hand this down to whoever I deem worthy to become an Eagle so they will know to find an apprentice of their own."

"Is *that* how you do it?" I was fascinated. "Everyone always wants to know how you become an Eagle."

"That's how," he acknowledged. "We find someone good enough with the right mindset."

"How can you be sure they will honor your code?" Nightfire demanded.

"As I said, it's the right mindset. Eagles don't just have the skill, they have honor, integrity, strength of will. Eagles are ready to give their lives to defend others. Eagles will never kill another for any reason other than defense. Eagles will not reveal who they are for pride, nor will they reveal who other Eagles are." He sounded as if he were reciting a creed, and I wondered how close this was to the oath he'd sworn. "Talent won't make you an Eagle. Talent will make you good. There are certain qualities Eagles must have. We have a reputation to uphold. In order to remain as we are, we can't afford corruption." He gave a thin smile. "And if one of us wavers from that mindset and breaks the oath and our laws, then the best hunters and fighters in Centralia are there to put a stop to it and make sure the corruption goes no farther. We take care of our own. That means keeping each other in line, and helping each other when help is needed."

Nightfire read something in how Raz felt, because I'd never seen him accept anything so quickly. "You are people of honor," he decided, then closed his eyes and started to contemplate a nap.

"I think he likes you," I said in amazement.

"And that surprises you?" Raz asked with humor.

"He didn't like me until days after he hatched, so, yes. I think you're the only other human Nightfire likes."

"Dillon is a good human," Nightfire interjected. "A human worthy of trust."

"Needless to say, it's a short list."

We rode for several hours until Raz called a break for lunch. I found myself warming to him more and more. He was happy to talk to me, although I quickly learned not to ask too much about the Eagles. Since I didn't bother him with more questions once he hinted he couldn't answer, he seemed friendlier. We talked and laughed through lunch, but as Nightfire settled for his afternoon nap, I suddenly couldn't stop yawning.

"Are you ill?" Raz asked, concerned about my sudden attack of drowsiness.

"No. I'm sorry." I rubbed at my eyes. "I get tired when Nightfire's sleeping."

"There's no harm in a nap. It's a long ride still."

"I'm not a child. I can stay awake," I insisted.

His tone didn't waver. "I'm not criticizing you. There's no harm in sleeping. It might provide some relief from the ride."

"Are you tired of talking with me?" I asked, wondering if I was disturbing him.

"If you want to keep talking, we have plenty of time. I'm only suggesting that if you're tired, you rest until Nightfire wakes up. We'll likely have a late night and there's no telling how long this meeting will go."

I gave a huge yawn and decided it would be acceptable to rest until Nightfire woke up.

The next thing I knew after I'd settled myself was that the sun was setting and Nightfire was nudging me awake. I blinked a few times, my body stiff from being too long in one position.

"Finally," Nightfire said with slight exasperation. *"You have been sleeping for hours."*

"I what?" I realized I was partially leaning against Raz and sat up to look around. We were much farther south. Looking back, the mountains weren't even visible. There was nothing but rolling plains covered in what I guessed to be crops for food. "Hours? How many hours was I asleep?"

"Five," Raz offered.

Far too many. "I didn't mean to sleep so long."

"It's all right," he assured me. "We're not far from our destination. We'll stop somewhere soon for dinner."

"Where are we?" There were fewer trees, and I couldn't imagine not being able to see the mountains. I'd been watching the mountains my entire life.

"The southern half of Centralia has plains until we reach the dead land near the southern border that we share with the Silons. We're about a two day's ride from the dead land, if we rode hard."

"We aren't going to the border, are we?" I asked apprehensively.

"Why do you fear the Silons?" Nightfire questioned.

"Because they're our enemies and they hate us," I replied. "They try to take over every few years, whenever someone with enough power rises up and convinces them to go back to fighting us for land and resources again. And we aren't going there, are we?" I asked again.

Raz shook his head. "No, we aren't going to Silon, or the dead land. We're well away from any Silons," he assured me. "Any more questions?"

"Where are all the trees?" I asked, bewildered. "And the mountains?"

He laughed. "This land is used for crops, and so the few trees have been cut down. If we headed west, we would eventually find the mountains again, but you'd have to reach the desert first. Have you ever seen a desert?"

"Not really. The School of Officers and Gentlemen was the farthest I've ever been from home." I rubbed at my arm, which had fallen asleep and was now returning, painfully, back to life.

"Not even to the capitol?" he asked.

I shook my head. "My mother didn't think it was safe. My father promised that he would take us, someday. And then someday never happened. My father traveled once to the mines near Anglarius when I was nine and that was the last time he went anywhere."

"The Silons also share a border with Anglarius, do they not?" Nightfire inquired. "Why do the Silons not go to war against them?"

"Because Anglarius is three times our size, with far more skill and many more people than us," I replied. "If Silon attacked Anglarius, the Silons would be obliterated. So they just attack us all the time because we're smaller."

"Does Anglarius not defend you?" Nightfire demanded. "Do humans not form alliances, or do you not trust each other enough?"

Raz answered this. "Things between Anglarius and Centralia have been...a little unstable since our shift from a monarchy to a democracy. We have a trade agreement, but Centralia is in the process of renegotiating an alliance between them. The alliance was made between the monarchs, and once our queen stepped down from the throne, that alliance was declared void."

"Cowards," I said matter-of-factly.

"The queen?"

"No, Anglarius. They were just waiting for us to collapse into chaos so the Silons could take over. That's all they're doing. Just waiting for us to collapse so they can take over or make a deal with the Silons. They're snobs who don't want a stain on their clothing."

Raz was grinning. "A pragmatic and open-minded view of our allies."

"They aren't our allies. A trade agreement isn't the same as an ally. An ally supports you in war. They probably have a trade agreement with the Silons too. They could keep the Silons in line if they wanted to. They're big enough."

Raz shrugged easily and pulled the horses to a stop. "Would you like to take care of the horses or find us a place to get food?" he asked, nodding to the town up ahead.

"Aren't we driving there?" I asked.

"I think it best if we stay out here with Nightfire. There are those who might be leery of a dragon."

"Oh. Right," I said, feeling stupid. "I'll take care of the horses."

Raz disappeared to town and returned with food while the horses fed and rested and Nightfire stretched out. We stayed there until the sun had nearly set, and then we set out again. We stopped after less than an hour and Raz staked down our horses next to the carriage. "The rest is on foot from here."

"How far?"

He pointed to a hill where I could see a large fire, and a second, smaller fire farther away on a smaller hill. "That's where we're going. The Eagles have already gathered."

I couldn't help the moment of wonder and anticipation. I was going to meet the Eagles.

I couldn't see them very well until we reached the top of the hill, and there I stared in awe at them all. The Eagles were a secretive group, known only to other Eagles. They were the defenders of our country who would rise in times of need, then fade back into the background until the next time of need. They were the best of the best; the best with staff, sword, arrows, fists, and weapons that I had never heard of, and I was seeing a lot of them. Some wore a chain around their necks with a symbol to show their weapon. Some didn't have that chain. I looked curiously to Raz and could see a chain, but I couldn't see the pendant attached.

"I like this place," Nightfire said. *"It is peaceful."*

I understood what he meant. There was no underlying feeling of derision, or fear. There was clear respect by the way they murmured greetings, bowing to me. Of the women, some of them were dressed like men, wearing pants. I felt a little more at ease, even if I felt uncomfortable with the respect they gave me. I was little better than working class, and they all spoke to me and deferred to me as if I were a powerful noble. It was a frightening and heady feeling.

"Lady Madara," a woman said, bowing to me even though she wore a skirt.

I couldn't help the wince. "Don't...call me Lady. I'm just Kaylyn."

She smiled, small wrinkles forming at the corners of her grey eyes. "Kaylyn. Welcome to you and Nightfire." Then she bowed to him as well.

Nightfire inclined his head gracefully in acknowledgment. I went into a nervous curtsey.

"You are in a unique position, both of you," the woman said. "The first human to have a relationship with a dragon, and a young dragon willing to live with and associate with humans."

Privately, I thought tolerate might be a better word than associate. Nightfire sent a feeling of agreement, which meant I hadn't controlled my thoughts again and allowed Nightfire and any other dragon to hear. "We didn't really have a choice," I said truthfully.

"The General's Council made it clear of their wishes and that they had plans concerning you both. And with all the interest and plans focusing on you, the Eagles have decided to give you and Nightfire assistance to make your own decisions and live in a place more...welcoming. Has Raz explained our decision to you?"

"Yes. I mean, he explained you wanted to teach us and give us a place to live. And we're grateful," I added in a rush.

The dark-haired woman smiled. "We didn't doubt that you were grateful. Before you start training, there are several things we would like to ask of you."

"Here it comes," Nightfire grumbled. *"You humans can do nothing without strings."*

"As you know, Eagles like to remain secret. Our identities as Eagles are only revealed in times of war."

"Eagles are only known on the battlefield," I said, remembering what I'd been told.

She nodded. "We would like to ask that you not mention our identities as Eagles. Would you swear to that?"

"Yes, of course. I swear."

Nightfire grumbled mentally.

"Do it," I ordered silently. *"It's not that big a deal. With what they're doing for us, we can keep their secret."*

"We will keep our silence, humans," Nightfire said with palpable annoyance, his eyes flashing light pink. "You may have your secrets. You are not that interesting."

I felt my face flush. "Nightfire!"

Raz laughed. "We aren't offended, Kaylyn. I've never known a dragon to be pleased with humans for anything."

"You've met a dragon?" I spun to face him, knowing Nightfire's eyes were locked onto Raz as well.

"Make your promises first," Raz said. "Then I'll tell you everything."

"There are more promises? You humans are suspicious and untrusting," Nightfire informed everyone.

"And you're just a wealth of trust and gullibility," I snapped at him.

Nightfire snorted. "You are the one who trusts too easily. You do not understand caution. You would trust the thief who promises he would not think of taking a loaf of bread from you."

"All they've asked so far is that we let them stay a secret," I hissed at him. "They have a right to their privacy, don't they? They just want to know we aren't going to proclaim we've met the Eagles and make their lives as miserable as ours. You should understand about privacy after having none of it for over a month."

Nightfire was mildly abashed and subsided.

"Will you keep the secrets of the Eagles? How we live, what we do, and all encounters with them?" the woman asked.

I nodded. "I promise."

"I will promise as well," Nightfire grumbled after my quick, pointed glare.

"Here." Raz passed a metal chain to me. Looking at it curiously, I saw an silver feather attached to the chain. "This makes you an honorary Eagle," he explained. "You aren't an Eagle, and you can never claim to be an Eagle, but this gives you the ability to talk freely with us and interact with us."

"Oh. Thank you." I quickly slipped it on.

"We have a place for you to stay," Raz said. "It's secluded. You won't find a lot of people there. And at least one of us will go with you." He nodded to the group. "You can choose."

"I thought you were coming," I blurted out, panicked at the thought of having to choose someone, sure I would somehow offend the rest. I liked Raz. He was also the only one here who didn't make me feel like such a child. Many of the Eagles were much older, and I was sure some of them would have little patience for an unwanted, awkward thirteen-year-old who was trying to raise a dragon. And if he'd met a dragon, maybe he'd know something that would help.

Raz was calm. "If that's what you want."

Nightfire may not have thought highly of Raz, but he understood the comfort of familiarity, however briefly we'd known him. "You made the offer, human. You will hold to your promise," he demanded.

Raz bowed to us. "Then the decision has been made. I'll go with you."

I wasn't sure I hid the relief, but I did try. I wished now I'd been a better daughter and had paid attention to all the rules my mother had attempted to teach me. My sisters would know the right response to give, and be properly polite and graceful. I was hoping I didn't offend all of them at once.

"If that's settled," the woman began, "I would ask that you wait over the next hill until we are finished here."

Nightfire was outraged. *"They treat us like children,"* he said angrily to me alone. *"They are no better than the fat generals you are supposed to obey! I will not be treated like a human baby who misbehaves and is sent away so the adults may talk. We have made our promises to them and they still keep secrets from us as if our word was not enough!"* His eyes flashed a light red. *"They should not doubt the word of a dragon."*

I flushed scarlet at Nightfire's rant and shifted uncomfortably at the weight of everyone's gaze on me. "Nightfire…he says we gave our promises and he doesn't like not being trusted."

Raz chuckled softly, guessing that Nightfire hadn't been so polite.

"We aren't keeping secrets from you." This was an older man, speaking politely to Nightfire. "But much of what we say won't hold much interest for you."

"I will decide what holds interest for me," Nightfire said, voice ringing with insult and anger. "You will not tell a dragon what he does or does not wish to know. You humans…"

"Nightfire! *Please!*" I begged. "It wasn't anything *personal*! They were trying to be *nice*!"

"They were trying to control us, like all other humans," Nightfire informed me.

"Are you feeling that from them, or are you just hating all humanity again?" I asked.

"I am tired of others telling us what to do."

I gave up. *"Are you staying or going?"*

"I will stay."

"Fine." I threw up my hands in exasperation. "He's staying. I'm going." I muttered to myself as I stalked towards the hill in the distance with the fire about stubborn, suspicious dragons.

The night wore on. The Eagles stood or sat and talked for a long time. Nightfire sat in a clear space among them, revealing nothing of his thoughts to me. I snapped twigs and threw them onto the fire, wishing I knew what they were talking about and fighting drowsiness.

As I started to consider lying down and sleeping on the ground, Nightfire rose and padded over to me.

"Anything interesting?" I mumbled.

"Not for you. You would have been very bored." He curled around me on the grass. *"I can still hear what they say."*

"Then I'll sleep and you can listen. I'm tired. Are they ever going to end?"

"Not for some time. They have much to talk of."

"How can they have so much to talk about and none of it be interesting?" I gave a yawn.

"You would not understand much of what they speak of. I do not understand all of it. And they ask Raz many questions about how he will protect his identity as an Eagle and whether or not he will still take an apprentice. They think you could never hide as an Eagle should be able to."

"I'd never be good enough to be an Eagle. I don't want to be an Eagle. All they do is fight." I let my eyes close, curled up to sleep. It took only a moment until I felt myself drift and the sounds of the world faded away.

Chapter 9

I didn't know how long the meeting lasted. I woke when Nightfire nudged me. I let out a groan and curled tighter, unwilling to get up.

"It is morning," he informed me. *"And Raz wishes to leave. He says we have far to go."*

I rolled over and found I'd been covered by a blanket sometime during the night. The fire had died down and was little more than embers smoking.

Since I was awake, Nightfire got to his feet and headed down the hill.

"Where are you going?" I called.

"There is a lake. I am thirsty."

I rubbed my eyes tiredly.

"Good morning," Raz said, coming around what remained of the fire. "Breakfast?" He offered bread and a canteen. "It's light now, but we'll have more variety when we reach where we're staying."

"Thank you." I took both and he took the blanket, folding it up and placing it beside his before moving to sit next to me. "Nightfire said we had a long way to go?"

"Several hours. It's military land, so we'll reach the property before we reach the building. But once we get there, we won't have to leave again."

"How will we get food?" I protested.

"It can be delivered from the town nearby, but there's plenty around that we can eat off of. Nightfire can learn to hunt. There's a river not too far away. And the building is plenty big for the three of us, even if one of us is a dragon." He flashed a smile.

I tore a bite off the bread. "I'm sorry for Nightfire."

"Why?" He took a stick and stirred the fire, watching the sparks. "We understand that he's capable, and willing, to speak for himself. We also understand the dragons don't trust humans. The one I met didn't trust me even after I'd saved him."

"*You* saved a dragon?" I sent this thought to Nightfire. *"Did you know?"* I asked after I'd relayed what Raz had said.

"He told me while you were asleep. I have heard this story."

I stared at Raz expectantly. "If you told Nightfire, I want to know."

Raz continued to stir the fire. "About a year ago, I was traveling in the desert."

My nose wrinkled. *"Why?"*

He grinned. "Because it was there. While I was there, I was attacked by wyverns and managed to fight them off. Unfortunately, they came back with reinforcements. I took shelter, and so they mobbed a dragon; Smokyscales. He's nice, as far as dragons go. He was polite enough after I'd helped him fight the wyverns off. One of his wings was injured, which was why he'd needed my help, and he allowed me to assist in repairing it. We talked while I worked. Before he left, he said he wouldn't forget what I'd done. I said if he ever wanted to find me, then he could find the Eagles and give them my name."

"I thought Eagles were supposed to remain secret," I accused. "How is he going to figure out who the Eagles are?"

"I explained we were supposed to be secret, but I also explained that we had meetings every full moon. He knows how to find me if he wants to. He wasn't as touchy as Nightfire is. He said he will remember that Eagles are people that dragons can trust." He shrugged. "I haven't heard from him since, but I might be able to call on him for help if we get in a bind with something Nightfire needs that we can't provide."

I finished my bread and drained the contents of the canteen. "I guess it's good to have some sort of help." I headed over to the four barrels. *"If we need to move, you should come eat,"* I thought to Nightfire. *"So I can oil you before we go."* I pulled the lid off of the barrel full of fish and dragged out the three largest fish. "How are we going to pay for everything?" I asked.

"Captain Durai said he'd take care of it. I have some money to start with, and then everything else will be paid for by the military post closest to us."

"Good. Because we're going to need a lot of food." I dipped my hand in the second barrel. "And lots of oil."

"What is the oil for?"

"It keeps Nightfire's skin from cracking and protects his scales. I have to oil him every day, sometimes twice a day." I decided the oil was liquid enough it didn't have to be warmed and wiped my hand off. If the oil turned too cold, it became more gel-like and didn't like to spread very evenly.

"That must take work. And dedication."

I grinned shyly. "Well, he gets grumpy if I don't oil him. And I don't really have much else to do. Nightfire and I just talk, mostly."

"Out loud?"

"No. Mentally." I fussed with the straps on the third barrel. "I can speak mentally to Nightfire. You could too."

"I could? How so?" He sounded intrigued.

"Nightfire said whenever he speaks he opens up a kind of pathway between minds because he only speaks with his mental voice. You can send thoughts to him. So it's a deliberate choice every time he speaks to someone because he doesn't always want to hear your thoughts. He does say if he doesn't keep speaking to them that the pathway fades and he can't hear their thoughts after a while."

"All I do is think things to him?"

"Not pictures. He can't do pictures. Only words."

"Last night, he could hear our thoughts then."

"Only some," Nightfire said, coming over the hill. "Momentary thoughts. Some I did not hear at all." A second later, he said, "Yes, I could hear yours sometimes."

Raz looked pleased despite the answer. "That's interesting."

Nightfire laid on the ground. "You do not need to shout it. I am not deaf." As he started to eat the fish, I oiled him, beginning at the tail and working my way forward. By the time I got to his neck, he'd finished eating and was relaxing contentedly.

Raz loaded everything onto the carriage while I hurried down to the lake to change and wash. When I returned, he was rolling the last barrel to the carriage and closed it inside. Seeing Nightfire was waiting, I went to the head of the horse and started to speak soothingly. She was a calm horse, very steady, but she didn't like this process. Nightfire rose on his back legs, hooked his claws in, and climbed on top of the carriage, the frame creaking in protest. Nightfire ignored any sounds and curled up for a nap.

I hitched the other horse next to the mare. This mare refused to move if she could see the dragon and any large movements by him made her nervous. It was only after she was hitched next to the first mare that I could remove the cloth over her face. Raz offered a hand to help me up after I'd finished. There wasn't any room inside the carriage, so we both sat up front. When I was seated beside him, he set the horses in motion and we headed for our next destination.

The drive took a little over four hours. Raz and I talked almost the entire way about anything we could think of. I listened eagerly to his stories, and he listened attentively to mine. It was nice to have somebody's full attention for more than a few minutes at a time. Everyone else always had somewhere else to be, or something that needed to be done. We ate on the way, finishing off an early lunch when I saw a sign that pointed towards Rillmyra.

To my relief, the closer we got, the more trees appeared. By the time we reached Rillmyra, the town Raz said was close to our destination, there were cliffs everywhere, very tall ones, and plenty of trees. We didn't go through Rillmyra, just close enough to see it, then we followed a path through the cliffs to a large clearing. The cliffs eased back to form a kind of barrier that showed what I knew once had been a grand building. It was four stories high, with textured stone walls and ledges that almost begged to be climbed. It might have been whiter once, but it was more of a light grey now, with windows all the way up to the top. To the right of the entrance was what I recognized as stables.

Raz pulled the horses to a stop and I climbed down, looking over the building. There was a faded sign and I squinted as I moved closer to see it. There was only one word carved in, and the paint over the letters had faded. Still, it was legible. "Vesta?"

"This was a meeting house." Raz pushed open the two wooden doors and headed inside.

I wandered around the room. "It's a big place," I said. "Was it for Eagle meetings?"

He chuckled. "No. Meetings when we used to have royalty. The king and queen and all the advisors would meet here."

"I wish we still had royalty," I grumbled.

"Despite what you may think, this is better in its own way. If the king wanted to be rid of you and Nightfire, all he had to do was order it and you'd be gone. This way, it takes more people to convince, which takes more work, but it also protects you from an immediate whim."

"It is harder to kill everyone who is important," Nightfire said, padding around the second level.

"There's that too. After the last king was assassinated, all the pressure went to the queen to provide a male heir."

"Because men are the only gender who can think for themselves and do anything important," I said bitterly.

"You humans have strange ideas," Nightfire commented. "It does not matter to dragons."

"I think the lot of you are smarter than humans most days."

"We are smarter than humans every day," Nightfire informed me regally.

I stuck out my tongue at him.

"Luckily the queen had enough power to remove the royal position, and elevate a kind of democracy before she left." Raz stuck his hands in his pockets, watching us explore.

"To save all the backstabbing that would have been done to marry the queen or her daughter, or prove themselves closest to the royal line so they could take over. People in power are nothing but greedy."

"Did you always have such a dim view of society?" Raz inquired.

"I'm a minor noble and a female. That means I'm close enough to see how nobility and those with power treat those just below me and those who have the misfortune to be unfavored or female. All my sisters think about are marrying someone of higher rank. It's stupid to want nothing out of life but to marry someone who thinks himself better than you." I ran my hands over a stone column. "I like this place. Is this all that's left?"

"Just this. The rest was torn down or destroyed during battle. It's not the best, but I think we could make a home out of this."

I looked around. I could easily envision this as a home not just for me and one dragon, but for others.

"You get ahead," Nightfire informed me. *"There is nothing to say there will be more."*

"If we can make it, then maybe others can make peace too."

"Dragons do not like humans and do not need humans."

"Do you enjoy hating all humankind? Shouldn't we want more than dragons killing humans and humans trying to kill dragons?" I asked aloud, looking to Raz for some kind of feedback.

"Humans cannot be trusted," Nightfire answered, his voice stating his finality.

That stung. "I can't be trusted, then? Or just by you because you're stuck with me and don't have a choice?"

Nightfire didn't answer.

Angered, I stomped down the stairs. "Look, dragon, if you want to go, I'm not holding you back. Go find someone you can trust. I'm *sorry* I'm not up to your standards, but I'm doing my best!"

Raz didn't say anything as I stormed out the door.

Temper was short-lived. I slung a few rocks moodily, then slumped to the ground, my head on my knees.

Nightfire sent an apologetic emotion, and I shut him out. It was hard enough to deal with people who looked down on me now. It was harder to deal with a dragon I was supposed to raise who trusted me less than the generals who wanted to control him.

"It is not the same."

"I thought you were busy hating my race."

"I do not hate you."

"This isn't going to work if you hate everyone except me. Who am I supposed to talk to? What about after you leave?"

"Why do you say I will leave?" I heard Nightfire's footsteps as he padded across the rocky ground.

"Because you hate it here and I don't know why you'd stay. There aren't dragons here. There won't be a dragon mate. And you don't want anything to do with my people or my country." I sniffed, my eyes watering at the thought. Not even three months, and I was in tears over the thought of him leaving.

Nightfire nudged me with his nose. *"I would stay for you."*

"Oh, stop it."

He nudged me again, more firmly. *"I would stay for you, Kaylyn. We share a mind link. It stays with us until death. With dragons, we stay until we are of a certain age, then we live on our own. It is different with us. There is...more. I do not understand it, but I do not want to leave it. Perhaps I will not live with you every day at every moment, but I will not leave you."* He curled around me, and his eyes, when I looked up, were brown with worry. *"Dragons do not trust humans. It is our way. It is not my way even though it should be. Trust comes more easily for you. I will try to be more trusting of your kind."*

I put my arms around his neck as far as I could. *"You aren't messed up. Maybe because you're around humans you're adapting. People change. Why can't dragons?"* I rested my cheek against his neck now. *"Besides, dragons can trust humans some. Your mother trusted me with you. Smokyscales trusted Raz. Maybe dragons just never found the right people to trust. There are plenty of humans that aren't worth trusting."*

"You are a human dragons can trust."

I hugged him tighter. It was the biggest complement he'd given me. It was perhaps the only complement he'd ever given me, and it meant a lot to me.

By the time Nightfire and I made it back, Raz had stabled the horses and unloaded the carriage. "I realize it's early," he began, "but we should probably eat now and then try and make the rest of the place livable for tonight."

My smile disappeared and became a look of dismay. "*This* place?" I repeated. "The *entire* place *today*?"

He laughed at my expression. "No, of course not. But the stables need to be cleaned out and hay put down for the horses, and at the very least we should get the walkways and this floor clean." He pointed to the stone floor under our feet. "The rest we'll work on one at a time."

"Oh." I felt relief. "Where do we start?"

"Have you ever cleaned a stable?"

I shuffled my feet, mildly embarrassed. "No," I said reluctantly, knowing hard work meant a lot to this man. "But it can't be that hard to learn, right?"

He inspected me a moment. "Perhaps you should start in here."

I protested, sure he thought I was ignorant or lazy. "I can do it! I can work! We had servants, but we didn't have a *lot* of servants! I'm not a pampered noble!"

"I never said you were." His tone was gentle. "But you aren't dressed to work in the stables and put down hay. If you'll start sweeping in here and set up for supper, I'll come help when I finish."

"I can start working now," I said immediately. "So we have someplace clean to eat."

He acquiesced. "If you're all right with eating late."

"Fine," I said instantly.

"Then I'll start in the stables."

I nodded, determined to get as much done as I could before he finished with the stables.

"Are you certain this is not human love?" Nightfire asked suspiciously as Raz headed out the door again. *"You are eager to please him."*

"I like him," I retorted. *"And I respect him, and I want him to like me. I'm trying to make a good impression."*

"Why should he like you if you are not acting like yourself?" Nightfire wanted to know.

"I am acting like myself! I just don't want him to get the wrong impression of me. He's an Eagle, and he's worked hard to be one. I don't want him wishing someone else had taken me."

"If he does, I will bite him," Nightfire vowed protectively.

I smiled at his sincerity. "Thanks. Do you see a broom or something?"

Nightfire helped me find a broom, but I didn't get much sweeping done before the amount of dust in the air made me feel as if I were choking. I pushed the front doors open instead and tried to find windows. The two I did find that had the capability to open were stuck shut, and I had to have Nightfire's help to open them. I started on the top level and swept the dirt down. Nightfire left to explore since he didn't enjoy the dust in the air any more than I did. The open windows and door helped. I managed to get all the walkways and the entire bottom floor swept before Raz came back. Pleased with myself, I decided to start on the lower rooms and try to clean them out a little. I opened the first door and headed over to the heavy curtain over the window. I fought them open, and as sunlight streamed in from the setting sun, something crawled on my foot.

I let out a shriek and jumped nearly across the room, shaking my foot to get whatever it was off, and dashing to the safety of the door. Raz ran inside in time to see six mice follow through the door and scamper across the stone floor. Seizing the broom I had clenched in my hand still, he swatted two of the mice towards the entrance, attempted to swipe at a third, and that one and another turned tail and ran back inside the room they'd come out of. Two of the mice disappeared.

112

I knew my face was flame-red. "I...I'm sorry," I stammered. "I didn't mean...They startled me, is all. I...I wasn't expecting anything alive. I'm not afraid of mice. Really, I'm not."

Nightfire stuck his head through the door, anxiety spinning through him, but calming at my embarrassment since he knew I was all right. *"You are hurt?"*

Wishing I could sink through the floor, I shook my head. "Just a stupid mouse," I muttered.

"What is a mouse?"

I pointed mutely to the little grey creature scampering from a shadow across the room. Raz swept it across the floor towards Nightfire. The creature was so frightened by Nightfire it didn't move. Nightfire eyed it curiously, bending down and sniffing it.

"You're going to scare the poor thing to death," I protested.

Raz was grinning. "I take it you harbor no ill will against mice then?"

I was still blushing and I knew it. "It just surprised me is all. It crawled on my foot."

"Perhaps now would be a good time for dinner." Raz went over to pick up the mouse.

Nightfire hadn't quite lost interest in the creature. "Does it taste good?" he wanted to know.

My nose wrinkled. "Yuck!"

"If you see more, you're welcome to eat them," Raz informed him. He carried the mouse to a wooden box and set the creature inside. "We'll dispose of the mice elsewhere." His eyes moved to the room I'd barreled out of, hearing the squeaks inside. "We're going to need to deal with the mice. Quickly. When we don't have much for them to destroy." He handed the broom back to me. "You work fast."

I still wanted to sink through the floor and didn't look up. "Thanks," I mumbled.

Nightfire came the rest of the way inside, pressing his nose against my cheek in a gesture of affection. *"Do not be ashamed. Fear is not bad."*

"It was a stupid mouse. You know who screams over mice? Rich ladies who don't do anything. They're the ones who jump on chairs and scream over a mouse."

Nightfire nuzzled in an effort to soothe me. *"It does not mean you are not brave. Even Raz can be afraid."*

Imagining Raz frightened over a mouse made me smile a little and I hugged Nightfire for a moment. "Would you really eat a mouse?" I asked.

"It is meat. I eat meat," he pointed out.

I felt my nose wrinkle automatically. "Don't eat it in front of me, please. I'll get you more fish."

He was more interested in fish than mice. I gave him some fish outside on the grass, and went inside to eat, my hand smelling fishy.

"I'm told there's a stream somewhere nearby," Raz mentioned, hefting a sack over his shoulder. "Let's go find it, let the dust settle."

"Did you finish in the stables?"

"Just finished when I heard you scream."

I felt my face heat again. "I'm really not afraid of mice," I felt important to repeat.

"There's no shame in fear."

"I'd like to see you scream over a mouse," I said sourly.

He laughed. "Who would rescue the rich ladies then?" he teased. He handed me a canteen and the box with the mouse inside it. "Any guesses as to where this river is?"

"Nightfire?" I asked.

"Southwest."

"Southwest," I answered.

Raz didn't argue. "It should be close. Let's see how far it is."

The river was three minutes away at a normal pace, but the walk wasn't bad. It was a fairly smooth path, and the path was even sort of visible in the fading light. There were shallow places in the river, visible from where we sat and ate, and the river was wide enough and deep enough to suit any purpose we might have, even cleaning Nightfire; although I suspected if he grew to the size of his mother we'd have a difficult time getting him to fit as easily as he would now.

"We're going to be roughing it for a few days," Raz said as he handed me an apple. "Although I've been promised that we'll have everything we need. However, nothing can be delivered until we're ready for it. We should have an icehouse, which will need to be cleaned. The mice will have to be dealt with before we can safely store food. I believe there might be some furniture left in the building, but we'll have to see what we have first so we know what we need."

"I can handle it," I responded, trying to seem tough in order to make up for my less than stellar moment earlier. I dropped a piece of bread in the box for the mouse. "I didn't see any buckets, or any rags. We'll need both to carry water and clean."

"I'm told we have water in Vesta. It was a royal meetinghouse once and they'd want nothing but the best. But I'll be sure to ask for both," he added. "I'm sure this isn't what you're used to, but we'll make it work in no time."

"Apples to pears," I said with a straight face, causing him to laugh. He toasted me with his canteen, then picked up an apple of his own.

Back at Vesta, after setting the mouse free near the bank, Nightfire groomed himself, feeling smug. "There are no more mice," he informed us. I wasn't sure if that meant he'd scared them all away, or eaten them.

Raz raised an eyebrow. "How did they taste?"

"Don't tell me," I said quickly. "I don't want to know. Are you sure they're all gone?"

"I could hear them move. Now I cannot. They are gone."

"One less thing to worry about then," Raz said cheerfully. "Ready to work some more?" he asked me.

I nodded.

Nightfire rose. "I am not interested in more dirt." And he trundled off towards the river.

Raz and I started working on the first room, cleaning up what remained of mice nests and mice droppings. I tried to open the window, but it refused to budge and only made my hands hurt. Raz struggled a moment, but managed to force the window open. It helped the room to smell better. I took the drapes down, since they would have to be cleaned.

We discovered the pantry next door and together cleaned out more mice nests, scrubbing the shelves with water and a bar of soap Raz produced from somewhere. When we finished with the pantry, Raz carried the candle we'd lit for light out into the main room.

I followed, a question on my mind. All the work today had made me curious about what kind of man Raz was. "What sphere are you in?" I asked curiously.

He looked mildly surprised by my question. "My sphere?"

I rolled my eyes. "Your rank."

"I know what you meant. I was surprised you asked. I thought being a noble or not didn't matter to you."

"It doesn't to me. It will to you."

He looked as if he were fighting a smile as I joined him at the table, pulling up the other chair. "And why is that?"

"Because you're a man."

He laughed at that. "And that will make a difference?"

"Men like to brag. I've seen it at the School. The instant someone moves up in the ranks, he goes and boasts about it and starts showing off to the women and those below him."

"And women don't?" He looked as if he enjoyed my view of his gender.

"What rank do we get to achieve unless we marry well?"

"Do you think women don't enjoy power just as much?"

I shrugged. "Sure. But I've seen women who become friends with their servants."

"I've seen men who have done the same," he countered.

"I haven't."

"What about Dillon Marcell?"

"He knows them. I don't know if he's friends with them. And he's weird. I like him though. He's one of the few nobles who are actually nice."

"So nobles can't be nice," he stated with some amusement.

"The higher sphere you are, the less any of them care. Men and women, but mostly men. Like Warren. He acts as if being a minor noble is something to be proud of." My voice was bitter on this. "As if it *means* something to be a step above working class when anyone above us doesn't think a minor noble is worth anything more than anyone else. We're just as little to them as a slave would be. And it only matters because you can't do anything in this country unless you have a name and money to back it up. A name will get you somewhere, and no one has money without a title." I drew a circle on the clean table moodily. "If it hadn't been for Dillon, the generals would have taken Nightfire away from me, and they would have never thought twice because *Miss* Madara, the female child, is nothing to them."

"That's not who you are now." Raz's voice was a little kinder. "You're Lady Madara."

"They gave me a title because a minor noble couldn't be important. They gave me a title so I could be worth the dragon in their eyes."

"Obviously the dragon thought you were worthy enough as you were. So did Dillon, and Captain Durai, and your brother, and the Eagles."

That improved my mood a little, but I still felt like sulking. "It's just another title," I muttered. "Some words to be proud of."

"I hate to tell you, Kaylyn, but titles matter to men because they matter to women." He sent me a smile at my suspicious look. "Follow my logic. Titles, as you said, generally mean wealth. Wealth means safety and comfort, and women want to know they will always have a meal and a nice place to live with things to own. And men want women. If women loved poor sheepherders, there would be more sheepherders than sheep."

I couldn't help but smile. "So it's all my fault."

"I'm afraid so. Would you love a poor sheepherder?"

"Long before I ever loved a noble," I said instantly.

He laughed. "Is that so?"

"Nobles can never be faithful because they love themselves first, and their wealth second," I stated, repeating a common phrase. "Which is why you can't be a noble. Not a high-ranking one, anyway."

His mouth curved in amusement. "Because I'm not self-centered?"

"Because you're not insisting on titles. The generals referred to each other by title half the time, not by their first name. The richest ones are always called Lord and Lady. And you don't bring up my status a million times to remind me of who I am by calling me Lady Madara. Lowerclass doesn't care. Upperclass does."

"You are now upperclass," he reminded me. "A higher sphere."

I scowled. "That was their choice. Warren can enjoy it. I don't care what I am."

"Men do," he reminded me gently. "Nobles will offer you marriage now."

I was quiet, considering that. "If I ever married," I began at last while Raz watched, "I suppose I could marry a noble. If any of them could love me first. I want to be…" I blushed faintly. "Never mind."

"Go on," Raz encouraged, clearly interested.

"No. It doesn't matter because I'm never going to marry. I don't *want* to marry."

Raz didn't push. "Also a choice. I suppose I won't have to worry about any suitors showing up then?" he teased.

"Not for me. And good riddance to them all," I said with feeling.

If Raz thought I was being young and foolish, he at least had the kindness not to say so.

Chapter 10

The next morning, Raz was up with the sun. I dragged myself up as well. "What's the plan for today?" I asked, smothering a yawn.

"I need to head to town for food and supplies. I have dealings to work out with the guards stationed here."

I guessed he wasn't intending to take me, and decided it wouldn't be that interesting anyway. "What should I do?"

"Whatever you like. You need to become stronger, and there's a lot to be done here." He gestured to the dark, dusty ceiling. "So you might consider a little bit of work."

I was sure that by 'work', Raz had meant sweeping, maybe moving the furniture a little, and dusting. I decided I wasn't interested in that as I stared up at the ceiling after I'd eaten. "Well?" I asked Nightfire. "Any ideas?"

"The railings make it hard to walk," Nightfire mentioned.

"All of them?" I tilted my head up.

"The ones on the first level. The rest have bigger walkways."

It was true that the walkway on the first level was the smallest. The rest had smaller rooms above, so the walkways were bigger. "I know how to fix that," I said cheerfully.

By the time Raz came back, Nightfire and I had knocked all the railings down on the first level. "What are you doing?" he shouted up at me, trying to be heard over the noise as Nightfire ripped out the final railing.

"You said I needed to work more, right? Get stronger? Well, I'm doing it!" I pulled the last of the nails out of the floor. "Besides, Nightfire needs to be able to move around. It's his home too." I dusted off my hands, then entered the first room. All the

119

trash was swept out or pushed out to the floor below. Raz shook his head, then started picking out pieces of the trash that could be reused. Soon there was a film of dust in the air.

I spent the most time above the area that Nightfire had picked out to become his. Raz entered to find me attempting to pull a warped board out of the wall and not having much success. "Let me." With a quick and almost effortless movement, he twisted the board out, then snapped it in half.

"Show-off," I muttered.

He held a hand up, palm facing towards me. "Hold your hand against mine and push."

I obeyed, pushing hard, and was barely able to move his hand back at all. Feeling about as strong as a newborn, I dropped my hand. "I already know I don't have any strength. You don't need to remind me."

"This is what we're trying to build up," he reminded me, pulling another board out of the wall, one that was rotting and needed to be replaced. "When you train every day for a couple months, you'll get stronger. When you train every day for a couple years, you'll be even stronger. I've been training, and you just started." He reached up for another board, one above his head. I went to work on the last wall, stubbornly prying the warped or rotting boards out of the wall. Raz broke them all in half. I was secretly impressed and disgusted.

"Can this room be mine?" I asked.

"If you want. It'll take some work, but we can start here." He stared at me a moment thoughtfully. "How much do you know about carpentry?"

"My father did some. His was mostly ornate, and some carving. He didn't build things."

"I'd find something for your hands. I'll make sure you have gloves tomorrow. Let's see how well you work with wood."

Raz showed me how to use a hammer and nails, and assisted as I started hammering in boards. I hit my hand twice and was infinitely more careful after that. That meant I had to hit the nails about three times as much as Raz, who quickly and

120

confidently pounded the nails into the wood. By nightfall, every rotten board had been replaced in my room and my hand hurt.

"I don't like carpentry," I said sullenly.

"You'll improve," he said with far too much cheerfulness. "With your room finished, at least this part, we'll work on tearing the rest down. I want to know where the water's coming from."

"Rain?" I suggested, not knowing where else it could come from. The water pipes didn't run up this section of the wall.

"Yes, obviously there's a leak in the roof somewhere, but I need to find out where. Preferably before it rains again. If we can follow the water trail upward, we'll find it."

"You could have Nightfire look."

"I may. Let's find something to eat. It's getting late."

The next morning, Raz disappeared while I oiled Nightfire, my aching muscles making it more of a chore than normal. Nightfire waited until I finished, then went outside. He stated I created too much dirt when I cleaned and didn't understand how anything was supposed to be getting clean when I was making it all dirtier. Raz returned to find that I was balanced precariously on a bedpost as I attempted to pull a stubborn board from the wall. "Don't stand there," Raz ordered. "Climb down."

"I almost...have it," I ground out through gritted teeth. The bed let out a groaning sound and collapsed. I yelped, clinging to the board as I dangled over the empty bed frame. Then the board came loose and I dropped to the ground with another yelp, crashing into the wooden pieces.

"There was a reason I said to climb down." Raz made his way over to me, avoiding the nails and broken boards. "Are you all right?"

"I think so." I sneezed.

He held out his hand to help me up, then picked up the board. "Why did you pull this one out?" he asked, looking at it. "There's nothing wrong with it."

"No, but the wall behind it is all wet and I was trying to figure out why."

"Wet?" He frowned, staring at the hole. "It hasn't rained here for over a week. It shouldn't be wet."

"I'm just telling you it's wet," I said defensively.

"I didn't say you were lying, Kaylyn; it simply doesn't make sense there would be water. Not that there should be water inside this building anyway. It should all be contained by pipes." He picked up a wooden box and moved it against the wall, standing on it and peering into the hole. I handed him a candle, watching him touch the wall and rub his fingers together, smelling them. "Mold," he said grimly. "And it's still wet." He handed the candle back to me. "Let's see if we can find the source of the water."

"It's only on this side. The other sides don't have any water at all."

"Sides? We're in a circular building, Kaylyn," he said with humor.

"You know what I mean," I muttered. "It's only here. My room, this room, and the room next to it all have the same smell and boards that are warped by water. None of the others do. And the largest room on the top floor has bees."

Raz grimaced. "Wonderful. We'll get to that later."

Our investigation showed us what had been the kitchen on the third floor; I covered my nose and mouth, making a gagging sound. Whoever had been here last hadn't bothered to clean up the kitchen. The sink was full of mold and furry things, and there was a slow dripping sound coming from it.

"I see," Raz said. "The water leak is here, and it all catches in this room, and then it slowly empties out, running to the other rooms below this."

"I think I'm going to be sick."

"That would be the smell of bad meat." He crossed over to the icebox, and opened it. A new wave of the stench came out, and he grimaced. "Someone forgot to clean up in here." He closed the icebox and studied the floor. Every board looked waterlogged and warped. There were obvious cracks in the wood. "This is going to take a lot of work."

"I'm not touching that thing," I said, pointing to the sink with the water in it. "Make Nightfire do it."

"He can help, certainly. Call him, please."

Although Nightfire wasn't pleased, especially with the bad smell, he came and shoved the heavy soapstone sink to the window and helped to tip it so that everything spilled out the window, including everything that had been inside it. They had been metal at one point, and crashed and clanged to the ground.

"I'm not sure I'd have felt safe eating from those again anyway," Raz commented as we lowered the tub back to the floor. "All right, Kaylyn, you can choose. Clean the tub, or empty the icebox and clean it."

I stared reluctantly at the icebox. "How do we get it clean?"

"If Nightfire will help, we'll carry these down to the river."

"I am not a pack mule," Nightfire informed us both, glaring at Raz, his eyes pink slits.

"Do you like this smell?" I inquired. "Because I don't. All you have to do is carry them. We're going to have to clean them."

Nightfire grumbled mentally, then gave in. "I will carry them. But only to make this room smell better," he decreed.

"Sink or icebox?" Raz asked again.

The sink was bigger, but the icebox still had the nasty, rotting food in it. "Sink." I trotted to the door. "I'll get the cleaning things."

With the help of Nightfire and the horses, we carried everything down to the river, where Nightfire dumped the sink and icebox in the middle. Raz opened the icebox and let everything wash downstream.

"You'll poison the fish," I said, watching it float by from the bank.

Raz splashed water at me playfully. "Come on, Kaylyn. This is better than hammering, isn't it?"

"Is the water cold?"

"You aren't afraid of a little water, are you?" he teased, splashing me again.

I stuck out my tongue at him and waded in. The water wasn't that cold, but it was running at a decent pace. I had to be careful not to fall down on the slippery stones.

We scoured for a good hour. Mine was bigger, but Raz had more pieces to clean. I had to be careful not to lose the soap, as I'd almost lost it twice as it tried to float down the river or sink to the bottom to be carried away. By the time I was finished, the soap was much smaller, but the sink looked worthy of use again.

"Do we have an icehouse? I think you said once we did." I asked as I tipped the sink over in the water to rinse off the last of the soap.

"We do. It's below the pantry."

"There can't be any ice left."

"Enough so that we can have an icebox. The military outpost is going to bring some for us to last until winter, as well as some fresh sawdust. We have to clean it out before they'll bring it, however."

"I supposed that's next?"

"It is. We're going to move the icebox down to the first floor until that room is replaced. I don't trust the floorboards to hold. Tomorrow, we're tearing it up and seeing what we can do about the mold."

"What are we doing today?"

"Tearing out the rest of the rotting boards and drying this place out as much as we can. A lot of the building is stone, which will help, but we're going to have to make sure moisture can't get in again and spread. Then do what we can with the icehouse. As soon as it's cleaned out, we can have the military make a delivery." He rinsed out the icebox one last time. "All clean?"

"Me, or the sink?"

"You're less likely to mildew," Raz pointed out. "Nightfire, help us get these out, please."

As Raz started to push the icebox over towards the bank, he slipped and fell, submerging in the water. I burst out laughing, then made my way over to help him. He grimaced and wiped some of the water off his face. As I offered a hand to him, he took it, then yanked hard, dragging me down next to him. I let out a gasp of outrage and shock as I pushed myself up to breathe. The water wasn't exactly warm.

Now he chuckled. "Let's see you laugh at me now."

I splashed water at him, and he splashed me back, both of us laughing and trying to splash the other more.

Nightfire flicked his tail dismissively at us. "You act like children," he sniffed.

We looked at each other, then simultaneously splashed at him. Nightfire was offended, then retaliated, slapping his tail in the water that created a wave to drench us from head to toe. I shrieked and giggled, taking cover behind the icebox in case he decided to attack again.

"I think Nightfire wins," Raz said, laughing as well.

Nightfire smirked as we hauled our way out to the bank.

"For a dragon not even four months old who just lectured us about acting like children, you shouldn't be so smug," I informed him, slogging my way to the rocky ground.

Raz assisted me up the bank, then worked his way back down to haul everything up the bank and we trudged our way back to Vesta. After we changed, we opened every window in the place and Raz set me to cleaning out the icehouse while he went to work on the mold with a cloth tied over his face and long sleeves and gloves. I figured I'd rather freeze than roast while scrubbing walls and whatever it was he was doing. I moved some ice up to the icebox so it could start cooling it down again. By the time Raz came down to check on me, everything had been cleared out and cleaned and I was shivering in the bottom of the icehouse.

"Looks good. Come on out before you freeze." He offered his hand, removing his coat and drawing it around me when I'd reached the top, feeling how cold my hands were. "Sorry," he apologized when I sneezed. "I need to wash it to make sure all the mold is gone. I think the rest of the rotting boards are gone, and I've gotten rid of most of the mold."

"I hope it doesn't rain."

"So do I. But we know what the problem is so we can fix it, temporarily if we need to." When I sneezed again, he took the jacket back. "You aren't going to thank me by the time this warms you up."

"That's okay." I sneezed again and headed outside. "Nightfire warmed me up last time. Should I bother cleaning up?"

"Go ahead. The sun's almost setting. We'll be done for the day."

I retrieved another set of clothes, all my dirty laundry, Raz's jacket, and hauled them down to the river where I scrubbed them in the fading light, fighting drowsiness. I'd worked hard today, and I ached all over. I laid the last skirt out to dry and plunged in the river. It shocked me awake long enough to clean myself from head to toe while Nightfire waited patiently by the bank. I climbed out and dressed again, stuffing everything back in the basket except Raz's jacket, which I laid carefully on top to let dry a few minutes longer. Then I climbed on top of Nightfire and let myself drift.

I awoke to find Raz gently shaking me, the last of worry lines disappearing from his expression. "Wake up, Kaylyn. Next time, maybe you should wait to do your laundry."

"What?" I looked around, blinking. I was in front of Vesta, still slumped over Nightfire's back, and Raz was holding a lantern.

"I was about to go looking for you. You've been gone two hours."

"Oh. Sorry. I was just waiting for your jacket to dry and I fell asleep." I rubbed at my eyes tiredly.

He slid his arm around my shoulders to steady me when I slid to the ground, then gathered the laundry while I stumbled inside. I curled up on my pallet and felt myself start to drift again, sinking quickly into unconsciousness.

I awoke to find my clothes stretched out across the room to finish drying. Blushing faintly, I quickly took them all down and stored them in my now-dusty trunk. Nightfire was already up. "Where's Raz?" I asked.

126

"He went to the military outpost. He says when you wake up to eat and avoid the room with the bees. He probably will not be back until midday."

I spent my time cleaning the room I'd claimed as mine. I moved everything out, scrubbed the floor and the walls, and what I could of the ceiling to get rid of spider webs, then I moved the bed frame back in and Nightfire helped with my trunk. I scrounged around the building until I found what would work as a bedside table and set my unlit candle there. Next to the candle sat the carving of a horse done by my father. It went everywhere with me. The few books and possessions I owned that weren't clothes went on the board that sat on the far wall. I didn't know what the board had been for, but it was there, ornately carved out of a deep, rich mahogany, sturdy, and wide enough so that nothing I put on would fall off.

Raz returned as I worked on Nightfire's room. I was sweeping all the dirt that had accumulated there when he walked in with the military group. "Good to see she can still do a woman's job," one of them said, carrying in a pallet that was loaded with ice.

My eyes narrowed and I clenched the broom handle tightly, imagining myself cracking it across the back of his head.

"Through the door in the floor," Raz directed, cutting his gaze to me. "Kaylyn, would you mind checking on the bees upstairs?"

I fumed as I stomped up the stairs to the top floor. The bees were buzzing around the far wall, just as they had been the last few times I'd been in here. I knew Raz had sent me here to keep me from saying things I shouldn't. I glared at the bees, then stomped my way back down with an entire litany of things to say to the man about what I thought about women's jobs.

Raz was wisely waiting for me at the bottom of the first set of stairs. "Easy, Kaylyn," he said quietly. "Don't make a scene. It won't help to get on his bad side."

"He shouldn't get on *my* bad side," I hissed. "A *woman's* job?"

"He is in charge of any deliveries here."

"Yeah? Well, I have a *dragon* and he won't dare cross Lieutenant Marcell."

"There are a lot of people who believe that women don't belong in the military. Even Eagles have to put up with it from time to time. Trust me, none of them are pleased about it. Show a little decorum, Kaylyn, and prove that you can behave as a woman would."

"Silent and sewing?" My tone was sour.

"Ladylike. Polite and demure. As if you were a ranking noble, worthy of the title of Lady."

I glowered at the floor. "I'm not a Lady. I'm a minor noble, no matter what the generals have done."

"You only aren't a Lady if you act as if you aren't one."

I gave a disgusted sigh. "Fine. But I'm not touching a broom or doing any *women's* chores until they're gone."

"That's fine. Why don't you look in every room we have?"

"I already did. I had everything but my side explored. That's how I knew about the bees."

"So you've claimed an entire side of the building now?" he teased gently.

I was faintly embarrassed. "The side my room's on. I've looked through everything else. The room over there has a lot of furniture." I pointed. "And the rest on that level are empty. The room with the bees has a fireplace."

"What about that one?" Raz pointed to the one above the kitchens. There was obviously a space there, and a large one, but I couldn't find any sort of door.

"I don't know," I admitted. "I can't figure out how to get in. It's the only room left."

He smiled. "Then I guess you're not done exploring."

"You're just distracting me so I don't tell that man he's an arrogant lout."

"That I am. But we also need to know what's up there. If there's another room we have to replace." He handed me a key. "This might help. I don't know if it's locked at all, but if it is, this key might unlock it."

"Raz! Where's this room with the bees?" someone called up. "Are we starting in there, or the kitchen?"

"Pulling boards or exploring?" Raz asked.

"As if you had to ask." I hurried back up the stairs.

I couldn't find any way in from the upper level, so I headed down to the kitchen. There was some kind of latch in the ceiling, but I couldn't get it to move.

"Can I help you?" a voice inquired.

Startled, I looked to see one of the soldiers next to the box I was standing on. "I can't get the latch to move."

"May I try?" he asked courteously.

I stepped down and watched him. Even with gloves on to protect his hands, he couldn't make the latch budge. Seeing he couldn't get it, another stepped up to try. By the third one, I decided they weren't getting it open and left to try another way.

Nightfire had informed me there was some kind of balcony outside the room and offered to carry me up. I hurried outside and wrapped my arms around his neck, stretched out on his back. "Be careful, okay?" I asked. "This isn't really comfortable."

"Do not fall."

"That's kind of the plan," I muttered, holding tighter.

Nightfire carefully, but quickly, climbed his way up the outside of the building. I squeezed my eyes shut tightly, not sure I'd be able to hang on if I got too curious to look around, or look down. Not until we reached the top did I open my eyes, jumping down to the balcony. Nightfire feigned disinterest, informing me he was going to sleep, but his head was tipped to watch me.

There was a door leading inside. It was the kind of door that opened by use of a key on both sides, and the key I held fit easily inside. The lock was a little stiff, and so was the door, but I managed to force it open and edged inside.

It was nothing like I'd expected. The outside had been tiled, which was expensive but not strange since it would protect the floor below from water. The tile had been continued inside. It looked like marble and was polished to elegance. There was a fireplace, made of another kind of rock, one that mirrored the elegance of the floor, in a beautiful, soft blue color mixed with a soft pink. The walls were marble part of the way up then turned into white stone, but there was no pattern like there was on the floor, just the hint of pink veins running through it. There were two large windows on either side of the fireplace that faced the west, where the sun set, but it wasn't simply glass. Inset in between where the corners of the panes intersected were little stones cut like a diamond to throw rainbows against the wall. This window was never meant to open. I didn't want it to.

Contrasting the lighter walls was a dark, mahogany bookcase built into the wall with a few books still sitting on them. The entire room was as large as the kitchen below and the room next to it. I could only imagine what it had been for.

I let out a shriek of delight. "Raz! This place is *beautiful!*" I raced over to the trapdoor in the floor and quickly used the key to unlock it, twisting the latch and pulling the trapdoor up. Raz was standing below, looking up at me. "You have to see this!" I said excitedly.

"How did you get up there?" he inquired, his expression telling me he already knew.

"Nightfire carried me up. He said there was a balcony. The key let me in. Raz, it's not a storage room! It's…it's like this belongs in a palace!"

"Is there another way up?" he asked.

"There's a door, but someone built a wall over the other side. I think this used to be a dumbwaiter. I have the pieces for one up here. And you couldn't get the door open because it was locked." I dropped the lock down for his inspection. "I guess whoever did this created a trapdoor to cover the dumbwaiter and then locked it, and went out through the door and told someone to build a wall over the door. Why would anyone do that?"

"To preserve the room. What's it look like?"

"Expensive. The floor is stone, even outside where the balcony is. Which explains all the water down there. It didn't have anywhere to go but through this trapdoor. There's a hole right above here, by the way."

"A big hole?"

"No. But any water caught on the roof would go here."

"So the water comes from the roof to the floor there, through the trapdoor which, incidentally, was right above where the sink was placed, and that poured here and then continued to trickle for days. If we fix that, that should prevent any more mold. Any cracks in the stone?"

"None that I saw. None on the balcony either."

"Who would tile a balcony?" asked the man who'd informed me I was doing a woman's job. He glared at me as if I'd done it myself.

"That would be a man's job, wouldn't it?" I said, unable to stop the snide tone. "So I suppose a man did it." I disappeared as Raz fought a smile, staring at his shoes. I returned quickly with a chip and dropped it down. "This is what the floor's made of. It cracked outside in one corner. Is that marble?"

Raz inspected it, as did everyone else. They'd stopped pulling up the floor and were crowded below the trapdoor. "Limestone," one of them decreed. "Good limestone. Polished. That won't soak up water, or hardly any at all."

"You have to see it," I told Raz.

"Later," Raz promised. "We need to get as much work done today as we can. Do you want to come down?"

I shook my head emphatically.

He grinned. "Afraid you'll have to pull more boards up?"

"No. I'm afraid you'll make me hammer again."

"You have an hour, and then you get to help somewhere," he informed me.

That gave me an hour of respite. If the men were really good, I wouldn't have to do that much. I immediately agreed.

"Kaylyn? Come down through the door, not the outside of the building," Raz said before he went back to work.

"Spoilsport," Nightfire thought to me.

Chapter 11

I spent my hour looking through the books and looking for any holes in the room. Nightfire helped me onto the roof so I could look there, and the only hole I found was the one over the trapdoor. The door was like the one to the balcony, and was only opened on either side by a key. I borrowed four nails and a hammer and carefully put a nail in each of the four corners of the doorway so those on the other side could see where the door had once been. Then I climbed down and sorted through the wood to see what was salvageable and what wasn't. I didn't care that it was delegated to me because I was female; I had no interest in the physical labor upstairs.

Half an hour before sunset, the men trooped wearily downstairs and left, informing us there were returning tomorrow to see if they could finish nailing the floor down and promising more equipment. They would even find a sealer for the floor just in case it rained before we got the ceiling fixed.

Raz handed me a hammer. "Come on, Kaylyn, time to work."

"Work? I thought we were stopping," I protested.

"You haven't worked up a sweat today. Don't protest."

"I worked this morning!"

"Doing women's work," he teased.

"That's not funny. This isn't women's work." I pointed to the boards I'd sorted and stacked and carried to various spots on the floor. "Besides, I don't recall being invited up to work with the men."

"I don't recall you demanding to help either."

"I was being...what was the word you used? Polite and something."

"Demure. And you, Kaylyn, were taking advantage of the man's judgment against women doing hard labor."

"Wouldn't you?" I trotted up the stairs. "After dinner, can I please show you the room?" I begged.

"Yes, I'll look at it. I'm curious. I just didn't want all the others up there too, or this might have taken another few days. I want to take a look at that hole in the roof anyway."

All the wood had been pried up from the floor, and we were now nailing down what was left of the wood that would be the floor. Raz moved quickly and efficiently. I had more problems. I couldn't manage to put in four nails without hitting my hand, I bent several nails, but the worst was when I managed to catch my skirt under one of the boards and nailed it down before I realized the problem.

Dismay and horror were my primary emotions once I realized I couldn't get my skirt free, despite my struggles. Then Raz said, "Keep going, Kaylyn. We'll use up the last of the wood tonight. No breaks."

"I'm stuck."

"You're stuck?"

"I'm stuck." Embarrassment was clear.

Raz came over, then started to laugh. I glared at him, my face warm with mortification.

"I suppose you can take a break then, until we get you free." He took my hammer and started to pry up the nails I'd just put down. He lifted the board enough for me to pull the material free, then handed the hammer back to me, his eyes still laughing at me.

"I feel like throwing this hammer at you."

"You have to learn to laugh at yourself, Kaylyn. How many people do you know nailed their skirt under the floor?"

"None. Because this is men's work, and women spend their time sewing."

"Did you ever sew your skirt to your needlework?"

"Twice. And don't you dare laugh at me. My sisters did it too. Skirts get in the way of *everything*."

"Then wear pants."

I stopped what I was doing. "*What?*" I spluttered, flabbergasted he would suggest breaking such a universal social rule.

"Wear pants," he repeated, focusing on his task. "It's not completely uncommon. And it's just us, most of the time. As long as only Nightfire or I are the only ones who have to know, it isn't going to be a problem. With everything you're going to be doing, you'll want pants."

A small burst of excitement nearly had me bouncing. "You're going to *let* me wear men's clothes?"

"I'm even going to admit to suggesting it. But only if you promise not to wear them outside of Vesta and its grounds."

"I promise!"

I sensed he was smiling as he placed a nail. "Keep working. I'll see what I can do to get some new clothing for you." He pointed to the boards. "Get the last of those nailed down, and I'll take a look at your room upstairs."

The anticipation of showing it to him got rid of the last of my temper. I even managed to somehow not smash my hand on the remaining four boards I put down. Then I watched Raz climb up and let him assist me in getting through the trapdoor.

He looked around, taking it all in.

"Isn't it beautiful?" I asked, beaming as if I'd built it.

"It is. What are the books about?"

"They're written by hand, so they're hard to read. Only one of them is printed. I think they're really old. The two I looked at, one was a history, and I think the other might have been a journal for someone. It was pretty script, but it wasn't easy to read. It mentioned a few names, like Kirkpatrick and some old noble lines, and I think it was written by Brianna Kay."

He paused in his inspection of the fireplace. "Brianna Kay? Princess Brianna Kay?"

I stared at the book. "I didn't remember that was her name. The last princess of Centralia?"

"I'd be very interested in reading that," he said, resuming his inspection of the fireplace.

"But if it was her journal, why would she leave it behind?" I protested.

"She was sixteen when she left. Perhaps she thought she didn't need it anymore." He rubbed his fingers over the fireplace. "Bluestone," he said. "That's what this is. I laid a floor of it once."

"Expensive?"

"Yes, somewhat. It's a type of sandstone." He looked around. "I don't see any work needed up here."

"Is *he* coming back tomorrow?" I asked.

"Sergeant Sample? Yes, he's coming back."

"Sergeant Sample?" I snorted.

"A sample of the finest, or that's what he said." Raz flashed a grin at me.

"I bet he worked really hard to come up with that one."

He laughed. "You really don't like him, do you?"

"He's just like the generals and all the idiots I left behind at the School. Women are stupid and the sooner we're married off so our husbands can control us, the better." I scowled.

"I've known very few women that were controlled by their husbands, despite wishful thinking on the man's part."

"Guess that's why he never got married." I opened the door to the balcony and started to climb onto the rail.

"Kaylyn." Raz's voice wasn't harsh or appalled, but mild. "What are you doing?"

I hesitated, one knee on the handrail, and leaned back to look through the door. "I'm going to look at the hole on the roof."

"Do you think that's particularly safe?"

"Nightfire's here," I pointed out. "He won't let me fall."

"Why don't you stay off the roof today? If we need to know anything about the hole, Nightfire can tell us."

Sighing, I lowered my other foot to the tile. "I wasn't going to fall."

"You don't plan on falling, but that doesn't mean you won't. It's a long way down."

135

"Spoilsport," Nightfire thought to me again.

I settled myself against the rail and watched him explore the room. "What's for dinner tonight?"

"Is there meat left?"

"No. Nightfire ate the rest of it. He's eating all the time."

"Likely means he's hitting a growth spurt. Humans are the same way. Does he need more oil?"

"I've had to oil him more than usual, but I have another barrel."

"How long should the barrel last?"

"I don't know." I frowned up at Nightfire. "Maybe…a month? But that's if I have to keep oiling him this much. Otherwise it should last two."

"I'll ask for more the next time I see Sergeant Sample. What kind of oil?"

"Dillon wrote it down. I think I know where the paper is." I headed down through the hole in the floor and to my room. By the time I made it back up, Raz was lowering himself through the hole in the ceiling and closing the latch. "I found it," I said, offering the paper.

Raz accepted the paper. "Have you ever fished?"

"No. But Warren has. I cleaned the fish afterwards."

"Then why don't we go fishing? We can have dinner by the stream."

I shrugged. "Nightfire, are you coming?"

"I will catch my own food," Nightfire decreed.

Raz and I passed an evening catching, cleaning, and cooking fish. Raz knew more about cooking outdoors and showed me how to cook over an outdoor fire using nothing more than sticks, several large leaves, a stone, and a few plants for seasoning. I, in return, showed him a trick my father had showed me to keep meat from falling into the fire without using a stone in the middle. Then I bathed my still-aching hands in the river, mentally grumbling about how I hated hammers while Raz sliced vegetables to go with the fish. I nearly choked twice in the meal because Raz told funny stories throughout the evening while he continued to fish. It seemed as if he'd gone everywhere in Centralia, and he had stories from all the places.

"I want to be like you someday, you know." I poked a piece of a wild onion further in the fire to season the fish. "You've been places and done things and you know all these people."

"You're young. You have time. Although the nomad's life isn't as wonderful as you might think."

"Nobody's life is glamorous. But yours is at least interesting. Nothing interesting happened at home. Not since a mule kicked Betty into the stream while she was flirting with someone her dad said she wasn't to ever flirt with."

"What happened to Betty?"

"She couldn't swim. Hardly anyone can. The man who buys and sells horses and saved her. He's big. Maybe the biggest man I've ever seen. He just walked in the stream and walked out carrying her. And then her father wouldn't allow her out of the house for four days because she disobeyed him." I shrugged. "It was all anyone talked of for a month."

"Do you ever miss home? Your friends there?"

"I didn't have friends there. I thought Amina was my friend, but she wasn't. All anyone ever talked about was looking pretty, and dreaming about balls, or talking about who they'd marry." I tilted my head to look at him. "Do boys care as much about marriage as girls do?"

"I can only assume so. Men spend a lot of time thinking about marriage."

"You don't *act* like it."

He chuckled. "I imagine it's hard to see sometimes." He pulled in another fish, killing it before handing it to me. I took the knife and went to work again while he cast the line out again. "This should be the last one to clean and cook tonight. The rest we'll just freeze."

"If Nightfire doesn't eat them all," I muttered. "If men spend as much time thinking about marriage as girls, why do you hide it so much?"

"Because we're nervous. Shy. We're worried about making a move and then getting turned down. We don't want to be hurt any more than you do."

"You aren't nervous or shy. Ever."

"I'm also not flirting with you, am I?" He smiled at me. "I've learned a few things, wandering through Centralia, and I've discovered what I'm looking for out of marriage and a wife. Until I find someone who might be who I'm looking for, I'm content to wait."

"If you married, would she be an honorary Eagle too?" I wanted to know, curious.

"It would be highly unlikely."

I frowned. "But she would know you were an Eagle, wouldn't she?"

"She might. She might not."

"You wouldn't tell her?" I was astonished.

He offered a half-smile. "Where are Eagles known, Kaylyn?"

"On the battlefield. But not even your *wife*?"

"We don't tell people. Oftentimes our closest friends and family don't know."

"But your *wife* wouldn't get to know?" I couldn't move past that.

"We have to protect our identity."

"I know, but…it seems *wrong*."

"It's something to think about when considering marriage. Either I have to keep this secret from her, or I have to find someone who already knows."

I had to think about that for a few minutes. The stream bubbled, bugs zipping by to be eaten by the fish darting through the water. I watched Raz as he patiently held the line, waiting for a bite on the other end. I couldn't imagine having to lie to my husband about something like being an Eagle. Not that I was ever marrying anyway, but that just made me shudder to think about the lies I'd have to tell. "That just makes courting worse," I said finally. "And it's already bad."

He chuckled.

"Humans think about love and courting too much," Nightfire stated.

"You have to find a mate eventually," I returned, looking around for him. I didn't know where he was, but he had to be close. "When do you find a mate?"

"Dragons can find a mate when we are two years old."

I finally spotted him. He was wading through the stream, washing off mud. "I think you're about done fishing," I mentioned to Raz.

Nightfire darted his head down, and came up with two fish. He spat them onto the bank, and came up with two more in two quick darts of the head. Raz wound up his line while I quickly collected the fish. "Did you get enough to eat?" I asked.

"Yes. But I will need more oil. I itch all over."

"Then we should head back. Get the fire, if you would, Kaylyn," Raz said.

I put out the fire while Raz collected everything we'd brought, put the fish in the basket, then handed me the water canteens. The three of us walked back to Vesta together. While Raz stored everything, I cleaned and oiled Nightfire. I went to bed shortly after because Nightfire turned in early and I knew I wouldn't be able to stay awake.

The men returned the next morning with a professional carpenter and a beekeeper. While the carpenter checked the rest of the building for any signs of future problems or further mold issues, the beekeeper, a woman to my delight, used smoke to make the bees drowsy and confused. Then she gathered what she could of their hive and all the bees she could find. Once she removed everything, the carpenter replaced the wood, and covered it with something he said would prevent any other bees from returning to build another hive. Since the beekeeper had been assured that the queen bee was among the hundreds of tiny, buzzing bodies, it was unlikely a new nest would be built. I ate the honeycomb the woman had given me, then watched the last of the floor go in. Raz wasn't helping either, there wasn't enough room, but made sure to get a few pointers from the carpenter about fixing the hole in the roof before thanking everyone and sending them on their way as the sun set.

"Well, Kaylyn, Nightfire, we have a place now," he announced as he closed the door to the outside. "A livable place to call our own."

"It needs much more work," Nightfire stated.

"The only big problem left is the hole in the roof," Raz pointed out. "Everything else is cosmetic. We have an icehouse, a clean icebox that has food in it, a pantry that is decently filled, no more bees, no mold, hopefully, and a brand new kitchen floor. Every room in the building can be used. We shouldn't need any more outside assistance, except for deliveries."

"He's secretly impressed," I whispered to Raz.

"I am not," Nightfire said.

Raz smiled. "I'm not expecting him to be impressed. His kind lives in mountains. This is a human concept of a place to call home." He looked at me. "I saw you'd fixed up your room. A mattress and sheets are expected in the next few days so that bed frame will have a purpose."

"What about you?" I asked. "Aren't you going to claim a room?"

"Eventually. I don't see any reason to claim one now."

"Of course there's a reason. That's the room we'll be cleaning next," I pointed out pragmatically.

He chuckled. "We'll work on that tomorrow. Let's find some food. Can you cook?"

"Not much and not very well."

"Then I have more to teach you. Grab the bread and the cheese from the icebox, and I'll grab the rest."

I'd wondered if Raz was going to teach me anything about fighting, since he hadn't made any mention of it since arriving at Vesta. Now that the immediate problems were solved, Raz started finding out what I could do. Mornings were spent outside, working with weapons such as the staff, hand to hand, and arrows, then we would break for lunch before starting work inside. We dusted and swept and mopped each and every room. Raz fixed the roof, but refused to allow me to help, stating that it wasn't safe and he didn't have the materials to spare. I grumbled a little for form and stayed inside while Nightfire sat on the roof with Raz and watched him work.

Nightfire spent his time learning to glide, knowing it apparently by instinct, and discovering how to hunt. He would occasionally bring back something for us, usually deer, which Nightfire informed us were very plentiful and very stupid. Raz advised him to leave the female deer alone in case they had baby deer to care for, and Nightfire quickly decided fish were less bothersome to hunt. He couldn't tell if they were girl fish or boy fish and he didn't care to.

After Vesta had been cleaned, Raz chose a room to work on, almost directly across from mine, and we started to repair it, finding furniture since he'd decided it was his room and adding things for him. He had a shelf in his room as well, and we added a wooden holder for his sword. Aside from that, his room was almost identical to mine. He lived just as sparsely as I did.

Raz informed me over breakfast a month after we'd arrived that I would be working full time with weapons now. "I know where you are and what you need to work on," he said, buttering his bread. "And it's time you started learning."

I sipped my milk nervously. "For how long?"

"Until the day you die," he stated.

"No, how long each day?"

"Morning and afternoons. Repairs can be done after dinner."

I was immediately grateful we'd started eating dinner before the sun disappeared.

As if he knew my thoughts, Raz smiled wickedly. "You'll be exhausted anyway."

"I'm not any good with weapons," I warned him.

"You'll improve," he said, unruffled.

"What about Nightfire?" I asked, grasping for anything to save me.

"What about Nightfire?" he inquired. He knew I was looking for an excuse.

"He needs to learn to fly," I pointed out. "Rosewing said I had to teach him."

"Luckily for Nightfire, I thought of that before you used it as an excuse to avoid training. A falcon trainer is headed here sometime within the next two months. Until she gets here, you get to spend your time training, and Nightfire will do whatever it is Nightfire does." He smiled at me. "Finish your breakfast. We're going to start with the staff today."

I'd known that Raz had been testing me before, seeing what I could do, which wasn't much beyond what anyone else learned, but it quickly became apparent just how easy he'd been on me. I would have said it was humiliating, but he was never anything but helpful; teaching, lecturing, occasionally teasing. He was aggressive, and didn't hesitate to relinquish my weapon from my grasp. He also didn't hesitate to cause bruises. I wasn't sure I ever caused him pain.

After having my shoulder whacked for the umpteenth time, knowing it would turn a lovely shade of purple soon, I tossed my staff on the ground in disgust. "I yield."

Raz rapped me none too gently on my head. "Yielding in battle means surrender, Kaylyn, and surrender is not an option."

"Of course it is! People surrender all the time!"

"Eagles don't."

I didn't hesitate to point out the obvious. "I'm not an Eagle."

He remained patient, but his words were solemn. "Realize, Kaylyn, that surrender most likely means your death, especially because of Nightfire. If he chooses to fight, and he likely will, he's a powerful weapon. That's a weapon any enemy would want to get rid of."

"And what if they wanted to use him instead?" I demanded.

"Then that's worse," he answered soberly. "How do you think they'd force Nightfire to change sides? Do you realize the kind of pain they'd put you through? Do you realize the dangers of surrendering as a woman?"

"They wouldn't…"

"Yes, they would. And you can't forget that. You also can't forget that you and Nightfire share a mindlink. I've watched you both. You get tired when he gets tired; when you feel pain, he flinches. What effect do you think killing you is going to have on him?"

"I will no longer wish to live," Nightfire said, joining the conversation.

I stared up at where he'd been sunning himself on top of Vesta. "You won't want to *live*?"

"Raz is right. I feel your pain and you, mine. If I die, you will no longer want to live, and if you die, I will no longer want to live."

I was simultaneously flabbergasted and terrified. I had no idea what to say.

Raz scooped up the rod and held it out to me. "Never surrender," he said simply.

"That's it? Nightfire just said if something happens to either of us the other's going to die, and all you have to say is never surrender?"

"What should I say?"

"I don't know! Something!"

He placed the staff in my hands. "Perhaps, from now on, you should be a little more careful with endangering your life, since it's more than your life now."

I felt myself shiver. "That didn't help."

"Is there anything I could say that would make you feel better?"

"I don't know." I held tightly to the staff. Suddenly I was aware of the new possibilities for my death.

Nightfire glided down, landing a little ungracefully, then nuzzled my cheek in an effort to soothe me. *"You are learning to protect us,"* he thought to me. *"You are learning so it will not happen, so you will never have to consider surrender. Raz is teaching you about battle to protect us from what you do not know. He is simply giving you the proper mindset to fight with."*

"I don't like this mindset. War scares me."

"Do not think of war. Think of protection. Others will not like you and they will not like me. You need to know to protect yourself from everyone who could hurt either of us. And giving up is never the right way to fight. It cannot protect you."

"I thought men had this strange honor system," I said, looking at Raz. "Not killing someone who yields."

"It's less honorable to kill someone who's yielded, but to those who don't care, it won't matter. And you're not a man. Those who see you as having forgotten your place or disapprove of what you're doing can use you as a lesson to other women not to forget where they belong. Female Eagles tend to fight harder, longer, because this honor system that used to be upheld by everyone won't protect them and will only rarely protect another man. The rules of fighting are forgotten in battle. There's no fairness. You do what it takes to win."

"You must always want to win," Nightfire said.

I felt young and small. A dragon less than five months old was joining in on lecturing me on how to be a fighter. I wasn't sure I had what it took to be what they were expecting.

"Try again," Raz suggested, hefting his weapon.

"No." Nightfire curled around me. "Tomorrow. Not today."

Raz didn't argue. "Let me know when you want lunch."

I sat down on the ground and felt Nightfire adjust as Raz went inside. "I don't know if I can do this," I whispered.

Nightfire pressed his nose to my cheek. *"You can. You must."*

"Nightfire, I'm not a fighter. I'm not anything. I could never fight in battle."

"You could. If you thought I was in danger, you would fight." I felt Nightfire press his nose against my shoulder to comfort me. *"Whatever happens to you also happens to me. I am a dragon. I can protect myself. You must also be able to protect yourself. If you cannot and you are killed, I will die. By protecting yourself, you are*

also protecting me. Danger is everywhere. Raz is trying to prepare you for it."

"I wish I could pretend this was the same, but it's not. This isn't like knowing how to protect my honor as a female. Before, all I had to do was escape. Now I have to win. And winning means I have to kill. And I don't think I could."

"Then do not think of killing. Winning does not always mean you must kill. Winning means they can no longer fight."

"I have to knock them all out? Or disarm them? I'm not that good."

"You can be. Raz is one of the best fighters and he is training you. If you try, you can make sure no one ever harms you again. No one will push you or hit you because you will not let them."

That appealed to me. Making sure no one ever thought they could bully me was one of the few reasons that would motivate me to learn to fight. I'd had enough of people like Lord Kipper. "Maybe I could do that."

Nightfire nuzzled gently, satisfied I was starting to consider it. *"Think. Decide. Raz will not make you a soldier who kills without reason. He will train you to protect, defend, and fight with honor. He is not like the generals who want a weapon."*

I had to consider that for a few minutes before I came to my decision. "Okay." I took a deep breath in, let it out quietly. "Okay, I'll try."

Chapter 12

Raz didn't make a mention of my hesitation when we went out to practice the next day. I was nervous, wondering what Raz's reaction would be to my fear, but all he did was hand me a bow and quiver of arrows and order me to shoot. I kept watching for a sign he wasn't pleased with what I could do, sure it would eventually come.

"Kaylyn, what are you waiting for?" he finally asked, telling me he'd seen my glances.

I rubbed my hand over my aching arm. I'd never shot so much for so long before. "I'm waiting for you to figure out I'm a lost cause."

"I hardly think you're a lost cause."

"You'd be the first, then," I muttered.

"Did everyone think you're a lost cause, or just the teachers?"

"Just about everyone, but the one who taught fighting and self-defense was worse."

He sighed. "Let me take a guess and say he wasn't very encouraging."

"'You couldn't hit the broad side of a barn if you were six steps from it'," I mimicked. "'How many arrows do you intend to waste today? Are you aiming for the target at all? If you ever practiced, maybe you'd get somewhere. I can't believe I'm getting paid to put up with you. It's a good thing your family has a son to defend your honor, because the worst you could fight off is a one-winged fly'."

It was the first time I'd ever seen Raz angry. "Do you believe that?" he demanded in a voice that was tightly controlled.

I hesitated a moment too long. "No," I answered slowly.

He closed his eyes a moment, as if searching for patience.

"Well, he's right that I'm awful, isn't he?" I demanded, defensive. "Or are you going to try and tell me *this* is good?" I pointed to the target which held three arrows and many more scattered arrows around the target.

He rested his hands on my shoulders. "Kaylyn, I'm not expecting you to be good yet. This only confirms my belief that you were never taught, never *really* taught. I'm not looking for a student who already knows everything, who can meet some vague standards and that's all. I like to teach. If I didn't, I wouldn't be here. You have talent and you have the ability to learn. That's all I need from you, besides the willingness to learn." His piercing, blue eyes held sympathy. "I don't believe in the method that abuse and insults will encourage learning. If those are the kinds of comments you're waiting on, you'll have a very long time to wait."

"Raz, can't you see I'm awful?"

He gave a half-smile that said he saw far more than what I did. "I've seen worse after more time with better trainers." He released me and held out his hand for the empty quiver. "Go put something on your arms. There's no sense in overworking. Once we get some stamina built up, we'll go longer."

After lunch, he handed me a staff. "Based on your lack of teaching, I think it's best if we start from the beginning," he stated. "You have a few bad habits I don't like that any decent instructor should have caught and corrected. So let's start over. This is a quarterstaff. It's typically used as a defensive weapon."

"Am I that awful?" I asked, disheartened.

"No, you aren't, Kaylyn. But if you don't have the basics properly grounded, it will mean we have to go back and re-teach it. I'm going to make sure you're taught right from the beginning." He offered his staff to me. "Imitate my grip."

I obeyed.

"Good. Try not to let your hands move out of that position so you have the best control of the staff possible."

Lessons for the first month weren't too difficult. I already knew most of what he was teaching. Starting from the beginning had its advantages because I became stronger through daily repetition of the basics. Mornings were archery, afternoons were with the staff. Halfway through the second month, Raz started to slowly introduce hand to hand fighting and the knife. I was hesitant with the knife, drawing blood wasn't something I wanted to do, so Raz suggested I learn to throw it. I found this entertaining even if I didn't do it well.

One day, during a day of rain, Raz decided we'd stay inside. I was given a few chores to do while he worked on repairing a room. He didn't make me help with carpentry very often since there were plenty of other things to do. Nightfire was lying in the doorway, watching the rain fall, somehow entertained. The scent of rain mingled with the wood Raz was working with as he shaved a piece here, adjusted another one there, trying to repair the broken cabinet we'd found stuffed behind one of the curtains in the upper rooms. Nightfire had helped us get it down, which was good because we'd almost dropped it off the first level to the ground floor with the railing gone.

Since the chores weren't going to take very much longer, I popped out of the room on the second floor and leaned against a support beam. "Raz?"

"Yes?"

"Eagles get tattoos, right?" I asked.

He glanced up. "Most do. A few don't."

"Did you?"

"I did."

"Can I see it?"

"It's not exactly available for show," he mentioned drolly.

"Why not? I know you're an Eagle," I pointed out.

"Because it sits here." He tapped the left side of his chest, over his heart. "And it isn't proper to show my chest to a female."

I put my hands on my hips. "I'm wearing men's clothes and a tunic with no sleeves, and my hair is too short. Any person other than you would have a fit about my outfit, especially since I'm showing my shoulders. Plus, I have a brother. I'm not going to tattle to my mother."

He grinned, then stripped out of his tunic. I clattered down the stairs to see. It was a shield, an Eagle feather crossing from the bottom left angling right, and a sword crossing in an X from the bottom right to the left, with the blade pointed up. I studied it for a full minute. "Are those your initials?" I asked. In the upper right corner was an RG in fancy letters.

"They are."

"What about for women? What if they get married?" I asked.

"It doesn't matter. Whatever their name was when they came in is what their name is for the Eagles." He put his tunic back on.

A thought occurred to me. "Could *I* get a tattoo?" I demanded, intrigued. "Tattoos are only for military, but I'm technically military."

"You could. I wouldn't."

"You *wouldn't*? You've already *got* one!" I spluttered.

"A tattoo for the Eagles is a way of proving who you are, or a way to identify us if we die. Your dragon proves who you are."

"Oh." I thought about this. "I wonder what mine would look like if I got one."

"That would be up to you. It's just another reason why you shouldn't rush into this. Tattoos are permanent. They aren't something for fun or to get on a whim. Getting this meant I had to spend time recovering."

"Recovering?" I asked, confused.

"Tattoos are ink that's been dug into the skin with needles hundreds of times," he said, watching as I winced. "And that leaves an injury the body has to deal with. Soreness. Scabs. Itching. For several months until it was completely healed."

"All this for a picture?" I complained as I headed back up the stairs.

"All this for a point of pride. That's what tattoos are. Something to be proud of." He resumed working on his project.

"It's always pride," I muttered.

"Sergeant Sample is coming later today," Raz said as I returned to the room I was cleaning. "So you might want to change before he gets here." His voice never changed from its calm, complacent tone.

I immediately turned around. "He's coming here? Why?" I demanded.

"Because he's bringing another bed. Natasha's due to arrive in the next two days."

"Who's Natasha?"

"She's a falconer. She'll be teaching you and Nightfire about flying."

"Is she an Eagle?"

"Yes, she is. And she'll be staying in the room you're cleaning out."

I was interested in meeting another Eagle. "How long is she staying?"

"No longer than a month."

Nightfire was irked, and now glaring out the door. Since I could feel him fuming, I went down the stairs to him. "What are you upset about?" I asked. "I thought you liked Eagles."

"I will not be trained like a human pet," Nightfire snapped.

"Nobody said you were a human pet. We're just teaching you how to fly. If Natasha's a good falconer, she'll know all about how to raise birds."

"I am not a bird," Nightfire informed me.

"Birds fly, dragons fly. Go with it." I couldn't imagine why Nightfire felt so affronted.

"I am not a bird and I will not learn to fly like one," Nightfire insisted curtly, his eyes green for stubbornness.

I put my hands on my hips and matched his stubbornness with my own. "Well, I don't know how else to teach you to fly. Falcons are majestic birds; the birds of kings. If you don't want to learn to fly like a falcon, we can teach you to fly like a canary."

He blew a breath at me, then settled his head on his front legs, grumbling softly.

I repented somewhat, feeling his insult to being compared to something so small and more like dinner. "Look, if Rosewing had told me anything about flying, we wouldn't need someone else. But she didn't, so if you want to learn to fly, we have to have outside help."

"Fine," he griped, but he didn't sound very cooperative. I left him to brood, hoping he'd accept the matter a little easier by the time Natasha arrived.

The rain lightened, then stopped within half an hour. Nightfire went outside to crawl on the roof. He warned me when Sergeant Sample and the military people were on their way, and I hurried to change into appropriate clothing, standing politely as they carried in the bed pieces and set it up. I waited until they left to finish the room. The rest of the day was mine to do with as I pleased unless Raz called for help. He didn't call very often so I wrote letters to my family and Dillon, then cleaned my room a little before climbing the ladder into the Queen's Room. Raz had almost gotten the door open, but I liked climbing the ladder more.

The Queen's Room was my little sanctuary where I could dream. I liked watching the rainbows on the wall, and looking over the grounds from the balcony. I liked looking through the princess's things too. I shied away from her diary, not quite comfortable reading something so private. The piece I'd read told me that this room had also been her sanctuary. I felt connected, in some little way. I wondered what it was like to be princess over a nation, and then watching that nation fall apart. The nation had lost a king, but she'd lost a father, and this had been her last home in Centralia before she'd left her country with her mother.

The day after next, when Natasha was due to arrive, Raz set me to practicing while he went Rillmyra for more supplies. When Nightfire told me someone was approaching from the town, I hurried out to meet her as she led the horse on foot down the path. "Hi!" I called.

She smiled. "You must be Kaylyn. I'm Natasha." She came to a stop, bowing since her hands were full with the horse's reigns and a heavier jacket. Her skirt reached the tops of her shoes and covered even her ankles. Her hair looked as if it had never been cut and the braid reached down the entire length of her back. I was sure when it was unbraided it went to her knees.

I couldn't help but stare. "How do you move?" I asked, bewildered. "Your skirt is so *long*!"

Natasha laughed, white teeth flashing against dark skin. "I am of a family that clings to the old traditions. I see your family is a little looser."

"Oh." I touched my hair reflexively. "No, not really. My mother would rather I be dressed like you."

"Then someone allowed you to leave the old traditions behind a little. I don't have many skirts that allow my ankles to show."

"But you're an Eagle," I protested. "Aren't you?"

"Do you believe that means I don't follow rules?" she asked with amusement.

"Does it?" I asked.

She laughed again. "Raz said I would find you amusing. My being an Eagle means I have to follow the rules more closely. I remain in secret, and I don't mind the long skirts. I only break the rules when the Eagles are called up."

"How do you practice?"

"My weapon is archery. The length of the skirt doesn't bother me. And I have enough freedom to do what I wish. Falconry is a respected profession, and no one can have an objection to a female falconer if she's good enough. It was originally a lady's profession, you know. Have you ever tried falconry?"

"My mother's afraid of falcons."

"A pity. Perhaps I'll have time to teach you."

"That would be fun," I said eagerly. "Only, is it all right if I wear pants?"

"I don't mind. You might find them a little warm." She clucked to her horse, rubbing his nose affectionately. Her dark skin starkly contrasted the horse's white coat.

"Did you ride sidesaddle all this way?" I couldn't help but ask.

"Unfortunately, yes. It's a downside of skirts, but I'm through now. Raz said you had a stable."

I nodded. "Raz is in town. He says he'll be back by lunch and that I'm supposed to get you settled in. He didn't know when you'd get here."

"I made good time today."

I remembered my manners. "Can I carry something?" I offered.

"Thank you." She unhitched her bag, offered it to me. "I'll just stable Snow and be right in."

I carried the pack inside, then pushed both the front doors open as Natasha left the stables. "Fresh air?" she asked.

"Nightfire," I replied pointing up.

Natasha looked up, then politely moved aside as Nightfire landed on the ground. "It's an honor to meet you," she said, bowing to him as well.

Nightfire eyed her mistrustfully. "I do not know you."

"I wasn't at the meeting when Kaylyn was brought into the Eagles. I lived too far away to make it."

"Be nice," I warned.

Nightfire gave me a grumpy glare and continued inside.

"Sorry," I apologized. "He doesn't take well to new people and he doesn't like being taught to fly by a human."

"Perhaps you could help me then. I haven't seen a dragon up close before, and I need to know what I'm looking at."

I gave Nightfire a dubious glance. Sure enough, he had something to say. *"A human cannot teach a dragon to fly if she knows nothing about them,"* Nightfire stated crossly.

"Give her a chance! She just got here!"

He flicked his tail and didn't answer.

"We'll see how this goes," I muttered. I crossed over to Nightfire. "What do you want to see?"

"Could you have him stretch out his wings?" she asked.

I glared at Nightfire. It took a moment, then he opened his wings with a snap.

Natasha moved closer, inspecting Nightfire's wings. "See these?" she asked, hovering a finger over Nightfire's wing and tracing it over a joint. "There's where the blood flows, and how Nightfire controls his flying. And over here," she pointed towards the base of the wing, "that's the muscle. The more he flies, the bigger and stronger those muscles are going to get."

Interested, Nightfire turned his head to watch Natasha work. She pulled out a sketchpad and started to draw. She identified different parts of the wing for me, and the major bloodlines and muscles according to the look and the movement Nightfire was capable of. Raz returned to find me attempting to identify the parts of the wing by memory.

"Nightfire, don't prompt me! I can get this," I insisted in mild exasperation.

"I see you made it," Raz said to Natasha, setting his purchases down. "And introductions have been made."

"Here." Natasha handed her paper to me. "This is for you."

"Thanks." I retrieved what Raz had brought. "I'll put this up."

"Thank you, Kaylyn. How was the trip?" he asked Natasha.

"It wasn't bad. I had a brief encounter with a grumpy innkeeper and Snow, but I tipped well and he was mollified."

With Nightfire much more pleased with Natasha, he let Natasha make sketches while Raz practiced and worked with me to set up lunch.

Mornings changed to practice with Nightfire, to teach him how to fly. Natasha showed us how falcons flew, her trained falcon had flown overhead with her, and Nightfire was eager to imitate them. He listened attentively as Natasha described different exercises for building up wing strength. In the afternoons, Nightfire was left to train alone and Natasha joined us. Both of them offered tips and advice. I was slightly ashamed at first, wondering why Natasha didn't state the obvious, my archery hadn't improved much, but after the third day and no comment on my abilities I stopped worrying about what she thought. Raz left archery to Natasha's care, and she spent time working with me on focus and control. She was as good as Raz on staffs, however, and thumped me just as much as he did. She was a little gentler with the blows, but I earned just as many bruises.

"Are all the Eagles good at everything?" I complained during the third week.

"We've worked hard to be proficient," Natasha answered.

"That means yes," I grumbled. "I bet you all can't do anything poorly."

"Then you haven't seen me dance," Natasha said with a grin. "I'm regularly called out as the worst dancer in Centralia."

"Right. So you're only good at everything that matters." Most days I didn't mind it. They were Eagles; they were supposed to be that good. But recently I'd found there were days when I was tired of the flawless Eagles who were just another reminder of something I could never be.

"This is what matters to us. What matters is different for everyone."

"Thanks to the generals, this matters to me." I glared at the target as I drew back the arrow. I'd learned not to yank when frustrated. The only part of archery I felt I'd improved on was the ability to draw the arrow back. It wasn't difficult, and my arms weren't exhausted anymore, but I still couldn't manage the complicated process to fire it. I had to keep my arm turned out so the string didn't raise a welt on my arm, although the arm guard did help. Raz had found one for me after I raised a large welt that had even Nightfire complaining. Since bringing up my previous teacher made Raz mad, I hadn't even mentioned my teacher's favorite phrase of, "You're so stupid, pain can't even teach you to do things right."

Besides how to draw the arrow properly, I also had to remember to sight down the arrow. I had to account for my tendency to pull to the right just a little. My worst problem was the wind. I could consistently remember to do the rest of the steps, until I was frustrated, but I could only rarely remember to account for the wind, and I hated its inconsistency. On the bad days, language my mother would have washed my mouth for uttering filled my mind, often about the wind.

Miraculously, my next three shots hit the target, one in the center zone, and then the next two didn't touch the target. I hissed in frustration.

"You have to find your routine," Natasha said. "Every time I draw a bow, I go through the same process." She drew an arrow, laid it on her bow, and drew it back with a smooth, easy motion. When she released, it struck where I'd been aiming every time and never hit. My following shot barely nicked the inner ring.

"See?" she said approvingly. "That's better."

I didn't mention that I'd been lucky. The arrow had hit to the left of the ring, and I'd already been compensating by aiming more to the right. I had no control where the arrow went on the target. Most of the time I tried to be grateful it was hitting the target.

"You'll get better at control," Natasha assured me, as if reading my thoughts. "Another month and you'll be able to hit the target every time."

"Are you staying that long?"

"No, I'm leaving tomorrow. I have to spend the rest of the day getting everything ready for my trip."

"Will I see you again?" I asked hopefully. Although Nightfire was through learning what she could teach on flying, I did like having another person around. Natasha being a female Eagle made me feel hope that I could possibly be a reasonably good fighter someday. I didn't imagine I'd ever come close to matching an Eagle, but her ability to outfight men gave me optimism.

She gave a mysterious smile and winked. "Maybe someday. You never know."

That evening, over dinner, Natasha discussed in length where she'd go. I didn't think much about it, other than trying to figure out where these places were, until breakfast the next morning. They were both sitting at the table downstairs, looking over a map when I exited my room. "Remember this one?" Natasha asked. "The noble's youngest daughter fell head over heels for you there."

Raz laughed. "Yes, but it was her grandfather who fell for you."

"You're a good, proper girl," Natasha imitated in an old, dry, shaking voice. "The kind of girl my wife knew how to be. Nothing like these mavericks today."

They both laughed. "We had fun, didn't we?" Natasha asked. "Exploring. I've heard of at least three more people who might be possible apprentices for me. One of them a ten-year-old. And I've heard of two possible apprentices for swords."

My heart dropped. Her suggestion and implication was clear.

"I haven't had enough time to look around here. How old are the ones you've heard of?"

"Twelve and fourteen. Cousins. The mother of the ten-year-old was considered an apprentice once, but Pentra was picked instead due to their ages."

"It's Marianna's son? I hadn't heard he was interested in weapons. It would be nice to see her again."

"It would be nice to travel together again. Visit all the little corners of Centralia. Follow rumors of talent."

I backed inside my room and closed the door, blinking hard against tears of rejection. I could already foresee the future. Raz would leave with Natasha, find someone who wasn't hopeless, someone who could become an Eagle so he could fulfill his duty, and I would be shipped off elsewhere.

I ran to my window and climbed down the side of the building, and then I ran for the stream before I screamed or cried and drew either Raz's or Natasha's attention. The last thing I wanted was pity.

I stayed by the river once I reached it, wondering miserably where I'd go now. Would someone else come to deal with me now? Or would I be sent back to the School for Officers and Gentlemen in apparent disgrace? I hated how slow I was. If I'd been a better fighter, maybe he wouldn't mind staying here. But he had high standards, and I couldn't put any more of myself into my training. It was as if he was searching for hidden depths of skill or strength that

I didn't have. Maybe it was something an Eagle would have, but I wasn't good enough to be an Eagle.

I sat in misery, threw a tantrum, cried, then became downright hostile. I was tired of being dumped elsewhere. I was tired of nobody wanting me. *So what if I'm not good enough to be an Eagle?* I thought angrily, stomping up and down the bank. *I'm not an idiot! It's not my fault women are never taught anything!* I slung a rock into the water and threw myself on the ground, miserable.

Raz came in search for me long after the sun had set. Nightfire had called to me and sensed that I was sulking so he hadn't continued to talk to me. He wasn't annoyed by my fit of temper and I knew he was always waiting in case I wanted to talk or if I needed consoling. I guessed he'd told Raz where I was, because I heard his footsteps approaching the stream without searching or any hesitation.

I didn't move a muscle, sitting in stony silence as he came towards me. He sat down next to me, setting the lamp he carried on the ground behind us a little. "Natasha's gone," he said conversationally. "Left a little after lunch. She did want to say farewell to you."

I resisted snorting in contempt and glared at the moon-lit river.

Raz didn't say anything further, seeming to contemplate deep things as he watched the water flow. Silence sat between us for several minutes.

"So?" My voice was clipped.

He turned his attention to me. "So?" he inquired.

"So, when are *you* leaving?" I asked derisively. "Going off on this wonderful little hike so you can find your brilliant apprentices? Having fun chasing down rumors of talent?"

"You shouldn't eavesdrop." His voice held disapproval.

"You were both *standing* in the *middle* of the *building*! I wasn't eavesdropping; it was *impossible* not to hear!" I seethed with the added insult. "How was I not supposed to hear your plans to go here and there and wherever and about all the fun times you have exploring the little corners of Centralia?" I shoved myself up and stomped three steps away. "Do I need to pack tonight or tomorrow? And where am I going *this* time?" I kept my back to him so he wouldn't see the angry tears returning.

Raz idly flipped a few stones into the water. "I wasn't planning on going anywhere. But I suppose if you want, we can go exploring into the little corners of Centralia. We should probably wait until Nightfire has built up a little more stamina; and you'll have to have more horseback riding or you won't be able to walk once we start."

I spun around, not quite sure I could correctly understand what he was meaning. It sounded as if he intended to take me with him. "What?"

He stood and flipped another stone into the water with a soft plunk. "Personally, I thought Vesta was rather nice, even if it does need some work. It suits every purpose we'd possibly need, for us and a dragon."

"Raz, stop teasing me. You're going to stay? You weren't going to leave?" My voice wavered with fragile hope.

"Of course not, not unless you and Nightfire came with me. I made a promise to train you, Kaylyn. I'm not about to abandon you." He rose and bent down to pick up the lamp.

I flew towards him, my arms wrapping around him in a fierce hug. It surprised him, and he shifted automatically to keep himself from falling before he rested an arm around my back in a return hug. "I gave my word, Kaylyn. I'm not leaving you."

"Thank you," I whispered.

He rubbed his hand gently over my back. "All right?"

I nodded.

He waited until I let go before releasing me. "Would you like dinner?"

"Yeah. I'm starved."

"Oil Nightfire, and I'll have food ready by the time you're done." Together we headed back to Vesta, while I silently promised myself I would make sure he didn't regret staying.

Chapter 13

Knowing Raz had chosen to stay with me instead of searching for his apprentice motivated me to work harder. I put in as much work as I could to making myself improve, hoping I would confirm his decision to stay. I wanted to show him I deserved his choice to stay.

Nightfire and I both worked hard. While Nightfire worked on strengthening his wings, and developed an infection on one of his back feet I had to deal with, I continued to train with Raz. He worked me over with staffs or hand to hand each morning, and after he'd given me my quota of bruises for the day, he dragged me outside to shoot or throw knives. Complaining and excuses weren't tolerated. Anything he told me to do I was expected to do. It was only with the sword that I got my way.

He handed one to me one afternoon, just as I thought we were going to stop for the day. It was his own weapon, the beautiful sword I'd seen him use with deadly precision. I backed away, shaking my head emphatically. "No. No way. Not a chance. It's too big!"

"This is a standard sword. You need to be able to use it."

"I can be good enough at everything else, can't I? Good enough I don't have to use this?"

Raz was smart enough to see the panic. "Kaylyn, it's only a sword. Why are you so afraid of this weapon?"

I swallowed hard. "I…I'm no good at fighting. I never was. I never wanted to fight. Some girls want to be in the military, but the military won't take them. I didn't want that. People can be good at the staffs, or at archery, or all these other weapons, but soldiers use swords. Swords only have one purpose. And I don't want to be a soldier. I don't want to kill."

"Someday that choice may be taken from you," Raz said quietly. "It might end up that it was your life against someone else's."

I stared at the ground, wishing I was strong enough to say, "Sure, no problem. It's just another weapon I need to learn to use." But I shook my head, refusing to look up and see disappointment.

Raz sheathed the weapon. "That's all for today," he said. "Go call Nightfire down. I'll get dinner ready."

Dinner was a silent affair. I picked at the food, shame at disappointing Raz so strong I couldn't find an appetite. I wanted to be able to do what he asked of me, but I couldn't picture myself fighting in battle without fear overwhelming me. I didn't have the guts for battle and I knew it. Swordplay was a battle skill.

"There are a rare few who are born for battle," Raz said.

I lifted my head to look at him.

"Those few are the ones who are always ready to fight, because fighting is what they love. They understand the play of battle, the strengths and weaknesses of others and themselves, and their life is usually ended on a battlefield, which is where they'd want it to be."

I shuddered at that thought.

"For the rest, battle is something that's learned. The moves, the skills, the things that come so naturally to the few are something the rest have to work their entire lives for. The problem with those who are born for battle is that killing is easy for them, if they have the right mindset. And that can turn a talented individual into a monster without a heart. It can happen to those who have struggled to learn all the parts of battle. I don't foresee that problem with you. What I do see is talent that extends to all areas. Those who can do staffwork have problems with archery. Those who can do archery can't seem to grasp knifeplay with the same consistency and skill. And knives are not interchangeable with swords to those who use them. You're doing well at all the ones you've handled so far. I'd like to see if the sword is the same."

I could feel myself drawing in. "I don't *like* swords. I don't know why I have to learn anything. Nothing's expected of me."

161

"Nothing?" he asked quietly.

I shrugged moodily. "My mother would like me to marry somebody wealthy and powerful, but then she'd also like my father to return from the dead to take care of her. She doesn't expect either to happen. She doesn't even expect me to marry. I may be in the military, but nobody expects me to be able to do this. They don't even want me to be able to fight. They expect a female to sit at home, sew something, and dream about happy, perfect marriages with happy, perfect husbands. Nobody cares what I do unless I'm bothering them or not doing what they want."

"Is that what you expect from yourself?" he asked.

"I don't expect anything. I know what I am. I'm a barely-noble girl who has two mirror images that are more appealing to everyone else for any reason you'd care to name. Nobody wants me. I don't know what I want except this isn't it."

He set his plate aside. "I know this isn't what you wanted, but maybe you could give it a try. We'll forgo learning swordplay if you'll give everything you have into the rest. Maybe you'll hate it, maybe you won't. We'll see what happens."

I felt crushed. I'd been giving everything I had. He obviously didn't think so.

"That was not what he meant," Nightfire informed me. *"He does not want you to stop trying because you are afraid."*

I didn't answer, still pushing food around on my plate. Inadequacy always managed to take my appetite.

Raz sounded as if he wanted to sigh. "Maybe we need a break. We've been working hard for several months. You haven't seen Rillmyra at all, have you?"

I shook my head. "You always go alone."

"Why don't you come with me tomorrow then? You can take a break from practice and I have some business with the military outpost."

"Sergeant Sample?" I couldn't help sneering his name.

There was a hint of a smile now. "Yes, Sergeant Sample."

"Do I have to go see him?"

"I think you're old enough not to get lost, right?"

"Of course," I said, mildly indignant. "I almost never get lost."

"Then we'll make sure we can find each other and I'll let you explore while I meet with Sergeant Sample." He set his cup on his plate and stood, carrying them upstairs to wash.

"Are you going to eat that?" Nightfire inquired.

I quickly ate the vegetables, then shoved the plate at him. It was cleared in two seconds. Nightfire disappeared into his room under mine, satisfied. I went upstairs to hand the dishes to Raz and disappeared in my room where I laid in bed and wondered if Raz was wishing he'd gone with Natasha. Part of me believed he should have. The rest of me wanted not to think about that.

Curiosity had me in a good mood in the next morning. I had the foresight to wear a skirt, the longest I had, and hoped it wasn't windy. The bottom of the skirt was at the edge of acceptable, right below my knees.

"Ready?" Raz asked when I clattered down the stairs two at a time.

"Ready," I replied. "What about Nightfire?"

"He doesn't want to come, which works out just fine. I'm not sure too many people would handle a dragon very well."

I shrugged. "Let's go then."

"I'll meet you outside."

A minute or two later, Raz returned carrying a piece of paper and a sack of money, both of which he tucked in his pockets. He paused when he reached me. "Are you forgetting about something?" he asked.

I looked down, confused. "I'm wearing a skirt."

He tapped just under his neck. I reached there and felt my pendant. "Oh." I quickly hid it under my tunic. "Sorry. I didn't know I was supposed to hide it."

"It would be best if those who know just enough about the Eagles to guess what that means didn't have reason to start looking for Eagles." He resumed walking.

The path, which I'd been down exactly once, was still familiar. Rillmyra was a little larger than where I'd grown up, but it

163

had more craftsmen. I could hear the blacksmith's hammer, saw stalls and a few street vendors set up and doing business, and could smell the bakery. I inhaled deeply, appreciating the buzz of conversation and the sounds and smells of a marketplace. There were fruit and vegetables mingling with the smell of cooked meat, metalworking, drying grasses for baskets, dyes for clothing, and salt for preservation all blending in the air.

"Remembering something good?" Raz was smiling as I opened my eyes. "You looked lost in a good memory."

"I was," I admitted. "I haven't been to a market in a long time. My father took me on my eleventh birthday and said I could have anything I wanted. I haven't been back since."

"Too far away?"

I shook my head. "Mother didn't believe I should go alone, and my sisters never wanted to go. The servant went to shop. I was supposed to be acting like a lady and preparing to be married. Every time my mother said I could go, I'd get in trouble somehow."

Raz dug in his pocket and pulled out the bag of coins. He set five in my palm of various worth. "Spend them how you please. I'm going to the baker's, the blacksmith's, and then to see Sergeant Sample. You're welcome to come."

"I'll go to the bakery."

"Good day to you, Raz," the dark-haired woman at the counter called cheerfully when we stepped inside. "Who's this?"

"This is Kaylyn Madara," he introduced.

I remembered my manners and curtseyed politely.

The thin woman's brow furrowed a moment in surprise, then she nodded back. "My pleasure, Lady Madara."

"Kaylyn," I corrected instantly. "Just Kaylyn."

Her green eyes warmed a little at that. "What can I get you today, Kaylyn? Raz?"

"The usual will be fine."

I moved to where the bread was displayed and spotted my favorite bread; dense, hard-crusted, and covered in a mix of white seeds and little black seeds. "Raz?" I asked, pointing.

He nodded. "And half of that loaf, please," he said.

"I can cut you a slice of it now, if you wish," she said, giving me a wink.

"Yes, please," I said eagerly.

"My son loves this bread. It's always his favorite." She cut a generous slice and handed it to me on a cloth after bagging the rest of it.

Raz handed her the money and said, "Blacksmith's?"

I shook my head. "You aren't getting more nails, are you?" I nearly pleaded.

"Yes, I am. That room needs a few repairs."

I blew out a disappointed sigh. "Might as well get some more ice from Sergeant Sample then."

The woman chuckled. "Fixing up Vesta must be quite a chore."

"We're over halfway done," Raz said.

"Only eight more rooms we haven't even started yet," I muttered. "And five others to finish fixing."

"Five?" Raz questioned.

"That window on the third floor?"

"Ah, yes. Thank you for reminding me." He nodded. "Eileen."

"Good day, Raz," she called.

I seated myself near the window and ate my bread, watching the people go by. It was a cloudless day out, with summer and fall battling for control over the weather. The nights were getting cooler and the cold weather was making longer appearances, but the day was warm as summer refused to relinquish the temperature entirely. I watched servants to minor noble families, judging by their dress and manner, disappear inside the dark door of a shop, then suddenly reappear into the sunshine with either more to carry, or less. I could already identify the few who thought themselves superior because of their bloodline, but most of the people I saw were courteous and friendly to all they passed, even to the servants. I was almost done eating when a man and woman came towards us carrying what looked like bags of flour.

"Are you expecting flour?" I asked Eileen.

"Is it the miller?" Eileen peeked out the window, then hurried to create a direct path to the door behind her. "And his wife. They must have fixed the mill."

Not knowing what else to do, I grabbed the door, holding it open while the couple carried the flour sacks in. "You're our last delivery of the day," the miller told Eileen.

"I have the money in the back." Eileen opened the back door and allowed them to carry the flour to the kitchen. "Is the mill fixed?"

"All fixed. And I found the toy my nephew lost."

"Children," Eileen said with fondness.

The miller's wife noticed me as she left the kitchen in the back, dusting off her hands. "I haven't seen you before."

"I'm Kaylyn. Kaylyn Madara."

"Did you just move in, or are you passing through?"

"I've been here for a few months," I said. Then I realized they would have seen anyone new. "I live west of here," I added helpfully.

"With your parents?"

"No, with Raz Greenclaw."

"Ah, so you're living at Vesta." The man looked satisfied. His wife didn't.

"I thought a boy was living at Vesta," she said suspiciously.

I couldn't imagine why. "Nightfire's a boy."

"A male child," she said impatiently.

"Did Raz say something?" I asked, perplexed.

The woman looked taken aback. "No. I don't suppose he *said* anything…"

I brushed that aside. Whatever she'd guessed or supposed, it wasn't my problem. "Do you know where the blacksmith is?"

"Right outside, take a left. He's at the end," the miller informed me.

"Thanks." I curtseyed politely, then headed off to find Raz. He wasn't at the blacksmith, but the kind man informed me Raz would be back if I wished to wait. "He had some dealings with the military post," he said, gesturing to the guardhouse up the hill.

Remembering the man in charge had me scowling. "I think I'll just wander. Anything interesting here?"

"The young girls like to spend their time three shops down," he suggested. "Plenty of baubles there."

I was sure my sisters would love it. I'd never had any interest in what my sisters liked. "How about a woodworker? Anyone in this place do any carving?"

The man inexplicably started laughing. "Raz was right; you're a girl with a good head on your shoulders."

"The miller's wife thought I was a boy."

The blacksmith's eyes twinkled. "Well, that would be because Raz is a man well-versed in the art of telling what needs to be told, and alluding to what doesn't."

"Meaning?"

"Meaning he told the tailor he needed some clothing, specifically pants, for someone about the size of a young lady who just so happened to be in the shop at the time."

"You mean he didn't tell anyone I was a girl?" I demanded, trying to decide if I was impressed, flummoxed, or angry.

"Why would he?"

"Why would he hide it?" I shot back.

He laughed again. "Why don't you go ask the tailor?"

I rolled my eyes. No tailor would make men's clothing for a girl. Female servants only rarely got to wear pants, and they were never tailored for them. "And nobody thought to ask the military?"

"Most of us knew you were living there with your black dragon. Not many know it's just you and the dragon." He winked. "Carpenter's behind me, one over."

The carpenter wasn't quite as friendly and welcoming as the blacksmith. "Miss Kaylyn."

"How'd you know?" I asked.

"Yer just how Raz described you." He gave me an offended gaze. "I heard ye don't much care for woodwork."

"Carpentry? No. Woodcarving, yes."

"Ornamental or figurines?"

"Both. But I prefer figurines."

He seemed disappointed, as if I'd somehow failed his expectations. "Most lasses do."

I spotted a line of figurines and inspected them eagerly as I approached. Some were average. Some were decent. A handful were actually good, carved by a master. I picked up the first one I liked, noting the detail.

"That's…"

"Oak. Very difficult wood, but this will probably last for a couple dozen generations or so. It's a beautiful grain."

I heard interest in his voice. "Tis known that oak has a beautiful grain."

"My father liked it." I picked up another figurine. "Black Walnut. This is my favorite. Lighter weight. Darker color. Butternut is a beautiful color, but too soft for me."

"Tis for looks yer speaking of?" he demanded, a look of glee in his eyes.

"No, for carving of course."

He almost did a little jig of delight. "A lass who understands wood! And yer father told me none of his lads and lasses carved."

I was astonished. "You knew my father?"

"Aye." He bobbed his head. "I lived nearby yer home until yer father died. He was a great carver, he was."

I gave a wistful smile. "He was." I turned the figurine in my hands. "And the reason he never told you I carved was because my mother wouldn't let him. She didn't want anyone to know I carved." I looked at him. "Were you the one my father sold his carvings too?"

"Aye, lass. Thomas Madara and I did business together many times, we did."

"Do you have any of his carvings left?"

He shook his head, a touch repentant. "Nay, miss. His work was liked by many. I sold my last few carvings of his less than four months after he died."

I shrugged, put the carving down. "I just wondered."

He bowed to me. "Malan Arrowood at yer service, milady."

I curtseyed back. "Kaylyn. Just Kaylyn. And I just wanted to look today."

"As you please, lass. Let me know if there's anything I can do to assist."

Raz came in several minutes later to find me looking at different woods and the different grains in them. "The blacksmith mentioned he sent you here. What did you think of the town?"

I looked at Raz. "They all thought I was a boy."

He shrugged easily. "They believed a dragon was too much of a trial for a young girl."

"You mean you *let* them believe."

"People will believe what they want to believe." He offered a pouch. "This came for you."

I looked inside, astonished to see nearly a dozen letters. "Who's writing to me?" I asked, plucking one of them out. I nearly choked when I read who. "General *Maddox*?" I quickly sorted through the rest of the letters, astonished to see letters from each of the generals. "Why?" I asked, perplexed, as I looked up at Raz.

"Perhaps to keep in touch with you."

"They hate me. *Especially* General Maddox. They tried to take Nightfire from me and then they punished Dillon when he made sure they couldn't. They don't like me and I don't like them. Especially not after what they did to Dillon."

Raz didn't say anything to that. "Are you planning on going anywhere else?"

I shrugged. "Are we leaving?"

"Not yet. But if you'll stay between the blacksmith's and the baker's, I may need you in a few minutes."

I nodded and stroked my fingers down a block of wood. "I didn't know Malan was here."

"You know him?"

"My father sold his carvings to Malan. This was my father's favorite wood." I turned the butternut wood in my hand, searching for flaws. "He thought butternut had the most beautiful color. All his favorites were in butternut."

"Any of your father's carvings left?"

I shook my head and reluctantly set the wooden block down. "They were good. I'm not surprised they were all sold." I waved once at Malan, and he called a farewell before turning back to his customer. "Where are all the nails?"

"They'll be delivered with the rest."

"Sergeant Sample?" The resignation was clear.

"It won't be long."

"Better make sure I'm doing a woman's job," I muttered hatefully. I slowed down to admire the sculptures on display at another stall. I didn't understand stone, but I always appreciated stone carvings, even if they weren't as beautiful as wooden ones.

"Kaylyn…"

"Between the blacksmith's and the baker's," I repeated. "I won't be long."

I'd been by the blacksmith's shop, watching the smith and the assistants work on what I thought were horseshoes for several minutes by the time Raz came back. My bag was lighter of coins, but heavier with the little stone statue I'd bought. Since I wasn't around Malan now, I asked, "When I went to see Malan, he knew who I was, even though I'd never met him. He said you'd described me. How exactly did you describe me?"

Raz wore something like a smile. "I believe rebellious, little spitfire was what I called you."

"Then how did he know me so quickly?"

He lightly touched a lock of my hair. "You don't exactly follow the traditional conventions. A new face in this town, female, and not following the rules, it wouldn't have been hard for him to guess."

"So my hair's a little short," I muttered. "I'm wearing a skirt, aren't I?"

"One that doesn't properly fit you."

"You can't see my knees!"

"If you grow at all, I'll be able to. Come on. The tailor's waiting."

Chapter 14

The tailor was the one person I'd met so far who showed an intense dislike for me. He glared at me almost constantly while he measured and only spoke to Raz, ignoring me. Disdain was evident in his expression and in the few uncharitable comments he sent my direction. I wasn't allowed to speak. I silently fumed, and only Raz's occasional warning look in my direction prevented me from giving the man an earful and then some. Raz ordered half a dozen new skirts in three different lengths while I was ignored. As soon as the tailor let me move, I stepped down off the stool and stormed outside.

Outside, I waited furiously for Raz to finish, growing angrier by the minute. I'd never imagined that Raz would allow someone to so abuse me. I vowed he'd know that was the one and only time I'd ever put up with it.

When he exited the shop, he said, "I'm finished. Are you ready to go back?"

I nodded once, hitched the bag holding the letters and the little statue I'd bought higher on my shoulder, and stalked off.

Raz patiently followed as I headed through the streets unerringly towards our road back to Vesta. "Kaylyn, stay with me, please," he requested.

I slowed down, but refused to look at him, wanting out of this town and storming over the bridge that marked the edge of Rillmyra.

"Are you interested in lunch?"

"Oh, am I allowed to speak now?" I asked sarcastically.

"Kaylyn," he warned.

I whirled on him. "You let him say and do anything he wanted! You didn't stop him from *anything*! You just made sure I

171

couldn't stand up for myself! If I have to put up with *this* every time I leave Vesta, you might as well just send me back to the School to deal with those idiots who think I'm better off married so I can be useful in life!"

He came to a stop as well and met my blazing eyes. "What would you have liked me to do, Kaylyn?" he asked quietly.

"You should have told him to keep his mouth shut! You *should* have let me tell him what I do is none of his business! I don't answer to him!" I was all but shouting at Raz, infuriated and hurt that he had allowed that behavior.

"And what would have happened once you offended him? Do you think he would have done his job or told us to get out?"

"You could have said something to make him stop and you did *nothing*!" And that rankled. He had every right to request that the tailor censor his comments, or at least imply they displeased him.

"I did nothing while you were in there. That doesn't mean I did nothing. But I appreciate that you did what I asked."

"I *don't* appreciate that you made me do it."

"Kaylyn, listen to me a moment." His voice was still patient. "I realize you don't like him, but you didn't give him anything more to hate you with. You acted with decorum by keeping silent when you wanted to say something. Even if it wasn't what you wanted, you didn't alienate him or anyone else he might have spoken to."

"He already hates me."

"It could become worse. All I ask is that you try not to make things worse. You'll have to endure the bad opinions of others, and you need to learn to deal with them with as much decorum as you can. If that means not saying anything, it's a better choice than creating more problems."

I didn't like that he made sense. "And you couldn't have said *anything*?" I pleaded.

"Saying something in front of you would be humiliating to him," Raz replied gravely.

"It was humiliating to have to *stand* there!"

"I know it was, and I'm sorry. But while I know you can take the insult, however badly, I also know he can't. And if he refuses to help us we'll be doing our own sewing and mending, which I'm certain neither of us want."

Raz was just logical enough, calm enough, and sincere enough that I lost almost all of my anger at him. "I didn't get to hear Doctor McDragon apologize, and I didn't get to hear you talk to the tailor either. And I should have gotten to hear both of them. It's not like anyone else is shy about embarrassing me in front of everyone."

"Have I ever embarrassed you in front of anyone?"

I frowned at the ground. "No."

"People like to keep their dignity and will take anything with more grace if they can keep their dignity intact."

I kicked a rock in the road and wished Raz had been a little less concerned about the tailor's pride and more concerned with my pride. "So when I have to go back, I have to be silent and stupid like he expects, don't I?"

"Dignity is preferred, with silence as the second choice. Stupid isn't something I encourage."

I kicked at a rock again. "All right," I muttered. I dug in my little satchel and pulled out what was left of the money. "Here."

He smiled some. "While I thank you for your honesty, it's yours to keep and spend how you want. I wouldn't mind knowing what you bought."

My temper eased some, helped by the fact he trusted me with money. My mother had never allowed any of her daughters to keep money. My father or Warren had been in charge of whatever money we were given, which had never been much. I was much more willing to pull out the statue and show it to him.

My statue was a man and a young boy, one teaching the other how to work what was supposed to be a block of stone but could have been a block of wood. It was a mentor and apprentice, and it had spoken to me in a way my father's pieces had always spoken to me, because it was something I understood or that tied to a memory. The piece had enough detail to make it cost more, but I felt it was worth it. "My father always said he wouldn't make a piece unless it meant something to him. This reminded me of him."

Raz inspected the piece carefully, taking it from me when I held it out for him. "Did he ever have an apprentice?"

I shook my head. "Mother wouldn't let him because nobles didn't take apprentices, only craftsmen. I don't know if he ever really minded because he had children. Mother didn't mind when he carved as long as it was considered a hobby and not a trade."

"Would it have been so bad to be a craftsman?"

"Mother wants us to marry well and be true nobles. We're minor nobles and so close to the working class that she was afraid people might think we'd sunk down to working class. Class and status were always what mattered to her. And now my sisters care as much as she does."

He handed the carving back to me. "It's a nice piece. Good stone."

I tucked it away again. "Are we practicing today?"

"No. Today, you'll be free. Read your letters and do what you want and I'll deal with Sergeant Sample and the others."

I interpreted that to mean I was to stay out of the way.

I took time to do some of the chores I'd neglected and spent some time with Nightfire, eventually winding my way around to the stack of letters. I went up to the kitchen to read them in case I needed to reply and to keep out of the military's way.

Raz found me half an hour later still in the kitchen. I was tossing the letters over my shoulder one by one. "Arrogant, pompous jerks," I muttered, tossing another behind me. "Do you know what these are?" I was riled as Raz walked in. "These are letters from the generals, reminding me of my duty to the country. Apparently the Silons have a new general for their army, or whatever. Somebody who the Silons are willing to follow into battle. They think we're going to war soon. And all they've said is that my duty to Centralia will require me to send Nightfire out there to kill them all." I ripped General Maddox's letter in half. "They're cowards. That's what they are. The first sign of possible danger, and they want to send a dragon out to frighten the enemy away."

"You are part of the military," Raz reminded me, setting the materials in front of me to clean and maintain my weapons. He started with his sword, and I started with my bow.

"So? Nightfire and I are not at their beck and call for every little problem. Nightfire isn't a weapon, and I *won't* let them treat him like one. They're just being paranoid. The Silons threaten every year, and every year some new person decides to take over, and then the Silons are too busy fighting each other for power to bother with us."

"Kaylyn, Centralia is a small country with a lot of valuable resources," he gently chastised. "And Silon is a larger country that could use those resources. We've had to fight them before, and we will doubtless have to fight them again. I'm preparing you for battle. When they come, and they will in our lifetimes I'm sure, you and Nightfire will have to go. Nightfire can't be commanded to fight, but you need to accept that one day there will be a war and you will be a part of it."

"I don't need *them* reminding me of it. I didn't choose to be in the military, you know. Everyone else gets to choose. I was stuck there because of Nightfire. And now you have to put up with me."

"Put up with you?" he repeated. "Have you been that difficult a student?"

"I'm awful at everything. I'm slow, I can't remember everything I'm supposed to, and I'm not getting anywhere." I glared at the bow as I set it aside. I didn't mention the fact I was supposed to be learning five weapons, but only learning four. I still couldn't even touch the sword.

His face didn't change. "You're learning. If you knew everything, you wouldn't have anything to learn."

"If I knew anything," I muttered under my breath.

He continued to care for his sword. "Are all the letters from the generals?"

"Yes. But there was a note from Dillon that said he had letters for me that were on their way. One from Madelyn, one from Warren, and one from my mother."

"We'll check back in the next few days for them." Raz stood, the sword in hand. "Can you make dinner with what we have?"

I nodded.

"Call me when it's ready then. I'll be outside."

I watched Raz while I made dinner. I couldn't help it. The patterns, the pace of his movements were different every time I looked out the window. It was more of a morbid curiosity than it was interest. I knew Raz could and would use that sword to kill if he had to. I wasn't ready to face the thought of being in combat and having to kill. Everything I was doing was defending myself or working on developing skill, but swords drew blood. I'd seen Raz practice once or twice with Natasha and had tried to hide my horror when they came in to bandage their cuts. The cuts were never deep or deadly, but they laughed over the injuries while I made sure they didn't realize my revulsion. It wasn't so much vanity as it was self-preservation. The worst that could happen in staff-fighting was that I got whacked. The worst in swordfighting was that I died or was horribly crippled.

When the food was done, I waited until Raz paused in a routine, then said silently, *"Tell Raz that dinner's ready."*

Nightfire relayed it to Raz and Raz lowered his sword. He carefully wiped off his sword, then mopped his face as he headed inside. By the time he had changed his tunic and reached the kitchen, I was setting the water in front of his place at the table.

"Thank you." He settled in his chair and I settled in mine.

"Do you have some to share?" Nightfire's mental voice was piteous.

"You have no pride," I said, picking up the piece of raw meat I'd saved for him. "Begging for food like a dog for table scraps."

"I do not beg."

"It sure sounded like it." I leaned out the window and tossed the meat up, hearing Nightfire's teeth snap as he caught it. "Go catch your own food," I called up as I closed the window.

Raz smiled. "He must be growing again."

176

"How do you know that?" I asked.

"There's a similar pattern with humans, and any other animals. We eat more when we grow. You've been oiling him more than usual."

"Is that why he got an infection? His skin is growing and it got too dry?"

"Likely," he agreed. He studied me a moment. "I think tomorrow we'll start something new."

"What?" I asked.

"Control."

"I'm working on control on everything."

"Not physical control; emotional control."

I was confused. "How do you work on emotional control?"

"You'll see," he said cryptically.

I spent all night and most of the morning trying to figure out what he was intending to do. I was perplexed at the thought of training my emotions. I held my questions, even though Nightfire had indicated he knew what the challenge was.

Two hours after lunch, Raz blindfolded me.

"How does this train my emotions?" I questioned.

"We aren't yet. We're going to walk." He tucked my arm in his, as if he were a suitor or gentleman friend escorting me. It allowed him to direct me. We walked for a while, most of it heading up. It was difficult to walk and not be able to see all the dips and rocks, and I stumbled more than once. I could feel the difference of shadow and sunshine, the moments where the breeze was strong, then gone altogether. I couldn't guess where we were. Scent didn't help me either. The forest smelled like a forest, with trees, flowers, and the sound of birds everywhere.

Raz paused and told me to wait. I could hear a few scratching and scraping sounds for a minute, then he rested his hands at my waist behind me and directed me to walk slowly forward. "Breathe," he said quietly.

I obeyed, wondering at the touch of tension in his voice.

"Breathe again, and take off the blindfold."

I breathed in and slipped the blindfold off. The first sight that struck my eyes was the rolling of the land in front of me, dotted with trees turning warm colors and beginning to drop leaves. I could see where Rillmyra was by the clear space of trees. Then I looked down to see a single step between my shoe tip and the edge of a cliff. I immediately tried to back away and slammed into Raz without thought of anything but safety. Adrenaline shot up my spine while cold fear clenched my stomach and the desperation to move away from the edge of the cliff fueled my racing heart.

"No, don't panic," Raz told me. "You aren't going to fall."

"Yes, I am! This isn't safe!" I fought to turn around, to move even a single step away from that terrifying fall.

"You need to learn to face fear," Raz said, forcing me to stay where I was. "You need to learn to control your reaction to fear."

"Raz…"

"Just breathe," he said. "You aren't going to fall."

I couldn't breathe. Tears blurred my vision and my hands clutched at him desperately, looking for anything to anchor me. The world spun and my body shook violently. I was nervous about heights, I wasn't afraid of them like others I knew, but being so close to the edge without anything to block me from this fall terrified me. If I'd been thinking, I would have remembered all the ways Raz had taught me to fight. All I could think was that if I moved I would fall.

A soft keening, the voice of my agony, fell on my ears. I didn't know who was making the sound. It wasn't me because I was sobbing. I closed my eyes and turned my head away, my body shaking so hard I wasn't sure I wouldn't shake myself off the cliff. "Raz, Raz, *please*! I can't do this! Please, Raz, I can't!"

Raz finally took mercy on me and pulled me away, all the way back to the tree I could see he'd anchored himself to with rope. I buried my face in his front and wept uncontrollably, still shaking. He rubbed my back and held me close. "All right, Kaylyn. Just breathe. You're all right. You're safe." Pity was evident.

I shuddered and tried to breathe, but I couldn't shake the terror. I was afraid I'd open my eyes and see myself at the edge of the cliff again.

The soft keening reached my ears and I turned to look for the sound. Nightfire, eyes dark grey with agony and brown for worry, was sitting a little ways away, tail lashing back and forth, desperately wanting to assure himself I was all right and soothe me. I broke from Raz and ran to Nightfire, my arms wrapping around his neck as I wept.

He nuzzled briefly, then curled around me. The quiet hum and his calming emotions helped beat back the fear until I could relax. I was safe here. Nightfire would let nothing hurt me.

Raz left me to myself for the rest of the day. Nightfire coaxed me back to Vesta, but I was in no mood to speak to Raz. When dinner came, we ate on the bottom floor instead of upstairs. Raz let the silence hang between us while I struggled not to glare resentfully at him. Finally, giving into my anger, I spoke. "I'm not standing on that stupid cliff again," I informed him tightly.

"Yes, you are," Raz said calmly. "Once a week."

"No. I won't do it." I crossed my arms stubbornly.

"You will," Nightfire commanded. "Whether you like it or not."

Aghast at having my backup against me, I turned to face him. "Nightfire!"

His eyes flashed green, his stubbornness against mine. "Or I will carry you up."

"Why?" I nearly begged the question. "After today…"

"Raz has good reasons."

"I don't suppose I could know what these reasons are?" I demanded, looking between the two of them.

"You need to learn to control your reaction to fear," Raz stated.

"That's ridiculous. You can't control fear."

"Reactions," Raz corrected. "The reaction to fear. And yes, you can. It takes practice, just like everything else. Exposure to what frightens you over time will lessen your overall fear. But for

179

now, you need to learn to fight panic. You were helpless today. If time comes that you're in a similar situation, you need to learn to use your training and not freeze up and cry."

"I was scared," I snapped.

He shrugged. "That's the point."

I tried to appeal to Nightfire. "You're going to go through this too. Don't tell me you enjoyed it today."

"It is not good to be afraid of heights if we will fly someday," he informed me.

That threw me. "We? *We're* going to fly?"

"Of course," he said with some condescension.

I glared at him now. "Right. Because so many dragons *like* humans that we just fly around on them all the time. You never mentioned that you'd be willing to carry me."

"I thought it was obvious."

"No other human I know of has ever flown, so don't act as if this is common knowledge," I snapped at him. I turned back on Raz. "And standing on the edge of the cliff will magically make me unafraid of heights?"

"It will teach you control, and hopefully lessen your fear of heights."

"I wasn't *afraid* of heights until you nearly had me standing in midair!"

"Nevertheless, it's something you need to learn. And once a week, we'll deal with it."

"Do I get a say in this?"

"No," Raz and Nightfire said together.

I shoved away from the table and stalked up the stairs. "I hate you both," I informed them before I slammed my door.

Chapter 15

I'd expected once a week to mean every seven days. That apparently hadn't been what Raz meant. Three days later, just as I was thinking about forgiving him for this, he announced it was time to deal with my fear and started to pull me up the hill.

I balked. "I thought you said once a week!"

"I did. That was last week, and now we're doing it again."

"Raz, does this *really* matter?" I pleaded.

"Kaylyn, I promise I wouldn't put you through this if it didn't matter. You may hate this, but it's important."

I debated my chances of running, but Nightfire was plodding up the hill behind us and he was siding with Raz.

"Could we stand just a little farther back?" I implored, hoping he would be open to negotiation.

"No."

I let out a whimper. Raz was unmoved by my anxiety and directed me to the cliff edge. I half-turned, closed my eyes tightly, and clenched Raz's arm with both hands. I wouldn't allow myself to look at how close I was to the edge.

"I won't let you fall," Raz promised.

I was unconvinced and refused to move.

"It's all right, Kaylyn. You're just fine."

"This is not fine! I don't *want* to look!"

"Kaylyn, you aren't going to fall."

"You told me I had to stand here, so I'm *standing* here!"

I felt his sigh, but he didn't press any further. My hands cramped around his arm, yet I wouldn't let go. Finally, he decided that was enough and pulled me back. He had to help pry my fingers from his arm before I could let go.

I spent an hour away from Raz until the anger was under control and the trembling stopped. Half an hour with Nightfire soothing me, and I felt a little more forgiving. It was harder to be mad at Raz when Nightfire understood what I was feeling and why and could convince me with reason and emotion that this was important and wasn't a punishment. He stuck around during the evening when he was usually out hunting. I knew it was for me. I wasn't feeling very talkative as we cleaned our weapons. Raz silently and patiently worked, seemingly content with my aggravated silence. I wasn't any happier with new letters from the generals. I'd tossed them on the floor and I currently had no intention of picking them up. I continued to work and silently simmered.

"Speak to him," Nightfire ordered.

"And say what?" I griped. *"How much I enjoyed standing over a cliff today?"*

Nightfire didn't say anything, flicking his tail with a touch of annoyance.

"I can't find anything to say." It was partly sullen and partly a whine.

"You are not trying."

While I silently grumbled about the downsides of having a dragon able to read emotions, I struggled to find something to say. "I think my bowstring is starting to fray," I muttered finally.

Raz set his sword down. "May I see?"

I held it out, barely managing not to shove it across the table. He came over to inspect it, drew it back once to check. "It'll have to be replaced soon. I think I have a bowstring that we can replace it with. Do you know how?"

"No. The instructor didn't think women were strong enough to do it."

"The man who attempted to enact teaching was likely incapable of teaching anyone how to do it properly and used gender as an excuse." Raz crossed over to the closet and checked inside. "It sometimes amazes me what people are allowed to get away with. Someday, I may have to have a talk with this man."

That caught my interest. "And say what?"

"That he should find another profession. In teaching others, there must be a higher standard. People will pay or not pay if a craftsman is good or bad. The same can't always be said for a teacher." He closed the door to the closet. "I don't have a bowstring. I'll have to go to Rillmyra to get one."

"Can I come too?"

I could barely see the relaxing of Raz's shoulders or catch the warmth that added to the tone. "Of course. After lunch tomorrow."

"See?" Nightfire told me silently. *"He does not want you angry with him."*

"Then he shouldn't stand me out on a cliff."

"You should not question your mentor. An apprentice does not teach the master how to do his craft."

I colored slightly. "Nightfire," I muttered at Raz's enquiring look.

Nightfire rose and trundled out the door, satisfied I wasn't going to sit silently and sulk.

"We'll work on staffs tomorrow," Raz said as he seated himself at the table again.

I nodded and went back to work. This time we worked silently, but without the lingering resentment hanging between us. Raz finished first. He stored the cleaning equipment away and picked up the letters on the floor.

"You don't have to do that," I began, embarrassed.

"Finish your work," Raz said mildly. "You have time to write letters tonight, and I will take care of these." With the gathered letters in his hands, he headed for the door. "And you should eat something."

I quickly finished my work and found something to eat while I read the letters I had left. Mother's was as expected, commanding a response. I wrote something I thought would be what a good daughter wrote, then turned my attention to the other letters with a little more eagerness. The letter from Warren made me laugh a few times, and I felt touched by Dillon's letter, which was more from a friend than it was from a lieutenant to a recruit.

I headed out the next afternoon holding four letters to send off. Aside from Raz's new lesson about heights, I was much happier here than I'd been anywhere else, and I made sure to relay that. I could read their concern easily enough in their probing questions and did my best to honestly answer them all. After sleeping, I was feeling more charitable towards Raz. Nightfire seemed content with my mood and flew off towards the river.

As we entered the marketplace, Raz held out his hand. "I'll take these, unless you want to carry them yourself."

"Why wouldn't I?" I asked, holding the letters uncertainly. Then I caught on. "It goes through Sergeant Sample, doesn't it?"

"It does."

I was more than happy to hand them over. In return, he handed me a few more coins. "Check in with Malan or at the bakery in an hour or so," he instructed.

"Thanks," I called, heading off another direction. I was determined to explore and see more of the marketplace this time.

This visit was a little more baffling. More people seemed to know who I was without any introductions. Most were formal and gave me some semblance of courtesy. Some eyed me warily. I heard soft mutters as I passed by. It only took me fifteen minutes to figure out they were calling me the Dragon Girl. It wasn't two minutes later that a young boy blurted out, "You're the Dragon Girl, aren'cha?"

"Kaylyn," I replied.

"Are you the one with the pet dragon?"

I felt myself bristle. "Nightfire is not a pet."

"Papa says you're in charge of that black dragon and Mama says you're the reason it doesn't attack anybody," he stated assertively.

"Nightfire doesn't want to attack anybody," I said in mild exasperation.

"But black dragons are always dangerous."

I rolled my eyes. "Doctor McDragon doesn't know anything about dragons, and he's the one that said that nonsense."

He squinted up at me. "He's not gonna eat people then?"

"He says humans taste bad. And Nightfire's not my pet," I repeated, hoping he got the point.

There was a call that had the boy's head turning. "That's my ma," he said. "Bye, Dragon Girl!"

I shook my head once as he ran off.

Raz laughed when I told him my apparent nickname as we crossed the bridge. "I think it suits you."

"I don't mind so much, but everyone thinks Nightfire is my pet, or that I'm keeping him from razing the town and eating them all."

"That's something for the two of you to deal with."

I blew out a breath. "I wish I knew how to deal with it."

Nightfire's voice was suddenly in my mind. *"I need to be oiled. My nose itches badly."*

I caught the irritation. *"We're almost back,"* I promised.

"Now!" Nightfire ordered in my mind and Raz's.

"Go deal with it," Raz said.

"Thanks." I raced down the path.

Nightfire was waiting for me outside Vesta. His nose had scrapes across it from where he scratched it, and there was dried blood. I could feel the pain from the scratches and underlying itching from what I guessed to be infection. "Nightfire!" It was a cry of worry and reprove. "You scratched!"

"It *itches*," he growled out, ending on a slight whimper.

I ran my fingers through my hair in agitation. "Well, that's all well and good, but I don't know how to be a doctor. I don't know how to fix this." I bit my lip. "I'm going to need some scales."

I was carefully dipping scales into the four different concoctions of basic medicine when Raz entered. I hadn't put any oil around Nightfire's scratches because I was afraid it might create an infection. In the bowls holding tiny amounts of blood Nightfire

185

had willingly given, if unhappily, I was testing the four medicines as well. "Nightfire!" I warned, sensing his intentions.

There was something like a whimper from Nightfire.

"Is everything all right?" Raz asked.

"He scratched." I laid the scales carefully on the ground to watch them for any signs of change.

"What are you doing?"

"Testing medicines."

He crouched down beside me. "How? What does this do?"

"Nightfire's mother said if I tested a scale and some blood in medicine, I'd know if it was going to hurt him. If it reacts somehow, I can't use it. If it doesn't react, I can use it. I don't know what will help or what will work. Nightfire, *don't* scratch." I knelt in front of him and rubbed my hands over his muzzle around the scratches, hoping to ease the sting. "Just a few minutes, and then if something works, we'll use it, I promise," I assured him. "They should help with the itching. I'm sure it's safe, but I don't want to hurt you in case it isn't. No, you *can't* scratch! You'll just make it worse!"

"One is changing," Raz observed.

I hurried over to see the bowl with the pale green liquid turning the black scale grey, then white, as if sapping the color from it. Above, the scale was turning the black blood a bad, green color.

"Where did I put that journal?" I spun twice, trying to figure out where I'd left it, then raced up to my room to dig through the trunk. I hurried back down with the little journal in hand and carefully wrote down the changes that the medicine was making to Nightfire's blood and scales and made sure to note what ingredients had been used. The other three showed no changes, even after half an hour, much to Nightfire's agony and mine, and I started to slather one on over the cuts. The pain eased almost immediately, much to our relief. I continued to rub it in until Nightfire was completely relaxed and the itching and pain was gone. I then oiled the rest of him, searching for more infections. There was another beginning on the other side of his neck, and I even dabbed on a bit of the soothing medicine to ease any itching.

With Raz's help, we made six more medicines, three of which reacted badly with Nightfire's scales. I carefully wrote down all the ingredients that went into the medicine, what it was called, and noted it wasn't usable by the reaction it had. We didn't make Nightfire give more blood.

There wasn't any practicing that day because I wanted to stay beside Nightfire. I was wary of him scratching more and I wanted to make sure nothing got worse. Nightfire told me I didn't need to fret over him, but I refused to let him out of my sight. "I don't know dragon medicine," I told him whenever he complained. "And I don't have anyone to go to if this gets worse, and I can hardly trek to the Esperion Mountains to find dragons who may or may not kill me to ask how to fix this."

"I am bored."

I settled in front of Nightfire. "Then I'll give you something to think about. We need a name," I stated. "Something for people to call us. I need to have a real title before they come up with something worse than Dragon Girl, and we need an official title to show we're partners and that you aren't my pet."

Nightfire nodded his head once, but didn't offer any suggestions.

"Dragonfriend. Dragonpartner. Dragon…carrier. No, that sounds like you're a carrier pigeon and deliver mail. Dragonfighter. That makes us sound like weapons. Dragon… dragon…"

"Dragonrider."

I thought it over a moment, letting it settle in my mind. "I like it," I said at last. "Are you sure it doesn't sound like you're a flying horse?"

"It is a measure of trust that you are allowed to ride on me. It shows a bond, a friendship, and commitment if you are my rider."

"Dragonrider," I repeated. "Dragonrider partners."

"May I get up now?"

"No. You said I was going to fly on you. How? Where am I going to sit?" I could feel him shift into interest; thinking, planning, preparing for something that had never been done.

The next morning, after checking on the scratches and applying the medicine so the scratches wouldn't itch, I found a leather strip. We'd talked about how I would hold on. I would sit just at the base of his neck, so I could see and my legs could fit comfortably and wouldn't interfere with his wings. The only problem with that spot was that there was nothing to hold onto. I wrapped the leather around the base of his neck once and tugged. "Does that bother you at all?"

"No."

I climbed up on his back and tugged again, harder. "Now?"

"No. It does not cause pain."

"If I yank on this, is it going to choke you?"

He shook his head. *"It sits on bone. You could not hurt me."*

"Okay, so we know how I'm holding on." I thought about being in the air, and falling. Falling ran through my head a lot when I stood on the cliff's edge. "What if I can't hold on?"

"Then I will catch you."

"Can you catch me?" I asked curiously. I didn't know what he'd ever caught in his claws before.

Nightfire was silent a moment. *"I do not know."*

I knew we were thinking the same thing. "You need something to practice on."

I asked Raz to get some fabric about my height and width, and he complied, returning with a heavy, thick bolt of fabric. The only sewing I'd ever been willing to do was for this as I created a bag that was my height and could be filled to match my weight. I filled the bag with rocks and dirt at first, but after having to fill it after patching up the holes Nightfire occasionally made in the bag, I just put rocks in and sewed it back up. He'd practice catching it for hours a day. Only very rarely did he drop the bag or miss catching it. I'd see him on occasion when I was outside training. He never practiced when I was standing on the cliff, saying my emotions were too strong for him to focus, and because I generally needed him whenever Raz finally decided to stop torturing me.

When Nightfire finally decided he was ready, he invited me to try flying. A little apprehensive, I hadn't done so well with heights lately, I wrapped the leather strip around his neck. *"You're sure you can catch me?"* I asked for what felt like the hundredth time.

Nightfire remained patient, knowing my worries. *"If you fall, I will catch you."*

Trusting his confidence, I settled myself, gripping the straps so tightly I felt my fingers start to cramp. Since I was still nervous, I closed my eyes tightly.

Slowly, Nightfire rose, angled towards the sky, wings extended. I felt him settle on his back legs for a moment, then spring towards the sky, wings pumping hard to gain height. I held tightly, wishing I had something besides a leather strip to help me stay on, and then Nightfire tilted his wings and eased into a glide.

"Open your eyes," he commanded me. *"Look."*

I opened one eye cautiously, then the other, looking around, marveling at the sight. The view from a dragon's perspective was different. Everything seemed a little smaller, and it took me time to recognize places or buildings from the top. I could see all the way past Rillmyra. "Wow," I breathed.

Nightfire seemed satisfied. *"You are not afraid."*

"I'm not," I realized. "I'm not afraid." I leaned carefully to the right to look straight down. "It is a long way down, though."

"Now you are a Dragonrider," Nightfire decreed.

I couldn't help the grin. "I like being a Dragonrider. How long can I stay up here with you carrying me?"

"A few hours. We will not be needed until later if you wish to continue flying."

"Absolutely!"

Nightfire gave a pleased cry and shot off, bringing a shriek of delight as he weaved in the air, leaving all worries and struggles behind at Vesta.

Chapter 16

Although the thought of magically getting over my fear of heights was laughable, I hoped that I had somehow gotten over it. After all, I hadn't been afraid of flying on Nightfire. But when I was standing on the cliff again, the same overwhelming fear consumed me. I clung tightly to Raz's arm, and saw the next day I'd created a bruise. When Raz dragged me up the cliff five days later, he wore an arm guard, one used to protect against falcon's claws.

"Raz, this isn't helping anything," I pleaded. "Just drop it."

"This is important." He calmly looped the rope around his waist and tied it firmly. "Ready?"

"Why can't I stand just a little farther back?" I asked.

"The point is to get you out of your comfort zone."

"I'm plenty far out of my comfort zone."

"You're standing where you are."

Anger rose. "Why don't you just dangle me over the cliff on a fraying rope? I'm sure that's out of my comfort zone too."

There was something like sorrow for a moment in his blue eyes, but he silently gestured to the spot. I guessed that meant I wasn't moving back any.

The cliff wasn't helping my practicing. I struggled to follow the directions Raz patiently gave. The times he set me to practice alone felt as if I wasn't able to meet his expectations. Feeling inadequate didn't help my concentration. There were several times I had to stop practice because I couldn't see through the tears. I hid it as much as possible from Raz, determined he'd never know how awful I felt. I was certain that Eagles wouldn't complain, that they could do what I couldn't. After all, Raz was always telling me no complaints, no excuses. The more I practiced, the more I tried to make myself like the perfect Eagles, willing myself to be better. And as I continued to fail, the more I started to doubt myself.

The only time I ever felt secure was when I flew on Nightfire. Aside from a few stomach-lurching moments when I slipped a little, I was steady on Nightfire's back. I managed to construct something like a saddle that provided a little cushion from Nightfire's scales and wrapped around him to hold the cushion in place while still allowing Nightfire free movement. It wasn't much, but it made a difference in my ability to stay on securely. Nightfire hadn't needed to catch me yet, and I didn't want to provide him with any more opportunities than I had to.

Time with Nightfire started to be the only reason I felt glad to get up in the mornings. The days leading up to whenever Raz decided to spring the cliff on me were miserable as I waited in agony for him to tell me it was time to work on controlling my fear. I couldn't make any improvement. And the longer the week went, the more reluctant I became. Once the cliff was over with, I was usually better with that weight gone for a few more days. I made it up to the last day of the week once, but it didn't make it better. If anything it was worse. Dread never left my stomach from the moment I woke up. I could barely eat. I knew what was coming. By the time lunch rolled around, I was so tightly wound with nerves I was starting to feel ill. Nightfire was a little sympathetic, he hated how I felt, but he said I had to listen to Raz. I was beginning to believe Raz didn't understand fear, or didn't understand what it was like to be this terrified.

"Ready?" he asked.

"No."

"Let's go."

"I don't feel well."

"Fresh air will do you good."

"Raz, I *really* don't feel well."

"Then if you feel like throwing up, you can do so over the edge of the cliff."

"I hope I hit your shoes," I muttered.

Raz was unmovable. But the nerves combined with the fear made my stomach churn as I overlooked the steep drop. I felt my stomach roil and closed my eyes, fighting the nausea. Suddenly, a gust of wind hit me, caused me to sway, and everything in my stomach came up. Raz's hands instantly tightened around my waist and he dragged me back, where my body continued to heave.

Raz tried to help, but I shoved away from him. "I said I didn't feel well!" I shouted at him, tears streaking down my face again. "I hate this! There's no point! Nothing's changing except I have to wonder every day whether or not I get to be petrified! I *can't* lock my emotions down until I can't feel anything; and what's more, I don't *want* to!"

Raz's eyes were calm, as if my anger didn't affect him. "The point isn't to make you feel nothing. It's to give you a chance to control emotion before it controls you."

"Just because you *Eagles* do it doesn't mean everyone else can! I *hate* having to be like you when I can't!"

Nightfire pressed his nose to my damp cheek, already humming the crooning noise to help.

"And *you're* no better!" I sat on the ground, pressing my knees to my head and continuing to weep.

Nightfire curled around me and refused to move, nudging me gently until I turned into him. Though I didn't want to let him console me, I found myself calming. When I stopped crying, Nightfire prodded me up to my feet, keeping his head pressed to my side. Raz was finished coiling the rope.

"Let's head in," he said quietly. "It looks like it's going to storm."

I knew my eyes were bitter. "You enjoy this, don't you?"

He shouldered the rope. "No, Kaylyn. There's nothing about this I enjoy. But neither do I enjoy the picture of you getting slaughtered on some battlefield because you panicked. You might not like me after this, but if it comes to that, I hope you have a long, healthy life to hate me with."

I resisted telling him he was well on his way to making sure that happened and stormed away, slamming the door to my room closed when I reached Vesta.

I skipped dinner and would have refused to come out of my room the next day if Nightfire hadn't threatened to drag me out. I had very little to say to Raz and he set me working alone. I almost preferred it. Anger at my own failures had me snapping out at Raz. I would have preferred that he yell back, but he never spoke a harsh word. His eyes would show quiet pain and sorrow and he would say nothing else. Time practicing alone kept me from saying more.

I was collecting the knives I'd thrown when I spotted a traveler coming down the road. Nightfire was watching suspiciously, informing me this man was not from Rillmyra or someone he knew. I ignored him and paced back to my spot to keep throwing. Throwing knives always put me in a mood of irritation. I'd do the same thing over and over, and I couldn't get consistent results. Sometimes I'd think I'd done something wrong, and I'd hit the target and stick it. Sometimes I'd feel I'd done everything right, and the knife would bounce off the target. I couldn't figure out what I was doing wrong, and I certainly wasn't in any mood to ask.

The man walked right up to me and said nothing about the clothes I was wearing. His own clothes were well-made, and based on the materials and the care shown in the work as well as the well-groomed appearance, I picked him as a noble. All that was missing was an arrogant sniff and a comment about my appearance and noble status. When I turned my glare to him, I watched him inspect me with a steely gaze under iron grey eyebrows. "So you're the Dragon Girl."

"Dragonrider," I snapped at him.

"Touchy, aren't you?"

"Rude, aren't you?" I shot back, not caring I was being just as rude.

"Do you know who I am?"

"No."

"I thought not." He rolled up his sleeve, showing a tattoo at the top of his shoulder, a shield with an Eagle feather crossing a sword.

"Oh." I let go of some of the hostility. "I thought you were a noble."

He gave a humorless smile. "Don't insult me. Where's Raz?"

I pointed to Vesta. "He's in there. He already knows you're here."

"How do you know that?"

"Nightfire told him." I heaved another knife, scowling as it bounced off the board.

"Half a step back," the man advised. "I'm going to go let my worthless protégé know I'm here."

This made me pause. "You're Raz's mentor?" I asked, surprised.

"That I am. Half a step back. Keep throwing."

"I see where Raz learned how to teach," I muttered as I heaved the knife again. This time it stuck, just at the edge of the red circle. Pleased, I tried again.

"Raz says you may stop," Nightfire informed me a few minutes later.

I gathered the knives and made my way inside, wondering what Raz's mentor was doing here.

Raz introduced me when I walked in the door. "Kaylyn, this is my mentor, Grand Pentra."

My nose wrinkled slightly. "Grand? That's your name?"

"My name's Pentra, and that's what I'm called, Dragon Girl," Pentra snapped at me.

"If you keep calling me 'Dragon Girl', I'm going to keep calling you Grand," I snapped back.

Pentra glared at me. "You're a disrespectful excuse for a female."

My temper was ignited. "And you're a grumpy relic who thinks being old makes his disrespect to others acceptable."

194

Pentra wore a humorless smile. "You don't like many people, do you?"

"No."

"Good. Shows sense. More sense than my worthless protégé has." He sent a pointed look to Raz.

Raz seemed familiar with Pentra's abuse and was even smiling a little. "I don't expect the worst of people, but that doesn't mean I like them all." He turned the conversation without a hitch. "Are you staying?"

"No. The village of Greensbrook is holding a tournament. I'm going to watch. Plenty of swordfighters there."

"Are you staying for dinner?"

"I brought my own food," Pentra said. "Eat if you want."

Raz declined. I ate alone and went to my room, waiting to be called out. Scraps of conversation drifted through. When I heard a chair scrape, I went to the door and stood at the edge, leaning against one of the columns. Raz and Pentra were standing by the door, Pentra's pack back on his shoulders.

"I'm meeting others at the village. I'll add on a room for you at the inn."

"That won't be necessary," Raz replied. "I won't be going."

"You aren't coming?" Pentra asked, surprised.

"I have training to do."

Pentra gave a disgusted snort. "I know you made a promise, but you need to find your apprentice and she isn't going to be it. She isn't good enough to be an Eagle."

Fury had my blood boiling. "Then I guess it's a good thing I never *wanted* to be an Eagle," I shouted down at him, watching his head turn. "If you want to find a future Eagle, clearly you won't find one *here*, so feel free to leave!" I whirled around and slammed the door to my room shut behind me. Then I climbed out the window and down the side of the building to the ground where I ran until my anger wore off. When my anger was partially spent, I circled back around to the stream, fuming.

Raz, of course, knew where to find me. Several hours had passed. I guessed he had been trying to let me cool down. He sat down next to me at the stream, watching the water flow by. I just wished he would leave.

"Pentra's gone."

"Good," I said heatedly.

"There's nothing wrong with not being as good as an Eagle," Raz said quietly. "It's a rare few we ask and expect to meet those standards."

"Does the rest of the world get the same comparison? Or am I the only one who people like to say 'she'll never be as good as an Eagle'? I never *wanted* to be like you!"

"I know." Raz kept his voice quiet. "Pentra simply wants me to remember that I have a duty to find an apprentice. It weighed on him all the years it took to find me. He doesn't want me to carry that same burden."

"I don't like him."

"He's a little abrupt. If it helps, he wasn't intending to hurt you."

"No. It doesn't help."

He sighed. "I'm sorry for…"

"It doesn't matter." My voice was clipped. "It's not important."

"It's not…"

"I don't want to talk about it!"

He finally let it drop. "All right then." He picked up a stone, rubbing his thumb over it a moment before tossing it in the river. "Are you ready to go back?"

"Sure." I got up, dusted myself off. Although Raz was right beside me and didn't say a word, I could see the lines on his brow. This was just another unresolved argument, another conversation with hurt feelings that would remain and linger, poisoning our relationship until there was nothing but animosity left.

The next day was pure torture. I just felt tired. I wanted nothing more than to curl up somewhere and tell Raz to go away and leave me alone. He set me to practicing alone, which seemed like punishment. This made practicing worse and my lack of talent even more apparent. For the first time since I'd come to Vesta, I closed my eyes and wished myself anywhere but here, and wondered if Raz was starting to feel the same way. And with his mentor pushing him to abandon me and search for an apprentice he'd sworn to find, I felt as if I were simply unwanted and in the way in yet another place with yet another person. Even Natasha had tried to get him to leave me and go elsewhere.

I turned in early but couldn't sleep. I sat on the floor and stared at the Eagle pendant they'd given me. I wasn't succeeding, and I wanted so badly to reach his expectations. No matter how hard I worked, I wasn't getting better. Every minute of training just showed how farther and farther behind I was, and I would never catch up. I couldn't even hold a sword, the one weapon I knew Raz loved. I wasn't meant to be in the military. I could fly on Nightfire, but couldn't stand heights. I could fight, but only with some of the weapons, and not even acceptably.

I thought of Raz. He was supposed to be finding his Eagle apprentice. I was holding him back, and putting him in misery as much as I was in misery. Eventually, he'd become so fed up with me that he'd say I would never be any good, and that would be the last day I'd ever see him. I'd hoped that in coming here I'd find someone who wouldn't see me as a failure. I had a feeling that wouldn't last much longer, and I'd be able to add to my list of inadequacies.

I didn't sleep that night. I second-guessed myself, wavering, then I gave up and packed everything I could into a bag. I refused to think about what I was doing. It hadn't been this hard to leave my mother and sisters, but I could already taste the feeling of freedom, the relief of not having pressures weighing me down every moment. I was leaving Vesta tonight.

Nightfire awoke half an hour before the sun stared to rise. Everything I was taking was already outside, but I crept back inside one last time. The building was quiet. Raz would still be asleep. I removed the pendant he'd given me, the silver feather glinting in the candlelight as I hung it over my doorknob before I snuck quietly outside and closed the door. I knew the pendant would be the first thing he saw when he came looking for me.

Nightfire wasn't convinced of my plan. *"Why are we running?"*

I shouldered my pack. "I can't do this, Nightfire. I'm not good enough. I could never fight anyone. How am I supposed to be in the military if I can't fight?"

"But why are we running from Raz?"

"Because I can't be *good* enough for Raz! Because he's just wasting his time trying to beat some sort of skill into me! I worked harder here than I have anywhere else, for any reason, and I'm still no good! I'm tired of being a failure! I'm tired of disappointing him and everyone else that matters! I'm going to the mountains. At least there we can find someone who can teach you all the things I can't."

Nightfire shifted unhappily. *"But what about Raz?"*

"Raz will be just fine. He doesn't need me. He's got his stupid Eagle apprentice to find." I wiped at my eyes. "I'm going. Are you coming with me or not?"

He silently laid down, and let me climb on, the leather straps wrapped around his neck. As he took off, I allowed myself one look back before I closed my eyes and told myself not to look again. This freedom, I realized, was bittersweet.

Chapter 17

Nightfire still had reservations about leaving Raz, but he was excited and curious to meet other dragons. From the maps we'd studied, he knew where to find the Esperion Mountains and he took a direct flight to them, passing over trees hibernating through winter and dead grass covered in frost while I tried to keep my face warm. We landed a close to where Rosewing had died and traveled west, towards the School for Officers and Gentlemen. I felt uneasy, but Nightfire assured me we weren't anywhere close to the School. *"There are many mountains,"* he said. *"Dragons do not live in all parts of them. Dragons would not choose to live close to humans."*

Our travels on foot up the mountains, because Nightfire's wings were tired, weren't exactly together. I'd travel one way, and Nightfire would another. Being a dragon, he could move more easily over large cracks, steep rocks, and loose ground. I had to be more careful. Often I would stop to see he was higher up a particular slope, and I was farther down it, and farther behind. He didn't mind taking it slow for me. I guessed flying this morning had worn him out more than he wanted to admit.

"Would you slow *down!*" I shouted at him two hours later. My hands and feet were sore, I was accumulating a layer of dust, I had scrapes on my legs and arms, and I was sweaty despite the cold temperature. None of these was putting me in a pleasant mood.

"If I walk any slower, I will stop moving," Nightfire informed me.

"Then stop *moving* until I catch up!"

I felt his sigh. *"Humans have little stamina."*

"I have been training with an Eagle," I muttered to myself as I hauled myself up another rock. "I *cannot* have that little stamina. It isn't possible."

Nightfire dropped my pack in front of him and settled himself to watch my progress as I fought my way up to where he was. It was as much a physical as a mental challenge. Not all paths led to where he was, and I was too tired to want to backtrack and try again. My final decision was to go almost straight up, and then follow what looked like a path over to where Nightfire was. Halfway up, I took a detour around a very large boulder.

"You are going the wrong way." Nightfire sounded amused at my paltry human struggles.

"I am not," I muttered rebelliously. I clambered onto the boulder, and saw a very large pair of eyes, red eyes, not that far from me.

Blinking in shock, I watched a grey dragon rear up, hissing at me. His voice was thunder in my mind; low, powerful, and frightening. *"Human, you are not where you belong!"* Then he opened his mouth, the sound of a great rush of air shrieking into his mouth as he angled his head towards me, eyes turning deep crimson.

I screamed and crouched down, as if to somehow protect myself from the flames. Quick as lightning, Nightfire circled around me, covering me. Before I could worry about him getting hurt, the fire struck him. I didn't feel any pain from either of us.

"It takes much fire to hurt dragons," he thought to me.

"Good to know," I answered weakly.

"Dragon, why do you protect this human?" the dragon thundered.

"I share a mindlink with her. If you kill her, I will no longer want to live."

The dragon was astonished. I peeked out cautiously to find the eyes colored light orange with surprise. "You created a mindlink with a human? And with *this* human?" The dragon eyed me doubtfully.

"She saved me as an egg from the wyverns. She has raised me." Nightfire lifted his wings slightly, eyes narrowed at the dragon, prepared to defend me.

"Lies," the dragon hissed. "No dragon would leave an egg open to wyverns."

"It wasn't left open. Rosewing was dying," I informed him, ready to duck in case he wasn't interested in hearing me.

The dragon stared hard at me, but his eyes weren't turning red. "Rosewing? How do you know Rosewing?"

"I told you. She was dying. I helped her fight off the wyverns and she gave her egg to me to protect and raise."

"If she was dying, why did you do nothing?" His eyes started to turn red again.

"What was I supposed to do?" I shouted at him. "She wouldn't let me touch her! You dragons are nothing but sheer stubbornness! How was I supposed to help her if she wouldn't *let* me?"

"You should have made her. You should have done something."

"Like what? I promised I'd take care of Nightfire, and there wasn't a way to keep my promise and do any good for her! If you wanted something done, maybe *you* should have showed up!"

He glared me into submission, or at least I assumed that was the point, but I wouldn't crumble. I glared back.

"I hear a human's voice." A green dragon walked over a large rock, staring at us. "I have not seen this dragon before."

There was a silent conversation between the dragons, and the grey one tipped his head back and let out a roar. The green dragon settled himself at the top of the rock he'd appeared over, scrutinizing us. Whatever was going on, Nightfire uncurled from around me, his wings folding again.

"They don't look happy to see us," I thought nervously to Nightfire.

"They did not know what happened to Rosewing's egg." Nightfire's mental voice was tensed still. *"They have called others."*

"Others?"

A black dragon, as black as Nightfire, landed suddenly before us, startling me. I fell backwards with a yelp and Nightfire had to save me.

"Why is there a *human* here?" the black dragon demanded, glaring balefully at me as I righted myself, rubbing my side where Nightfire's tail had collided to stop my fall.

Nightfire hissed at the dragon, but said nothing I could hear. As more dragons started to land, I moved closer to Nightfire nervously, not liking the pink tinge to their eyes.

Somebody spoke first, but I only heard the reply. "Humans are liars and cannot be trusted," the black dragon in front of me decreed.

"She did not lie," the dragon I'd first met said. "I would have known."

"Why does a human have Rosewing's egg?" someone else asked. This was a female. "I would not trust a human with an egg."

I felt insulted. "He's alive, isn't he?" I said snidely "Alive and well thanks to a *human*."

All eyes turned to me. "A dragon would do better," the female said. She was a blue dragon, her pink eyes narrowed in displeasure at my existence on her mountain.

"I don't remember any dragons offering to do it better," I snapped at her. "I remember a dying dragon telling me I had to take the egg. I remember making a promise to raise and protect it. Any other dragon would tend to stick in my memory."

"She has done well, for a human." This was grudging from a different dragon. I couldn't figure out which dragon the voice had come from.

"Then let her live and send her home." This was from the giant black dragon that had startled me.

"We cannot do that, Ironclaw. The human shares a mindlink with the young one."

"Ironclaw?" I vaguely remembered the name. I tipped my head back to look up at him as realization hit. "You almost ripped General Maddox's arm off."

He gave a terrifying grin, his eyes yellow with pride with a touch of orange for what I thought was arrogance. "For a fat man, he moves very quickly."

"He says you tried to kill him."

"If I had wanted to kill him, he would be dead."

I didn't doubt it.

"This human is familiar to me." The green dragon, still perched on his rock higher up, was still studying me.

Heads turned to the dragon. I was puzzled as to how another dragon would know me. To my consternation, he rose and padded down towards me, his eyes intent. I wanted to crawl under Nightfire and hide, but I held very still as he stopped in front of me, his great nose moving as he breathed in the air.

"I know your smell," he said. "You were there with Rosewing. You took the egg."

"I was *given* the egg. I didn't steal it," I said defiantly.

"It was not an insult, human. We were afraid wyverns had eaten it. I did not understand why a human had been there and nothing was gone."

"Then you didn't think I'd stolen the egg?"

"Rosewing would not have allowed it," he stated. "And I knew you could not have taken the egg by yourself. One human cannot move a dragon's egg. I understand now why your scent is familiar to me."

I didn't know whether to be flummoxed or awed. "You remembered my smell after all these months? I don't smell that much, do I?" I looked at Nightfire for confirmation.

"A dragon has a better nose than a human, and a better memory. A human presence in a place for half an hour will leave a scent that any dragon could smell. You lingered with Rosewing."

"Over an hour," I said cautiously. "Then you were Rosewing's…" I searched for the word.

"Clan," he supplied. "I was among the clan, as was my mate. The rest did not know her."

"Oh. Well, I would have taken the egg to you, but Rosewing said you would have killed me."

"She spoke the truth." The giant, green dragon settled in front of me.

"Prove that you speak the truth," the female dragon ordered. "Prove that Rosewing was alive when you took the egg."

I thought back to what Rosewing had told me. "Rosewing told me her mate was Courageheart and that he was dead."

There was a silent murmur among the dragons. Beside me, Nightfire shifted restlessly.

"Very well," Ironclaw said. "You speak the truth." He brought his face close to mine. "Why have you come?"

I fought nerves. "Nightfire…Nightfire needs to know about dragon things. I…I don't know how to teach him. I could barely teach him how to fly. I…I was hoping you could help me make sure I'm raising him right."

His eyes narrowed. "Why is there fear?"

"Because you look like you want to eat me?"

"Humans taste terrible," he said dismissively. "That is not what I meant. There was always fear. It drove you up the mountains. Why does fear bring you here?"

Embarrassment had me shouting an answer at him. "That's none of your business, dragon! If I wanted to tell you, I'd have told you!"

He pulled back, surprised. Nightfire nuzzled gently to calm the familiar mixture of shame, failure, disappointment, anger, and fear.

"She has spirit." The green dragon seemed to smile, his eyes turning a shade of golden-yellow. "I like her."

"A *human*? Embereyes, have you forgotten all you know about humans?" the grey dragon demanded.

"I have seen many humans, Stormscales," Embereyes replied. "I have not forgotten that they are capable of much bravery and sacrifice. This young one has shown admirable qualities. She has cared for a hatchling, and now risks the dangers of our mountains to ask for help. Humans do not travel as deeply into the mountains as she has without good reason. They know we do not want them here. But I like this one. She is not like many other humans I have seen."

I felt myself relax some.

Stormscales wasn't ready to accept me. "Surely you do not suggest she stays with us?" he complained. "Humans smell."

I glared at him. "Nightfire got over it. You can get over it too."

Embereyes's voice was still placid. "They must be together. There are many mountains, Stormscales. If you do not like her scent, move to another mountain. I do not mind."

I felt a little better that at least one of them was willing to accept me.

After some complaining and arguing, of which I only heard part of, Nightfire and I followed the dragons up to the caves. Nightfire chose a cave among the labyrinth of dark corridors and I settled myself in.

The dragons weren't pleased at first, and made no secret of it, but after the third day, they started to at the very least not hate me. One by one, they started to open their conversations to include me. From there, we progressed to replying to my questions, not glaring on seeing me, and occasionally calling me Kaylyn instead of 'human'.

Embereyes was the first to initiate a conversation with just me. I found myself liking him more and more. He was about as kind as I figured a dragon got, although he was still abrasive and blunt. I was far more appreciative of that, especially once I remembered the way the generals had treated me. The dragons may have despised me and thought there was much I was incapable of, but they also thought that of all humans. They didn't dislike me any more or less than any other human; although Crystalscales, the blue dragon who had said she wouldn't trust a human with her egg, seemed to harbor a kind of resentment that I thought I could be a dragon mother like her. Blackstar was Courageheart's sister, and she was much kinder than most of the others. The family tie to Nightfire wasn't strong for either dragon, but she gravely stated one day that she was grateful I had saved her brother's egg. Stormscales didn't spend a lot of time around, but when he did, it involved frequent complaining about my human stench, no matter how often I bathed. I would have called it whining, but he was bigger than me.

Nightfire spent his time learning from the other dragons. He tried to brush me aside at times, but after we had a very loud and very long argument, he relented and agreed there wasn't any reason why I couldn't listen to him learn from the other dragons too. The other dragons were rather amused and gave me the first complement they'd ever given me; I was decreed as stubborn as a dragon. It was used often as I struggled to survive and put up with dozens of dragons who weren't fond of humans. I wasn't sure if it was the fact I was young, or the fact that I was a girl, or both, but Nightfire confirmed that the dragons were far less wary and suspicious of me than any other human.

I'd forgotten to get oil for Nightfire when I left, and berated myself for five hours, wondering how I was ever going to get more. Embereyes solved the problem once he understood what I was fretting over. "Dragons rarely use oil," he stated. "We live in caves because it is good for us. There are minerals and life inside caves that are good for dragons. And humans," he added. "Do you not feel the moisture in the air inside the caves? It is good for your skin also."

"Yeah, but don't you eat…things…in there?"

"It is food for dragons, not humans."

"I wouldn't eat that if I was about to die," I informed him.

"If you ate it, you would likely die."

"But Nightfire won't, right?"

He blew a breath at me. "He is a dragon. He will be fine. You worry too much, human."

"You know what, dragon, I promised to take care of him. I don't have a *clue* what you dragons do or anything that would help or hurt Nightfire. So anything *you* might know because you've lived with other dragons for your entire life, Nightfire missed out on. I'm allowed to worry."

"Very few things are dangers to dragons alone. Only when things are mixed do they hurt dragons."

"What things hurt dragons?" I asked.

"The baby horn."

I was puzzled. "The baby horn? It's hurting Nightfire?"

He shook his head. "Dragons lose their baby horns after one year. Dragon horns can be used to hurt dragons. When the horn is lost, dragons hide it. When Nightfire loses his, it will be your responsibility to make sure it cannot be used to hurt him."

"Should I bury it?"

"There are not many places to bury things in the mountains, but humans stay off these mountains."

"Should I keep it with me then?"

"It is your choice. As long as you are sure no one can ever access the horn, you may keep it with you."

"What else would hurt him?"

His eyes were colored yellow with amusement. "Go get the book you write in. I will wait."

I hurried to grab the little journal and raced back, seating myself in front of Embereyes with the ink and pen ready. I carefully copied everything Embereyes had to say, dipping my pen into the ink again and again and wrote until my hand started to cramp.

"You may stop. That is all for today," Embereyes said when I started to stretch out my hand.

"You don't have to stop," I insisted. "I'm fine. I can keep writing."

"There will be plenty of time for more writing. We will do more another day." He rose and plodded outside, taking flight. I hurriedly caught the ink jar before the wind from his wings knocked it over.

While I let the pages thoroughly dry, I pulled out the other book I'd brought. I'd taken Princess Brianna Kay's journal with me on a whim. I'd held off reading it because it felt wrong. Now I cracked it open, leaning against a rock as I started to read the journal. The writing was, several times, difficult to read. It was in a beautiful flowing script, but a few stains on the pages or a word scribbled out made it tricky. However, the more I read, the more connected I felt with the princess I'd never met. She wrote about struggling with studies, about the problems in court, about suitors of every age vying for her hand, about missing her dead father, and about having to give up the throne. She'd been close with her mother.

She also mentioned Vesta and its grounds. She hadn't been able to go explore unescorted, but she loved what she'd been able to see. The guard with her, Brodrick, had been a close friend, and I could see the transition as they went from princess and guard to best friends. It was an interesting look into the life of a woman I felt in some ways I could relate to. She was independent, and she fought the rules of society, which was harder as the princess of the country and with so many men in charge of everything she did. She wrote about the excitement of being able to wear a skirt that didn't touch her ankles.

My mother says that while ruling men must be the first to make a change, ruling women must be the last. I have expressed my displeasure to her regarding it, but there is little we can do. My father has said privately that he does not care what I as a princess wear regarding skirt length, so long as it does not become indecent by reaching my knees, but my mother as queen must be more lady-like according to the old customs. I asked if I will be allowed shorter skirts when I become queen, but he only said it would depend. When I asked Brodrick why my father hadn't been clearer, he said much of it depends on who my husband is and what the advisors to my father think. As I entertained Lord Castleman tonight, one of my more elderly suitors, I prayed Father would find a man closer to my age. I fear my father will be rushed to make a decision, since I am already fifteen. Brodrick assures me that my father does not need to rush. A princess is one of the few females that will not be considered a spinster even if she turned twenty without being married. A princess always has marriage options.

I put the journal away when the dragons started to return. Nightfire wanted me to stay close when he was hunting in case wyverns came, but once dragons had returned, I was allowed to explore. I said aloud that I was going out, ignoring the uncaring silence, and started off. I knew one of them heard, and would let Nightfire know.

There were always new places to explore in the mountains. I could take the same path five times and end up somewhere new every time. It wasn't that I got lost; it was that with such rocky ground, I would choose to go up instead of right, or left instead of back down, and then I would find new directions to explore. Many of my choices were controlled by the steep climbs or sheer faces of rock that didn't allow any handholds.

I was working my way down, following the bleating of mountain goats, when I stepped on a loose rock. I let out a yelp as it slid under my feet and frantically tried to maintain my balance. The rock didn't stabilize and slid down. I threw myself to the side, frantic to prevent myself from tumbling down the mountain, and let out another yelp as I slammed down hard on something sharp. My hand instantly moved to my arm and I gritted my teeth as the blood seeped from under my clamped hand.

Nightfire's concern surged at the pain in my arm. *"You are hurt."* I sensed him taking flight, searching for me.

"Cut my arm." I looked up, spotted him. He circled slowly downward, landing nearby.

His neck stretched so he could inspect the injury. *"It is bleeding too much."* He was concerned, eyes going brown.

I had a sudden memory of Warren teaching me about a tourniquet when I'd stayed at the School. "Can you help me back?" I asked. "I think I have something that could help."

Nightfire helped me onto his back, and instead of flying, he walked up the mountain to the series of caves. I hurried to fish a long strip of cloth out of my pack, then, using my teeth and other hand, pulled it tightly just above my injury, watching with fascination as the bleeding slowed. "I guess he was right," I muttered to myself. "Tourniquets do help." With the bleeding slowed, I worked at making a bandage. Nightfire had a better memory than I did and told me step by step what to do. As I worked, other dragons gathered one by one to watch.

"I smell human blood." Embereyes walked in, inspecting me as I worked. "You are hurt."

"I fell."

"Will you need a human doctor?"

"I don't think so." I gingerly untied the tourniquet and noted that no fresh bleeding started with some relief. "Not unless I get an infection." I fingered the hole in my sleeve and eyed all the blood. "I don't think I have anything to repair this with, however. And I'm going to need more bandages."

Embereyes tilted his head slightly, considering something. "Come with me."

I climbed to my feet and followed, Nightfire right behind me.

We wove through various passages that were only vaguely familiar before we stopped at a smaller cave. I was speechless for a moment. It was packed with things. Clothing, jewelry, packs, jackets, pieces of wood, things that clearly belonged to humans. "I thought you said dragons didn't hoard things," I managed to say to Nightfire. "You called it shiny trash."

"We do not want human things," Embereyes said. "Humans have left them on our mountains. We move all human items here so we do not have to see them again. We have no need for any of this. You may have it if you wish."

"Oh. Well, thanks." I set my candle down, the only thing giving any light to this room, and started to sort through the pile of items. I found several clothing items that were my size, or close, including a silk top, light pink, and big enough that I wouldn't outgrow it quickly. Inside the two packs, I found a supply of candles and matches. Their smell of sulfur-drenched pinewood was familiar, and with them was a flint and steel set for starting a fire. I also, to my astonishment, found a general's jacket. I didn't know whose it was, but had a guess that it might belong to General Maddox since the sleeve was torn from the jacket and the jacket wasn't small.

I left with clothing, General Maddox's jacket, and a handful of jewelry pieces that I couldn't resist taking. The packs were now filled with anything I could use, including a handful of knives, two quivers of arrows, and a bow over my shoulder. Nightfire carried the pack in his teeth that I guessed had belonged to a doctor at one point. Many valuable medicines were inside, including a small bottle of golden liquid that I knew cost a gold coin almost any time it was used. It was the best medicine money could buy, and it took a lot of money to buy it.

Nightfire insisted I use what was inside the doctor's pack on my arm, and my protests got me nowhere. Reluctantly, I fished out the bottle of liquid that would prevent my wound from getting infected, using a piece of my old tunic to soak up a little of the liquid. I carefully peeled off the bandage and washed my arm, gritting my teeth against the pain. Nightfire endured it, then pressed his nose to my side after I'd replaced the bandage.

"I'm going to be fine," I promised him. "Really. I'll be more careful."

"You must. You cannot die. I need you." It was one of the few times Nightfire had ever seemed vulnerable.

I rested my cheek against his muzzle, stroking his face until he started to calm down. *"I'm not going to die,"* I promised silently. *"All right? I'm not going anywhere."*

He hummed softly, a sound of relief mixed with contentedness. I leaned against his neck, feeling his knot of anxiety slowly fade. We sat there until the sun set and darkness fell, both of us calm, content, and at peace.

Chapter 18

I woke up one morning realizing my birthday had passed sometime, and that Nightfire's had as well. I was fourteen now, and he was a year old. When I told him, he said it didn't matter much. Two days later, his baby horn fell off. I stuck it in my pack with my most valuable things until I went exploring next. With Nightfire following me, I found a little tree farther up and proceeded to bury the horn as close to the roots as I could. Nightfire and I were satisfied that the horn was safe, so he invited me to climb on his back.

"I don't have any straps, so be careful, okay?" I asked as I climbed on.

Nightfire waited until I was settled, then carefully took off, soaring gently over the mountain. We decided we'd get the straps first, and then continue flying, so Nightfire wheeled around and landed on the ledge outside the caves. It wasn't more than a minute before I was back outside, lighter of the pack, winding the straps around Nightfire's neck.

"Why do you tie things around Nightfire's neck?" Crystalscales asked, her eyes a curious blue.

"So I can hang on," I replied. "Otherwise I might fall off."

"You *carry* this human on your back?" Crystalscales demanded, disbelief and disapproval in her gaze.

"What's wrong with that?" I shot back, defensive on Nightfire's behalf.

"Dragons are not slaves to humans. Horses carry humans."

"Horses don't have a choice. If Nightfire doesn't want to carry me, he won't let me on. I'm not forcing him to do anything."

"It is demeaning."

"I saw you carry a hatchling the other day. Why wasn't that demeaning?" I crossed my arms and glared.

"Because it was a hatchling and not a human," Crystalscales stated, as if the answer were obvious.

This riled me. "Look here, dragon; being a human doesn't mean I'm the lowest form of life on this earth. I'm not some crazy, diseased creature. I'm capable of intelligent thought, just like you, and just because I don't have wings and a tail does not make me jealous or controlling, or whatever else you expect of me."

She huffed a breath at me. "Your kind is greedy and uncaring, human."

"And yours is disdainful and thickheaded, dragon."

Crystalscales growled at me with that insult.

"Disprove me," I challenged. "How long have I been here? When have I ever been greedy or uncaring?"

Crystalscales didn't answer, flicking her blue tail in obvious annoyance.

I slung my jacket on. "Guess we aren't *all* greedy or uncaring then."

Nightfire nudged me with affection. *"You are as stubborn as a dragon,"* he complemented. I felt his pride and humor.

"And don't you forget it," I teased back. I climbed carefully on top, grabbing the straps.

Although most of the dragons seemed to share Crystalscales's disapproval, Nightfire didn't mind. We often flew together. When Nightfire wanted to hunt, he let me off and I wandered around until he was finished. We occasionally saw wyverns in the distance, but Nightfire easily avoided them, commenting that wyverns were slow and stupid. All the same, when we saw a group of them not far away one crisp, clear day, we headed back to the cave. Neither of us wanted to encounter them.

As we landed outside on the ledge, I paused in folding the leather straps, staring at the black-colored liquid on the ground. Nightfire could smell something and his eyes were starting to change to grey.

Hoping I was wrong, I followed the drops inside and came to an abrupt stop, aghast. The smell was unmistakable and the number of drops confirmed a dragon was hurt and bleeding. I stared, astonished, at the smeared puddle of black blood. Aside from Nightfire's mother, I'd never seen an injured dragon. Bewildered, worried, I looked around, casting my gaze up into the dark heights of the caves where the dragons liked to perch. "Embereyes? Crystalscales? Blackstar?"

Crystalscales came down and landed in front of me, eyes brown with worry and grey with fear. "Ironclaw is hurt," she said to Nightfire and me, shifting restlessly.

"How? What happened?"

"Wyverns. They travel in packs always. Ironclaw was not careful enough."

"Is there something I could do to help?"

"There is nothing anyone can do to help," she retorted. "Ironclaw is hurt too badly. He has gone to the cave for sick dragons and he will die soon."

I was thrown by the utter belief in her tone, and the lack of emotion. There was anger, unease, but no misery or mourning. I could feel tears already gathering and her eyes didn't hold a hint of blue. "Maybe…" I began.

"No." Crystalscales cut me off. "Stay out of this human. It is not your concern." Then she took flight, leaving me feeling whipped and near tears.

"Do not take Crystalscales's words to heart." Embereyes laid against the far wall, sadness in his eyes. *"She is angry now. She will mourn later. Ironclaw is one of the strongest among us and it pains us to be reminded again that even the strongest must be careful."*

"I just want to help. I can mix medicine you don't have. Surely I have something that would help," I pleaded.

"Then do what you can. You cannot make things worse by trying. But be careful. Ironclaw is stubborn and in pain. He will not take kindly to help from a human."

I sniffed hard and wiped my eyes. "You don't call me as stubborn as a dragon for nothing."

I didn't know what to expect, how bad it would be, but I guessed since Rosewing had died from a wyvern attack, Ironclaw would look similar. With my pack of human medicines on my back, I crept softly into the cave for sick dragons.

The cave was dark. Ironclaw, being a black dragon, would have been hard to spot if he hadn't been breathing too loudly. I lit a candle with one of my matches and recoiled at the sight.

Ironclaw was sprawled ungracefully on his side, one wing stretched out as blood dripped slowly down it. He was covered in scratches, all but stripped of his scales, with barely any place on him not bleeding. I swallowed hard. I wasn't sure how he'd made it back.

Ironclaw's neck was curved around, and his eyes cracked open to glare hazily at me. *"Have you come to stare, human?"*

I shook my head. "I want to help."

"I do not want your help."

I squared my shoulders. "That's what Rosewing said. But you can't get rid of me like she did."

"It is a waste of time, human."

"Then it can't hurt anything, can it?"

He hissed at me in warning as I stepped towards him.

I took another step closer. "If you want to waste your energy hissing at me instead of getting better, that's fine with me, dragon. Whether you want my help or not, you're getting it. I don't know about dragons, but humans don't tend to sit around and wait for people to die. No matter how sick they are, how hurt, we like to do what we can because we value life. If you want to die with honor, or whatever this dragon pride thing is, it's no less any honor because you tried to get better." I unshouldered my pack and pulled out more candles, lighting them around the room.

"The light hurts my eyes," Ironclaw grumbled.

"Then close your eyes. I need to see what I'm doing." The more light I brought into the room, the worse Ironclaw looked. There was so much blood, so many injuries. I hurried out of the room, down to the cave with all the human items, and hurried back with an armful of clothing. Ironclaw had blown out half the candles in the room. I patiently relit them, then started to make the nasty grey drink Raz had taught me to make. It was safe for Ironclaw to take, and it would make him sleepy. I was fairly certain that if I touched him, he'd bite me, even if only in a reflex to pain. I wasn't interested in being bitten by a dragon.

One of the medicine ingredients had to be boiled for half an hour, so I built a fire and started it boiling. While I did, I started a second, larger fire and started to boil more water for washing the clothes. I let the clothes soak for a few minutes, then laid them out to dry on the part of the floor I'd cleaned.

"Can a dragon not die in peace? Must I smell your human medicines and be bothered by the noise?" Ironclaw complained.

"You aren't dying, not if I have anything to say about it," I returned grimly. "You may have given up, but I haven't."

"You are wasting your time."

"I don't have anything else to do right now." I carefully poured the contents of the smaller pot into a bucket through a layer of cheesecloth, straining out the water. I strained it two more times, then began to mix the medicine together. It took nearly an hour to set, and by then I'd laid all the clothes out to dry. Every medicine in the bag had been tested in Ironclaw's blood and a few loose scales to make sure of what he could take. I'd marked the ones I couldn't use in case I became tired and didn't remember.

"All right, dragon." I set the bucket of medicine down in front of him. "Drink it."

Ironclaw snorted and didn't move. His eyes had been closed for the last few minutes, and I wasn't sure he hadn't been asleep.

I crossed my arms and glared.

"You are wasting your time, human."

"It's mine to waste. Drink."

"No."

"Why? What is it going to hurt? It would at least make you feel better."

He didn't answer and didn't move.

Frustration built. "Would you stop fighting me and take it, you stupid dragon?" I yelled at him. "You are the most ungrateful creature I've ever met!"

He opened his eyes to slits and growled at me, but it was pitiful and weak.

"Dragon, either you take this of your own will, or I'm going to pour it down your throat as soon as you faint. Nightfire's taken this before, and unless you're weaker than him you're drinking it too, one way or another."

Now he hissed in defiance, but I didn't flinch, watching him through narrowed eyes. I was finally rewarded when he scooted his big head forward. I picked up the bucket and carefully poured it into his mouth a bit at a time. He made a dragon sound of disgust as he laid back down and closed his eyes. *Your human medicines taste terrible. Almost as bad as humans.*

"I don't even want to know how you know what humans taste like." I went back to ripping up materials. Fifteen minutes later, Ironclaw was unconscious thanks to the grey drink. With Nightfire's help, I clambered up on Ironclaw's back to begin my work. It took lots of time, lots of cloth, all the bottle of golden liquid except for a few drops, and half of the rest of the medicines in the bag, but by the time I crawled wearily down, every injury on Ironclaw's body had been attended to.

Nightfire was waiting outside the cave for me. He dragged me to him and curled around me without hesitation.

"What are you doing?" I demanded, rubbing at my sleepy eyes.

"You must sleep. You are tired."

"I can't. I need more cloth for bandages."

"We can help. We will tear cloth."

"I thought you were just waiting for him to die."

"We do not want him to die. When a dragon refuses help, we do not force him to take help. We respect the wishes of the sick dragon. But if he has allowed you to help, we will help as we can." He nuzzled gently. *"Sleep. We will work."*

It took very little effort to sink to the ground and fall into sleep. When I woke, I staggered upright and fumbled in my pack for something to drink or eat. There was a large pile of cloth strips at the entrance to the cave Ironclaw was in. There was also another pile nearby of wriggling things. My nose instinctively wrinkled. "What…?" I began.

"It is what dragons eat to remain healthy," Embereyes informed me. He was lying nearby. "It will help sick dragons to get better."

I nodded. "Does he eat all of it?"

"All that he can."

I gagged twice, but I loaded the wriggling creatures into a large bucket and hauled them in. Ironclaw looked more alert today, and was certainly more energetic. By the time I returned with the strips of cloth to boil clean, the bucket was empty.

"If you ate those that quickly, then you have no right to turn your nose up at my medicines."

"Your medicines taste bad."

"And those things tasted better?" I shook my head and started to mix the nasty, grey drink.

Ironclaw must have believed I was doing some good, because he allowed me to climb on him and inspect all the injuries. For those injuries that had soaked the bandages in blood, I noted to strip them off and replace them. I was relieved to notice that there weren't any that had infection so far. "I guess that stuff really is powerful," I murmured to myself. "No infection yet."

"The dragon medicine will fight infection."

"You weren't up to taking dragon medicine yesterday. Until whatever you just ate kicks in, that medicine probably saved your life." I retrieved the nasty grey drink and set it in front of him. "Drink."

He stared at it doubtfully, distaste clear.

"Dragon, drink it or I'll make the next one worse. I swear I will." I turned my back to deal with the bandages, and heard him drink it. After the medicine had been taken, I replaced the bandages that needed it, and Ironclaw was too sleepy from the potion to react immediately to the pain. By the time I finished, he was asleep.

The next day, Ironclaw still showed no sign of infection, to my utter amazement. He refused the nasty, grey drink, stating he wasn't going to be put to sleep like some weak human. I ignored the insult and made another medicine, and he drank three of them a day.

At the end of five days, Ironclaw was well on the mend and grumpy about it. He didn't appreciate not being able to go where he pleased and do what he wanted. Unfortunately for the rest of us, he was still too injured to be able to fly or do anything that wouldn't tear open his wounds again. So we were forced to watch him and make sure he stayed for another week. It was during this week, in a rare moment of lucidity where Ironclaw agreed he wasn't well enough to leave, that he spoke to me.

"You saved my life." It was almost grumbled, but still somewhat grateful. *"I owe you a debt, human."*

"You're welcome." I folded what was left of the clothes carefully, the pile in the room of human trash much smaller now. "What exactly does that mean to a dragon?"

"It means you may call on me to help you in some way to repay the debt."

"You owe me one?"

I felt his sigh in my mind. *"Yes, human. In your words, I owe you one."*

I searched for a proper reply, and ended up with, "Thank you."

Ironclaw grunted and turned on his side to sleep.

Embereyes was one of the dragons that stayed the most often to keep Ironclaw from leaving. As I was usually there as well, he invited me to pull out the journal and gave me more to write down. The other dragons didn't seem appalled, and instead added more things for me to write. It was during one of these sessions that they mentioned mindlinks.

I came to an abrupt stop. "You mean I'm *not* the first human to have a mindlink with a dragon?" I demanded, hopeful.

"You are the only human that has lived longer than a day with a mindlink," Blackstar informed me.

I was taken aback. "Why?"

"Because dragons create mindlinks with humans who are about to kill them. What hurts us then hurts them."

"You mean you use the mindlink as a weapon?" I asked, astonished.

Nightfire shrugged. "If the human is going to kill us, we create the mindlink. When we die, he will die also. That way, he will not be able to celebrate winning and kill more of us."

I was disturbed. The mindlink I shared with Nightfire wasn't a weapon, it was a measure of trust. It created a bond between us. "So, did you create a mindlink with me to protect yourself? Or for some other reason?"

"It was my choice to make us partners forever. I did not have to create a mindlink. It protected me, and it protected you."

I decided not to ask any further questions about why. I was certain I'd get answers that would infuriate me and lead to arguing. I dipped the pen back into the inkwell. "So you don't know if anything different is going to happen because I've been mindlinked with Nightfire for a year."

"If you have not become crazy, then there is very little reason to worry," Embereyes informed me kindly. "Unless Nightfire dies, you likely will not have any harmful changes."

I had the brief thought that he'd intended to comfort me, and just shook my head, imagining my sisters in tears if they'd heard this news.

When the dragons were tired of talking, Nightfire invited me out and we flew over the mountains. The winds were changing direction, with cooler air from the north coming down. There weren't very many trees and not much grass either, so the brown leaves weren't blowing all over the place and the mountain goats were looking for something else to eat. The temperature was the biggest indicator that winter storms were coming. The mix of the incoming winds gave me a few bad moments when I was afraid I would fall off. Nightfire was good at adjusting to keep me on, but as a particularly violent gust of wind hit us, I was jolted off to one side. I slid off and let out a scream, clutching desperately to the leather straps as I dangled in midair. "Nightfire! I'm falling! Land! Land, please! Hurry!"

"Let go."

"No! Are you crazy? I'm not letting go!"

His mental voice was calm and confident. The emotions attached told me he was absolutely sure of himself. The panic and fear were all mine. *"Let go, Kaylyn. I will catch you."*

I swallowed hard, fighting fear, latching on to his assurance for the nerve to obey. Instinct rebelled, telling me to hold on. Closing my eyes tightly, I let out a small whimper and let go.

The fall through the air was both exhilarating and terrifying, and somehow curiously addicting. The rush of adrenaline made this almost fun. I didn't have more than a few seconds to wonder about this conclusion before Nightfire's claws closed around me and he eased my descent into a controlled spiral. He landed gently on the ground, letting me go. My heart was still pounding, but I stared up at him with a sense of wonder as I gained my feet. I was absolutely at a loss to explain what had happened.

Nightfire understood. *"Again?"*

Curious to see if this feeling would hold, I started to climb back up, settling myself and reaching for the straps. Above us, there were half a dozen dragons standing at the ledge, watching us. "Ready," I said. Nightfire took off, his powerful wings beating hard as he took me higher and higher, then easing into a slow, gentle glide.

Half of my mind screaming at me, demanding to know what I was doing, I got to my feet, using the straps to maintain my balance as I looked down. Then I let go and jumped. There was the same curious rush of excitement and fear, but my mind was calm. I felt Nightfire's claws circle me and wrapped my arms around one of his claws. I understood what had happened. I'd learned to trust.

Chapter 19

The cold set in with a vengeance and it snowed two weeks later. Nightfire was fascinated with the snow and played in it for hours as this was first real snow we had seen. I spent half an hour in the snow, then went back to the fire. The next time I went out, I put on layers and didn't travel far. The layers made it more difficult to move, and the snow made the rocks treacherous to travel. Still, I piled up a few rows of snowballs and pitched them at Nightfire when he reappeared. He couldn't avoid them all, and he batted drifts of snow at me with his paws in playful retaliation. The dragons were entertained by my winter antics and spent plenty of time watching me play in the snow, sometimes with Nightfire, sometimes not. I started drinking tea, there was a pack full of it in the cave of human trash, because it was warm. I had plenty of water when I melted the snow.

Nightfire brought in the meat, and I skinned it. There was very little fish and a lot of mountain goat. With the packet of herbs in the same pack as the tea, I experimented with different combinations of spices with my goat. Any food that was brought in was brought by the dragons. Despite the snow, they seemed to find plenty to eat.

After about three weeks of snow, I became tired of the cold. That was when the big storm hit, adding a record amount of the white flakes. It snowed for almost two straight days. The dragons were patient and didn't mind it as much. I kept building up the fire for light. It was during then that Nightfire blew flame for the first time. He practically strutted around the cavern the rest of the day, continuing to blow flame and keep my dying fire alive. When the snow stopped, the dragons, with Nightfire, used flame to melt the snow out of the cave and took off in search of food. I did a little exploring over paths I'd traversed before and knew fairly well. Another storm came three days later and lasted two days again, but the dragons had stocked up meat in preparation. The food lasted us months as the piles of snow became taller, then smaller, then larger again, then slowly shrinking back down. I had no idea what the date was and only a hazy clue of what month it might be. Time didn't really seem to matter in the mountains with nowhere to go and nobody else to see.

The cold weather lingered, infringing on springtime and I became sick for ten days. Nightfire worried over me and only rarely left my side, pressing me to take medicine. I refused the first day because moving took energy I didn't want to think about. The second day, I took something that I knew all sick people took. By the fourth day, Nightfire had stopped worrying so much because I felt better. The final three days was a lingering cough and a tendency to get cold easily.

The days I spent ill gave me plenty of time to think. And as the snows finally melted and the days got warmer, I found my thoughts drifting more and more to Vesta and Raz. At first, it was with anger. As days passed, I became less angry and more guilty. I would find myself sitting beside the entrance to one of the caves and looking in the direction Vesta was, wondering if Raz was still there, imagining the trees blooming and the sounds of new life. I tried to ignore those thoughts at first, but I found myself contemplating more and more how things had played out.

The dragons were grooming themselves in the evening nearby while I stared across the landscape.

"You will not find your answers by sitting there, human, no matter how many hours you may sit," Ironclaw informed me.

"She is reflecting, Ironclaw, maturing," Embereyes lectured. "It is good she takes the time to think."

Ironclaw gave a derisive snort. "Thinking should be followed by actions. She does nothing but sit in confusion and wallow in her emotions."

"Ironclaw, you don't have emotions," I informed him. "And I'm not sure you ever think about anything but your stomach."

There was dragon laughter to my comment. Ironclaw hissed in displeasure and returned to his cleaning. "I do not waste my time believing that thinking and wishing will solve problems."

"Would you prefer that she keep running?" Embereyes asked in return. "It has taken her these months to stop running and start thinking. I do not expect her decisions to come quickly when she has only just begun to slow down."

I felt slightly insulted they were talking about me as if I couldn't hear them. "I'm not running from anything," I informed them.

Crystalscales sighed. "She lacks much maturity. Like a hatchling."

"Humans progress slower, but in time they can possess the same understanding as dragons. For those that are more stubborn, understanding does not come as quickly." Embereyes was sounding like a wise, old sage. "She will learn. Has she not changed since she has arrived?"

"Her smell has not changed," Stormscales grumbled.

I stopped listening then, already familiar with the argument about a human's stench to Stormscales's sensitive nose. The dragons finished their grooming and headed off to their own caves, a few remaining behind. Nightfire started to chew on a plant that dripped creamy sap. I was told it kept dragons' teeth healthy.

I couldn't get my mind off of Raz. I couldn't help but wonder what he'd been doing all this time. Had he stayed at Vesta? Had he searched for me? Did he think I was dead? Did he even care any longer?

I stared out at the scenery that held no answers. "Do you think Raz is mad at me?"

"I do not know." Nightfire continued to chew. *"If you do not want him mad at you, why did you leave?"*

I sunk lower. "I don't know. I thought it would be worse if I stayed and disappointed him. But now I'm always worried about whether or not he's angry at me. If he's disappointed in me."

"You did not want to disappoint him, so you left to disappoint him."

"It's not that simple," I muttered.

"It is exactly that simple," Embereyes informed me. "You are like other humans. You let fear control you."

"Raz doesn't," I pointed out.

"It is not the fear you are thinking of. You think fear and you think of a feeling of fear. The feeling if I were to drop you in midair."

"What fear are you talking about then?"

"You are afraid of trust. You are afraid to believe in anyone, even yourself, because you do not want to be disappointed."

"That's not true!" I protested. "I trust Raz! I trust Nightfire!"

"Only two that you trust?"

"Can you top that list?" I countered. "You don't trust humans. None of you trust humans."

"Humans have not proven worthy of trust. You trust Nightfire because you share a deeper connection than you do with a human. He feels your pain and you feel his. You do not trust Raz."

It hurt that anyone would believe that, especially dragons who could feel my emotions. I trusted Raz just like I trusted Warren and Dillon. "How do you know I don't trust Raz?"

"Because you are not afraid to fly." Embereyes sounded infinitely patient. "You can stand on the edge of a cliff and have fear, but not be afraid. Self-preservation is a strong will to fight. You know it is your choice to stand there, to move away. If someone stands behind you, you become afraid because you are forced to depend on someone else. It is someone else who allows you to step away, or who could push you over the edge."

"Raz would *never* push me off a cliff!" I shouted at him.

Embereyes blinked very slowly. "You need to learn maturity," he informed me. "Shouting does not make you right nor does it make your point stronger. You must control your anger."

I bit my lip at the censure. "I'm not a child," I muttered rebelliously.

"If you act as a child, I shall treat you as a child. You may think that Raz will not push you over the cliff, but if you believed it you would not be so frightened. Fear is why you keep running away."

I didn't want it to be true. Was I really so awful a person that I couldn't trust?

Nightfire came searching for me the next morning when I didn't appear to eat. I was curled up, my head pressed to my knees, shaking with sobs that were now empty of tears.

"Why do you cry?" Nightfire demanded anxiously as he landed, curling around me.

"Embereyes was right." I hiccupped. "I'm a coward. I don't trust anybody. How horrible do you have to be to not be able to trust Raz? Dillon? Even my brother?" I hiccupped again. "I'm a terrible person."

"You are not." Nightfire sought to comfort me, rubbing his great head against my arm. *"You are young, like a hatchling. You make mistakes."*

"Raz will never forgive me. Look at what I did to him! He *shouldn't* forgive me! He's probably gone by now. After everything he did, I...I..." I couldn't finish that thought, so ashamed of myself I didn't know how I could bear it. Everything I'd been forcing myself not to think about was slamming hard into my conscience. "I'm a terrible person."

Nightfire tried to soothe me, but I was inconsolable. It was Embereyes that eventually came out, flying to where I was, and settling on the rocky ground. Nightfire must have explained what I was upset about, because Embereyes went straight to the point. "You torture yourself for nothing."

I refused to answer, sniffing hard.

"You cannot know what will happen until it does. You cannot know what Raz will do."

"I wouldn't forgive him if he did this."

"You are young. A hatchling struggling to fly. Raz has already learned to fly. Do you think I will react the same as Nightfire?"

"Raz isn't that old. He wouldn't trust me ever again. And he shouldn't trust me. I'm a horrible person."

"I know from your thoughts and Nightfire's thoughts that he is mature and has gained much wisdom for his years. He is not you." Embereyes nudged me gently. "You doubt yourself too much. Can you not see there are levels of trust? Do you love equally? Do you hate equally?"

"Of course not."

"Then you do not have to trust equally. Dragons trust you, but not other humans. That does not mean we will trust you with everything, but we have trusted you to live with us, have we not? To be among us and not harm us? We have told you secrets that have never been known by a human before. Nightfire has reached a different level of trust than others in your life, and you have gained a level of trust with us that other humans have not. It does not make you a bad human or a good human."

"You said I couldn't trust." I raised my head to look at him, blinking away more tears.

"I said you had fear. And you do. You are afraid to trust because you are afraid of being hurt. There is time to learn to fly, young one. Part of flying is falling to the ground."

"I wish it were as easy as flying." I scrubbed at my gritty eyes.

Nightfire pressed his nose to my cheek again, and this time I wrapped my arms around his muzzle and let him console me. "I wish I knew if Raz was mad at me," I whispered. "I wish I hadn't left."

"Then it is time you found out," Embereyes said placidly. "It is time you went back."

I turned to look at him, my stomach already twisting in knots. "You want me to leave?"

"There is nothing more for you here. You do not need to hide here any longer." There was no censure, but simple advice from one who knew far more than I ever would. "Go to Vesta, Kaylyn. There is a place for you there."

"There was once." I let my eyes close.

"There will still be," Nightfire assured me.

As afraid as I was of going back, I hoped fervently he was right.

Chapter 20

We left the next morning. I fretted the entire way, terrified of the possibilities. The closer we got, the more anxious I became as my thoughts raced. Raz wouldn't be there. Raz would be there and he would be furious. The Eagles would have shunned me. Raz would hate me.

"Stop," Nightfire ordered. *"You are making me feel ill."*

"I already feel ill."

"Worry will change nothing."

"When you tell me how to stop worrying, I will. Until then, deal with it."

It took most of the day to reach Vesta. We stopped so Nightfire could rest and eat, but I could stomach nothing but a few sips of water. I'd nearly told Nightfire to turn around several times and go anywhere else, but Nightfire told me I was facing Raz. *"You can face him with dignity, or I will carry you in my claws and you will face him as a child."*

I slid to the ground when Nightfire landed in front of Vesta, my knees almost shaking, feeling myself shrink in. I had no idea what Raz would say and I had absolutely no courage to find out.

I might have stood outside until Nightfire pushed me in, but Raz came out. As he stepped out the door, seeing me, he paused. "So you came back." His voice was even, not displaying temper or welcome.

I nodded.

"I see." He went back inside without another word.

The sting of rejection hurt deeply. I crossed my arms tightly over my stomach and fought not to cry. I'd ruined things with Raz. I'd hurt the only real, human friend I'd ever had.

Raz came out again and crossed to me. I sniffed hard, trying to swallow the tears. I felt myself hunching for the lecture, the statement about how ungrateful I was, and the anger, whether hot or cold.

"I would prefer," Raz said, "that you not leave this." He held out the pendant with the Eagle feather. "I don't know if you could have used it, but I would have felt better knowing you had it."

I looked at it, at him, then cautiously reached for it. I kept waiting for him to say, 'Now get out', and go inside, but he didn't. Instead he said, "You missed lunch, but I can make some more if you're hungry."

I shook my head dumbly.

"Well, come on inside. It looks like it might rain." He went back inside.

I looked up at Nightfire, confused. "I don't understand."

He put his nose to my back and pushed me forward. *"Go,"* he ordered.

"What about you?"

"I know when to come in out of the rain." And he took flight, settling on his favorite spot on the cliff.

I went hesitantly inside. "Nightfire…he's going to take a nap outside."

"We'll leave the door open in case he wants to come in." Raz was sitting in his usual chair, working on something with wood. It was as if I'd never left. I couldn't believe he was still here, doing the same things.

He flicked a glance up at me as I lingered uncertainly by the door. There was even a hint of a smile. "You don't have to stand there, Kaylyn. What are you waiting for?"

"You to start yelling at me."

"I'm not going to yell."

"Why not?"

"Yelling wouldn't solve anything."

"That doesn't seem to matter to anyone else," I muttered.

There was a hint of a smile again. "I don't often lose my temper. I'm not going to yell, Kaylyn."

He was angry. He was the kind that would never say it, but it would be there. "I wish you would yell," I mumbled.

"Why?"

"Because the people who don't yell are mad forever. I don't want you mad at me." Misery was evident. "I'm sorry, Raz."

"I don't want an apology."

I flinched, my eyes filling with fresh tears as I hung my head in shame.

"That wasn't what I meant." Raz laid his tools down on the table, seeming anxious to reassure me. "I meant that you don't have to apologize. I'm glad you came back."

"I don't understand!" I cried, tears streaking down my face. "You should hate me! You should want nothing to do with me! You shouldn't *be* here offering *food* and talking about *rain*! I left for *months* and you're glad to *see* me? You don't even know where I've been or what I've been doing! You shouldn't want to *be* here!"

He rose and walked towards me with deliberately slow steps. "And would you prefer that I gave you what you wanted? Yelling at you while you cry? Saying things that you'll remember for years and use to doubt yourself? Punishing you and making you so miserable you'll wish you had never come back?" He stopped right in front of me, holding my miserable gaze steadily with his blue eyes. "I'm afraid I'll have to disappoint you. I have no intentions of doing any of those. I would like to know why you left."

I gulped in air. "Because I'm no good. I knew I wasn't and I tried anyway, and I wasn't getting anywhere. You're an Eagle, and you deserve to work with someone who's better than me."

"Kaylyn." For the first time today, I heard a rebuke in his voice. "When did I ever say you weren't doing enough or that I was tired of teaching you?"

"You didn't *have* to say it! It was obvious enough that you were wasting your time." I clenched the pendant tightly. "I thought you'd be glad when I gave up. I've disappointed everyone else. I didn't want to know I wasn't good enough again." Tears were never-ending as they came in a fresh wave. "I don't know where else to go. I don't know what I'm supposed to do. I know I messed up, Raz, and I'm *sorry*! I'm so sorry."

He enfolded me in his arms, letting me weep into his tunic. "I know," he said quietly. "It's all right, Kaylyn. I understand."

A soft drizzle began to fall outside. Raz let me cry until I finally ran out of tears. "Did it help? Wherever you went?"

"I don't know. It helped Nightfire. We went to the mountains. We've been living with the dragons." My fingers were clenched into his soft, cotton tunic as I spoke, my head resting against his chest. The smell of rain filled the air.

"The mountains? The dragons took you?"

"After they tried to kill me."

"That sounds more like dragons." He heaved a deep sigh. "If you want to tell me what happened, then I'll listen. If you don't, then I'll respect it."

"I just want to be here. I'll train and I'll work, and I'll do everything I'm supposed to." It was less of a promise and more pleading that he would allow things to go back to the way they'd been.

"If that's what you want."

"I don't know what else to want." I pulled back to wipe uselessly at my face. "I'm sorry, Raz."

"I know." He handed me a cloth so I could wipe my eyes. "You don't have to apologize."

"Yes, I do. I ran off and I shouldn't have. It was a childish thing to do. You're responsible for me, and I should have said something instead of just leaving. I hurt you, and you didn't deserve it. And I'm sorry."

His eyes were smiling a little. "You've grown."

"I have?" I looked down, realizing the skirt I wore barely reached a decent length. "Oh. I guess I did."

The smile touched his lips now. "That wasn't what I meant. I meant that you've matured a little, not grown taller. But you have grown taller, I can see. At least half a head. I'll visit the tailor." He glanced towards the door. "Nightfire's coming in. I left everything of yours alone. It's all right where you left it."

I nodded, then hurriedly fished an old tunic from my pack as Nightfire trundled in, water dripping from his scales. He settled in the middle of the floor, allowing me to dry his head first, then closing his eyes to nap.

"What's this?" Curious, Raz picked up the silk top that spilled out of the pack.

"Oh. Well, the dragons had all this stuff that people leave on the mountains, and they said I could have it. There were a lot of clothes. I really don't know how they have that many clothes. There's a jacket in there that I think belongs to General Maddox."

Raz sifted through what I'd brought back, looking intrigued at the medicine pack. "This must have belonged to a wealthy doctor." He held up the small bottle that had maybe a drop or two of the expensive and powerful golden liquid pooled in the bottom. He whistled softly as he weighed it in a big, callused hand. "A very wealthy doctor to afford this. And wealthy patients."

"It was nearly full when I found it."

Raz raised his eyebrows in surprise. "This was full? What happened?"

"Ironclaw was attacked by wyverns. I had to use it so he wouldn't die."

"Then it was put to good use." He replaced the vial. "I take it you didn't need it then?"

"No. Not for me."

"I'm glad to hear it." His blue eyes were grave. "I was a little worried after so much time and no word about a black dragon or the girl with him."

I focused my gaze on the droplets of water on Nightfire's wings, shame returning as I worked silently. Raz was suddenly by my side, a cloth of his own in his hand. He sent me a smile and started work on a leg. "In case I haven't said it, welcome back, Kaylyn."

I felt some of the guilt ease and sent a smile back. "When do we start practice again?"

"We'll wait until after tomorrow. We're going to need more food, and you can get settled in again." He glanced outside.

"Why don't you get settled in now? Clean up from your travels. I'm sure you haven't had warm water since you left."

"Mountain stream," I replied. "And I have to finish drying Nightfire first."

"I can finish this. Five months is a long time to depend on a cold mountain stream."

I paused. "I was gone five months?"

He looked as if he wanted to smile and shake his head, but he merely said, "Yes. Go clean up. Nightfire and I will be fine."

I obediently lowered the cloth and headed for the stairs, scooping up my pack along the way. I was looking forward to still water that was warmer than I was.

"I see you lost your horn," Raz said to Nightfire as I entered my room. "I hope that was supposed to happen."

I lounged in the bath, scrubbing myself head to toe twice before I climbed out. My hair had grown long enough that I could braid it somewhat, but I left it alone since I had no reason to keep it out of my face. I put on the pink, silk top, something I'd wanted to wear but had been afraid to in the mountains in case it ripped, and paired it with a white skirt I hadn't taken with me.

Although it was still early, I could smell Raz cooking and made my way upstairs. "Can I help?" I asked.

Raz glanced over at me, then suddenly went very still. Confused, I looked behind me to see if I should be concerned, then back at Raz when I saw nothing there. "Raz?" I asked.

Raz's eyes moved to mine, and then he spoke. "You look like a beautiful young lady, Kaylyn. If you want to get drinks, I'll be done in a few minutes."

I looked down at myself, trying to figure out Raz's reaction, then shrugged and reached for the drinks. "Upstairs or downstairs?"

"We'll eat upstairs."

"Why so early?"

"Nightfire mentioned you would be hungry." He set some vegetables on the table. "So what did you learn in the mountains?"

I talked straight through dinner about the dragons, all the different things they told me about dragon care. I showed him the journal that I'd written everything down in. He seemed interested in the part about the mindlink and that Nightfire could now blow flame. We talked until dark. When I yawned, Raz wished me good night and turned in. I followed quickly, nearly groaning with how soft the bed felt after months of sleeping on rock.

Raz spent the morning in town. I washed all my clothes down at the stream, letting them dry before I headed back. Raz laid out our weapons after dinner and we cleaned them, preparing mine for use again. I took a long bath afterwards, still reveling in water that wasn't straight from a mountain stream. Especially one that had been recently fed by all the snow. Nightfire needed oiled since we were no longer living in caves, and the trip had been rough on his wings. The familiar smell from the oil filled the room while Raz fiddled with some arrows. Every time I looked over at him, he wore a smile. Even Nightfire couldn't deny that it felt good to be back.

I held onto that homecoming feeling as I dressed the next morning. Raz wanted to start with the staff, so I picked up mine and carried it outside. I resigned myself to doing poorly again as my hands settled where they were supposed to and I braced myself for the attack.

Raz was a little easier on the pace and the strength of blows, knowing I hadn't practiced. What surprised me was that I didn't need it. All the practice I'd put in six months ago came flooding back and it was easy to protect myself and return blows. Curious, I tried my hand at a block and strike combination I'd seen and felt Raz use on me dozens of times. To my surprise, I saw him quickly adjust in a movement I'd only rarely seen; one that said I'd gotten him off guard. As he met my strike, his eyes started to smile. "Is that how it's going to be?" he inquired.

Before I could react to that warning, he put all his strength into shoving me backwards and came at me. I ducked his swing and surged upwards. He met my staff with his and forced it to slide downwards, pitting his body strength against mine as we struggled for balance. We mutually shoved each other, keeping our feet and immediately moving to protect from the oncoming strike. I wasn't wondering how I was capable of doing this; I was too busy trying to make sure I wasn't disarmed. And when, a minute later, our staffs met in an X that had the full strength of both of us behind it, there came a crack. We both backed up a step to see both our staffs had suffered and would break in half if we went any further.

Raz burst into laughter, eyes shining with pride and delight as he tossed his staff away. I just stared at him, then at my staff, stunned, wondering now how I'd been able to match him. It was the first time I hadn't lost. "I don't understand."

"You don't understand? You did exactly what I knew you could! Kaylyn, that was exactly what I was expecting out of you!"

"But I haven't practiced. And you didn't beat me."

Raz took the staff from me and tossed it aside, next to his. "I've been training you so that you *can* beat me, Kaylyn. I haven't been doing this to make myself feel better about my fighting skills. After all the time you put into practicing, you were supposed to be able to do this." He looked down at me with pride, pride because I'd done so well. I couldn't remember the last time anyone had been proud of me for something I'd been able to do. A warm glow kindled and started to grow.

Raz was still smiling, nearly beaming at me. "I guess we're done with staffs for the day. I'm going to need some new ones. Let's see what you can do with archery."

Archery was less of a surprise. I'd done some shooting up in the mountains, but as Raz continued to move the targets back, I couldn't believe it was this easy to continue to lock on. I knew I didn't hit the exact center, but Raz seemed proud enough that I could hit the red zone shot after shot. I attributed my knife throwing ability to the few times I'd played around with it in the mountains, and it wasn't as good, but it was clearly better. Raz continued with the knifeplay, and I found his instructions were easy to follow. I was capable of controlling how the knife hit the target, adding more strength, or spinning it more times or fewer times before it hit the target. I was even capable of doing it with my left hand, but it wasn't as strong.

The next morning we spent on hand-to-hand. All the work I'd done had made me stronger, and he couldn't overpower me. I was even starting to see a pattern with his moves, and instinctively know what came next. Raz always had a proud smile in his eyes despite the studied calculation on his face.

After lunch, I went down to my room briefly, and came back to find a sword laid out on the table. Raz was downstairs with the leftover food. More curious than afraid, I unsheathed the sword, studying it with a sense of contemplation. I'd watched Raz fight with this, train, and wondered if I was capable of making the same beautiful, practiced control of movements. I could know how to use this without having to kill with it. Being a warrior didn't frighten me as much as it once had and I wasn't sure why.

I heard Raz coming back up the stairs and continued to study the weapon in my hands. When he appeared in the doorway, he didn't say anything, pretending as if he couldn't see me holding a weapon that had once terrified me. He went over to close the window against the threat of rain thundering in the distance.

"So how exactly am I supposed to hold this thing?" I asked.

"That would depend on what you're intending to do with it and what kind of sword it is." Not betraying a hint of what he was feeling, he came over and adjusted my grip on it, his fingers light as they rested over mine. The hilt of the sword was long enough for both my hands to wrap around it. "Feel how heavy it is?" he asked. "This is a practice sword, made heavier to build up muscle. That way, whenever a real sword is used, it will be easier to fight with."

"Where's your sword?"

"I won't need it today."

Without saying anything further, we both went upstairs. There, Raz taught me how to swing, how to grip the sword with one hand or two, and taught a few exercises that I could practice on my own for control. By the time we stopped for the day, my arms were aching with this new series of movements and muscle strain.

"The ice packs are in the icehouse," Raz said, offering the sheath.

I slid the sword inside. "Where do I keep this?"

"With the other weapons. I'll make dinner tonight while you ice your arms. Spicy or not?"

"Spicy, of course," I answered, heading for the door. "Not a lot of spice up in the mountains."

I caught his smile as I headed out, and was fairly certain it had nothing to do with spice and everything to do with how I'd gotten over my fear of swords.

The following three days were exhausting for my upper body. The sword was heavy, and I felt totally uncoordinated as I struggled to make it move in an imitation of what Raz showed me. Mornings were one weapon, evenings were always swords. It ended up that I made lunch and Raz made dinner because I was always icing my arms after practice.

"Can I have tomorrow morning off?" I inquired as I chewed the deer meat Nightfire had brought and Raz had cleaned and cooked. "Nightfire needs some attention and I need to practice flying on him."

"Then take tomorrow morning," Raz said. "I'll put some work in on the staffs."

"You know, you could just ask the military to buy some more," I pointed out.

"Why bother? I like working with wood. The military can save some money and I can make good use of the wood around here. If we ever did jousting, you'd be spending time making lances."

I winced. "We aren't jousting, are we?"

"No. Jousting is no longer a battle skill; simply entertainment for old men who refuse to let go of the past. You won't need to learn it."

"Good. Because I wasn't looking forward to wearing armor."

"Armor is a waste of energy and money," Raz stated briskly. "Those who know what they're doing won't need it. Those who don't know what they're doing won't be protected for long. All it takes is a strike at a weak point, or a big enough sword, and armor becomes useless. That's why Eagles don't use armor."

"Eagles don't use armor at all?" I asked, curious.

He shook his head. "There's other battle gear just as effective and better at allowing us free movement, so we don't use armor. It's rather distinctive to ask for black armor anyway," he pointed out. "We wouldn't be secret for long, and any noble with enough money could ask for black armor and pretend to be an Eagle. We have our own uniform that doesn't require a blacksmith."

"Can I see it?"

"Someday."

"Does someday mean 'whenever the next battle is'?"

"Someday means someday. Although with our neighboring country, there is a chance that war will be the reason you see an Eagle uniform."

"Do you ever wear your uniform outside of battle?"

"No."

"Not for anything? A funeral or initiation or something?"

"There are times."

"Like when?" I pressed.

He wore a glimmer of a smile. "You're pushy today."

"Raz, you're an Eagle, revered throughout the country for everything you and other Eagles can do. I have the pendant that says you can let me know things and I promised I wouldn't tell." My voice was plaintive.

"I don't doubt your word. And I'd have thought that with all the time you've spent here the Eagles might have lost a little of their shine."

My brow furrowed in perplexity. "You think because I met you I'll have lost respect?"

"I think that most people have an idealized picture of Eagles and forget sometimes that we're human. And we are only human, Kaylyn," he added.

"So you say. There are days I don't think I believe it. Humans make mistakes on occasion and you don't."

"I've made plenty of mistakes." Raz took a drink of his water. "And the only other reason we might wear our Eagle uniform is when we're acting under Eagle laws."

I wasn't aware Eagles had laws. "What laws?"

"One law is that we never betray the vows we took. Eagles are not assassins for hire. We don't kill for sport. We don't kill outside of protecting ourselves, others, or battle, and it has to be life or death. About a year before I met you, there was an Eagle who broke this law. He killed for money. And the Eagles banded together to hunt him down."

I just stared at him. "You killed him?"

"We did, yes. And then we buried him as an Eagle."

"Because that makes everything better," I muttered sardonically.

He sighed. "Kaylyn, we take these vows seriously. We hold ourselves to a higher standard and we try to make sure that each Eagle understands they could back out before they take the vow. This man had other options. He didn't have the right reasons to kill another."

"Didn't you have options? Couldn't you have flashed your tattoos or pendant at a few military people and have him locked away forever?"

"No, and for two reasons. One." He held up a finger. "Eagles are secret. Much of what we do never leaves our group, not for our families, not for our friends, not for anything. A man who betrayed the Eagles by using his skills to kill another for money is not a man who can be trusted. Eagles are alive because we are secret. It's for our own protection. That man could have named off who we are, how we meet, the laws we hold. And every Eagle could have then been hunted down and killed. I could have a target on my back because that information might have gone to our enemies. Our secrecy makes us mysterious, and that man could have given up the information for any number of reasons, including torture by those too curious."

I couldn't fault that reasoning, but it still made me uneasy.

"Second." He held up another finger. "That man died in battle. He fought us, and he lost. He knew the punishment that was coming, and he tried to escape it. And when he didn't, he chose to die fighting. He had plenty of opportunities to surrender. He didn't want it."

"Then you saw it. You were there."

"I was. The only time I've ever had to use my Eagle uniform was to stop another Eagle. It's not something we're proud of. But it isn't something we can let slide."

I contemplated that for a minute as he went back to eating. "You know, my brother always told me I was odd because I never wanted to be an Eagle. And I still don't. You make me grateful I can't be an Eagle."

Raz laughed. "I suppose your brother dreamed of being an Eagle."

"For years. He probably still does. He could never get good enough at anything though. I think the reason most people join the School is because they hope they'll be good enough to meet an Eagle."

"That's not how we find our apprentices. In fact, it's extremely rare that we choose someone under military control."

"Well, it's not like anyone *knows* how you become an Eagle, now is it?" I pointed out. "Most people don't even know you have apprentices. They think Eagles see how good you are, and then you become one." I drained the rest of my glass and rose.

"You're back in a skirt," Raz noted. "Is is possible you're seeing the merits of being a female?"

"No. The pants are getting tight. They aren't comfortable."

"All you had to do was say something."

"You usually notice those things. You noticed when my last clothes were getting too small."

"I'll order new clothes," he promised. "The tailor will have to come measure you."

I made a face. "But he glares at me the whole time. Like I'm an abomination for wearing men's clothes."

"You could stop growing," he offered.

"I don't *want* to be this small for the rest of my life."

241

"Well, then I guess your only other option is to sew your own clothes." He gave a teasing smile as he placed his dishes in the sink next to mine.

I made a face again. "Not a chance."

"Then be nice to the tailor. We're paying him to allow you to flaunt convention."

"I'd be nicer if he didn't look like he'd been sucking on a lemon," I muttered as I started to wash the dishes.

True to my suspicions, the tailor arrived to glare at me. Nightfire asked what it looked like when someone sucked on a lemon.

"All squinty-eyed and puckered up."

"The man looks like he has eaten a lemon," Nightfire agreed.

The tailor took notes while Raz patiently observed, working on his staff. We were going to practice after I was done being fitted. Raz had agreed that Nightfire and I could practice the following morning, since the tailor had come right away and we hadn't expected him to be free.

The tailor had brought two tunics for me to try. As I was trying on the second one, the first being too small, I heard the tailor start to complain. "It isn't right that a woman wear pants," he informed Raz, his tone indicating his displeasure. "She is becoming a woman, and if she is not trained to act as one, she will never be sure of who she is."

"Lady Kaylyn is quite aware that she's a woman," Raz said calmly.

"Think of her image!" the tailor insisted. "A woman her age is preparing to be presented to society. A woman is accomplished in the feminine arts and readying herself to find a suitable husband. How will she ever find a husband here? As her uncle, you should be acting in the place of her father and presenting her to society."

"I don't want to be presented to society," I said, walking out with the other tunic in hand. "I don't want to become nothing more than Lord Somebody's wife. And I'm only fourteen."

The tailor spoke to Raz, since he thought Raz was the head of my family. "A woman can't be kept out in the middle of nowhere. A delicate lady should be able to interact with other women of her age."

"The last women of my age I interacted with made me want to scream," I said. "I *like* being here. Could you just size me, please?" I offered the tunic in my hand. "This is too small."

Raz raised his eyebrows slightly. I'd said please when the man was busy insulting me.

The tailor wasn't pleased, but he came over to take the tunic from my hand. "I don't think it appropriate that you wear clothing not meant for women to wear."

"Female Eagles wear pants," I pointed out. "Why can't I?"

"You don't know what Eagles wear," the tailor responded snippily.

"I know I never heard any stories about Eagles wearing skirts in battle. The thought of it is ridiculous, because I've tried wearing skirts while being trained for battle, and it isn't possible. And if you ever tried to take care of a dragon, you'd know that's not possible in women's clothes either."

He inspected the sleeves on my shoulders, then marked something down. "I have what I need." He gestured back to the room I'd changed in. Peeking out, I saw he hadn't quite given up on convincing Raz that I needed to be elsewhere. I didn't hear what he said, but I heard Raz's reply.

"Kaylyn is connected to a dragon. I think she's allowed to have a little leeway with the traditional conventions. Kaylyn needs to find who she is, and that may not be the traditional woman. When she decides she wants to be presented to society, or be around more people, I will make sure it happens. Right now, this is where Kaylyn chooses to be."

I opened the door and came out and handed the other tunic to the tailor. "Raz, where's my staff?"

"It's leaning against the door."

I shrugged on a jacket. "I'll wait outside," I said, accurately interpreting that he needed to conduct business of some kind.

The conversation wasn't long, but the tailor left looking irritated and disapproving. Raz didn't seem concerned. He came out and watched the tailor go.

"Do we have to do all our own mending?" I asked.

"No. He's simply unhappy with people who don't follow the expectations of society."

"It's kind of hard to do with a dragon."

"You couldn't be accused of trying to follow them either."

"Yeah, well, since when have you been my uncle?"

"Since I decided I didn't want any questions as to propriety. So I informed the tailor that I was your mother's brother. And since your brother is very young, I took responsibility for you." He lifted his staff. "Ready?"

"But Raz! I'm a delicate lady!" I protested in a mockery of a feminine voice.

He laughed.

We practiced until an hour before dinner. Then Raz said, "Take the last hour and go over the different blocks and strikes. Practice them on your own."

I tried to swallow the look of disappointment, but didn't do it quick enough to hide it from him. "What?" he asked.

I shook my head. "Nothing."

"If you'd prefer more time against me…"

"I thought I was doing well. That's all. I thought I was better."

He frowned, a furrow in his brow. "You are. You're doing very well. Why wouldn't you think so? Because I wanted you to practice alone?"

I shrugged, looking the end of the rod planted in the dirt.

"Kaylyn, why do you think I'm asking you to practice alone?"

I blew out a sigh. "Because I'm not doing something right," I muttered.

"Why do you think that?"

"Because that's how it is. I earn the right to train with someone else. Otherwise I practice alone."

He looked as if he wanted to laugh. "That's never been why, Kaylyn. Sometimes it helps to work things alone, to get the moves under control. Do I need to stand beside you and watch every arrow you fire or every knife you throw?"

"No, it's just how it always was," I said, confused. "I thought you were supposed to."

"That explains quite a bit. Why didn't you say anything if you thought you were being punished that much or you thought you were that bad?"

"I thought it went under the no-complaints-no-excuses rule."

He shook his head once, gave a long sigh. "Kaylyn, that rule doesn't mean you can't ever complain about anything. It means that you can't whine that you want to do something else, or that something's too hard. You're allowed to tell me that you're unhappy, or struggling, or that you don't think it's fair that you practice alone."

"Then I'm not behind."

"No. This is for you to solidify moves, fix mistakes, and work through things at your own pace."

"Oh. Okay." I felt relieved. I hadn't known what I was supposed to fix. I hadn't thought my strikes and blocks were so bad they needed work and I was relieved to find Raz agreed.

"I'll start dinner. It should be ready by the time you're done." He tapped the rod on his way past. "Work on not locking your elbows when you block. It's not consistent, but it's a bad habit to form."

I felt ridiculously pleased. The notion that practice alone was something good made my entire time here take on a whole new light. I wasn't all that good, but I'd never been hopeless. Maybe I'd turn out to be a real fighter someday.

Chapter 21

I awoke early the next morning and instantly sprang out of bed. Nightfire was waiting for me outside for practice. Half an hour later, I'd had a light breakfast and had the straps in hand. Nightfire was still until I was in place, then he rose onto his hind legs, spreading his wings. I felt his muscles coil, then he sprang in the air, wings beating hard to push us until we were soaring.

We took a few turns into the air until we were both settled, soaring over Rillmyra before wheeling around back to Vesta. After over an hour of flying, when Nightfire indicated he was ready, I rose to my feet and sprang off. Nightfire dove down and caught me easily. I was so used to the energy rush I could calmly think and analyze what I was doing and what Nightfire was doing. Thanks to the adrenaline, I noted more things faster as my brain raced. In order for Nightfire to more easily catch me, I had to figure out the right way to fall. I learned that stretching out, but keeping my arms at my sides, allowed me to be caught quicker. I had a habit of bending my legs that I was trying to fight. Nightfire set me on the ground and I climbed back on. I rolled off this time, pushing myself away from his body and already moving into the position that would best allow him to catch me. There was a shout below, then Nightfire caught me. *"I do not think Raz is happy,"* he thought to me.

I opened my eyes to see Raz running towards us. As Nightfire landed, I gained my feet a split second before Raz grabbed hold of me. "*What* in the name of *anything* did you think you were *doing?*" he bellowed at me. His hands were holding me so hard they hurt and he was nearly shaking me.

"I was falling," I explained, astonished at the mix of anger and terror in his eyes. "So Nightfire can practice catching me. We do it almost every day."

"Did you lose all sense up in the mountains?" he demanded of me. "What *possessed* you to do that?"

"It's what Nightfire's been practicing for. We can't assume I'm going to stay on no matter what. Raz, I was fine."

"*Fine?*" Abruptly, he let go and stalked back towards Vesta, nearly ripping the door off its hinges and slamming it shut behind him.

"I think you're right," I said to Nightfire, at a loss. "Raz isn't happy."

Of all the things I'd said or done, I'd never seen more than a flash of anger in Raz, and he was always quick to cool. Nightfire and I quit practice for the day, and after taking my time oiling him, I went in. Normally Raz would be preparing something for lunch, but instead he was sitting at the table, finessing what would become a staff. I guessed he was calm, able to be rational. "Lunch?" I offered.

His gaze lifted to mine and the anger slammed into me. I actually backed up a step. "I'll…I'll just get something for me, then."

Raz didn't say anything. I seated myself at the opposite end of the table, quietly eating, while Raz ignored me and worked. If I hadn't known him so well, I wouldn't have seen the subtle signs of his fury. His motions were smooth and controlled, his expression intent on his project. But his eyes were hard, his hands gripping too tightly, and there was a palpable sensation of barely controlled rage in the air. I wisely remained silent, knowing he wasn't interested in conversation.

When I finished, I put my things away and returned to the table, prepared to wait.

"You're on your own today." His voice was clipped, hard.

I met his anger with my own. "What about tomorrow?"

He ran his fingers over the wood, then turned it over. "We'll see how it goes."

"And the next day? The day after? A week from now? Are you going to keep punishing me for doing something you don't approve of, or would you just prefer that I leave?" It stung that he was pushing me away. It hit harder because he'd never done that before, and I didn't feel I deserved it this time.

He wouldn't look at me. "When you grow up, you'll realize one day that running away won't solve your problems."

My hands clenched at his cold hostility "I wasn't talking about running away. I was talking about you preferring me to be somewhere that you aren't. If you want to get rid of me, then *say* so. Don't leave me wondering day after day if you're ever going to want to deal with me again."

His eyes were equal parts of impatience and frustration and anger as he finally looked at me. "I suppose every time someone got angry at you they sent you away."

"Everyone except my father. Sometimes it was a day, sometimes it was a week, sometimes they told me to go away and never come back. Which one are you?" I threw out the challenge, waiting with coiled anger for the response.

"I don't know." He went back to his project, dismissing me. "We'll see."

Rising, I headed for my room, muttering, "Men make no sense at all."

"What?" Raz barked, a challenge in his voice.

I was halfway up the stairs and spun around. "I said you make no sense!" I shouted at him. "I don't even know what I did wrong!"

"You threw yourself off a dragon into midair!" Raz rose to his feet, the same anger scorching out. "And you've been doing it for *months* if I understand you!"

"Not always. Sometimes I threw myself off a cliff."

He shook his head. "I cannot believe this," he muttered.

"*You're* the one that's always saying I have to prepare! Would you prefer we waited until we were in the middle of battle and I fell off to find out if Nightfire could catch me? I *thought* I was doing something *right* for once!" I stomped up the rest of the stairs.

"You were." It was said with less anger.

I swung around a column to stare at him. "What?"

"I said you were." Raz didn't sound pleased to admit it. "You're right, it's something you need to work on."

I threw my hands up. "You can never accuse me of being irrational again, Raz, because you've topped anything I might have done! I *leave* five months, come back, and you aren't even *angry*! Then I do what you just agreed I'm *supposed* to do, and you're ready to kill me! Are all men like this, or is this irrationality just you?"

"Do you think I was never angry at you for leaving?" Raz demanded. "There were days when I woke cursing your name and waiting for you to come back so I could light into you. Other days I didn't even know *why* I was waiting. Do you think I was happy to find out you'd taken off in the middle of the night, slinking away without any sort of explanation or sign to say you were coming back? No, Kaylyn, I was exactly what you expected for three of those five months."

I didn't say anything, staring down at him silently as he gave a long sigh and pinched the bridge of his nose in an unfamiliar gesture of weariness.

"Kaylyn, I watched you jump into space and drop to earth, not knowing if you were going to survive it. If Nightfire was going to catch you. That kind of fear takes some time to handle."

"You said you could control fear."

"I controlled it enough that I didn't drag you inside and chain you to the floor, didn't I? You had time to come to terms with throwing yourself into midair, with one chance at living each time. This isn't a safe practice, and it isn't a controlled practice."

"It's a trust exercise, sort of," I pointed out. "Like standing on the edge of that cliff with you."

"And how many times did you beg, scream, and cry while standing on the edge of that cliff?"

"I guess you'll have to trust I know what I'm doing." But it wasn't as assertive as I'd thought it would be. "Raz, I promise I'm safe. If I die, so does Nightfire. You don't get anyone more motivated."

"Do you think everyone who dies plans on dying that day in that manner?" Raz asked.

"You're an *Eagle*. You got your tattoo so someone could identify your dead body which I assume is going to somehow be beyond normal recognition."

"That doesn't mean I *want* to die or that I plan on dying any day soon." He blew out a sigh. "Look, I know you need to know this, but I need some time. Give me a week, and then you can go tumbling towards the ground from the air."

I nodded, still leaning against the stone column. "Am I still on my own today?"

"You should do some work with the sword today. Just be a little more familiar with it. We'll start work tomorrow morning."

"Raz...I'm sorry." My voice was troubled.

"I know, Kaylyn. I'm not angry at you."

"Liar." Then I disappeared inside my room to try and figure out how I was supposed to handle this sword.

The next day, I went out to practice with some trepidation. I didn't know if he would still be angry, or if he would be here because he felt he had to. I'd had that before. But when he adjusted my grip, and moved through a step with me, it was apparent the anger was gone. He might not have been pleased with the thought of my practice with Nightfire, but it wasn't affecting anything now. He was just as patient, just as firm, and just as unyielding as before. He helped me when I struggled, was unbending about complaints or protests, and teased me during our practice time about one thing or another.

A week after our fight, I waited hesitantly for some signal from Raz on what to do. He hadn't mentioned my Dragonrider training, and I hadn't either. Nightfire waited patiently outside while we ate breakfast. I was trying to figure out whether or not to bring it up, but couldn't bring myself to speak.

After eating every last drop of oatmeal, waiting for Raz to finish eating, I started to fuss with my silverware.

"Well?" Raz asked.

I looked up from my spoon, nervous. "Well, what?" I asked.

"Aren't you going to train with Nightfire today?" he inquired.

Hope rising, I got up, but hesitated past that. "Are you sure?"

"You need to know this, and so does Nightfire. Go on."

Gratitude was evident in my expression as I quickly dumped my dishes in the sink and dashed towards the door.

"Raz said he would let you practice," Nightfire pointed out as I wrapped the straps around his neck.

"That doesn't mean he would have liked it. I don't want him angry at me again." I hauled myself over Nightfire's back, settling myself just behind his neck. *"Ready?"*

He was ready. He took off, winging his way up higher and higher, delighted to be able to share this experience with me again.

We practiced a few falls, just to make sure Nightfire was quick enough to catch me no matter what, then he started doing tricks in the air. The hardest part was being able to hold on when he twisted upside down, then flipped over again. I usually went hurtling out into space and he dived to catch me. After two hours of it, Nightfire settled into a lazy glide and we circled over the area, the sprawling, rugged landscape below.

"I am glad we came back," he thought to me.

"Yeah," I thought back. *"Me too."*

Chapter 22

Raz showed no apparent anger of my training with Nightfire any longer. If Nightfire felt any anger, he didn't mention it. We spent two mornings a week in the air, and the rest of the time I worked with Raz. After dinner, we worked some project in Vesta, repaired something, did laundry, or we cared for our weapons while Raz taught me. We covered a variety of topics, from politics to tactics, to managing horses, to the proper way to address everyone from royalty to a prisoner. It was always interesting. Even Nightfire loved to sit and listen to our conversations, asking questions. Raz occasionally had a book for me to look at, but almost everything he taught me was from his own memory, fueling my admiration and respect.

It was one evening after dinner that I left my room, ready for my next session in battle tactics, that I found Raz sitting at the table in the middle of the room on the bottom floor. He had a block of wood in front of him, and his knife, but the wood was in a curious shape.

"What's that?" I asked, dropping down instead of taking the stairs. I set the wooden carving of a horse, the carving my father had made, on the table, wondering why Raz had asked me to bring it.

"Just another project. I've been working on this for a while now." He offered the wood block and set it next to the wooden carving of a horse. "I haven't been doing so well," he said wryly. "If you have any help to give, I'll take it. I heard you knew how to carve."

I could see the basic outline of a horse, but his legs were a little too thin and very stiff, not like a horse would usually stand. The head was left alone, and the horse had no tail to speak of. I bit my lip to stop the smile as I picked up the knife and set to work on the wood. It had been a while since I'd done this, but it came back quickly as I sculpted out the rough form of a head.

"My father taught me how to carve," I said as Raz watched me work intently. "It was what he did in his spare time, when he wasn't working on a project. We were nobles, so we were supposed to gain money from our workers and lands, but we made so little, especially during the bad seasons, that it was good he could do something to supplement the income. We sold the figurines he made, all except this one. I wouldn't let them sell it." I could almost see the familiar room, hear my father's laugh. "He made it when I was eight. I always loved watching him carve and one day he said he'd let me help. I sat on his lap and held the wood at first, then he'd help me make a few cuts, and then he was letting me work it with him. I practiced for hours on scrap pieces of wood."

"Did any of your sisters carve?" he asked.

I shook my head. "No. They weren't interested. They were more interested in sipping tea, or pretending to, and dressing each other up and sewing things for their dolls. I always spent my time watching or helping my father. Like Warren. Warren worked on the crafts with my father, but he wouldn't often let me work on the crafts. He said anyone could use a hammer, but it took skill, true skill, to use a knife for something other than the purpose of hurting others." A lump rose in my throat, pain that I hadn't felt in a long time returning.

"You must have missed him when he died," Raz said quietly.

I nodded. "We buried him with my first carving. It was terrible, I hated to let others see it, but he was proud. He set it on the shelf next to his best carvings. After he died, Mother wouldn't let me carve. The few times I tried, Lisa would tattle on me and Madelyn would cry, so I just stopped."

"What was the carving? Your first carving?"

I was silent, carving out the rough form for the second ear. Raz didn't press. I knew he wouldn't ask again.

"It was an eagle," I said with a wry smile in remembrance. "At least, it was supposed to be. It didn't look much like one. Warren loved hearing tales about the Eagles, and Dad loved telling them. He'd fought in battle beside one, but he never told us who. All he said was that she was a marvelous fighter who saved his life. I remember wondering what your tattoo looked like, so I tried to create it. And when I finished, Lisa said it looked like a cross between a vulture and a wyvern and teased me for days."

Raz smiled a little. "But your father loved it."

"He would have loved it if it'd had one wing and no feet." I handed the carving back. "I have some tools. Some of his tools. Warren saved them for me and I've been carrying them ever since. Some of them would help, if you wanted."

"Maybe you could use some of them too," Raz said quietly. "We have plenty of scrap wood around, and I won't tell your mother." He started to work carefully on the nose, glancing at the horse standing proudly on the table for reference.

I just stared at the horse, and my father's signature etched into it. "What about your family?"

"They're still living. I was sent away to school when I turned seven, sent to study here or there, not just in school but in tradecraft. I spent six months under a blacksmith, nine months under a jeweler, three months under a painter, and two years under a carpenter. I could build things, not well, but I understood structure. I was sent to a potter, but that only lasted a week and then I went back to the carpenter. One day, I was practicing swordfighting out back and one of the carpenters saw and offered to go against me. I didn't understand the rules yet, and he taught me a few. When I tried to learn from someone who taught swordfighting, it wasn't the same. He had more rules that I didn't like and didn't want to follow, so I went back to Pentra and asked him to teach me. Eight months later, I was brought before the Eagles and made one of them. I was seventeen, almost eighteen then. I traveled around with the man who'd made me an Eagle for a while, then one day I decided to go my own way. If I needed money, I picked up a job here or there. I wasn't ready to settle down some place and make my name as a craftsman or find some other way of living."

I felt guilty. "You must hate being here."

"No," he replied. "Not at all. I have plenty to do. There's always something more to be done. A new room to start repairing. I'm not working for anyone other than me, and you," he added. "But it's not the same. I can be flexible with what I do. I can roam and explore and have a place to come back to. I can find people if I want them, and be alone if I don't. This place seems to have the right balance for the both of us." He frowned at the horse a moment, then carefully tried to sculpt the neck. "It was a little lonely with you gone."

I felt myself flush slightly and quickly moved the conversation along. It was one of the few skills my mother had managed to teach me that I excelled at. "Do you ever miss your family?"

"I check on them every now and again. They're rather like the dragons in their way of children. They raised me, and then one day I was ready to be on my own. If I show up one day, they'll be glad to see me. If I don't, they'll be content. They gave me everything they thought I would need to make it alone and believe I can make my way without them."

"Don't they want grandchildren? Or to know you're going to marry? Don't they have some sort of plans for you?" I asked, confused. My entire life had been spent under the notion that I would marry and provide children. I'd assumed it was the same for men.

"They wouldn't mind seeing grandchildren, but they'll live on without them. Being a craftsman who had plenty of workers around, my father didn't care if I followed in his footsteps or not. If a grandchild of his decided to follow his path, that would be fine. My parents expect nothing more than what they have. They both found what they were looking for out of marriage; a stable home in a good place and a partner who would let them do what they wanted."

"Was it an arranged marriage?" They were rare, but still around.

"It was. My grandparents got what they all wanted, and my parents found a way to make the marriage work for them. My father works in the shop, and comes home to a house that will give him company or solitude. My mother has her friends that she spends time with. They love each other, but it's nothing that storybooks would tell of."

"Is that what you want?" I couldn't imagine such a household. It seemed almost as if Raz hadn't been loved.

"I would like something more. With my life, it would have to be something more. There's no easy living for Eagles, so a woman would have to be more…volatile. Unpredictable. Impulsive. A woman who would be just fine with picking up her household and settling down elsewhere. It would have to be a woman who wouldn't mind country living, something less grand." He flicked a glance to me. "Is that what you want?"

"I don't know what I want," I said. "I don't know if I could find someone Nightfire could stand. He gets really jealous." I blushed, running a finger over the table. "Besides, I'm hardly old enough for marriage. I wouldn't know how to find someone to marry. My sisters were the ones who made themselves look pretty and learned how to catch a husband. I never did. I didn't want to. I've never really wanted to marry, mostly because everyone expected me to."

"I always found that phrase insulting," Raz commented. "'Catch a husband', as if we were a fish."

I giggled. "And do you think 'choosing a wife' is any less insulting? As if we were for sale in the market, lined up against all the rest for your inspection and critique?"

Raz smiled too. "I'm sure some of the men would prefer it." Then he laughed as I kicked him. "Careful! I'm trying to carve a horse here!"

"You won't, not like that." I got up and trotted upstairs to my room. "And unless you want to cut your thumb off, you need to not cut like that."

"It's what works best for me."

I swung around a column to face him. "Do you remember all those lectures about how I wasn't allowed to complain? No whining, no excuses? Well, same goes, Raz. If I don't get to complain about that awful sword, you don't get to argue with my carving lessons. You'll adjust and adapt and you'll do it without complaint." Feeling pleased to finally turn his own words back on him, I disappeared into my room while he laughed.

To his credit, he didn't complain. Other than a few questions for clarification, he mimicked my movements and my holds. I gave him a lump of wood for a practice piece and had him carve it into a square, and his second practice piece into a circle. Then he went back to the horse with a better idea of how to do straight and curved lines.

I didn't know how often Raz wanted to complain, but I was sure I had him beat. I fought with the sword every day, trying to make it move like I wanted it to. Everything else was easier, almost effortless at times, and the sword made me feel like I was starting all over again. Hours of practice a day went into the sword, sometimes with Raz, sometimes alone. It was only when I wasn't stumbling inside at the end of the day, too exhausted to think, that I thought I made any improvement. There was so much to learn. Every move had a block. Every block had a counter strike. And every counterstrike had its block. I could remember those consistently; it was when Raz would throw something new at me that I didn't know what to do with that I was driven to frustration.

"How am I supposed to block that if there's no block?" I demanded, rubbing the new bruise on my shoulder. "How am I supposed to fight if you're making things up?"

"You learn to improvise. There are only so many moves with a sword."

"Yeah, but a million combinations," I grumbled.

"So improvise," Raz suggested cheerfully.

"I'm not *good* at improvising! If you do A, then I'm supposed to do B. If you're doing some letter that's not in the alphabet, I don't have something to follow with!

"No excuses, Kaylyn." He gestured with his sword. "If I make up a letter, make up one of your own. It might work, it might not, but standing there and complaining that's not in the alphabet isn't going to protect you on the battlefield."

"We need a language with more letters," I muttered, starting the familiar circle pattern that began most matches.

In the evenings, after I'd tended to every cut, scrape, and bruise, Raz and I would sit down and carve. He was nearing the end of his horse, and I was putting the finishing touches on my carving. I had a tree, old and dead, with two owl hollows. Two faces looked out of the tree at the world curiously while staying safe inside their home. It was something fairly simple, to test my skills and find the familiarity. It felt good to be carving again. When I finished, I carved my name in the bottom of the tree and watched Raz etch his initials in tiny letters on the horse's hindquarters before smoothing the rough edges from the cut with a brush of a sanding stone.

"Well?" I asked.

He looked musingly at the horse. "I could do better."

"I like it." I ran my finger over the neck. "At least it looks like a horse."

He laughed. "Only because you helped. My horse would have looked silly with no tail and no ears." He picked up my tree and ran his fingers lightly over it. "Did it feel good to carve again?"

I nodded. I hadn't missed my father as much as I had before. Over half the times I'd tried to carve before, I'd ended up in tears myself. It didn't hurt as much as I'd imagined it would. "Dad would be proud," I said softly, so softly I didn't know if he heard.

"Your father would be proud of you no matter what," Raz said, setting the tree down. "I'd guess he'd be the kind of father who would make sure everyone knew you were his daughter so he could brag on you."

"He wouldn't have had much to brag on lately." I turned the tree around, imagining the owls' faces painted to make them stand out.

"You're too hard on yourself, Kaylyn. You're progressing."

"I've progressed to the point where I can actually make some real improvement and learn what I'm supposed to. If anyone else saw me, they'd probably laugh. I'm not anywhere as good as you."

"I am an Eagle," he pointed out.

"But your weapon is the sword, which I'm certain I'll never understand. You have to be weaker in some area, and the fact I've never come *close* to beating you means I'm still way behind."

He stared at me musingly. "Maybe we should find someone else to test you against."

"Like who? A ten-year-old?"

"You're too hard on yourself," he repeated. "You shouldn't judge your progress against me."

"Who else do I have?"

"That would be the point I'm trying to make. You need someone else to test yourself against." Raz studied me. "Every year, there's a competition for all the recruits of the military under nineteen. They compete with the weapons you've been training with."

"At the stadium just outside the capitol. Warren told me about it." I couldn't figure out why he'd brought it up. "All the boys compete with their best weapon, typically."

"It's open to anyone in the military," Raz mentioned. "Perhaps you should join."

I looked up at him. I'd been wondering if he wanted me to watch. "Me? But what if I fail?"

"Then you fail. You pick yourself up, you accept what happened, and you fight to do better. You won't be the best at everything in life, Kaylyn. You don't have to be the best."

"Yeah, well, you and everyone else are," I muttered. "You're part of a group that says you're the best. Dillon's going to lead the School someday. My sisters are catching husbands far above what any minor noble gets." And bragging about it, as if I cared.

"And you have a dragon," he reminded me. "Kaylyn, why do you have to compare apples to pears? Can't you be good enough

259

for just yourself? Don't you think Nightfire believes you're good enough? You won't ever reach the standard everyone else sets. You have to be who you are, and the rest will happen. Even if you try to make yourself who others want, you won't be happy. Do you think your sisters are happy? Looking not for love, but for an expectation of marriage?"

I stared at the table, shrugging. "As happy as they'd ever be, I guess."

"If your sisters are half as smart as you are, they'll want more. Your biggest problem is self-confidence because you think you have to be someone other than who you are. It's about as useless as you trying to become a dragon. Kaylyn Madara is enough of her own person not to need to be more."

I was silent a moment. "All right. I'll try."

"Good. We have a week. And then you'll be able to see how far you've come."

"Not that far," I muttered under my breath.

For five days, Raz put me through intensive training, as if I were in competition. He explained to me the process of how it would go, and we both agreed it would be best if I hid my face. I practiced with a head covering to get used to it, and wondered in the back of my mind how quickly I'd lose.

The sixth day, Raz only had me practice for two hours, one in the morning and one in the afternoon. He said it was better not to over-train the day before and injure something. I wouldn't train at all the day of the competition, just warm up before. I thought it odd, but decided to go look for herbs in the free time. Raz had found a book of herbs and edible plants and berries, and I'd decided to see if I could identify them. I promised Raz three times I wouldn't eat anything, that I would bring it back first, and took food with me just to appease him that I wouldn't get overcome with hunger and eat a poisonous berry. I wandered the countryside for hours, appreciating the solitude. I'd been working hard for this competition. And although I was sure it was a waste of time, I figured I could do decently at archery. And maybe not lose immediately in hand-to-hand.

Something about my thoughts must have shown on my face as I displayed my findings to Raz, identifying them one by one.

"You're too hard on yourself, you know," he said as he deposited the blueberries and blackberries in a bowl to wash. "You're going to amaze some people, including yourself."

"You do realize that all anyone expects out of me is the ability to defend my honor with a staff, right? The fact I know how to hold a sword at all is going to astonish them. The rest..." I shrugged self-consciously. "They won't laugh too hard, will they?"

"No one will laugh," Nightfire stated imperiously.

I sent him a half-smile. "Thanks." I plucked up a twig. "I'm not sure what this is."

He inspected it a moment. "Dill. I'm surprised. I didn't think dill would grow here." He set it aside to keep. "Do you think I'm going to send you out to humiliate yourself?"

"I think the recruits are better than I am."

"Apples to pears."

I shook my head. "Not here. This is one time when comparison matters. Any enemy would have to be at least as good as they are, and I'd have to beat them. I don't think I'm worse because I'm a girl, I think I'm worse because I'm just awful at this. But they'll think I'm worse because my hair's longer and I usually wear a skirt. Well, I'm supposed to wear a skirt," I admitted.

"Before you cut your hair off, why don't we just see how tomorrow goes?" Raz suggested. "I think tomorrow you'll be the most astonished of anyone by what you can do." He plucked up a flower. "What's this?"

"I just thought it was pretty."

He handed the flower to me. "Evening Primrose. It's edible too, but I suppose we have plenty of food."

I remembered my sisters had tucked flowers in their hair and tucked this one behind my ear. "Just in case I get hungry, then."

He smiled, but pensively. "We leave at dawn tomorrow. Nightfire isn't carrying both of us."

"I'll stay up a little longer. I want to carve a little."

He headed up the stairs, then back to his room a few minutes later. I called an absent goodnight as I worked on carving a delicate hand. Before long, when being delicate seemed like a difficult task, I put the tools away and left the carving on the table, placing the primrose on the table next to it.

The next morning, I was wide awake when it came time to leave. I was suddenly nervous about the possibility that I would humiliate myself, embarrass my brother, and give more credit to those who said I didn't belong in the military. I didn't think I belonged there either, but it seemed like the best home at the moment. And I hated to disappoint Raz, as if I'd fail his teaching if I didn't succeed.

"You are a Dragonrider," Nightfire said sternly as he took flight.

"I don't even know what that means."

"It means you are what no one else ever has been. You can be nothing but the best Dragonrider. I would not have chosen you if you did not deserve it."

"You didn't pick me because I could fight."

"You are willing to learn. You have learned. You will see. You will not fail."

By the time we reached the competition grounds, just outside the capitol, I was strangely settled. I was certainly distracted as I promised dozens of times that Nightfire wasn't going to hurt anyone. I had less patience for frightened women who had shown up to support their chosen man, or the recruits they admired, than the men. Of the men who asked, I told them Nightfire wasn't interesting in hurting anyone, and they seemed convinced. The women wanted to argue.

"But Doctor McDragon said black dragons were unstable, uncontrollable," whined a girl perhaps a year older than me, wringing her hands as she eyed Nightfire fearfully.

"Doctor McDragon is an idiot and a fraud," I snapped. "And anyone who takes his word doesn't deserve to claim to have common sense."

"Are you sure you can control him?" she pressed.

"I don't control him. He does what he wants. However, if I ask him to bite you, he probably will."

With a gasp, she hurried away in a swirl of brightly-colored fabric.

"It's almost time," Raz murmured.

"Good," I muttered, itching to get out of the skirt hiding the pants I wore underneath. "If I have to hear one more person quote Doctor McDragon as an expert on *anything*, much less dragons, I'll scream."

Raz handed me the cloth for my head. "Go make your entrance."

My entrance was to present proof to the judges that I was military. Most of the contestants here were from the School itself, but some were trained by those at military outposts. Those who couldn't leave their families for one reason or another could be trained by any graduate of the School, and most graduates on the officer side of the school were stationed at a guardhouse somewhere around the country. Those who did exceptionally well, or those who stayed in longer than a year, were added to the roster as military-in-training, just like those at the School. The competitors here could choose to show off their skills with all five of the weapons, but some would only perform with their best weapon.

I'd been worried that they'd look too closely at the document, but they merely looked to see Dillon's signature and directed me to an area with other recruits and marked something down on the list. I didn't have to linger more than a minute before someone showed up and handed me a bow and arrow.

"Who trained you?" asked the man who handed out the quivers of arrows.

"Raz Greenclaw," I answered, hoping he wouldn't be able to tell I was changing my voice.

He didn't notice. "Not heard of him."

I shrugged, accepted the quiver, and slung it over my shoulder. He moved on and we all were led out.

The crowd was settled. I saw Raz nod to me from the front row. Nightfire had perched at the top of the stadium, with a clear space around him. The stadium was enclosed, as it was fairly new, but there was plenty of room for him. Everyone paused to stare at the dragon as they entered.

"Is that Dragon Girl here?" I heard someone mutter. "Do you see her? I don't even know what she looks like."

The generals all sat on the front row in the middle, and they looked slightly irked. I guessed it was because I was here. I caught sight of Dillon as he searched the crowd for me, but he settled as the order came to begin.

As I faced the targets, I was startled to notice that they were considerably closer than they'd been with Raz. Putting my arrows where I wanted them wasn't difficult, but I noted with surprise they were for some of the others. Granted a few of them were young, probably first year cadets without even a rank, but I hadn't expected this many to struggle. I shot off my ten quickly, waiting for the next quiver to be handed to me. To my shock, that was declared the end of round one. Those who did well went up to round two.

Round two was ten more arrows and the target three paces back. I rolled my eyes and shot my ten, watching everyone else shoot theirs.

"Do you see that boy? The one in black?" I heard a general murmur. "He's good. Shows a lot of promise. I haven't seen an archer shoot that well at the School in nearly a decade."

"I wonder who he is."

"If he's any good, we'll find out soon enough."

They think I'm good, I thought with wonder.

"You must never get nervous," the boy next to me said as the final ten were chosen after we fired our third set of arrows. He'd made it, and so had I.

I shrugged and headed for Raz, curiosity burning.

"Well done," Raz said, smiling at me. "You're into the final round."

"Raz, is this the easy competition or something?" I whispered. "This isn't that *hard*! I never shot at targets this close with you!"

His eyes smiled. "I pushed you hard, Kaylyn. Perhaps I should have mentioned how hard before you reached that point of frustration. It's been my experience that those who are pushed harder to succeed, and are expected to succeed, will do it. I never said this is far beyond what the military trains you in. I never said that recruits are trained half the time you are. I expected greater things from you and you achieved them."

I glanced over at the boys drinking water vigorously. "How can they possibly be tired? We only shot thirty arrows."

"The past year and a half for you, Kaylyn, has been a huge transition. You've grown stronger, smarter, and wiser. I sent you through immersion to see how fast you could learn, and you learned quickly. Whatever happened on that mountain was a turning point for you. You'd shown flashes of comprehension, understanding, but somehow it all clicked one day."

"Is that what you were trying to do? Make it click?"

"I kept pushing, waiting for it to happen. I never dreamed you didn't see how much you were progressing."

I ducked my head down. "I'm sorry."

"It was a mistake on my part. I didn't pay attention." He handed me the next quiver of arrows. "Go show them what you're made of."

I saluted to bring the grin to his face, then lined up in front of my target. While others hesitated, waited for just the right moment, I coolly shot. I'd discovered that waiting only led to second-guessing myself. I also didn't try to pressure myself with the best. I didn't aim for that pinpoint spot that said I had perfect accuracy; I aimed for the center circle. I felt satisfaction as I hit it again and again. I even hit the pinpoint in the middle once, and was vaguely pleased. The crowd noticed too, and murmured with approval as they applauded.

The fifth round had only four people shooting, including me. The targets were pushed back five paces this time. The pale boy next to me started to sweat, the one next to him wiping his hands nervously over his pants, as if to dry them. The one on the end started to chew on his lip in concentration. I drew the first arrow and strung it to my bow.

I realized after I'd shot that we were taking turns, going down the line. I shouldered my bow and watched the other three, wondering at their nerves. I'd thought that surely recruits competed all the time, but judging by the boy nearly hyperventilating at the end of the line, I was beginning to rethink my assumption.

They all did fairly well. Each of them hit the dead center of the target at least once. I somehow managed to hit it twice. The pale boy next to me hit it three times, but completely ruined his last shot so that I won by points. It was more a mild shock than anything when I was named the winner. I shook my head momentarily, then headed towards Raz.

"Excuse me! Young sir!" General Maddox puffed his way over to me. "You've got quite the talent there, young sir. Quite the talent."

I bowed silently.

"That is talent, isn't it?" Raz asked easily, coming over. "Quick and accurate."

"Yes, yes, I must agree! I see a bright future for you, young man."

I felt the flush starting and bowed again to cover it.

"The next competition is beginning," Raz mentioned politely.

"Yes, of course. He needs to get into position." General Maddox winked at me, which floored me, then he puffed his way back over to his spot.

"Am I going to have to fight with swords?" I asked softly.

"You are."

I groaned softly.

Raz slapped me on the back in what I thought was supposed to be an encouraging gesture. "Buck up. You've got one of the competitions down. Only four more to go." He handed me a rod. "Go get 'em."

I almost felt sorry for my competitors. Raz was an aggressive fighter, and he'd trained me to be aggressive as well. I'd started to notice that hits I received were a lot less painful, and this was even more noticeable. The hits I took from Raz in the beginning had throbbed for hours. These lasted barely longer than a slight sting, a flare of pain, and then faded to the back of my mind. I wasn't sure if it was the fact I was used to getting bruises, or something else. Not one of them came close to beating me, and I saw some of them nursing sore hands as they left defeated.

I was congratulated after I defeated my last opponent, winning the staffwork competition, and Raz pulled me out of the way while the floor was cleared to prevent me from answering any questions. "Next is hand-to-hand," he said.

"When's swordfighting?"

"The sport of nobles is last."

I sighed. "Of course it is." I took a drink of water, then adjusted my head covering. "The boys could use some endurance training."

Raz's eyes flashed with amusement. "I'll mention it."

"She is right," Nightfire told Raz and me. "They tire easily."

"You're first," Raz said. "Go."

"Why am I first?"

"Because I put you first."

I knew everyone was curious about who I was. I'd caught the mutterings and excited whispers, and it appeared my opponents weren't any less curious. Three went for my head covering. Three were summarily flipped on the ground where they wheezed for breath. I was astounded at my strength. I had muscles, could clearly see the muscle definition from all the training and labor, but men bigger than me weren't able to overpower me. A suspicion was growing in the back of my mind as I defeated the last opponent who had to weigh twice what I did, leaving me still undefeated.

Curiosity mounted higher and the crowd was buzzing throughout the entire fourth round of knife skill. I was taken aback to find that most people viewed knives as a throwing weapon rather than a close-combat weapon. Almost everyone could throw their knife and hit the target provided, although getting the knife to stick and close to the center of the target was an entirely different matter. I'd thought it was something Raz had made up to get me used to using a knife. Fighting was being able to slash through a cloth in one swift motion. I wondered if swordfighting would be the same while I wondered how in the world I'd been declared the winner again.

Some opponents were given a sword. Raz gave me the one I'd used. It was worn, not as flashy or shiny, but I was comfortable with it. "Do you want armor?" he asked.

"I wouldn't know how to move in it," I replied. "I don't think I *could* move in it. It weighs more than I do. Do I need it?"

"Not if I trained you as well as I suspect I did."

"We only trained this for three months. I can't be that good."

"Immersion training, Kaylyn. We fought for a long time every single day."

I studied him. "It's more than that, isn't it? Something's changing about me."

"Ah, so you're noticing it too."

"Do you know why?"

"I can only suspect." He pointed up towards Nightfire. "You're the first that's ever made this connection to a dragon before. We're in uncharted waters."

I held my hand up, palm towards him. He rested his hand against mine and pushed. I felt the muscles contract, strain, but his hand wasn't going anywhere and I wasn't pushing as hard as I could. "I shouldn't be this strong," I said quietly, letting my hand drop. "I'm fourteen. I shouldn't be able to do this." I stared at him with troubled eyes.

"You are who you are, Kaylyn. If this is something because of your connection with Nightfire, then you're doing exactly what you're supposed to."

"Excuse me," Dillon said politely, coming to join us, "but you're up."

I nodded, hoping our voices had been low enough that our conversation didn't carry. I was pretty sure Dillon wouldn't mind, but I knew others would have something to say about my being here. As I passed by, Dillon rested his hand lightly on my arm, drawing my gaze up to his. He stared at me intently. "I wonder," he said softly, "if you are who I think you are."

You'll find out, I thought as I saluted him and headed for the middle of the arena.

"Where's Kaylyn?" I heard Dillon ask Raz. "The generals are wondering as well."

"Kaylyn had little interest in watching this," Raz replied. I noted humorously it could be interpreted as that I hadn't come, or that I was somewhere in the capitol. Then I was forced to focus as I saw my opponent approach.

Swordfighting was still a struggle. It didn't flow easily. My movements were clearly uncoordinated at times, but effective. It helped that some of my opponents were using armor they obviously weren't used to. It weighed them down. It also made it easy to topple them to the ground. Only one went without armor as well, wearing a leather jerkin similar to mine. He moved with grace and was elegant at defeating his opponents while the women cooed over his midnight hair, almost too long, and the mysterious brown eyes that stole their breath away. I was more to the point, abrupt, but it got the job done.

The crowd hushed in excitement as we lined up for the final match against each other. I understood why when I heard General Maddox, who was quickly becoming an excellent source of knowledge, say this man had won the swordfighting part of the tournament every year for the past four years. I decided he wouldn't get five if I could help it.

I nearly lost on the first stroke. He had strength, and he used it. I staggered from the sheer force of the blow, then gave a return strike with all I had. He quickly backed away, giving us both a moment to recover. When he came forward again, he used a stroke I'd seen with Raz a thousand times. And suddenly everything clicked.

My arms moved to block and counter, just like I had all those times before. Without pause, I swung around in the move that

Raz was always prepared for, but that would give me a chance to regroup. To my surprise, he wasn't as quick and nearly got sliced. I pulled back a little, then pressed forward. As he fought harder, his face got redder and redder under his golden skin.

I stepped back when he stumbled. It was possible he'd give a wild swing to protect himself, but I wasn't betting on it. He was too controlled. It gave him a moment to collect himself and prepare. I saw the question in his eyes as he circled with me. He wanted to know why I hadn't gone in for the kill. Then a sparkle lit up his eyes.

The next blow was testing, almost playful. I was enjoying the fun of the match. It was no longer for blood, for the win; it was the sheer delight in the rapid calculation of his moves and mine, the flow of movement, and the dance between two swords and the people that held them. If he'd been intent on beating me, if my moment to let him save face had incited his temper to protect his ego, I wouldn't have found the fun of this game. But here, I found it, and he played with me, grinning on occasion when I used a particularly good strike or block.

The dance continued between us, to the delight of the crowd. All the moves I'd been taught were slowly coming back to me. I'd occasionally throw one in to see how he responded. He'd toss one back and see what I did with it. And when I finally found the opening I needed, I used the one move he hadn't been prepared for, and took advantage of the slow reflex to shove him to the ground with a full body push. He didn't hit the ground like a falling brick as some of those in armor had; instead he let go of his sword to catch himself, but couldn't get the sword back in time and nodded as my swordpoint lightly touched his jerkin. "I yield."

Laughter bubbled out of me as the crowd burst into applause for us both. I lowered my sword and offered a hand to help him up, and then I pulled off my head covering. "That was wonderful!" I exclaimed, knowing my eyes shone with delight. "I've never fought like that before." I turned to Nightfire, still perched on the stone wall. "Nightfire, did you feel that?" I called up. "I finally got it!"

The applause had suddenly stopped as people gasped in astonishment. Nightfire let out a roar, pride evident, then launched himself off and glided down to me. I was still laughing as I hugged Nightfire's neck tightly. "Looks like we've gotten somewhere after all," I whispered. Then I turned back to the man I'd fought. He was standing there still, looking bemused.

"Are his eyes always yellow?" he asked.

I gave a shy grin. "No. It means he's proud." I crossed back over to him. "I hope you don't mind."

He started laughing. "Mind? I haven't had that much fun swordfighting in months! If a woman can have that much fun doing what I love, I'm not going to complain! I'm going to hope she has a sister!"

"I do," I informed him. "Two of them. Triplets."

"Any of them as good?"

"Doubtful. Last I knew, they were the more traditional women." I bowed to him. "Kaylyn Madara."

"Raphael Yett." He bowed back. "My utmost pleasure."

"He is flirting," Nightfire warned.

"I think I like it."

General Maddox huffed his way over. "What is the meaning of this?" he barked at me. "This competition…"

"Is for military only," I said sweetly. "Perhaps you've forgotten, General, but Nightfire and I are both part of the military. We were moved under military jurisdiction after Nightfire hatched. I was enrolled in the School and everything."

"But you're a girl!"

"The rules don't limit gender. Just military." I couldn't contain the happy grin. "And a girl just beat all your men in every competition."

He was appalled at the reminder. "This…this is…"

"A shock. You men aren't pleased with the fact that a woman is just as good, if not better, than you are. And you said yourself I was good. That I had talent. A bright future." I enjoyed the unhealthy flush on his face.

271

"That's enough, Kaylyn," Raz murmured, standing behind me, a hand on my shoulder. "Be proud, but not arrogant."

I turned to face him. "Raz, did you *see* that? It clicked! Just like you said the rest did! It was just *there* and I could do it!"

A smile touched his features. "I told you it would." He handed me the scabbard. "Sheathe your blade before you hurt someone."

"Well done, Kaylyn," a familiar voice said warmly. I looked up to see Dillon grinning at me.

"Well?" I asked. "Was I who you thought I was?"

"As a matter of fact, you were exactly who I thought you were. Your dragon gave you away. He was always more intensely focused whenever you fought, and I could see his eyes change sometimes." He let out a laugh. "I see the last year has done you some good!"

"Apparently so."

"Pack your weapons," Raz said. "Be sure to clean the blade."

I hefted the sword and headed towards where my other weapons were. It took several minutes to pack it all up. I looked over at Raz and Dillon on occasion to see them talking with the generals, nobody looking very happy, but I couldn't hear what they were saying from where they were thanks to the crowd of people who were busy talking loudly about today's event.

I had just finished packing when Raz and Dillon headed towards us. "Are we leaving?" I asked.

"Soon. We need to be back before dark." Nightfire had stated his strong objections to flying in the dark.

I gave a sigh. We had no time to explore Vicoma at all. I wasn't sure I was ever going to see the capitol at this rate "Where are the generals? Aren't they going to yell at me?"

"The yelling is over with." Dillon handed me a metal token on a ribbon. I inspected it curiously. "You're one of a dozen or so to ever win this," he informed me. "Winner in every category. The generals weren't pleased about not being informed, but they can't argue you didn't win this."

I looked up sharply. "Did they do something? You aren't going to be in trouble, are you?" I demanded of Raz worriedly. "You aren't going to be arrested?"

"No, Kaylyn, I'm fine," Raz assured me. "They couldn't arrest me."

"Maddox would if he could," I muttered. "And he'd arrest me too if he didn't want Nightfire so much." I went back to the token. It was engraved with all five weapons, and the seal of Centralia on the back. "Are you in trouble because you stuck up for me again?"

Dillon gave a half-smile. "I'm fine. I'm glad you're doing well where you are."

"Better than I thought I was," I murmured almost to myself as I traced the edge of the token. "Do you think you could give this to Warren?" I asked him, looking up again. "My sisters and mother won't care, but I want Warren to see it."

"Of course." Dillon accepted it back and slid it inside a leather pouch. "You should be proud of what you've done today. And stop by sometime. It would be nice to talk."

"I'll do my best." I smiled as Nightfire nudged me. "All right, Nightfire, I'm moving."

Nightfire sprang in the air once I was on his back, and I waved to Dillon as we took off. Once in the air, I let out a shriek of delight. "I'm good! Nightfire, I'm actually *good!*"

"Raz said you were."

"I know, but…I beat them all!"

"You are a Dragonrider. You can do more than what is expected, even of yourself."

I hugged his neck tightly. "I don't know. I'm expecting some pretty big things of myself now," I teased. "Maybe I could even beat an Eagle." I laughed. "I can't wait until my brother hears about this!"

Chapter 23

Despite my new understanding, I still couldn't beat Raz. The more mistakes I made, the more I started to get annoyed with myself. Raz was quick to reassure me that I was doing fine. I only half-believed him.

"Kaylyn, you're making progress. You're never going to reach the day when you always win and do it flawlessly."

"Why not? You do it all the time. I bet the Eagles always win."

Raz shook his head. "Kaylyn, Eagles are not perfect."

"You aren't awful either," I muttered.

"You're working for perfection, and it isn't possible. Perfection is something you should work for, but never expect to achieve."

"Well, that's just silly. What's the point of working for something if you're never going to reach it?"

"Why bother doing something at all if you're never going to be the best at it?" he returned. "Why bother carving?"

"Because I like it."

"Why else?"

"Because you don't always have to be the best."

"When you carve, do you give your all into it, or just do half the work?"

I could see where it was going. "You know I don't cut corners," I muttered.

"Why?"

"Because it matters that I do it right."

"Even though you'll never be the best at it? And it isn't ever going to be perfect?"

"Yes."

"That's why perfection is something to work for but never expect to attain." He lifted his sword. "Now try again."

"Should I ever think I can beat you? Or is that something else I should never expect to attain?"

A smile flickered across his face. "We'll see."

"Raphael Yett is coming towards Vesta," Nightfire said, displeasure in his tone. *"And he is looking for you."*

I looked up. "What?" I asked, startled.

Raz paused. "What did he say?"

"He said Raphael's coming to see me."

"Raphael?" he questioned, thinking. "Ah, yes, the swordfighter." He offered a hand. "Go find out what he wants."

I handed him the sword. "I don't think I should be long," I called as I hurried towards the path.

Raphael was within sight as I rounded the building. He sent me a smile as I got closer, and I noted his midnight hair was a little shorter than it had been. "I guess you knew I was coming."

"Nightfire," I explained, pointing to the cliff. "He likes to nap there."

Raphael glanced up at him. "I see. Well, I guess I couldn't surprise you then."

"It was a surprise," I assured him. "What are you doing here?"

He laughed at my genuine puzzlement. "I came to see you."

"Oh. You did? Why?"

He chuckled, a little softer now. "Let's take a walk and I'll explain it to you."

Still confused, I walked beside him. "Where are we going?"

"We're just walking. There's not a planned destination in mind, although we will have to end up back here eventually as you live here."

I was left to my confusion as we walked in silence down the path. The breeze stirred his hair, while mine was in an untidy braid to keep it out of my way. He was dressed well, and I rubbed my hands over my pants a little self-consciously. A quarter of the way to the stream, he finally spoke. "Were you ever courted, Kaylyn?"

"Me? No." I waved that off with a laugh. "Never."

"Never had anyone interested?" he inquired.

"Why would they be? I had two prettier sisters."

"If you're all triplets, then you can't be any less pretty than they are."

I shrugged, a bit embarrassed. "Well, they were more proper than I was. I was usually in the woodshop with my father or outside. Suitors aren't looking for someone covered in grass stains and sawdust." *Or one wearing pants,* I thought to myself.

"I still find it hard to believe by sixteen you haven't had a suitor who was interested."

I was taken aback. "Sixteen?" I laughed. "I'm only fourteen. I'm not fifteen for several more months."

He looked surprised. "Only fourteen then?" He came to a stop.

I came to a stop too as it finally hit me. "You...you weren't coming to *court* me, were you?" I asked, shocked.

"Why wouldn't I?" Raphael touched his fingers lightly to my hand. "So young," he murmured. "And despite the rebellious streak I find in you, I can still see a beautiful woman."

I flushed clear to my toes.

He laughed at me. "A woman such as you are, and you still blush like a child." His dark brown eyes were full of teasing laughter, and something else I'd never seen before; something like slowly-melting liquid. "I wonder," he said softly, "what else I could do to make you blush."

I went very still, hardly breathing at the touch of his breath on my skin. My heart was pounding so loud I wondered if he could hear it. I wanted to make some move, sure I was supposed to make one, but I had no idea what that move was. As his lips pressed to mine, he slid his hand to my back and pulled me closer. It was a swirl of shocking sensation that left a void when it ended.

"Oh," I whispered, confused.

Raphael laughed softly. "So you liked it too."

I couldn't make myself not blush as much as I tried. Not knowing what to do, my mind still reeling from the sensation, I said the first thing that came to mind. "I know why people are kissing all the time now," I blurted out.

He started to laugh and I wanted to sink into the ground. I started to push free as Raphael started to press his lips to mine again. Before I could free myself, he tightened his grip momentarily, one hand at my chin to guide my head into position. I subdued, but there wasn't the same magical sensation. I just wanted him to let me go.

He smiled as he pulled back. "You're such an innocent," he said, chuckling.

I kept my eyes firmly on the ground as I used what Raz had taught me to push myself free. "I'm going back now."

He looked surprised as he caught my hand. "Wait! Kaylyn, please," he said, pleading. "I'm sorry. I, well, I forgot what it's like the first time you court somebody. Or I guess in your case the first time somebody comes to court you. Stay, please?"

"Why? So you can laugh at me?"

"No, of course not. Because..." He cleared his throat, looking slightly embarrassed. "Because I want to be with you."

I couldn't imagine saying that, sure I'd die of mortification first. It eased the sting of his laughter. I remembered Raz had said that men risked rejection and were just as shy and awkward as women and felt a little more lenient towards him. "Don't laugh at me, okay?" I mumbled.

"I won't. I'm sorry." He moved closer. "I guess I'm not that good at courting, am I?" he asked with some apology.

I scuffed one foot on the ground. "I wouldn't know."

"Well, I know I'm not supposed to upset you." He offered a half-smile. "Can I at least walk you back?"

An answer that I knew was right floated miraculously to the front of my brain from somewhere. "There's no rush. We could take the scenic route," I offered.

He gifted me with a dazzling smile and held my hand more firmly in his. "I don't think we'll cover the area, as much land as you have out here. Maybe I could come back and we could explore some more," he suggested. "I'd like to see you again."

I felt my face go warm, but replied, "Me too."

Hands still clasped, we started to walk, disappearing into the woods.

After Raphael left, I slipped inside Vesta and spotted Raz working on his carving at the table. I felt uncomfortable because even though he didn't look up, I knew he knew I was here. "I…I'm sorry I took so long." I silently cursed my nervous stammer. "I didn't know he…" I stopped, not quite sure how to phrase it.

Raz chuckled. "Luckily for you, I knew better. Will Raphael be returning?"

"Not today. We just went for a walk. That's all," I excused quickly.

"It's nothing to be ashamed of, Kaylyn. You're of the age to court." He set the carving on the table. "What do you think of it?" he asked, turning the conversation.

I gratefully took the change and inspected the cube. He seemed to have gotten the hang of edges and making something with dimension. It had taken me three pieces of wood whittled down to nothing before I'd been able to finally grasp it. "It looks good." I laid it back on the table. "I guess it's time to try carving again. I have to get some wood first."

"We have wood," Raz said, gesturing to the stacks in the small room to my left.

"Not those. Aspen's a softer wood. It'll be easier for you."

"I'll let you make the trip into town tomorrow, then. Pick up the bread and anything else we need on the way."

"Something for these bruises, probably." I looked ruefully at my arms and legs. "How is it possible that I'm getting more bruises when I'm actually good at fighting now?"

"You can take the blows now. You couldn't before," Raz replied. "Are we finishing up practice, or eating?"

"I'm hungry. I'll go fix lunch."

I had a hard time focusing the rest of the day. I fought to keep my mind on what I was doing, but Raphael continued to surface over and over again when I least needed him to. Finally, as we were training with the staff before dinner, a memory distracted me enough that I didn't properly block Raz's blow, and the force of it knocked the end of my staff into my face.

I stumbled back with a yelp of pain, clutching my eye with one hand and trying to stem the flow of blood with the other while the world swirled around me.

"Kaylyn!" Raz was instantly by my side, guiding me to the ground and pulling a cloth out of his pocket. "Head back," he instructed as I stuffed the cloth against my bleeding nose.

"Is my nose broken?" I managed to get out, my eyes watering with pain. I could feel Nightfire instantly springing into the air to come to me.

"Let me see." He gently took my face in his hands and inspected it, touching it lightly here or there. "No, I don't think it's broken. How's your eye?"

"Throbbing. Everything's blurry."

Nightfire landed and pushed his head against mine, making worried noises.

"I'm okay, Nightfire."

"You are hurt," he snapped anxiously.

"I'm okay. I promise."

"I'll go get ice. Keep your head back," Raz ordered.

Nightfire curled in a half-circle around me, nuzzling gently on the uninjured side of my face as he slowly calmed.

"You've got to stop getting in a twist every time I get hurt," I informed him. "I'm not about to die."

"You are a human. Humans are fragile and weak."

"I am not that fragile, and I'm not weak. Just because we can't handle a dragon sitting on us doesn't mean everything in the world could kill us. It's just a bloody nose and probably a black eye." I gingerly touched my eye and winced. "Ow."

"Here." Raz was already back with some ice in a cloth. "Everything all right?"

"Yes. Nightfire doesn't think humans can handle any pain without dying." I pressed the ice to my nose and eye. "You don't have to say it, you know."

"Say what?"

"About not being focused. Distractions and learning to deal with them. I've already figured it out."

He smiled a little. "Can you walk?"

"Of course I can walk. I don't think I can stand, however. Having one eye does nothing for my depth perception."

Raz offered a hand and assisted me to my feet while Nightfire kept right beside me. I could feel his worry. He thrust his head under my hand to help me maintain my balance.

"Nightfire, for pity's sake, I'm just fine," I muttered.

"If you were fine, you would be able to see out of both eyes, stand, and walk without assistance," he snapped.

"It's just temporary," I insisted.

Despite my arguments, Nightfire insisted I stay on the bottom floor so he could keep a close eye on me. I laid my head on the table and placed the cold cloth over my face, wishing for the throbbing to ease. Raz came down the stairs with a cup of something he said was for the pain, and returned a few minutes later with something to eat. My nose had stopped bleeding, but everything around my eye was swelling.

Finally, after half an hour, the swelling stopped and started to recede. An hour later, the pain was gone. Raz inspected me one more time, then looked satisfied. "You'll have a bruise," he stated. "But I think your vision is fine. Let me know if anything gets worse."

I nodded. "I think Nightfire will let you know before I can," I said dryly. "He's as bad as my mother. Worse."

"You must rest," Nightfire ordered me.

"Nightfire, for pity's sake…" I said crossly.

"There's nothing else we'll be doing today," Raz intervened. "Keep ice on the bruise for a little longer. If your eye isn't too bad tomorrow, we'll put in some more practice."

"Fine," I grumbled.

I glanced in the mirror the next morning, and winced. My eye was vivid purple with a hint of blue, and slightly swollen. The longer I stared, the more I tried to convince myself it wasn't so bad. By the time I left, I was assured it wouldn't be that noticeable.

One step in the bakery, and I realized I was wrong.

Eileen let out a gasp. "Land sakes, child! What happened to you?"

Startled, the women at the counter turned and gasped as well.

I let out a sigh. "It's nothing. A rod hit me. I'm fine."

"Nothing?" a woman said in disbelief. She clutched her gloved hands together, as if in pain at seeing me. "You poor girl; you look terrible."

That didn't improve my mood. "I'm headed to see Malan. I'll be back to pick up the bread. Raz says the usual." Then I headed out the door.

Malan let out a whistle when he saw me. "That's a beauty, lass. What hit ye?"

"A staff. Is it really that bad?"

"Ye have a sunrise coming up on your face."

I let out a sigh. "I was hoping it wasn't as bad as I thought. I may need something to hide it if everyone's going to stare. Maybe I can carve a mask."

"Is that what ye want today, lass?"

I shook my head. "I need some aspen wood."

"Aspen's a wee bit soft for ye, isn't it?"

"It's not for me. It's for Raz. He's learning to carve. He needs a softer wood to carve on."

By the time I'd picked out a block of wood and paid for it and returned to the baker's shop, there was a larger crowd of people. I frowned in annoyance, then resigned myself to more stares and comments about the black eye.

The woman who'd commented in the store was standing next to a man I guessed was her husband. As I approached, she spotted me and grabbed her husband's arm, pointing at me with one, gloved finger. "There she is," she said anxiously, dark curls bouncing around her face. "Darling, *look* at her!"

The group of men turned and almost simultaneously frowned. "That's quite a bruise you have there, Lady Kaylyn," the husband stated, keeping his voice gentle, as if I were afraid of him. "Do you mind if I ask where you got it?"

"A staff," I replied, stopping outside since there were people standing in the doorway.

"When did it happen?"

"Yesterday."

"How did it happen?" asked another man with evident caution.

I frowned, confused. "I made a mistake," I replied, wondering how else I would have gotten a bruise from a staff.

For some odd reason, this made faces grow grimmer, darker, or more sympathetic.

"You poor dear," the woman from the bakery said. "How could you put up with it?"

"Put up with what?"

"You're covered in bruises and cuts, Lady Kaylyn," she said sadly. "Does your brother know about this?"

I was bewildered. "Of course he knows. He gets the same cuts and bruises."

The women shook their heads sorrowfully. "All this time, and no one knew," said one to another, and they nodded.

I had a feeling I was missing something. "I had a chance to defend myself," I interjected. "It was my fault."

"Dear girl, it was never your fault," said the woman from the bakery. She stepped forward, resting one gloved hand on mine, but so lightly I felt she were concerned about touching me. Her brown eyes were filled with pity I didn't think I'd earned. "You don't have to live like this. If we had known, we would have said something sooner."

"Known about what?" I finally asked.

"My sister, Doreen, she used to say she was just clumsy. And pardon me, but you don't seem clumsy."

"I'm not clumsy. What does Doreen have to do with this?"

Another woman latched on to me, her hands gentle on my arm. "It's all right, Lady Kaylyn. Cathleen helped her sister through the fight and divorce with her husband, and now she's doing just fine. The judge ordered that the man split the estate after her husband nearly killed Doreen. She'll tell you. You don't have to live with this. The bruises, the cuts, the black eye, it'll only get worse."

Cathleen nodded. "That man can't hurt you any longer," she said firmly. "We won't allow him to strike you again."

I gaped at her as it finally sank in. "You think Raz is *abusing* me? Raz would never hit me!"

"You said yourself he hit you with a staff yesterday," Cathleen reminded me. "We so rarely see you, and now you're covered head to toe in bruises with a black eye. I don't care if he is your uncle; you should not have to endure this and I won't stand for it a moment longer."

"Raz isn't abusing me! I was distracted, and I…"

"You see, darling," Cathleen said, ignoring me. "She's too frightened to admit to it. I want that man arrested."

"We'll send for the military right away," Cathleen's husband promised. "I'll go get the doctor."

"I don't need a doctor!"

"You're lucky you can see out of that eye at all," Cathleen said sternly as she pulled me up the steps, the other women around me giving me no choice but to follow.

My arguments were ignored while they all tried to convince me to admit I was being abused. The military stopped by, and two men headed to Vesta to fetch Raz. The military man left was too busy listening to the others give their reports and suspicions to talk to me.

Eileen moved by the table. "Can I get you anything, Kaylyn?"

"Can I get something for the headache?" My frustration and the cooing of the sympathetic women were making my head start to pound, which resonated in my sore nose and eye. Cathleen was insistent that even if I wouldn't admit to being abused by Raz, she would take care of me. She was planning on everything but adopting me, and I was certain it was because she was too busy vowing to bring Raz to his knees where he would beg my forgiveness.

I'd downed two helpings of the medicine by the time Raz showed up. He ignored the frigid glares from the women and stepped inside. "Kaylyn, are you all right?"

"I'm sorry, Raz," I sighed. "Apparently 'I made a mistake' means you're abusing me." I sent a glower to everyone else.

"Don't apologize to him, Kaylyn," Cathleen said, moving beside me to offer comfort. Her fierce look could have melted iron. "He should be apologizing to you."

"He hasn't *done* anything to me! I keep telling you, I'm *fine*! We were *practicing*!"

"Lady Kaylyn says you've been abusing her and her brother," Cathleen snapped.

I threw up my hands in despair. "Will you make her listen? I don't see how she'll believe you either, but she certainly won't believe me!"

Sergeant Sample bustled his way forward through the crowd of people in the bakery. "Raz Greenclaw, would you please explain how Lady Kaylyn received a black eye?" he asked sternly.

"Pretentious, egotistical narcissist," I muttered under my breath.

Raz didn't seem the least bit flustered by the glares or the accusations. "Kaylyn missed a block yesterday during practice and I didn't have time to correct the blow."

Cathleen set her jaw, dark eyes narrowing to slits amid the riotous curls. "Is that how you punish her? By making her fight you?"

"I wasn't being punished," I growled out for the umpteenth time.

Everyone ignored me. I felt like screaming.

"Kaylyn is being trained as an officer would at the School for Officers and Gentlemen. Under orders from Lieutenant Marcell, she is to be trained to the best of her abilities. You have copies of the orders, Sergeant," Raz reminded him patiently. "And you should be well aware of her abilities as she won the recruits' competition with all five weapons."

"She has bruises all over her," the miller's wife accused, the rest of the women nodding in agreement.

"How else am I supposed to learn to fight?" I snapped out, impatient. "That's how fighting works! You hit people, you get hit!"

"The doctor's here," Cathleen's husband announced.

"I don't need a doctor."

"It would be a good idea to let him look at that eye," Raz said.

"You said I was fine," I accused. "It's not my first black eye."

"You've been hit before?" Cathleen asked. "You poor dear. By your father?"

This had me on my feet. "Don't you *dare* accuse my father of harming me!" I shouted at her, nearly glowing with rage. "My father never laid a hand on me, and neither has Raz! Maybe Raz will put up with this, but I won't have you slandering my father's name!"

"Kaylyn." Raz's tone was simultaneously warning and gentle. "Cathleen meant nothing against your father. Please, sit down and let the doctor look at you."

I clenched my jaw for a moment, then I sat down. While Raz explained the training and why I was so bruised, I underwent the doctor's thorough examination. Finally, he nodded once. "She's fine." He sent me a soft smile and a secret wink. "Just as bruised up as any recruit I've ever seen. I'd say she's in good health and fine spirit."

I gave him a dubious glance. Anyone could tell I wasn't happy.

"I said fine spirit, not fine spirits," the doctor said, patting my hand twice before getting slowly to his feet, knees creaking.

"There's plenty of fire and gumption in you yet. Keep ice on that bruise and you'll be fine."

"Thanks," I muttered with the only manners left.

Cathleen had finally been appeased. "I am so sorry," she said sincerely. "I just didn't want to see someone else going through abuse."

"It's quite all right," Raz said graciously.

"All right?" I rose. "How can you say that?"

"Kaylyn," Raz said, giving me a level look.

I ignored it. "After this, you think this can all be smoothed over with an apology? Every single one of you turned on Raz! He's been in town to speak to you at least once a week for over a year, and within five *minutes* you're accusing him of abusing me! You gathered up a crowd to do everything but lynch him because of a black eye! Some friends you are!"

Cathleen looked humbled. "We were simply looking out for you, Lady Kaylyn. We were…hasty."

"Hasty? You were ignorant! You'd think that if you were so bent on protecting me you could have at least listened to me! I wasn't anything more than your spearhead. You were too busy saying 'poor girl, you look so awful'! You didn't even *doubt* that Raz was guilty, and he's done nothing to deserve that reputation." I was seething as they endured my tongue-lashing, shame-faced.

I stormed up to Sergeant Sample and got right in his face. "If you think for one minute that Nightfire would allow this, a dragon who feels every ounce of my pain, then you don't know anything about dragons. You had a duty to Raz, and he deserved more respect than you gave him." I sent a defiant stare to the entire room. "And just so we're clear, if I thought for one minute I was being abused, I'd leave, and not any dragon or human would stop me."

The room was silent as I pushed my way to the door.

Raz found me by the stream. I'd already changed back into pants and something that would cover the bruises. My face was buried in my knees to hide the bruised eye. Raz seated himself beside me and didn't say anything.

"I'm sorry." I whispered it. "I'm sorry for losing my temper and yelling at everyone. I tried to make them listen to me. They shouldn't have treated you like that."

"I was touched by your defense," he said, tossing stones in the water. "Honored."

I didn't answer.

Raz didn't push. He continued to toss stones in the water for several minutes. "Is Raphael coming soon?" he asked.

"I don't know why he'd bother."

"Why is that?"

"Poor Kaylyn, you look so *terrible*," I mimicked.

Raz paused a moment mid-throw, then flipped it in the stream. "The black eye isn't permanent. A week or so, it'll be gone."

"It doesn't matter. I'm not the kind of girl he wants anyway." I tugged the sleeves a little farther over my wrists.

"I don't believe that's true. He's seen how you fight. He sought you out anyway. I can't say I know Raphael, but I don't think he's going to be appalled by the black eye."

"Raz, I'm no good at courting. I can't even look pretty."

"It's a little early to decide courting is a bad idea." He tapped my arm gently and waited until I lifted my head enough to see him. "There's beauty I see in you that no black eye can hide."

That did make me feel better. "Thanks."

He returned my half-smile and offered a hand. "Shall we have some practice time today?"

I nodded and let him help pull me to my feet.

After practice and dinner, we sat down at the table downstairs. Raz worked on his new project and I worked on a circle just to see if I could. It was mindless work. I didn't have to focus like I did with more complex figurines. I was almost done with it anyway. It was becoming our new ritual.

"What did you tell everyone when I wasn't here for those five months?" I asked. "Apparently they thought something had happened."

"I said you'd gone away to visit and I didn't know when you were coming back."

"How did you know I was going to come back?"

"I didn't sometimes. Then I decided until I heard word of you or something from you, I'd wait."

I carefully shaved off an uneven patch in the wood. "Why weren't you mad when I came back?"

"Why do you keep bringing up your mistakes?" he returned with a hint of exasperation.

"Because I want to understand. Nobody else would have stayed two months, much less five. You stayed, and then you let me come back and start over. You had every right to toss me out."

Raz muttered under his breath as he chipped the corner of whatever he was working on and started to carefully smooth it out. "I didn't toss you out for several reasons. One being I'd promised to train you. The second reason being that it was as much my fault as anything."

I paused in what I was doing. "Your fault?" I was astonished he thought he was to blame.

"I watched you struggle, day after day, become frustrated with yourself to the point of tears more than once; yes, I saw them," he added as I tried to deal with the fact I hadn't been as sneaky as I'd thought. "And I didn't take steps to fix it. I allowed you to beat yourself up and thought it was just your way of learning. I didn't allow you to complain so you didn't think you could tell me how much you were struggling. It was my fault, and the day I realized and accepted that was the day I stopped being angry. I didn't like thinking that I'd run you off." He muttered under his breath again as he chipped another spot.

I slid another tool towards him. "I shouldn't have run off anyway."

"I shouldn't have given you the reason to," he countered. "I know you wouldn't have left if you hadn't thought you had to. You fight too hard to just give up." He picked up the new tool and went to work. "So we were both at fault."

I went back to my circle. "I thought you'd leave. Go find your apprentice."

"I have my life to find an apprentice. I don't have a deadline." He paused in his carving. "I wondered," he said quietly, "if I'd pushed you too hard. I know you thought I was immune while you stood on the cliff, but I wasn't. I was trying to help, but maybe I went too far. And when you left, I wasn't sure if it was because you were angry, or scared." His blue eyes were strangely vulnerable.

I fiddled with my knife. "A little bit of both. Mostly shame. I was getting nowhere. I thought you deserved better." I shrugged, a little embarrassed. "Someone who wasn't shoved into the middle of something she didn't want. It wasn't the cliff, not entirely." I turned my wooden piece in my hand, searching for flaws. "Is that why we haven't done any emotional training?"

"If that was what made you run last time, why would I repeat it?" Raz inquired. "It wasn't your choice last time, but it's your choice this time. If you don't want to, we'll find another way to help you deal with battling fear."

"No. I'll try. Everything else is easier. Maybe this will be too." I set the ball on the table and let it roll, spinning it in place to test for bumps. "I'd hate to know what you replaced it with."

"Something less traumatizing." Raz caught the ball as it spun towards him, running his fingers over it.

"Where's the fun in that?" I inquired.

He grinned, and tossed the ball to me. "You're showing me up. My ball didn't look that good after sanding."

"The day I beat you at *anything* is the day you can complain about my years of woodcarving."

"It's not a lack of skill. Your skill is fine, and improving daily. I'm still winning because you haven't figured out the mental game that goes with it yet. You're seeing moves one at a time, and occasionally two ahead. You're very good at reacting, but you need to start planning. I know what moves you prefer, and what moves you're weakest on, and combinations you like to use. That's what allows me to beat you."

"How nice of you to mention that *now*."

"You're starting to get it. I wanted to see if you could understand on your own what made you lose and what made you win. You understood it well enough that you beat Raphael. You knew the move he hadn't been prepared for, and you used it." His eyes twinkled. "The difference between Raphael and me is that Raphael wasn't good enough to learn from his mistake, and it takes a few more calculated steps to beat me."

"A few hundred?"

He just grinned and shook his head. "If you're feeling brave, we'll try the cliff tomorrow." He set his carving on the table and put his tools into the pouch.

Nightfire landed outside with a downdraft of air that brushed over us inside. He trundled in, a tiny creature shivering in his jaws.

"What are you doing?" I asked, pushing aside my revulsion. "You aren't going to eat that *now*, are you?"

Nightfire opened his jaws and let the thing fall gently to the ground. "What is it?" he asked us.

"It's a rabbit. Haven't you seen them before?"

"Not many." He eyed it. The little black rabbit was too terrified to move. I wondered if rabbits fainted. "What does a rabbit do?"

"They eat gardens and they jump really high."

"Is that useful?"

"No. Rabbits are pretty much like mice, except rabbits tend to stay outside."

Nightfire eyed the rabbit again. "Then why do humans try to keep these as pets if humans are terrified of mice?"

"Rabbits aren't scary. They're just pests. Look, are you going to eat it or not?"

"No. I am full." He gently picked the rabbit up by the back of the neck and carried it outside, depositing it at the door before trundling to his room for the night.

Raz and I watched as the rabbit stirred, the nose twitching, looked around, then shot off into the darkness. "That was...bizarre," I said at last.

"Dragons are intelligent creatures and seem to like knowledge."

"I thought he knew what a rabbit was. How can somebody understand tactics but not know what a rabbit is?" I asked.

"Rabbits were never used in battle," Nightfire answered from his room.

Raz laughed at that. "I'd imagine that's true. Blow out the candles before you turn in. Good night to you both."

Raz's quiet chuckles as I closed the door and blew out the candles reached my ears as I headed up the stairs to my room. Blowing out the candle, I decided my next carving would be of a rabbit. My father had carved pieces that had been inspired by a conversation. Sometimes he would just look at a particular carving and laugh at the memory it brought back. This moment in time, feeling at home, was a memory I wanted to hold.

Chapter 24

I started work the next morning before breakfast, trying to get my mind off of what was coming. I wanted to be able to face this challenge and not fall apart like I always had. If I kept falling apart, it meant that I didn't trust Raz. I didn't want to think that. Raz smiled when I told him what I was carving but simply said he'd meet me outside for practice.

I ate very little for lunch, conscious of Raz's attention.

"If you don't want to," he began.

"I said I'd do it." But I played with my spoon restlessly. With the autumn season bringing the cooler weather during the days and getting progressively colder during the night, we had oatmeal or other warm foods for breakfast to combat the morning chill.

"No one will think less of you if you change your mind."

"I will."

"You don't have to be so hard on yourself. This is asking a lot from you."

I thought of what Embereyes had said and felt myself blush faintly. "According to Embereyes, this wouldn't be a problem except I apparently don't trust anyone very much."

"I don't find it so much a lack of trust as I do a lack of control," Raz said placidly.

"That is the whole point of this," I muttered.

He shook his head. "I don't mean control over your emotions; I mean your biggest challenge is your lack of control over anything. Where you stand, how long you stand there, how far you're able to move, it's all dependent on what I allow. That's why this has been so hard for you."

I was startled into looking up at him.

"Kaylyn, you've spent your life fighting for some control of your life. You picked friends others didn't approve of. Your hair is this length because you want it to be, not for anyone else's wishes. You fought your mother and sisters about what's expected of you. You're aware that you have the capabilities to do a lot, but society's conventions won't allow you to do that, and it drives you crazy. Putting you on the edge of the cliff, you were suddenly powerless and it terrified you. Heights weren't your problem. Climbing down Vesta and flying on Nightfire never bothered you, but that cliff did. The difference was that one allowed you a choice, and the other didn't allow you any choice or control."

"You could have *mentioned* that was the problem!"

"It took me time to figure it out. I had no idea why you could be calm so easily in one situation, but then completely lose control in a similar situation. By the time I had it figured out, you'd already been gone a month." He carried his dishes over to the sink. "Take an hour, do what you want. I'll call you when it's time."

I picked up my block of wood and worked very hard on the rabbit's ears. I knew exactly how I wanted it to look, what angle the ears were at, the direction they were twisted, but forming two separate ears took careful control. When Raz's call came, I headed down the stairs quickly, hearing Nightfire take flight overhead.

Nothing was said on the way up the hill, or while Raz tied the rope around him. While he was busy doing that, I stepped cautiously towards the edge of the cliff. I was still a decent distance from the edge when I felt the first tinge of nerves that came near the edge of any cliff. With Nightfire, I'd always had to do a running jump so my courage wouldn't fail me and so Nightfire could more easily catch me. This required me to stand still and hope I didn't need to be caught.

When I was less than twelve good steps from the edge, I came to a stop. This, I discovered, was the point I could safely stand, where anxiety was manageable.

Raz moved behind me. "Ready?" he asked, hands hovering around my waist.

"Ready."

Raz guided me eleven steps forward, then stopped. I felt my entire back tensing up. Half of my brain was ordering me back, the other half was insisting I stay and do what I was supposed to. I forced myself to take a deep breath and relax my shoulders as much as possible.

"Good." Raz's voice was quiet. "Now that you're capable of thinking up here, I want you to figure out what about this is causing fear. Knowledge is your greatest weapon. What you think, or can convince yourself to think, can free you from being consumed with fear. When you stand up here, I want you to feel as in control as you do when you're holding onto something that gives you some power. Convince yourself that you're in control and be able to think without fear controlling you."

I stood there for half an hour, thinking. When Raz finally pulled me back, I wasn't shaking, crying, or angry. Nightfire's eyes were a satisfied yellow. Raz was smiling. "Am I still unreasonable and setting unreachable expectations for you?"

I shook my head. "No. I don't know why it was so much easier."

"Knowledge is power. The more you know and understand, the more weapons you have. You found *why* this exercise bothered you, and you can now fight it." He coiled the rope and left it at the base of the tree. "It's the same as fighting blindfolded. You don't know what you're fighting and you're almost certain to lose. Having one eye free allows you some information. Having both eyes wide open gives you the best chance of winning."

Nightfire rubbed his muzzle against my cheek a moment, then took off. I could sense his hunger and his intentions to sate his growling stomach.

"Let's see what you know about wildlife," Raz decided.

"That's a squirrel," I identified as it scrambled up a tree.

Raz flashed a quick grin. "What is it climbing?"

"Ash tree."

"Good. What about the tree next to it?"

The cliff exercise was replaced into the weekly schedule. Along with the cliff, I was given time to see Raphael. My black eye was down to a bluish-green ring when he showed up. He promised he had the universal cure and kissed it better, much to my slight embarrassment and secret delight.

I spent one evening a week with Raphael. The following morning usually found me tired because I had things to finish once Raphael left, but I was happier. He made me feel special. He was interested in hearing about anything I had to say, especially concerning Nightfire. A few times he brought a weapon and we sparred, but we stopped after teasingly saying he couldn't ever beat me. I wanted to practice more with him, but at the dark look in his eye, I quickly agreed we had better things to do and never mentioned it again. Since Raz had mentioned the mental part of fighting, I'd been working on it. Raz was harder to understand and predict than Raphael.

Without play-fighting, we had plenty more time to do other things as Raphael taught me how to go about our unorthodox courtship. He was willing to ignore my mistakes, and I made lots of them. How I spoke, what I wore, what we did, he was always there to correct my missteps. Despite the fact it almost seemed like a lesson rather than courtship, I always looked forward to him coming.

Once, Raphael showed up in the morning. One imploring look was all it took before Raz waved me off. "Go on. I have my own project to work on," he said. "But be back by lunch."

Since Raphael never came inside, I didn't guess it would be a problem.

We didn't do much exploring that day. We moved just out of sight, towards the river, and then Raphael drew me to him and started kissing me. We didn't stop for a long time. We talked, him about his estate and running it during the winter months, and he listened patiently and attentively as I talked about Nightfire; he was always curious about dragons. When our time was up, he leaned into me and started a last, long kiss, then walked with me to the edge of the tree line where we split, him going towards the path, and me heading to Vesta.

Raz took one look at me, then pointed to the chair across from him. He wasn't working on a project, which worried me. "Am I in trouble?" I asked, the remainder of my bliss evaporating quickly.

"You aren't in trouble."

I wasn't appeased. "You aren't mad because Raphael showed up, are you? I didn't know he was coming today, and he only comes once a week. I'm still working hard," I pleaded.

He cut me off when I would have continued, holding up a hand. "Kaylyn, we need to talk is all."

I bit my lip and nervously took my seat.

His face was calm. "Did your parents ever give you the talk about love?"

I was confused. "What do you mean?"

"About courting, Kaylyn, and what's acceptable, and what isn't."

"What's..." It hit me and I blushed clear to my toes. "Raz!"

"Kaylyn, this is something you need to know. If your mother or father never gave you this talk..."

"We had it," I blurted out. "Dad talked with Warren when he turned eleven and started talking to me after that. Mother sat me and my sisters down when we turned eleven and told us how babies were made. I know what's acceptable, and what isn't for courting." I hoped with that covered, Raz would drop it. The entire conversation was awkward and uncomfortable.

Raz wouldn't let it go. "And what did they say?"

"Raz!" I nearly wailed it. "Can we *please* not talk about it?"

"This is to prevent problems later, Kaylyn. I want to know you understand."

I closed my eyes and groaned, hiding my red face in my hands. "I promise, I understand! Why does it matter *now*?"

"Because you're courting someone now, and these walks in the woods are concerning me. I want to make sure you know what's too far."

"Raphael is a gentleman," I snapped out, my eyes opening quickly to glare at him.

Raz was unaffected. "Raphael is a boy who has a hard time thinking clearly around a female. He might very well get carried away."

"He's nineteen. *You* aren't that much older," I accused.

"I have discipline over what I do and how I do it. Raphael doesn't have that discipline, and that worries me. You clearly didn't do much walking today or you walked into a selective windstorm."

I flushed again and tried to smooth my hair out, which Raphael's hands had explored in some of the more heated moments.

"Do you realize the consequences if Raphael forgets to be a gentleman and you go too far?" Raz pressed.

"I could get pregnant, it'll shame my name, the reputation of my honor and my family's honor, and society will think I'm a tramp. Raz, *please* stop. I'll swear on anything you want that I know where the lines are. I'll talk with Mother again." I was all but begging for this conversation to end and never reoccur.

He sighed. "I just want you to be careful, Kaylyn. I won't say anything more as long as I'm sure you know when to stop. Sometimes the lines get blurred in the middle of all the feelings you're discovering."

"Got it." I got up quickly. "I'm not hungry. I'll skip lunch. I'm going to practice archery." I nearly bolted out the door and let out a breath in relief. "I'd give just about anything to never have that conversation again," I muttered as I headed over to the targets.

That night I wrote a letter to my sisters and mentioned a man wanted to court me. Knowing my sisters, they'd tell Mother. Sure enough, a letter from my mother arrived two days later, containing three pages that reiterated the lecture I'd gotten at eleven about courting and marriage. I handed the letter to Raz the next evening when Raphael showed up. "I've had the talk about love and courting," I stated. "Again. Can I go now?"

"Go."

Raphael had to leave earlier than usual and apologized multiple times with clear regret. "I have business I have to attend to.

I promise, it's nothing that holds more interest than you. I'd much rather be here, but some things can't wait."

"I understand," I assured him.

"I found this for you." He pulled out a wooden square, with my name carved in simple letters. It wasn't particularly well done, but it was spelled correctly. "You mentioned you liked woodcarving, so I thought you'd like this."

I was touched. "I do," I said earnestly. "I like it a lot."

"More than me?" he teased.

"Never," I replied instantly.

He gifted me with a warm smile. "I'm glad to hear it. I was worried for a second."

"You've given me plenty of gifts, and I've never liked any of them more than you. And I've liked all of them." I'd tried to give him a gift back once, but he'd stated that wasn't how courtship was done. Women were supposed to be given treasure to show how much they were treasured. Men were rewarded with affection. I thought it bizarre but I'd tucked the gift away, trying to ignore the sting that had lingered for several weeks.

Raphael moved closer, kissing me. "I wish this made up for tonight."

"You came earlier, so this means I get to see you more than I usually do," I reasoned.

He flashed a grin at me. "I'm still going to be thinking of you all tonight. I don't suppose you'd want to come with me?"

I shook my head regretfully. "I can't."

"If it's your reputation you're concerned about..." He dragged me flat to him, a wicked grin in his brown eyes. "We could go ahead and get married and solve that problem."

I was shocked a moment, then I gave a nervous giggle. "Wouldn't that throw all of society into a tizzy? We haven't even courted for half a year, and they want fourteen months from the proposal." Part of me was worried that he wasn't joking. My mother's letter for some reason flashed into my mind, and the warnings it had contained.

"I should think society would be the last of your concerns."

"What about Raz? Nightfire? Nightfire isn't ready for me to marry."

Raphael raised an eyebrow. "I never considered I'd ever be asking a dragon's permission to marry his Dragonrider," he teased. "I'll have to think over how to propose it then."

I felt as if I'd swallowed my tongue. "You mean...you're really going to ask him?"

"I think I love you, Kaylyn. And I can wait the entire fourteen months if you prefer, but I don't need the fourteen months. I have enough money to support us, I already love you, and if I can get Nightfire's and Raz's approval, don't you think that would be enough? I want to have you to come home to. I want to be able to truly show you what I'd be willing to do for you, and what I would give you." He brushed a lock of hair out of my face. "You're growing more beautiful by the day. Once your hair grows a little longer, it'll be the perfect length for how I envision you in a wedding dress and saying you love me." He paused here. "You do love me, don't you, Kaylyn?" he asked.

"Of course," I stammered quickly. "I mean...I think I do. I'm at least as sure as you are."

He smiled, warming my heart. "Then think it over. When I see you again, you'll have to tell me what all I have to do before I marry you. All right?"

I nodded.

He kissed me once more, then, with all the grace and control of an Eagle fighter, he spun me around and dipped me low to the ground, his hands around my waist, eyes sparkling at my shriek of surprise. As he pulled me upright, we both started laughing.

"Just so you look as if you've been walking long distances. I wouldn't want Raz to think I was up to anything dishonorable." He kissed me once more. "I really need to run, Kaylyn. Think of me, all right?"

"Of course," I replied, and waved as he hurried down the hill and off to his destination.

My mind was crowded with thoughts when I reached Vesta. Raz was carving on his wood block. I retrieved the rabbit, but my movements were slow as I worked.

"Heavy thoughts tonight?" Raz asked, eyes on his carving.

I looked for anything to put off telling him about Raphael's proposal. "What if Raphael was your apprentice?" I asked suddenly.

"It's possible." Raz said nothing more than that.

Curious, I put the carving down. "That sounded…like you were saying no."

"It has to fit. Something about him doesn't fit. I can't say what, but there's something about him I don't like." He held up his hand to prevent the angry protest. "It's nothing against you, Kaylyn. I know you like him. But something about him makes me think he isn't the kind of person who would make a good Eagle."

I didn't say anything, but I fumed.

"I see Raphael left early tonight."

"He had to work."

"He wouldn't have had to leave so early if you'd stayed here."

"He likes to walk."

"There's no need to get defensive, Kaylyn. I'm simply stating he doesn't have to avoid coming inside. Or avoid me."

"He isn't avoiding you. He wants to spend time with me. He loves me."

Raz didn't even pause in his strokes of the knife. "Has he said so?"

"Yes. Today."

Raz looked at me, blue eyes grave. "Do you love him?"

I bit my lip, struggling with an answer. "I don't know," I said at last. "I should love him, shouldn't I?"

"Not necessarily."

"But I don't even know if I know. Shouldn't I know if I love him?" I felt awful.

"Right now, you have plenty of time to find out," Raz said. "You have fourteen months at least after he proposes, and I trust he won't propose until he's sure of your love and his."

"Plenty of people don't marry with any kind of love."

"You wouldn't marry a man unless you loved him, Kaylyn, of that I'm sure. You have very few people to answer to in terms of marriage, and your brother knows better than to try and set a match for you. No one can ever force you to marry, not with a dragon."

I thought of Raphael. Maybe I'd ask him to wait a few months. Until I was sure. He said he'd do whatever I needed. Once I was sure, I'd have him ask Nightfire and my brother. And I'd introduce him to Raz. Raz would see. Raphael had been the only person to ever make me consider marriage seriously. That had to be something like love.

"I do not like him." Nightfire's eyes were bright green, and I could feel the jealousy in waves.

"You never like anyone at first."

"I will not like him."

"Why not?"

"Because he has secrets. Because he has greed."

"You haven't even met him," I protested silently.

Nightfire flicked his tail. *"You are my Dragonrider. He must have my approval first. I do not like that he has not come to me."*

"He doesn't think you're inferior or anything."

"Then why has he not spoken to me?" Nightfire demanded.

I shook my head. *"You sound like a grumpy father. Nightfire, I wouldn't disappear on you. I wouldn't do anything without you. I'll make him talk to you. You'll see."*

Nightfire wasn't buying it. *"He would have taken you today and left. If he had honor, he would not have done so."*

"How do you know what he did today?" I accused, my arms folded as I glared at him.

Nightfire didn't sound the least bit repentant. *"I watched him. I heard him. He did not act like a good human. He acted like a thief trying to trick another into thinking someone else stole what he has taken."*

"Nightfire!" I was furious and offended. Raz looked up briefly, then back at his work.

Nightfire's eyes showed his determination. *"He will not take you from me."*

I held my sigh. *"Nightfire, I'm not going anywhere without you. You're part of me. I can't leave you behind any more than I can leave my leg behind. Would you just please give him a chance? He loves me."* I felt like squirming. *"And nobody's ever loved me like that before. Not...not like someone they'd want to marry. He picked me, Nightfire, out of everyone else he could have picked. Nobody's ever picked me for anything, except you. And Raz."*

Nightfire relented at that, pressing his muzzle to my cheek in comfort. *"His emotions are not what they should be,"* he said. *"I do not want him to hurt you."*

"Can you just give him a chance? If he comes to you and we have a long engagement, will that be enough?"

"No," Nightfire replied. *"But it will not matter until he behaves as he should."*

"He will," I promised. *"I know he will."*

Although the conversations with Raz and Raphael left me somewhat uneasy, I managed to push it away and focus on my training. When Raz called me outside for some emotional training, I looked around, searching for Nightfire in my mind. To my consternation, Nightfire wasn't in range.

"Kaylyn?" Raz asked.

I hung back, hesitated. "Nightfire's not back yet."

Raz just grinned. "Is that what your security blanket is?"

"You said to find something that gave me control."

"You'll be fine."

"We already trained every weapon today. Why aren't we putting this off? It's almost dinnertime."

"You're making excuses."

"I am not." I started up the hill anyway. "I'm simply asking why we're doing so much today."

"Because I want to do everything today."

I blew out a sigh. "I hate the 'I said so' reason."

"Today, that's your reason."

Nightfire appeared halfway through the training, but he perched himself on top of Vesta and ignored me.

"Hey!" I protested, calling to him.

"You do not need me."

"What if I fall?"

"Raz will not let you." And he started preparing for a nap.

"Dragons," I muttered.

"What?" Raz inquired.

"He's taking a nap!"

"Obviously he thinks you're fine."

I glanced down at the sheer face of the cliff and the steep drop. "Right."

The reason for all the work became apparent the next morning when it occurred to me it was my birthday. I had almost forgotten. The letter Raz brought back from my mother and sisters and the gift from my brother told me they hadn't forgotten. Warren had found a woodcarving tool I'd seen once or twice and was interested in using.

Found this tool and remembered Dad never had it. The man at the woodshop was certain I was teasing when I said this was for you. For my birthday, I want to see one of these carvings. Oh, and your sisters got bracelets. I know you'd prefer something else, something more personal. Happy fifteenth birthday, sis. And tell Nightfire happy birthday in a few days. Do dragons celebrate birthdays?

Love you,

Warren

"I see your family remembered your birthday as well," Raz stated.

"I almost didn't," I admitted. "I guess you did yesterday?"

"I did. Today you may do whatever you want. And I also have this." Raz handed me a little box. "Just a little something for your birthday," he said.

Curious, I lifted the lid to the box to find a black stone attached to a gold chain and a gold, six-pointed star in the middle of the stone.

"It's called a black star sapphire," Raz explained. "The way the stone is formed, it creates the star. I thought it would suit you."

I stared at him, stunned. "But...but why?" I asked, falling back to my nervous stammer.

"Because you're a beautiful woman who deserves beautiful things." He said it simply, as a fact, while Raphael always said it with a touch of teasing or seduction. "Fifteen marks the year when most women are presented to society. You may not necessarily want that, but just in case, you have this."

I held the stone tightly in my hand. "Thank you," I said softly.

His blue eyes were soft with affection. "You're welcome. Enjoy your day."

I did enjoy my day. I wandered to town and back, used my new woodcarving tool, discovered that dragons did not celebrate birthdays but that Nightfire wouldn't object to something, and wrote letters back to my sisters, mother, and brother. The only disappointment was that I heard nothing for Raphael, but I couldn't remember if I'd told him when my birthday was or not.

The next day, Nightfire warned me during lunch that someone was coming. Raz went down to greet whoever it was, and when he called up the stairs, I could glimpse her stabling a horse loaded with packs. The horse's light brown coat was just a few shades darker than her skin. "Who's this?" I asked, sending a cautious smile and wave to the girl. She sent me a friendly smile back and nodded, speaking soothingly to her horse as she unstrapped what I recognized as a sword.

"This is Carmella." Pride was evident in Raz's voice. "This is my Eagle apprentice."

I was momentarily speechless. Then, because Raz was watching me carefully, I managed to find something to say. "When did you find her?"

"When you were in the mountains. I promised to train her."

"Does she know?" I touched the pendant, prepared to hide it.

"Yes, she knows. She's here because she was sent here. Some approval has to be met before we get to tell our protégés what they're becoming."

"You could have said," I said with a bit of reproach.

"Yes, I could have. Should I have?"

"It might have been nice."

He nodded once in acknowledgement. "Are you all right with Carmella joining us?"

"Of course," I said indignantly to hide how unsure I really was. "She's your protégé after all, and it's not like we don't have the room." I approached the few steps and bowed since I wasn't wearing a skirt. "I'm Kaylyn Madara," I greeted. "That's Nightfire." I pointed up to where Nightfire sat, glaring suspiciously down at Carmella.

"Carmella Kennit," she introduced. She bowed back, her long, dark hair spilling over her shoulders. "It's a pleasure to meet you. Raz has told me all about you."

"Really? He told me nothing about you."

"Well, he didn't know for sure when the Eagles were sending me to him. I came with the letter, or you would have had some sort of warning of a new house guest." Her dark brown eyes sparkled wickedly. "I hear you decimated the School's recruits at their last competition."

"I guess I did. Have you been here before, then?"

"Earlier, when you were gone visiting your relatives. I was passing through town and Raz pointed me towards the blacksmith. My horse needed new horseshoes and then I stayed in town for a couple weeks once I figured out he taught fighting."

"So you're going to be an Eagle?"

"Once I prove I can fight well enough and that I didn't trick them all into thinking I was trustworthy and honorable and everything else." She slung a pack over her shoulders.

"Here." I grabbed another one for her.

"Thanks. Which room is mine?"

"Probably the one with the bed."

She grinned. "Raz said I'd like you. I do."

I liked her too and I grinned back. "It's been a long time since I found another female who wasn't stuffy and didn't spend an hour in front of her mirror every morning."

"Not if the prince of Anglarius were coming to court me," Carmella said instantly.

I couldn't help but laugh, figuring I'd found a new friend.

Chapter 25

A letter from Raphael arrived the day after he usually showed up. It contained an apology, but he had to leave the country for at least a month and wouldn't be in touch with me. He sent a bracelet with little gemstones as an apology gift and even called me his future wife, telling me again that he loved me. I wasn't sure I was happy to have that included. The bracelet went on the mantle. It held more use as decoration than it did as jewelry. Despite my disdain for sparkling stones that were protected and only occasionally worn, somehow Raz's gift meant something more to me. I kept it in the box beside my father's carving, carefully preserving it from the dust that was created as Carmella moved in.

Carmella fit right into Vesta, and Nightfire had quickly warmed up to her. Carmella hadn't seemed overly fazed by meeting a dragon, and the fact that she didn't quote Doctor McDragon on anything put her a step ahead of most people in my mind. She didn't shirk from work and slid herself into the rhythm of our home without undue difficulty.

While the daily routine took a little time to adjust, for all four of us, practices took very little adjustment. I was actually glad to have her. Carmella joined us for morning practices, then Raz would set one of us to practice alone while working with the other, then switching. Occasionally he had us fight each other; and while she had the sword skill, I had the quicker reflexes that put me ahead. Once she started training with Raz though, she picked up more quickly on his instructions concerning swordfighting and I started losing more often. She made practicing fun and entertaining, and whether we were practicing or not, she made me laugh. She was a good friend.

After the first month, Raz took me aside and quietly asked if it was all right that he work more with Carmella. "She could use more individual attention to her training," he explained. "She's used to practicing alone, but what she needs is more things to practice, and people to practice against."

"It's fine," I promised him. "I understand." Carmella had told me that after a nasty fight with her father she'd left her home to pursue her dream of being a warrior. Even if the military wouldn't take her, she had a passion for swordfighting and a skill that nobody could deny. She'd been living on her own for about two years and had discovered six months in that her father had disowned her and she wasn't allowed to return home again. "I can practice alone."

"If you need more time with me, just say so," Raz said, blue eyes piercing. "I'm just as responsible for you as I am for her."

"I will." I brushed off his concern, making shooing motions. "I don't mind practicing alone anymore."

He gave a half-smile. "What's the one mistake you need to fix on staffwork?"

I rolled my eyes. "The best defense is not always a good offense. It takes more effort to attack than to defend." I had a tendency to attack hard, and to keep attacking. I knew the defense blocks; I simply preferred to adjust the attacks to counter his.

"Stay on staff for the rest of the day. Work through the exercises I taught you." Then he headed over to Carmella.

At first I didn't mind the time, but I gradually became more and more jealous as spring wore on and the days got warmer. Raz would no longer spend half his time with me, and he always talked about Carmella. I could only stand it for so long.

As he started off on how well Carmella had done today, she was walking the horses around, I got up, carried my plate to our makeshift sink downstairs, and headed to my room. I was busy swallowing snide comments.

Raz's quiet laugh followed. "You aren't subtle enough to hide your anger, Kaylyn, or you aren't mature enough to want to."

"I'm tired of being called a child," I said, my tone clipped.

"I didn't say you were a child. You've matured. The first week we met, if you were angry you would have yelled at me and stomped out of the room. You simply aren't good enough to hide that you're sulking about something."

My tone was downright petulant as I muttered, "I am not sulking." I flicked my towel over my shoulder and slunk into the bathroom.

My mood wasn't helped by Raphael's letter. After over three months, he wrote to say he was back at his home, but he wouldn't be able to visit for at least another two months.

Things have gone bad here, and with the harvesting months approaching I have to do everything I can to prepare for it. I want to be able to spend my first months as your husband with you instead of desperately trying to fix things that could have been fixed before. Just wait a little longer, my future wife, and I promise I'll be ready. I love you.

I wrote back that I understood and, after much hesitation, wrote that I loved him too. I put my indecision down to the fact that I hadn't seen him or spoken to him since before my birthday. I didn't care any less for him, so that had to mean I loved him. Maybe once I saw him again, I'd feel more secure.

Another month and a half passed and the heat swamped us day and night. The insects chirped and zipped through the air. Raphael's letter continued to nag at me. I didn't feel comfortable marrying so soon. I had technically known Raphael for far less than a year and we hadn't courted very long. I couldn't imagine living the rest of my life with Raphael when I barely knew him. Drawing up my courage, I wrote a letter asking to observe the standard fourteen months of engagement. An anxious three weeks later, Raphael wrote back a missive, as it was far too short to be considered a letter, stating he understood. I tried to compose a reply, but the curtness of the missive made it hard to find something to write, so I gave up and decided I'd see if the next letter was a little more loving and understanding than this one.

Raz continued to devote more of his time to Carmella. Pride wouldn't allow me to ask for anything more than he gave me.

One day I realized it had been three weeks since I had stood on the cliff. While I should have felt happy about that, it wasn't my favorite part of training by any means, I instead felt hurt. It seemed as if he'd forgotten, as if he were replacing me. He hadn't said we were stopping, we had just stopped.

I stopped talking as much, struggling to push down my feelings. As they discussed tactics or weapons, or anything else in the evenings, I silently worked on my woodcarvings, one after another. Raz had finished his and hadn't started another, busy working with Carmella. Any questions I might have had about what to do about Raphael and love and marriage I no longer felt I should ask. Carmella knew about Raphael, she'd told me about a few of her suitors over the years since she was eighteen, but I had never been good at sharing private feelings and I didn't want her to think badly of me for not loving Raphael when he so obviously loved me.

Raz started noticing that I was withdrawn and worked to include me more in conversations, spending more time in practice with me. It didn't help. Carmella wasn't trying to deliberately intrude, but she had a few questions for Raz that took his attention from me. I realized I was starting to resent her for it, for being an Eagle, for being here at all, and felt ashamed of myself.

"Swordfighting today?" Raz asked me during lunch.

I shook my head. "No. I need the afternoon off. You can work with Carmella."

"Any word from Raphael yet?" Carmella asked. "Is he coming?"

I shook my head again. "He says not yet, but maybe in two or three weeks he can come."

"I guess you'll be glad to see him. It's been...what? Six months?"

I nodded. I was afraid he might propose when he came. His anger had apparently passed because he'd sent instructions on what I should do for the wedding when I started planning were locked away. A knot of cold fear lodged itself in my stomach every time I thought about it. Then I felt miserable that I could be so unsure.

310

Raz moved the conversation along. "I'll see if I can find the ropes today, and then we'll work on the next exercise. They should be here."

"They're at the cliff."

Raz paused a moment. "They are," he said. "I'd forgotten."

I wondered if that meant he'd forgotten the ropes were at the cliff, or if he'd forgotten that he'd trained with me up there. I stood and carried my plate to the sink. "I'll bring the rope back today."

"See you tonight!" Carmella called. "I'm making dinner!"

I forced a smile. "Maybe I'll eat with Nightfire then."

She laughed. Raz didn't.

I wandered restlessly across the grounds around Vesta, making my way eventually to the cliff. I untied the rope, wound it up, then carried it down to Vesta. Carmella and Raz were training, laughing as they sparred together. I dumped the rope just inside the door then left again, swallowing sudden, unexplainable tears.

Instead of the stream, Raz found me at the cliff, leaning against a tree and overlooking the now-familiar view of the ground below. The dry grass crunched under Raz's boots. The smell of water was in the air, storm clouds starting to roll in for a much needed rain. I didn't change position as Raz moved to sit beside me.

"The last time I saw this look on your face was right before you ran off to the mountains for five months," he said quietly. "I don't want to go through that again."

"I'm not going to run off and disappear."

"You aren't happy either." When I didn't offer an explanation, he said, "Kaylyn, if you won't tell me what's on your mind, at least give me some way to make this less miserable for you."

I didn't say anything. I hated feeling replaceable. I hated it more knowing Raz didn't see it that way. He had his duty as an Eagle to train another Eagle. Fading to the background wasn't an easy thing for me to live with. I'd found a place that made me feel unique and good at something, and now Carmella had the attention I craved.

311

"Kaylyn."

"It's nothing, all right? It's nothing that matters."

"You matter."

For a moment, I was afraid he'd figured it out. Then he said, "Is there anything I can do to make whatever it is better?"

The only thing that was possible would have shamed me to ask. He'd never halfway teach his protégé, and he'd never pretend he wasn't proud of Carmella and her skill. I felt utterly self-centered and egotistical. I didn't want him to know how ashamed I was for wishing Carmella gone. Carmella hadn't had a wonderful life with people loving her and offering her whatever she wanted; she'd struggled and been abandoned, just like me, and she deserved this feeling of acceptance that I'd found. It was becoming more and more apparent, however, that I couldn't share it.

"Kaylyn." He shifted, trying to see my troubled gaze. "Is there anything…?"

"No." I closed my eyes and rested my forehead on my knees. "There isn't."

He rested his hand over one of mine. "I'm sorry, then, that I can't help. If you need anything, let me know. I'll do what I can."

That hurt, because he meant it. "You'd do nothing less," I said too softly for him to hear as he headed down the hill.

Raz tried to make things better. For nearly three weeks, he spent time working with me and even picked up woodworking again. Carmella stated she was hopeless with what I was doing and she knew it. I tried not to be petty, but I couldn't help the internal gloating that I had found something she could never do.

"I'm headed into town tomorrow," Raz said as he carefully chipped out a bad part of the wood. "Does anyone need anything?"

"Nightfire could use some oil. The last barrel is halfway empty," I said.

Raz nodded. "I'll be gone a while. Why don't you two practice against each other? Staffs."

"I'm going to beat you this time," Carmella said, brown eyes sparkling with her challenge.

"You said that last time," I shot back. "If it isn't sharp, you don't know what to do with it."

"My weapon's better anyway."

"There's a reason swordfighting is called sport of nobles; because it's a weapon for those with money. Those without money deal with rods or weapons like them. That means you're in trouble if you ever face anyone who isn't a noble."

"Sword beats staff every time," she said cheerfully.

"So much for honor," I said, giving a fake, disapproving sniff.

"There's honor, and then there's stupidity."

"Carmella, keep your staff high and that will solve half your problems," Raz said. "Kaylyn, how do I reach…"

I was already sliding a tool over to him.

"Ah, thank you."

"What are you making anyway?" I asked.

"I haven't decided yet. We'll see if inspiration strikes by the time I'm done with this. Take it easy on my apprentice tomorrow."

"If I have to."

He smiled at me. "Not that she needs it, but you have to."

The next morning, Carmella and I decided it wasn't too hot outside, despite that the wind wasn't blowing and it wasn't cloudy at all, and started practice. Nightfire caught a deer early and decided to take a nap. Thankfully he was far enough away, across the field in an especially sunny patch behind some trees, that I wasn't too sleepy through the emotional link.

Carmella tended to lean into her strikes, trying to meet my strength enough that it threw her off balance. I was trying to figure out how to make her quit leaning so far forward when a pain wrenched my side; a sharp, slicing pain. I gasped, instinctively cupping my hand over my side as the staff dropped to the ground. Through the emotional link, I felt Nightfire's surprise, his pain, and then his utter fury in rapid succession. His roar of pain and challenge echoed over the ground.

"Kaylyn?" Carmella asked, confused and worried.

"Nightfire," I whispered. Then I turned and ran. *"Nightfire!"* I screamed. Every instinct was screaming protect. My side burned, but it was faint, just a reminder there was an injury; it didn't jar me like any injury I carried would as I ran. There was a second roar of earth-shattering fury that rang across the rocky ground and echoed in my mind as rage rolled though me.

I ran faster than I'd ever run before. *"Fly! Fly!"* I screamed through the mental link to him because I needed all my air to run. The fact Nightfire could fly was the only advantage I was sure of right now.

I saw Nightfire take flight in the distance, and the lone person standing where Nightfire had been. The person lunged after Nightfire, sword flashing, and fell short, cursing under his black head covering. My scream of rage rang to the man, and he turned as I approached. He had a moment to strike with the blade in his hand before I reached him, but his reaction wasn't near as good as mine.

I slammed the man to the ground, hitting him with everything I had. With a snarl, he leapt right back up, but his swing was a blind move. I was too angry to think about the fact I didn't hold a weapon, or that I somehow knew what move to expect from him, and moved in. I caught his wrist, and used every bit of my strength to push his arm down, and then I slammed my palm up, into his chin. He staggered back, shaking his head, and I ripped the knife from his belt. Bringing the blade by my ear, I watched his eyes widen, watched the surprise light his eyes as he tried to put distance between us, backing away. And then I slung the blade as hard as I could and watched it sink into him with deadly precision.

He jerked back, which even in my fury shocked me. Targets had never flinched. They never made a pained whimper either. Targets didn't crumple slowly to the ground while blood spilled around the knife, around his hands clutching the area, as if he could push the blood back inside. There was a sound I couldn't identify, as if he were trying to speak, but he couldn't make it out before his body slumped, the eyes remaining open.

I found I wasn't quite breathing and moved forward. I hoped if I saw his face, I would somehow assure myself this man had wished me harm. Or it would somehow not be a person. Ripping away the cloth over his face, I reeled backwards, staring in horror at Raphael. I blinked once, then twice, something like a scream echoing distantly in my head as I stared into the unseeing eyes of the man I'd courted. I now realized why his movements had seemed so familiar. I sank to my knees over him. The rage gone, I was becoming aware of what I'd just done.

Carmella finally reached me, panting from the run. "Good throw!" she said, grinning as if I'd just performed a trick. "That was excellent fighting! No wonder Raz says you're so good!"

I stared up at her, not comprehending. "What did I do?" I whispered, guilt consuming me.

"You killed him. That's exactly what you meant to do. Wasn't it?" she asked.

I closed my eyes. I had. The drive to kill had been there, but it wasn't just that that frightened me. Killing this man hadn't been an accident; it had been a decision. I'd made the choice. I covered my face and bent over. "Yes," I moaned. "I meant to kill him. What have I done?" I started to weep. "What have I done?"

Carmella was confused. "Haven't you killed before?"

I didn't answer. I couldn't answer. I pushed myself up, stumbling once, then started to run. I ran as fast as I could, pushing myself faster and farther away from that place and the consequences of my actions.

Nightfire circled overhead. I clutched my side with Nightfire's pain. With a sudden downdraft he landed and I staggered to him, weeping. "What have I done, Nightfire? What did I do back there? And you're hurt! And...and..." I didn't know what to do first, what to feel first. I didn't have anything to tend Nightfire with and I was so shaken by what had happened I couldn't think straight. I blindly ripped off my jacket and moved instinctively to his side, pressing my jacket over the injury.

Nightfire tried to calm me, but I couldn't control this morass of emotions. It didn't help that his pain kept throbbing in my side and his anger and sense of betrayal were strong. Betrayal was one of many emotions, but panic was first. I stayed where I was kneeling beside Nightfire, holding my jacket to stop the blood from spilling out, and whispering the same sentence over and over. "Don't die. Don't die. Please don't die."

"Kaylyn." Raz rested a hand on my shoulder and I jerked, a full-body ripple of fear and protection. Nightfire let out a soft growl.

"Easy," Raz said softly, to both of us. "Easy now. It's all right. Kaylyn, he isn't going to die." He eased down beside me, taking in the reaction I was experiencing. "I have medicine right here. We can fix him. You'll both be all right."

My body trembled uncontrollably. "Did you see him? Did you see what I did? He did this. He did this and I...I..."

"One step at a time, Kaylyn. Breathe. I'm going to fix Nightfire." He rested his hands over mine. They were white, clenched tightly to the blood-drenched cloth. Very gently, he eased my fingers loose from the fabric. "Go calm Nightfire. Make sure he doesn't bite me. I'll take care of him."

It wasn't so much that I calmed Nightfire as it was that he calmed me. I wrapped my arms tightly around his neck, shuddering and sobbing while Raz tended to Nightfire's side. I felt the occasional twinge of pain in my own side, and Nightfire let out a shudder once on a particularly strong one, but it was, for the most part, painless. Nightfire hummed a crooning sound that helped, pressing his nose to my side in a bid to seek comfort and give comfort. I worked my way down from sobs to sniffles.

"Kaylyn, what medicine can I give Nightfire?" Raz asked, voice calm.

I didn't answer right away, struggling to think.

"Kaylyn." Raz's voice was slightly sharper, commanding an answer.

"I'm thinking! I think...Echinacea. It's safe for him. And...the numbing gel. You can't use the...the pink powder, and the nasty, grey drink makes him sleepy." My voice wasn't steady. I stared at my hands, the black streaks of blood from Nightfire's injury. I remembered the sword coated with Nightfire's blood, and knew the knife I'd sunk in Raphael's chest would look the same. I could even remember the sound, and the reaction of the vivid memory brought such a strong wave of nausea that I twisted away and heaved. It didn't bring any relief to my tortured mind and body.

Raz came around Nightfire and uncorked a vial under my nose. The strong scent jerked me back and would have brought tears to my eyes if they hadn't already been filled with tears. "Breathe." His voice was filled with quiet compassion. "It will help."

I breathed the scent in twice more, then started to cough. Raz corked the vial. "Nightfire is fine," he promised. "Nothing vital was hit as far as I can tell. It was a deep cut, but Nightfire's going to heal. And so will you." Very gently, he took one hand and wiped it off, then the other. I felt a little steadier by the time he finished, enough so that I managed to stagger to my feet.

Raz looked at Nightfire a moment. "It would be better if you stayed here for a little while, gave that time to heal. I'll find something for the pain."

Nightfire nodded, settled his head on the grass, but kept his eyes on me, the strongest color brown for worry.

I swallowed hard. "Am I in trouble?"

"No. No one is going to blame you for this. But we'll have to talk to the military. They'll need to see it."

"No! No, I can't go back! I won't!" I started weeping again, shaking, wishing I could fold in on myself and disappear. "I can't see him like that. Not like that. Please, Raz."

Raz stripped out of his jacket and slid it around my shoulders. "Go back to Vesta," he said quietly. "Clean up. Carmella and I will take care of it." He pulled me to him, let me shiver into his chest. "You're all right," he murmured. "I know you don't feel like it, but you're all right."

"I'm a monster."

"No, you're just scared. Everything seems frightening and out of control. It's going to be all right, Kaylyn."

Tears burned my throat. "I hate him."

"I know."

I stumbled back towards Vesta alone. Instead of washing off, I dumped cold water in a bucket over me, looking for a way to feel connected to the world again. Dripping, shivering, I stripped out of the wet clothes as soon as I was in my room and curled up in dry clothes in bed, staring at nothing for a long time until I pulled the covers over my head and pretended I was a dragon in an egg, safe from the world full of betrayal.

Carmella came back with Nightfire not long before the sun set. Carmella looked a little nervous now. "Raz says you need to take it easy on Nightfire for a few days."

My voice sounded rough. "Where is he?"

"He's going with Sergeant Sample to deal with Ra-"

"Don't say his name!" I screamed at her. "I don't want to hear it again!"

She quickly changed the rest of her sentence. "We found letters to him. He wasn't in it alone. Dillon Marcell has been contacted. Raz went with the military to find the accomplice and sent a message that he'll be back by tomorrow. He said…he said he was bringing something you needed to see."

Nightfire nuzzled me tiredly, his eyes grey with pain. My side throbbed from his injury.

"I'll get some medicine," I whispered, my arms linked around his muzzle. "The nasty grey drink, or something else?"

"Sleep will be enough. We will both need sleep tonight. I am sorry for the pain he caused you."

"I'm sorry too." I slowly released him, half-turned to Carmella. "Do you know why? Why he did it?"

Carmella shook her head. "Raz knows. He just told me to stay with you and Nightfire."

I nodded and headed to the pantry for ingredients. I made some of the nasty grey-colored drink, watched Nightfire drink it, then curled up against his neck for the night. He slid into sleep and I let his drowsiness pull me down with him into dreamless oblivion.

Chapter 26

I knew the next morning that I'd overslept. Nightfire said Raz had already returned. He and Carmella had gone to take care of some things and there was something for me on the table downstairs. I staggered out of Nightfire's room to the stairs, hoping that I'd feel better once I woke up completely. Mostly I felt tired.

I forced down a few bites of food, but that was all I could manage. Nightfire headed outside to find his own food, but that cut in his side wasn't going to allow him any strenuous hunting, so he was heading to the river. I scrubbed listlessly at my dishes, struggling to stop thinking and not having much success. When I decided they were clean, I dried my hands and headed down the stairs to find what it was Raz wanted me to see.

I found a letter on the table and opened it curiously. There were three sheets of paper folded together. What I saw inside sickened me.

I've managed to romance her enough to find out what we need, the letter said in Raphael's handwriting. *The dragon takes a nap every day, and I know the time. I've studied Doctor McDragon's books very carefully, and I know how to dispatch the beast quickly. Kaylyn will die as well, which will provide enough of a distraction to take what we need. Let the buyers know to expect the forthcoming riches within the week. If we're very careful, we can sell the dragon's body after it's dead, or acquire some of the internal organs. The government will do almost anything for a profit and will care very little about a girl, military or not.*

My hands shook as I pulled out the next letter, in a different handwriting.

Are you certain the girl won't pose a problem? I don't want to give my buyers false beliefs. They're very good for our business.

Don't blow this, Raphael. They believe we're protecting the nation. Black dragons are notoriously short-tempered and liable to go out of control in a moment. Why else would it be kept in the middle of nowhere?

Raphael's response was the third and final letter. I could almost hear his voice reading it, the boast in his tone. *The girl isn't a problem. She's like any other woman; eager to please and entertained by cheap trinkets. This one doesn't know the difference between worthless sparkles and treasure. I have her completely under control. She'll do anything I ask if I provide the right kind of...encouragement. Send word to your buyers that soon this menace will be under control, and they'll have their trinkets to prove it. I'll join you after I finish grieving over her grave.*

I couldn't breathe, struck hard by the callousness and carelessness in these letters. My heart felt as if it were being torn in half. Raphael, and whoever this other person was, had been plotting to kill me. Had always been plotting to kill me. I hadn't realized his questions about Nightfire had been anything more than normal curiosity about dragons. Seeing how worthless I'd been to Raphael, I let out a soft gasp of pain, hands clapped over my mouth as I dropped the last letter to the table.

I lurched to my room, feeling as if I were going to be physically sick. From the doorway, my eyes were drawn immediately to the trinkets lined up on the carved shelf. The gifts from Raphael that I thought had been unique and personal were carefully arranged so I could see them all. Anger rose for a moment, scorching the tears that were attempting to build. I snatched the baubles up, carried them up to the Queen's Room, the room I'd spent all my time daydreaming in, and slung everything hard on the floor. The bracelet shattered into pieces, the gemstones glittering brightly as they slid across the floor in different directions. The wooden carving of my name cracked in half but still remained intact as it laid on the limestone. Everything else rolled every which way across the room. I stared at them all, the fragments and scattered pieces very similar to my heart, then I whirled around and slammed the door shut, locking it before I burst into tears.

Raz and Carmella didn't return until the sun had almost disappeared completely. Nightfire had crept inside hours ago to console me as I raged and sobbed. The injury in his side only made it worse, because Raphael had come that close to killing Nightfire. I was the fool that had never seen what he really was, despite the warnings. It was a slight comfort to know that one of the only real friends I had would make sure the letters never appeared again.

I sat on the bed, my feet resting on the cooling floor, and stared at the lines in the wood. I followed their pattern with my eyes, never taking my eyes from the floor as footsteps came up the stairs. They moved quietly, with pity in every movement. "Dinner?" Raz ask, his voice soft with the same pity.

"No."

He didn't press. "I'm sorry, Kaylyn."

I closed my eyes and didn't respond, staying silent until his footsteps traveled down the stairs again.

My dreams were fragmented that night, vivid even though I couldn't remember many of the details. I didn't feel rested, and I felt, if anything, more miserable. I wasn't sure if Raphael's death or betrayal hurt more, but I was suffering for both. Memories returned to taunt me and nothing I did made them go away.

Nightfire tried to get me to come out, and I refused. I didn't want to go anywhere or deal with him or other people. I wanted to be left alone until I could forget. The rising sun didn't chase the nightmares away, because my nightmare had already happened in broad daylight.

"Kaylyn!" Raz called. "Kaylyn!"

"She is in her room," Nightfire said, making sure I could hear him. "And she will not come out."

I heard Raz move lightly up the stairs, then around to where I was. I refused to look up, keeping my eyes tightly closed as I wrapped my arms a little tighter around my knees.

Raz moved to sit by me. "I'm guessing we aren't training today," he said quietly.

I shook my head and didn't look up.

"I contacted the military outpost," Raz said. "They investigated and cleared you. You aren't going to get in trouble for what happened. There's no family to want revenge. You did what you had to do. It's going to get better, Kaylyn, I promise."

"You knew. Didn't you?"

He sighed quietly. "I guessed. I didn't want to hurt you by saying anything. I thought if he was like I suspected, then you'd realize it."

"He was using me. The whole time. I never figured it out. I'm so *stupid*!"

"No, you aren't."

"I am too." Old, familiar tears of hurt and shame spilled down my cheeks again, following familiar paths. "He knew what would happen. I told him that if Nightfire died, I would too. He would have killed Nightfire anyway. He said he loved me and that he wanted to marry me. But he never cared. And everyone knew it but me."

Raz put one arm around me and drew me against his side, rubbing my back silently.

"I'm never going to marry." I choked it out. "I don't ever want to court again."

"They aren't all like he was. There are men like your father out there. Men like Warren. Dillon."

"I don't care," I wept. "I hate them all. I hate marriage. I hate courting. And I hate *him*."

"I know." He continued to rub my back.

I cried for a while. The world seemed an exhausting place, but Raz made it bearable, helping me to breathe without feeling like I would cry again. Nightfire also sent soothing emotions to ease the storm thundering inside me. Raz didn't try to use words to heal me. No assurances I would be okay, no promises it would be better, and his silence was healing. The longer he sat there, the more I felt a piece of the pain was leaving that wouldn't return.

Eventually he moved, just a little, testing if I was ready to leave his hold. "I'll have dinner brought to you. If you need me to stay…"

I shook my head, forced myself to sit up and not cling to him more. "I'm just tired. Carmella's your apprentice."

"Carmella isn't the only person I have a duty to. Carmella doesn't need me as much right now."

I sat up straight, pride forcing me not to beg him to stay longer. "I just need to do something. I'll probably clean a little."

He let his hand fall. "All right. If you need me, all you have to do is say so."

I nodded and listened as his feet crossed my floor, the walkway, down the stairs, and the opening and closing of the door.

"Clean," Nightfire said skeptically.

"Clean," I replied.

I found cleaning somehow therapeutic. Once I started, I couldn't stop. Nightfire, sensing I wasn't going to sit and wallow in self-pity any longer today, left to hunt. When he came inside with Raz and Carmella, the sun was nearly setting. I'd cleaned the kitchen from floor to ceiling, and every remotely dirty dish or utensil we owned had been washed. The pantry had been emptied, cleaned, and organized. Every walkway had been scrubbed and every window washed, except the Queen's room. I couldn't make myself go in that room. I left dinner made for Raz and Carmella and disappeared into the bathroom, knowing they'd assume I'd eaten.

I bathed for half an hour, soaking in the water, then I climbed out. My hair was still wet when I seated myself in front of a mirror with a pair of scissors. My black hair was a decent length now, almost acceptable. Raphael had liked my hair long, had requested that I let it grow out. I split my hair painstakingly down the middle, brushed it a few times to get it straight, parted my hair so half rested in front of each shoulder, then I picked up the scissors and cut it off so it brushed my shoulders, first the left side, then the right. I did a little more cutting, evening a few things, then I opened up the window, gathered all the strands of hair, and let them fall outside the window. I felt a kind of release as the black locks disappeared in the dark. I was my own person, looking how I chose to look. It freed me just a little.

Despite being exhausted from little sleep and hard work, I continued to stay awake. Finally, well into the night, I got up and made my way up the stairs with a lit candle in hand. I pulled the book I wanted from the shelf, but dropped it loudly on the floor. It took that much more effort to bend down and pick it up. Next, I took the vial of powder that would knock me out and settled at the table. If my mind wouldn't allow me to sleep, I was determined to go around it. I flipped through the book, searching for the right series of ingredients that would send me into dreamless unconsciousness.

"What are you looking for?" Raz's voice asked quietly from the door as he came in. He picked up the vial, studied it a moment, then carried it over and replaced it in the cabinet. "This isn't the right way."

"I just need something to sleep. I can't sleep. And I don't want to see *him* when I do."

Raz gently closed the book. "I don't want you dependent on potions to get you through this."

I let him draw the book from my hands and stared at the shadows cast by the candle flame. "I'm sorry I woke you."

"It's all right." Raz returned to the table with a block of wood and a knife, his callused palms pressing the familiar items into my empty hands. "If you need to settle, this is how you settle down. Not with medicines or you'll be tempted to take them every time you struggle. You have to fight through it until one day it no longer hurts and it isn't so hard."

I stared at the block of wood for a very long time as if I didn't know how to carve. "I don't know what to make," I whispered, wanting to cry. I'd never had a lack of inspiration. It was as if Raphael would take everything from me.

"Carve a flower. You like primroses."

I had to close my eyes to see it, to bring up a picture. Slowly, I gripped the wood, turning it, searching for flaws that would have to be dealt with, then I made the first cut. Nothing was said as I started to work, already imagining the delicate petals, knowing I would have to go get one to be sure I knew the leaves, the length of the stem, the smell. I understood wood. Last time, carving had given me a few moments of peace that I'd needed while it helped me grieve for my father. This time it gave me an escape as my mind worked over cuts, grips, strokes, shavings, planning how this would become a flower that could be as close to reality as possible.

I didn't hear Raz leave, but I felt him come back when he draped a blanket over my shoulders. I realized I hadn't made a cut in a while, that my hands had stilled and my eyes had closed and not reopened. I started awake as Raz gently took the knife and wood block from my hands. "Sleep here tonight," he murmured. "Your body may not thank you in the morning, but you need rest."

I groaned something as I rested my head on my arms, my eyes closing and my mind already falling into blank peace.

I awoke in the morning to Carmella moving quietly about the room. "Sorry," she apologized, brown eyes showing obvious regret at taking a few more moments of forgetfulness. "Raz said not to disturb you."

"S' okay," I managed, rubbing my face. "Time?"

"Almost eight. You all right?"

"Sort of." I pulled the blanket to my lap and started to slowly fold it. "Training?"

"Raz and I are about to start. Join us if you want," she offered, wanting to help.

I shook my head. "Cleaning."

I could see Carmella didn't understand. But fighting had always been a part of her, and it hadn't been a part of me. Fighting wasn't an escape for me. "Have fun then. I guess."

I spent my morning in the stables with the horses. I cleaned the stables, walked both horses to the stream, plucking several primroses that still survived as a reference to my carving, planning on drying them for preservation. When I got back, I did more cleaning in the stables before going inside.

Raz found me after lunch as I was finding things to stack on top of the pages with the flowers. "You can't have much more to clean."

"No, but I can find something to do."

"I think you should spend a little time on this today." He withdrew the sword from the sheath and offered it with both hands.

I looked at the blade silently, then looked away. "No."

Raz raised his eyebrows. "No?"

"No. I won't fight. Not anymore."

He sighed. "Kaylyn."

"I can't be this person." I stared at the floor, my voice tight. "I never wanted to be this person. I never wanted to kill. And I won't kill again. I won't fight again."

"Fighting doesn't mean killing."

"Then what's the point?" I shouted at him. "You're teaching me to *win*! And after I win, I'm going to let them back up so they can try again? You're training me to be a *warrior*, and I'm *not* a warrior! I never *wanted* this!"

Raz sheathed the sword and set it on the table. "I know you didn't," he said quietly. "But before…"

I tensed, ready to scream at the sound of Raphael's name.

"Before what happened," he continued, "you had a different idea of being a warrior. Why has it changed?"

"Because I was a stupid, little girl who thought killing would be *simple*! You never told me they *haunt* you forever! You never mentioned *any* of what I'm going through!"

"You had the right to do what you did. You killed to defend. If you remember that, it'll make it easier."

"*Easier*? Do you think having the *right* to kill *matters*? It makes absolutely *no* difference! I hate myself for *living*!" I broke into tears.

"Kaylyn." Raz attempted to make contact.

I shoved him back. "Don't *touch* me!"

Raz wasn't deterred. Perhaps having gone through this before, he understood what I wanted more than I did. I was a raw, emotional mess, and ashamed of the tears as much for shedding them as I was for being alive to be able to shed them. Guilt I didn't think I'd have to deal with was slowly tearing me apart, and the fact I'd cared for Raphael didn't help any.

Raz gathered me into him, holding tightly until I ceased struggling to get free. I wept, but there were fewer tears. I wondered if there would ever be a day when I'd be able to stop crying.

"You'll be all right," Raz promised against my hair. "You'll make it through. He won't haunt you forever. Being a warrior is never easy. But I wish for you it wasn't this hard."

I clung to the hope it would get easier as Raz pressed a kiss to my temple, murmuring it would be all right.

It didn't get easier. It didn't help that Raz had to train with Carmella either. It wore on me more and more, no matter how hard I tried to fight it, that I couldn't have Raz's attention as much as I wanted. I refused to ask or interrupt their practices and so I spent my time watching them fight. Raz had the same patient but brutal style with Carmella. I stayed inside, wishing I was out there and knowing there wasn't anything that could get a weapon in my hand. Dreams at night and memories during the day were enough to keep me from joining them. I had to force myself to touch a staff, a quiver of arrows and a bow, reminding myself I hadn't killed with this and I didn't have to. Swords were as much a fear to me as they had been the first time Raz had offered me one. Knives were only for eating or carving.

Nightfire knew things were falling apart. Vesta didn't feel comfortable now, and the way things stood, it wasn't going to change. He didn't argue it. *"It is time to go,"* he stated one day as I finished oiling him and checking the injury. His side was healing well.

"Not if you don't think so," I thought back. *"If you want to stay, if you aren't healed enough…"*

"It is time. We are not happy here. You are not happy here." He nuzzled me, spreading oil across my face.

"I'm a terrible person. I should be happy here. I shouldn't be jealous. I shouldn't be like this, but I can't get better."

"You are doing the right thing for Raz, for Carmella. Staying is not best for any of us. Going will be best for us. There will be no memories of him elsewhere. Perhaps with no memories, there will not be so many dreams or thoughts you do not want."

Nightfire's distress for me was evident. He wanted me to be happy again, to be able to forget what had happened, and he knew it wouldn't be forgotten here.

I sighed. *"I hate running out on Raz again."*———

"We are not. Tell him we are leaving. He will understand."

I nodded. *"When do we leave?"*

"Tomorrow. There is no reason to stay."

I let out a slow breath. *"Okay. I'll tell him. Anywhere you want to go?"*

"I do not care. I will go where you need to go."

"Home," I said aloud, picturing my family's little estate. "I need to see home." I got to my feet. "I'll tell Raz and Carmella."

The two of them were inside, cleaning their swords and sharpening blades at the table after practice. I stood at the entrance. "I'm leaving," I said, watching them turn their gazes to me. "Tomorrow."

Carmella wanted to protest, but Raz knew better. "Where?"

"Home. At least for a while. I don't know. I'll see how things go."

A murmur from Raz had Carmella getting up and leaving, the whetstone and her sword in hand.

"Why are you doing this?" he asked quietly when Carmella had gone. "You had the right to kill him."

"No, Raz, I had the right to defend Nightfire. I had the right to defend myself. If I'd taken a step back, forced him to talk, I could have stopped him. I could have given him a chance. I didn't. I didn't *want* to."

"Mastering anger is like mastering fear or any other emotion. You don't always succeed, but step by step it's easier to control."

"It wasn't anger; it was bloodlust. I've heard the stories about men in battle, about how wild and crazy they become, killing without mercy or thought. I won't go down that road."

He sighed quietly. "Why do you have to leave to stop yourself?"

"Because you know as well as I do that I can't pick up a weapon and use it anymore. You have an apprentice who needs training, and I'm only getting in the way."

"You aren't the same. You don't learn the same. You don't need the same things."

"I know." I stared sadly at the fire, unable to meet his gaze knowing what I was doing to him. "And I can't find what I need here."

"This is more than him, isn't it?" It was less of a question and more of a statement. "That's just what's going to give you your reason for leaving. Whatever's been making you miserable, you've finally decided you can't stay." He sounded sad. "Will you be coming back?"

"I...yes," I said at last. "Someday. I don't know when. At least you won't be alone this time."

"It's going to be a little lonely here with you gone. We'll miss you and Nightfire. Kaylyn?" His voice called me, asking that I look at him.

I moved my gaze from the fire to his blue eyes that held regret and sadness.

"If you ever need me, all you have to do is ask. If you'll just let me know where you are, I'd appreciate it. Unless I get word, I'll be right here."

That made me feel a little better. "I know. Thank you."

He rose and approached, pressing his lips to my forehead a moment. "You'll feel better, I promise. Can I see you off tomorrow morning?"

I nodded.

"Then I'll see you in the morning."

For the first time, it didn't matter that I couldn't sleep. I spent the night cleaning and packing until I fell asleep leaning over two different bags. I woke up before the sun and finished storing the last few items. Before I headed downstairs, I went upstairs and left the finished primrose on the table, then hauled everything down to the stables. Raz came outside as I was loading the last of the bags into the carriage. "Going home as a lady, I see," he said lightly.

"My mother would have a fit if she saw me riding in a way that was actually comfortable. I figured bringing Nightfire was pushing it anyway." I was in one of the longest skirts I owned. The brown fabric brushed my shoes.

"Will your sisters be excited?"

"Madelyn might. Lisa won't. Not unless her noble suitor's managed to get her to be less of an uptight snob. Which is highly unlikely, but I can hope."

He smiled a little. "All packed?"

"I think so." I scuffed my foot on the ground. "I feel like I'm running out on you again."

"You aren't. You need time to think and settle what's happened."

I still felt bad. I stared unhappily at the ground until Raz took my hand and held it palm up, placing his horse carving in my hand. "If you have room for this, I'd like you to keep it."

"But it was your first," I protested. "And it's a *good* first."

"I have an excellent teacher. I can make another." He closed my hand over it. "From student to teacher."

I swallowed hard, suddenly feeling as if I were about to cry. Raphael had said I couldn't tell trash from treasure, and I knew what this was worth, emotionally. "If you make me cry again, I'm going to be mad at you."

"Making the transition to become like your sisters already, I see," he teased. "Next thing you know, I find you stopping by the tailor's shop on your way back to visit for some gloves and a pink, silk gown."

I winced at the picture.

He laughed, then went over to adjust the reins on the horse. I carefully tucked the carving in my pack with my father's tools and the other carvings, watching as Raz spoke silently to Nightfire. Whatever he said, Nightfire nodded once, then playfully butted Raz's shoulder. Raz smiled and good-humoredly shoved his muzzle away, then came back over to me, his eyes gentling. "Take care, Kaylyn. Write every so often so I can hear from you, all right?"

I nodded. "I will." Then I threw my arms around him.

He hugged me close, holding tightly for a long moment before letting his arms relax. "Safe travels."

Nightfire let out a trilling cry and jumped in the air. I waved once I climbed into the carriage, then set the horse in motion. We had almost reached the cliffs that would hide Vesta from sight when Carmella leaned out a window, letting out a piercing whistle to catch my attention and waved. "Success and safety!" she called to me.

I waved back, drinking in one last sight of Vesta before it disappeared from view. Then I sat down again, faced front, and pushed the horse faster while Nightfire soared overhead.

Chapter 27

We reached my mother's house before sundown, but not by long. The lone manservant came out to assist with the horses. "Welcome home, Lady Kaylyn," he said sincerely.

"Are my sisters and mother here?" I asked.

"Nettie's fetching them now."

"Kaylyn!" Madelyn raced to me, eyes alight, her black hair left loose, dressed in a soft cream dress printed with a dark green design. She hugged me tightly. "I'm glad to see you!"

I couldn't help but grin. Madelyn was the sister I preferred. She had a touch of an independent streak, and she hadn't tattled on me like Lisa had. "I thought you would be taller."

She made a face. Madelyn had always wanted to be a tall, elegant beauty. "Well, I didn't grow. Lisa and I are the same height with maybe half an eye difference."

"How is Lisa?"

"She's engaged, so, you know, worse than she usually is."

"Engaged already?"

"Lord Oliver Lewis Devillier started courting her not a month after we became true nobles."

"I thought he died."

"No, that was his father, the second. This one's the third. He proposed four months ago. He's due any minute to visit."

"Does Warren know?"

"Of course Warren knows."

"Kaylyn!" My mother swept out of the house. Her gaze slid over me, a slight frown marring her brow for a moment before she leaned down and brushed a kiss on my forehead. "Welcome back." Her black hair brushed my cheek, smelling faintly of jasmine. My mother wore a dress in a rich, red color, one that spoke of elegance.

"Thank you, Mother," I replied.

She touched my hair gently, the frown back. "I see you've cut your hair."

"Of course she did." Lisa swept out of the house. Her black hair was swept into an elegant bun. Unlike Madelyn, she was dressed in what I guessed to be her best dress, something silken in purple, and even wore new jewelry. I assumed they were from her betrothed. "She could never look like us. She always had to be different."

"Since your noble status is thanks to my being different, I'll assume that was supposed to be a compliment," I said sweetly.

"Speaking of your dragon, where is it?" Lisa asked, looking around, as if Nightfire were hiding behind the house or the wagon.

I instinctively bristled. "Nightfire is not an *it*."

"He did come, didn't he?" Madelyn asked, looking both excited and nervous. "I've never seen a dragon before, you know."

"Of course he came. He's waiting to make sure you won't faint when he lands."

"He won't muss my dress, will he?" Lisa asked.

"Not unless you're afraid of a little wind."

"Wind?"

Nightfire suddenly landed in the open yard. Madelyn let out a muffled shriek of surprise. Lisa clutched at her hair with a distressed wail. Mother, to my admiration, refused to so much as flinch. As the two servants rushed outside to gape, she strode across the grass to Nightfire and curtseyed. "Welcome to our home, Nightfire." She folded her hands primly. "I trust you won't be ruining our property or eating our animals."

"Or eating us," Lisa muttered under her breath as she continued to smooth out her hair.

"Humans taste terrible," Nightfire stated. "And I prefer to hunt than to eat lazy animals that wander around, overfed and stupid."

My mother seemed satisfied. "I don't know if we have a place for you to stay in. There's an old barn, it's no longer used, but it might be big enough to suit you. It's in the west field."

"I will find a place to stay." Nightfire rose and padded past my mother. Madelyn just watched, mouth open wide.

"Madelyn, dear, close your mouth before you swallow a fly!" my mother ordered her as she headed inside. "Lisa, stop fussing with your hair."

"Amazing, isn't he?" I asked, pride in my voice.

"Yes," Madelyn said in a hushed voice. "He's beautiful. Nothing like wyverns at all!"

"He has wings and a tail, and wyverns have those," Lisa said, annoyance clear.

"Your suitor's arriving," I said. "I don't think he's going to want to marry you if he finds you acting like a shrew."

Lisa instantly pasted a smile on her face and rushed inside. "Mother! Mother! Lord Lewis is coming!"

"She still calls him by his title?" I asked Madelyn.

Madelyn shrugged. "He hasn't insisted otherwise."

"I bet he's a snobby, self-centered noble."

"We're noble too, you know," Madelyn pointed out.

"I refuse to be a noble. Not with the way they all act."

"They don't all act like that. I haven't gotten the chance to tell you about my fiancé."

"You're engaged too?"

"Not for very long. Only a few weeks. He's very sweet."

"Well, I guess I'm happy for you then." I glanced down at myself. I was rather dusty. "I should change before Lisa's fiancé gets here."

"Probably, or she'll be embarrassed all night. Unless Nightfire needs you?"

My silent query was quickly returned. "No, he says he's fine. He's going to fly around a little before the sun sets."

"Warren said you can speak to dragons with your mind. Is it hard?" Lisa breathed.

"No, you just think, and he hears it."

"He hears everything I think?"

"You learn how to figure out what he hears." I shook out my skirt and watched a cloud of dust sift to the ground. "Tell Lisa

I'll look proper when I show up," I said as Lord Lewis's carriage pulled into the entrance of the path to our house.

It took only fifteen minutes before I was excusing myself politely and settling myself in the sitting room. It had been my father's workshop, but after Father died it had been converted to a parlor. I glanced at the mantle where my father's carvings had always been. It now held candles. I carefully smoothed out my fresh, clean skirt and folded my now-clean hands properly.

Lisa's suitor had stood as I entered, as manners dictated. "You must be Lady Kaylyn." He flashed a smile which, with golden hair and blue eyes, was likely very charming.

After Raphael, I was immune to charm. "I am. You must be Lord Devillier."

"Lord Lewis," he corrected with a genteel smile.

I flashed a sidelong glance to Madelyn as I took my seat by her.

"I hear you have a dragon, Lady Kaylyn," Lord Lewis inquired.

"It's more like a dragon has me, Lord Lewis." If he was going to play the title game, I was going to see if I could use more titles than he could. He'd used two, I'd used two. "We're partners."

"Rather like a marriage?"

"More like…we're part of each other."

"Soulmates then," Madelyn offered.

I shook my head. "Not in the way you're thinking. It's not about love; it's about being like one instead of two sometimes."

That seemed like too much of a strain for Lord Lewis to contemplate. His brow furrowed a moment, then he moved on. "I should think it interesting, living with a dragon, Lady Kaylyn."

"Oh, it is, Lord Lewis. Always." I gave a genuine smile at that.

"How long until you go your separate ways? Surely, Lady Kaylyn, he'll have to part ways sometime."

"Oh, no, Lord Lewis. Nightfire and I are staying together forever. There would be no reason he wouldn't stay with me."

He raised an eyebrow. "A husband and family might be a reason, Lady Kaylyn."

"Doesn't your suitor mind having a dragon around?" Lisa asked me.

"I don't have a suitor." My tone was completely cool and calm, despite what the statement did to my heart.

My mother's disappointment was obvious. "My poor dear. What happened?"

"He tried to kill Nightfire, then me. He's dead now."

That brought conversation to an utter halt. Awkward silence filled the room. I simply smiled at Lord Lewis who seemed taken aback at my news. "So you see, Lord Lewis, a husband and family aren't likely to happen any day soon. Right now, I have decided that until I find a man I can truly trust, I will wait. For years if need be."

Madelyn took my hand in comfort, her sadness for me plain and sincere. "I'm sorry, Kaylyn. I hadn't heard. I'm sure my fiancé could introduce you to better men. Or even Lord Lewis. They know many nobles of high society."

"That's true," Lord Lewis acknowledged. "There's Lord Pennington, for instance. A decent fellow. Then of course there's the McBride family, Lord Dain's eldest son, or his middle son, and even the youngest son of Lord Blackworthy would be a good husband. If you're looking for an officer, I do know quite a few."

"Thank you, Lord Lewis, but I already know most of the men at the School for Officers and Gentlemen. Nightfire and I stayed there for two months after Nightfire hatched. Lieutenant Marcell and Captain Durai weren't able to let me take classes while I was there, but I had plenty of time to be introduced to other recruits, like Lord Kipper, and Lord Leolin, and the Lennox family." That was three titles and a family name for him, five titles and one family name for me.

Lisa shot me a dark look for controlling the conversation. Either that or she suspected my private, little game. "I'm sure during the next formal event we can introduce you," she said. "Lord Lewis, have you heard anything from Harriet?"

I fell quiet and listened with half an ear to the rest of the conversation. Lord Lewis didn't stay long once the sun set and gave his farewells. Lisa turned on me when his carriage was gone, anger marring her pretty features. "Why did you have to embarrass me?" she demanded.

"How did I embarrass you?" I wondered aloud, genuinely perplexed.

"He was *trying* to help so you don't end up a spinster and you spurned him!"

"Would you have preferred that I stated that all men are liars and that I have no inclination to ever marry, or even court?" I couldn't help the touch of amusement. The announcement that I *wanted* to remain a spinster wouldn't have gone well at all. Men seemed to take offense at the notion that a woman could be happy without having a husband and bearing their children.

"Just because you can't make a man want to marry you…"

"Oh, no, Lisa, he wanted to marry me." My voice was cold, all amusement gone. "Or so he said. He promised me love and marriage. He promised me I was everything to him and that all he wanted was to come home to me at night. And then he tried to kill me for money. I never thought my life would be worthless if I didn't marry, and now that I have a glimpse into what you and Madelyn have, I think I can do without it. There's nothing you have that I need or even want. You can marry Lord Oliver Lewis Devillier III and be his wife, and I won't envy you. Now if you don't mind, I have had a long day of traveling and I want to see Nightfire before I turn in tonight. I will see you all in the morning."

My mother said not a word as I headed outside.

The path to the old barn wasn't quite as worn as it had been when I'd left. I'd traveled it frequently. Before I'd left, Madelyn and Lisa and I had gone to the barn to play. Lisa had been the first to stop, and she had convinced Madelyn not to go in order to dress up and flirt with the boys that passed along the road. Madelyn hadn't always gone with Lisa, but I was sure she didn't go to the barn much now that I wasn't here.

The barn doors were wide open. Nightfire had pushed them both open, but that was odd to see since the doors had never been opened. We had never been strong enough to force them more than a large enough gap for us to squeeze inside. There were a few more broken boards and a smashed stable door that Nightfire had broken while moving around, but he'd formed a place to lie down comfortably.

"Is this all right for you?" I asked.

"I will be fine here."

"Should I close the doors?"

"No." He nuzzled me gently. *"Your sisters are nothing like you."*

"Lisa and Madelyn and I have always been different. I was the rebel, Lisa was the daughter Mother always wanted, and Madelyn was the one stuck in the middle, with more sense than Lisa but wanting to follow the rules more than I did. We just look alike. Mother used to dress us in the same dresses so no one could tell us apart."

"I find Lisa shallow and vain."

"Lisa is what most women are supposed to be."

"Why are women supposed to be so foolish?" he wanted to know.

I shrugged. "Because most men want us to be that way. We're supposed to be good wives. And I guess wives aren't supposed to be smart or interesting. I don't understand it. I never wanted a dull husband." I rubbed his nose affectionately. "Do you need oiled tonight?"

"I can wait until tomorrow."

"I probably won't be allowed to ride on you much since I can't get away with wearing pants here, but I can go with you tomorrow morning and show you what's around. Then I'll have to assure the townspeople that you aren't a wyvern and aren't going to destroy them." I rolled my eyes. "They probably still believe Doctor McDragon and his books of lies."

"Your mother does not believe them."

"What do you think about her?" I asked. I was still in awe and slight admiration that she'd stood up to Nightfire without a hint of fear. I hadn't done that well facing a dragon the first time.

He was silent for a moment. *"She is stronger than you believe. But you will never understand each other because you see things differently and expect different things."*

"Well, she has Lisa and Madelyn, at least. And Warren is being a good son. I just wish she didn't expect marriage out of me and nothing else."

"Marriage made her happy and gave her children. She wants the same happiness for you."

"Kaylyn!" I heard my sister's voice calling me. "Kaylyn!"

I sighed. "I guess I have to turn in."

Nightfire nuzzled me again, comfort against the dark and the nightmares it now brought me. I hugged him tightly, then hurried back, leaving him to sleep.

Madelyn was waiting for me at the back door. "I wasn't sure you could hear me," she said. "I wondered, do you want to stay with Lisa or me? We haven't shared a room since Warren said you weren't coming back, but someone will have to share."

"I think it would be better if the two of you shared. I haven't been sleeping well." Warren's room had been smaller, so it didn't surprise me that Lisa had claimed the larger bedroom for herself. I couldn't stomach sharing with Lisa again and there wouldn't be much space in what was now Madelyn's room.

"I'm so sorry about your…about the man who was courting you."

I nodded silently, thankful she hadn't said his name.

"I'll tell Lisa that I'm sleeping with her, and you can have my room. Well, it used to be your room, so at least it's more familiar to you."

I managed a smile. "You'll get it back. Once Lisa marries and moves out, you'll have a few months on your own, if I even stay that long."

"Do you know how long you'll stay?"

"No. I needed...something different. I don't know that this house will have what I need."

Madelyn nodded, as if she understood my vague explanation. "Well, I'll be out of my room in ten minutes. Have Nettie make you some tea. Maybe it'll help you sleep."

I heard Lisa's whining about sharing a room while Nettie heated the water for my tea. I'd tried to insist I would do it, I did just about everything for myself now anyway and she'd already unbraided her blond hair for bed, but she was adamant it was her duty. By the time Nettie had poured the hot tea into the cup, Lisa had given up complaining and my mother was wishing them good night. As she passed near the kitchen, I called, "Good night, Mother."

Her footsteps paused a moment. "Good night, Kaylyn," she replied, then closed the door to her room.

"Will you be needing anything else from me?" Nettie asked.

I shook my head. "Thank you, Nettie. Good night."

"Good night, Lady Kaylyn." She slipped quietly from the room, leaving me with my tea and my silent thoughts.

Chapter 28

I woke the next morning at dawn slightly bewildered. I gazed around blankly, trying to figure out where I was. The bed, the window, the furniture, all were unfamiliar. It came back to me slowly. I could recognize some of Madelyn's items that she still kept. Among them was a letter that looked well-worn, addressed to her from the man I guessed to be her fiancé. I shook my head, but couldn't help but think back to Raphael's letters that I'd kept with me. I felt better knowing they were now a pile of ash.

I rose and dressed, fetching my own water. By the time Nettie got up, I had already bathed, redressed, and had a bag slung over my shoulders. I was wearing my long, brown skirt to hide the fact that I was wearing pants.

Nettie looked startled as I strode through the kitchen. "Good morning," she managed. "Breakfast?"

"No, thank you," I said. "Tell my mother and sisters that I probably won't be back until lunch. I'll be with Nightfire."

"Lady Kaylyn, what does Nightfire eat?" Nettie asked hesitantly. Already a slight girl, she seemed to shrink a little farther at the idea of Nightfire eating, fidgeting with her braided, blond hair in anxiety.

"He hunts his own food, but he likes raw meat. I'll handle his food. Oh, and he says humans taste bad, so he won't be eating anybody," I added kindly to help calm her.

I managed to carry or roll the barrel of oil to the barn where Nightfire was stretching, still a little sleepy. I oiled him, then I wrapped the straps around his neck and climbed on, hiking up the skirt. "Ready," I informed him.

He shifted his weight, angling himself, then leapt into the sky, wings stirring up clouds of dust that we left below, soaring into the sky. I found myself smiling at being in the air again.

We soared through the air for several hours. I showed him the river, the town, the different barely-noble families that we'd associated with, then Nightfire took me to the countryside. There were places here I'd never seen before. I had never been able to go so far on foot. Nightfire liked what he saw. I wasn't sure the townspeople were so thrilled. I had Nightfire land at the edge of town and waited by him for the first passerby to scream. It inevitably came. Her scream brought more people, and with them came men armed to fight the wyvern.

After a few minute of persuasion, the men lowered their weapons and moved close enough to talk without shouting. It took a further hour before I convinced them as much as possible that Nightfire had no interest in them or their livestock. After promising that Nightfire wouldn't raze the town, I hugged Nightfire's neck and wished him success and safety in his hunting. Nightfire left, eliciting some squeals and causing one girl to faint as he soared overhead. I walked towards my family's estate, the leather straps hung over a shoulder.

My mother said very little, giving me a frown when I said where I'd been. Lisa made a scene about how unladylike I was and how it reflected back on her. I ignored her and quickly changed out of the pants, tucking them away where I was sure no one would find them.

I spent some time unpacking and walking around the property alone until Nightfire showed up, then I joined my family for dinner. Lisa was pacing this way and that, her skirt twisting around her legs as she spun around. There were a few light bruises on her calves. The pretty shawl she wore, something I never had the patience to fight with, was draped over her shoulders and arms. As she settled at the table, I saw more bruises on her arms, of varying colors.

"Why do you have so many bruises?" I asked, frowning.

"I fall down a lot," she excused. "My balance…the doctor thinks it's a temporary condition. I'm just not eating healthy enough." She quickly took a bite of her salad and adjusted the shawl to cover her arms.

Nightfire offered a comment. *"How can people do so little every day?"* I'd explained that the very little activity done in the household today was typical for us.

I bit my lip to stop the smile. *"They think they are doing something every day."*

I could feel Nightfire's disbelief. *"If I rolled over and yawned I would do more than they do all day."*

I couldn't help the giggle, earning looks. Lisa just shook her head in disgust that her deranged sister was laughing at nothing again.

While I couldn't say I was happy at home, I could feel myself healing some. The second night, I awoke after an hour, unable to return to sleep. I fought with the bed and covers for several hours, then I gave up. My mother found me carving the next morning, a small pile of wood shavings showing I'd been at this a while collected under my chair. The next night, I couldn't get more than three hours of sleep. I was exhausted, but unable to turn my brain off. I seated myself at the table again in the silence of the night, knife and block of wood in hand, and went back to carving.

My mother woke during the night. I heard her moving about her room, her slippered feet moving quietly over the wood floor. She seemed surprised to see me working by the light of two candles. "Kaylyn, aren't you going to sleep?"

I rubbed at my eyes tiredly. "I'd love to sleep. I just can't."

"Perhaps if you put your mind to it…" she began, reaching for the carving.

I pulled the carving closer, protectively. "No. I know when I can't sleep."

Her hand paused. I hunched possessively over the carving and continued making little cuts, tensed in case she tried to take this away from me, as she had many times before.

"Would you like some tea? Something calming?" she asked in the silence.

I shook my head. "Carving works better. It helps me stop thinking. So I can't remember."

My mother was silent for a moment, then she retrieved another candle and her latest needlework. She lit the candle and started to stitch, still in her nightgown, her black hair braided and draped over her shoulder. Her brown eyes focused on the threads, occasionally looking over to me before moving back to her work.

We worked in silence for at least two hours. It was the closest to bonding we'd possibly ever had. We didn't talk, but the silent work somehow brought us closer. I'd never carved in front of my mother before. She'd considered it unladylike and any work I'd done in front of her had usually included sewing, which made me less than cheerful. My mother could sew beautiful pillows, fix any outfit, and could wield a needle with as much skill as Raz with his sword. There was very little my mother had ever been unable to do with fabric. I hadn't been blessed with her skill, or the patience to try and develop it. My patience was usually thin because my mother always spoke about what it meant to be a lady, and it always seemed that the lectures were aimed at me. Silence gave us peace.

I didn't remember falling asleep, but I awoke when Lisa swept into the room, loudly calling for Nettie. I started up, blinking stupidly at the bright kitchen. The candles had been blown out sometime, and my carving and the tools sat in the middle of the table. I studied the carving. It was easily recognizable now. A woman held a flower in her hand and was gazing at it, holding it in such a way it was obvious it had come from someone she loved deeply. As much hatred as I felt towards Raphael and men in general, love had somehow come out of me through this carving.

"What is this?" Lisa snatched it up before I could grab it. Her eyes narrowed at it. "Where did this come from?"

"Give it back," I snapped, getting to my feet.

Lisa finally pieced together the tools on the table and the carving in her hands. Her eyes narrowed at me, but there was something like triumph as she headed quickly for the parlor. "Mother! Mother, Kaylyn's carving again!"

I couldn't help the amusement as I gained my feet, following slowly. I also couldn't help but wonder what had happened after I'd fallen asleep. My mother had never approved of my carving, but she hadn't taken my tools from me last night. I wasn't sure she wouldn't take them from me now, however.

My mother was seated in her chair in the parlor, calmly sewing. Lisa was holding out the statue. "Mother, look! Kaylyn stole Dad's tools and now she's carving!"

My mother glanced up at Lisa. "Did you want your father's tools, Lisa?"

Lisa was taken aback. "No, but..."

My mother was serene. "I believe that your brother took the tools with him to the School. If Kaylyn has them, I can only assume he gave the tools to her. My daughters are not common thieves."

Madelyn was drawn to the parlor by our argument. Curious, she leaned over Lisa's shoulder to look at the carving. "Kaylyn did this? It's really good!"

Lisa whirled around. "Craftsmen carve! Ladies don't carve! Kaylyn was told to stop after Dad died! We're noble ladies!"

"You're noble ladies thanks to *me*!" I snapped at her. "And I'm going to keep carving whether you like it or not!"

Lisa ignored me. "Mother! Tell her she has to stop! Tell her she can't carve!"

I was prepared to tell her I'd leave the house in an hour if she did, but my mother spoke first. "Lisa, dear, you are far too old to be tattling on your sister. Now hand the carving back and sit down."

While Lisa gaped at our mother, Madelyn nimbly snatched the carving and inspected it more closely now. She gently stroked a finger down the woman's face. "This is beautiful, Kaylyn," she said as Lisa flopped in a scat and pouted. "This as good as any of Dad's."

I shook my head immediately. "I'm not better. Besides, I'm not done with it anyway."

"Lord Lewis is going to be appalled when he finds out," Lisa wailed dramatically. "He'll be ashamed of me, having a sister so unladylike. First a dragon, then *this!*"

I bristled at her tone. "I'm not marrying your fiancé, Lisa, so I don't care what he thinks. Though based on his choice of wife, I'm not certain he does a lot of thinking."

"Girls," my mother interrupted as Lisa started up, furious. "Both of you sit down. Madelyn, close the door, please."

I took my seat across from Lisa as Madelyn quietly closed the door. A closed door with my mother meant we were in trouble. She continued to serenely sew as Lisa and I glared. We sat in silence for a few minutes once Madelyn had meekly taken her seat as well, running her fingers admiringly over the carving. We knew better than to speak when a lecture was coming.

My mother finally put down her needlework and looked at Lisa. "Lisa, Kaylyn is your sister. However opposite you may be, I expect you to respect her and her decisions. Her actions are not shameful to the family or to our reputation. You cannot dictate her actions any longer. Considering all that Kaylyn deals with, raising and caring for a dragon, I am glad to find that Kaylyn can spend her time sitting quietly in a calm, ladylike manner, even if she cannot do it while engaging in a ladylike activity."

I felt as if I'd been simultaneously slapped and praised. Before I could decipher exactly what she'd said, my mother turned her imperious gaze to me. "Kaylyn, you know I don't permit you to scorn your sisters. As a Lady, you represent our family in a much more esteemed group of people than you have previously. Frankly, I worry some days about what comes out of your mouth, but somehow your actions have managed to endear you to those in power. I do not know this man who has been taking care of you, but I hope he has been teaching you to show respect and decorum, at least."

"Raz is a good man, Mother. He isn't corrupting me."

"I have my doubts about a man who could encourage you to engage in battle skills." She continued before I could protest and defend Raz. "I have stated my wishes that you not carve, but should you continue, I hope at least you will remember your position and keep this as a hobby, not a craft." She waited expectantly for an answer, the brown eyes all her children had inherited telling me what answer she expected.

"I hadn't thought about selling my carvings," I said honestly.

"Good." And she picked up her needlework.

Lisa was aghast. "You're going to let her keep carving?"

My mother didn't look up. "Yes, Lisa, I am."

Lisa let out a wail and stormed out of the parlor. Madelyn and I sat silently, partially stunned at this change of events.

My mother glanced up from her sewing. "Kaylyn, please remember that I do expect that my daughters make a family."

"You're more likely to get it out of your other children."

"I know, dear. But I reserve hope that you'll be a proper woman someday."

I didn't bother to say I would probably never be a proper woman in her eyes. "Thank you, Mother." I stood and carried the carving to my room.

Lisa sulked for an entire day. I couldn't go elsewhere since I could no longer ride on Nightfire. I knew my mother wouldn't allow it, and I figured making things worse wouldn't help anything. Nightfire spent a good deal of the days hunting anyway since he had to go farther to find animals that weren't owned by someone. At night I gained more and more time asleep, which was the only peace home brought. There were too many things that were the same that I still couldn't stand. Gradually, I started to feel restless at being stuck at home.

Home was made worse by the violent sickness we all got as the weather turned. My sisters were just as miserable they couldn't see their suitors as they were from the fact they couldn't go an hour without throwing up. My illness passed more quickly and I moved to a different corner of the house where their wails would be quieter. I was discovering my hearing was vastly improved. If Raz had noticed, he hadn't said anything. It felt like my entire family was deaf in what they couldn't hear. I added my enhanced hearing to the list of changes I thought I was going through and curled up with Nightfire for hours at a time, sometimes talking, sometimes saying nothing at all. I contemplated my life, trying to figure out where I belonged. It wasn't here, of that I was sure, but I didn't know where it was and I didn't know where to find it.

Three days later, my sisters were over the worst of the sickness. Since Lisa's suitor, Lord Oliver Lewis Devillier III, was coming and she was too sick to go outside, she begged me to meet him. "We always meet in the rose garden," she explained, eyes imploring. "Just tell him I'm inside, please? He's expecting me out there."

"All right," I promised. "I'll go meet Lord Oliver."

She winced. "Don't *call* him that."

"What? It's his name isn't it?"

"He doesn't like being called that. He's Lord Lewis."

I rolled my eyes. "All right, I'll go meet him." To my mind it was as good an excuse as any to get out of the house.

I wandered the rose garden for half an hour, dressed warmly and in a shawl, reveling in the silence. There wasn't much left still alive, but the view was decently pretty and allowed me to watch the road for anyone coming. When I heard a horse and carriage come down the road, I seated myself on a bench and waited. Lord Oliver Lewis Devillier wasted no time in coming to find his fiancée among the roses. "Is anyone else around?" he asked, not starting with formalities.

"No," I replied. "Everyone's inside. We've all been sick." My voice clearly displayed that. It was low and raspy.

I was about to mention Lisa was waiting inside when he grabbed my arm, yanking me up. "How many times have I told you to refer to me as Lord Lewis?" he hissed at me. "Lisa, I'm growing very tired of your memory slip-ups."

I was outraged. "Let go of me!"

He let go and shoved me back so that I fell to the ground where he glared at me. "I've told you again and again that I'm not your equal. You should be grateful you're marrying me!"

348

"Grateful?" I bounded to my feet quickly, anger and outrage surfacing at his words. "Why, you pretentious upstart! You arrogant lout!"

Furious, he grabbed my arm and squeezed in a grip that told me how Lisa got all her bruises. "Don't you dare speak to me that way!" he commanded.

In one quick move, I ripped free and shoved him back, glaring at him. "Don't you ever lay your hand on me again." I didn't care if he thought I was Lisa or not.

"A proper wife wouldn't *dare* speak back to me. A proper wife wouldn't *dare* to fight against me."

A proper wife, to his mind, meant taking all the abuse he wanted to give and saying nothing about it. And remembering all the bruises Lisa had, I shot my fist towards his jaw and sent him toppling towards the ground. "I am not your wife," I hissed.

He gained his feet as quickly as I had and clenched his free hand, his other touching his jaw where I'd socked him. Seeing Nettie come hurrying around the corner in alarm, he didn't dare touch me again. "This engagement is finished!" he shouted.

"Good riddance!" I shouted back. Then I stormed inside.

The scene between me and my sister rapidly dissolved into shouting and tears.

"How *could* you?" she wailed. "How could you *destroy* my happiness?"

"Happiness? Are you going to tell me you were *happy* being his punching bag? Listening to him tell you that you ought to be grateful he spares his time to call you stupid and knock you around?" I bellowed at her. "How's your *balance* problem, Lisa? Maybe it's from too much Devillier!"

My sister descended into sobbing wails of how she would never marry, draped pathetically over a couch.

"With men like that, I wouldn't know why you'd *want* to marry!" I said disgustedly, flopping in a chair.

"There now, dear," my mother soothed Lisa. "This will turn out all right."

"Mother, if you'd just let me go find him," Lisa started to beg, standing as if to go now.

I shot to my feet. "You're going to *apologize* to him?" I screamed, watching her flinch. "You're going to try to *fix* this? He was ready to hit me! He bruised me and thought it was *you*!"

"This can be fixed," she insisted.

"I don't think it can. He said the engagement was finished and I think he meant it."

Lisa sank to the floor, utterly distraught. My mother pulled Lisa's head into her lap and stroked her hair, soothing her eldest daughter who believed she'd lost everything. "My dear, was that really your place?" she asked me quietly. "If your sister was happy there…"

"You cannot tell me that Lisa was happy being shoved to the ground! How could you stand up for him, Mother? Do you want your daughters beaten every time someone's not around?"

She continued to stroke Lisa's hair. "What happens between a man and his wife is between them alone, Kaylyn. It is not our place to interfere. Lord Lewis is a very powerful noble. It would have been an honor for our family."

My lip curled in disgust. "I can't believe this," I spat, nearly shaking with anger. "That you would condemn me for standing up for myself. That you could *approve* your *daughter* being treated like a *slave* so that you can live more *comfortably*! And I can't believe *she* was willing to do it! Does nothing matter to you but society? Not even family? Or was Dad the only one who cared about any of us?"

At that, my mother flinched slightly. "Your father was a good man," she said quietly. "And he cared very much for his family, as do I."

"Really? My father would have been *proud* of me for protecting Lisa! My father would have whipped that man like a dog for what he did to Lisa! That you would condemn me for doing what he would have is sickening, Mother! It's bad enough putting up with men who think women are next to worthless; it's worse when it's the women in your own family who wouldn't care to see you dead at a man's hands if he gave you gold for it. You disgust me!" I whirled around. "Nettie!" I shouted. "Bring my pack! I'm leaving right *now*! I can't put up with these people and their cowardice and greed for one more *minute*!"

"What have I missed?" Nightfire inquired. His presence, lingering at the edge of consciousness, was suddenly clear as he came within range. He felt my anger and was curious to know why.

"My idiot sister's suitor was using her as a punching bag, and now everyone's upset I stopped him." I slammed my door open.

Nettie jumped. "Ma'am, what about your trunks?" she inquired timidly.

"Send them to my brother. I'm heading to the School. I know there are people there who have enough sense to fill a thimble." I stormed around the room, then whirled on her. "Did you know?"

Nettie shook her head frantically, blond curls escaping her cap. "No, ma'am. I didn't know. I swear it."

"Then stop acting like I'm going to beat you next," I snapped. "I'm not like *him*."

"Then maybe you should stop acting like him." Madelyn twisted her hands in the doorway, worry taking the sting out of her rebuke. "Kaylyn, do you really think this is the best idea? Leaving? What if he comes back?"

"Then my mother and sister will welcome him with open arms and hand him a rod so he can beat them senseless." I narrowed my eyes at her. "Did *you* know?"

She shook her head. "Not really. I...I suspected when she started...falling...so much."

"Then why didn't *you* do anything?"

She looked bewildered. "I'm a woman."

"Who else was going to do it?" I demanded. "Our father's dead! Warren's at the School! If you didn't *tell* anyone, how was it going to matter?"

She looked a little ashamed. "I'm sorry, Kaylyn. I didn't think I should bother Warren. He's so busy."

"It's his *duty* as the man of the family to take care of us," I snapped. "Which is utterly ridiculous. This should never have gone on so long. You should have stopped it."

"But how? I'm a woman, Kaylyn."

"So am I," I pointed out furiously. "It may be expected that men come to the rescue, but it shouldn't be like that. You should have never allowed this to continue on for months. Female or not, you care about her so you should have made sure it stopped." I held out my hand for the pack. "Nettie, if he ever comes back, you let me know. I will not let my sister, however stupid she is, be miserable for the rest of her life." I whirled on Madelyn. "How's *your* fiancé?"

"He isn't like that, Kaylyn. He's…he's like our father. He would never strike me."

"At least *one* of my sisters has sense." I slung the pack over my shoulders. "I'm off. Tell anyone who cares where to find me."

Chapter 29

My arrival at the School was a public event. It just happened wherever Nightfire and I went. The only good part about it was that Warren and Dillon were there to greet me. "Hey, sis!" Warren exclaimed, rushing forward to swing me around. "Look at how tall you are!"

I laughed. "You've grown too! I thought I was finally going to have some sort of advantage over you."

"Sorry. I just keep growing." He grinned unashamedly. "What brings you here?"

"I'm staying here for a little while." Quieter, I said, "Warren, we need to talk. Not now, but sometime. You need to know what's going on at home." Then I turned and smiled. "Dillon, I'm finally coming to visit!"

He chuckled. "How long a visit?"

"No idea. A month. Maybe two." I rubbed Nightfire's nose. "Is there a place where we can stay?"

"We have a new place for you. Come along, I'll show you." He nodded to another recruit. "Go inform Captain Durai that Lady Kaylyn and Nightfire have arrived and will be staying here for an unknown period of time."

"Yes, sir!" he said as he rushed off.

"So how are you?" I asked, matching his stride easily. "Anything exciting happening?"

He gave a proud smile. "My wife is expecting our first child."

I grinned delightedly. "That's wonderful! When?"

"We just discovered it, so it isn't soon. My wife has already picked out the names."

"What are the names?"

"Richard Leviticus Marcell, or Kaylyn Donna Marcell."

I came to an abrupt stop. "She wants to name it after *me*? She's never even met me!"

"She likes you. She thinks you're a brave and special person."

"I'm not either."

He raised his eyebrow. "Well, you would be mistaken. You're fifteen, so that can be excused." He continued to walk. "I wouldn't try to argue it. My wife has the stubbornness of a dragon and is proud to say so."

I looked up at Nightfire. "Yeah? Well, dragons are pretty stubborn."

"And humans are not?" Nightfire asked me.

"All dragons are stubborn. All humans are not."

"You are stubborn."

"I get it from you," I teased.

Dillon smiled as he unlocked a large door and pushed it all the way over to one side. "What do you think?" he asked. He gestured to the large, circular kind of barn sitting at a corner of one building. I was intrigued to see it was made out of both wood and metal, and was big enough for Nightfire. "I had this made for Nightfire," he said, as if reading my thoughts. "He is military, and I thought it only fitting that we have a place for a dragon to stay in."

Nightfire went in first, looking around. I could tell by the color of his eyes, light yellow, that he was surprised and pleased. The room was three times my height, and in a circular shape, with a curved roof. It wasn't quite big enough that a fully-grown dragon could stretch completely out, but it was cave-like. "It feels like a cave," Nightfire said, echoing my thoughts. "It feels like a dragon's home."

"Your room, if you want it, can be here," Dillon informed me. "There's plenty of space. There are pieces for a bed stored through that door." He walked inside. "The roof is retractable. The engineers here had fits trying to build a roof that would do that and have it consistently work, but they did it. That way you can have your privacy, and also be able to enjoy fresh air. It's just a little place here to call your own."

I threw myself at him and hugged him tightly. "Thank you," I whispered. "Thank you for this."

Surprised, he patted my back awkwardly. "Just have Nightfire be careful. It's mostly wood."

Nightfire nudged me gently to have me let go, then curled up on the floor. "You are a good human," he said to Dillon. "We are grateful."

Dillon patted my back once more and clasped his hands behind his back. "Is there anything else you need?"

"No. We should have everything." I walked over to the shelf and pulled out my father's carving, setting it down in the middle of the shelf. Then I wandered into the small room with the bed pieces stored inside and studied it. "Well, except a mattress."

"One will be coming soon. Let me know if there's anything else you require."

"I will," I said distractedly as I started to crank the ceiling open and closed.

Warren showed up as I was putting the bed together. "Someone would have done that for you," he said, holding the headboard to help.

"Why when I can do it?"

He just grinned. "Because most women expect the men to do it."

"Just hold the headboard. I'm almost done." I finished fitting the last piece together and surveyed my work with satisfaction. "That should hold."

"What's going on at home that I should know about?" he asked.

I made a noise of disgust. "Have you met either of Lisa's or Madelyn's fiancés?"

"Briefly when they proposed. Why?"

I told him everything. Warren listened to my tale with disbelief. "And she was going to marry him?"

"Mother encouraged it! She and Lisa are upset with me because I broke up the engagement."

"I can't *believe* someone didn't tell me," he muttered.

"What could they do?" I asked bitterly. "They're just women, and you're so busy."

"My duty to them comes first," Warren snapped, scowling. "Maybe I need to make a visit home."

"Please do. See if you can talk some sense into them and make sure that Lord Oliver isn't returning."

"That lowlife," he muttered, pacing back and forth. "That arrogant *noble*."

"I know. I already told him that."

"It's good somebody did." He ran his hand through his hair in agitation. "Now I feel like I should have known. That I should have done something."

"I'm her triplet, and I didn't know."

"You've lived out in the middle of nowhere for two years."

"No, actually I lived in the mountains with the dragons for five months."

He came to an abrupt halt. "You *what*? For *how* long?"

"Lived with dragons. Five months. That was before I showed up everyone at your little competition." I couldn't help but smile a little maliciously.

He blinked twice, then shook his head. "That's still the middle of nowhere, it's just a different middle of nowhere. I hadn't realized you'd gone anywhere."

My face warmed slightly. "I...needed a change. I was having...difficulties."

"Raz, he's treating you all right?" Warren pressed.

I nodded. "I wouldn't have gone back to him otherwise."

"I know, but I didn't know that you'd even left that place, and now you've left it again."

I fiddled with the material on my skirt. "I couldn't be there right now. It just reminds me of...him. And I don't want to think about him any longer."

"Are you all right?" Warren's voice was quiet, sympathy clear. "We got Raz's and Sergeant Sample's letters explaining everything. Dillon let me read them. It sounded pretty bad."

I shrugged wearily. "I killed him. I hate him. I was as stupid as Lisa."

"You weren't either," Warren contradicted fiercely. "He lied to you, but he never struck you. He wasn't any better than Lord Oliver, but he wasn't the same kind of bad." He hesitated. "You know you can talk to me, right? You know I'll always be there for you."

I couldn't help but smile a little. "Yes, I know."

He cleared his throat, uncomfortable with this, and quickly stood. "Good. I've got stuff I need to do. You know how to find me."

"I do. Thanks."

He nodded and headed for the door.

A glance around the dining room that evening showed that very little had changed. There were a few who gawked at me, but I ignored them and took my place near the end of Warren's table. I ate quickly, then left. The scribes in the library weren't too pleased to see me, but I ignored them as well. To prove a point, I picked up a scroll and read over it, just because I could, then carefully replaced it when other recruits started coming in to do their homework.

I was summoned to Dillon's office after dinner had ended, where I was informed that I would be joining a few fighting classes and one of Warren's classes.

"Not swords," I said immediately.

There was something like pity in his light brown eyes for a second. "Very well, I'll tell the swordmaster. I have a grasp of what Raz has been teaching you, so you shouldn't have too much trouble. If you have problems, let me know."

"It's not with that dim-witted professor, is it? The one who thinks I'm a little hellion who should be married by now?"

Dillon swallowed a smile. "No, it's not Mr. Quallis. Captain Durai didn't think it prudent to put the two of you together."

"Okay. When do my classes start?"

"Warren will set you up in two days and let you know where to go. He's leaving in the morning to take care of personal business back home."

I had an idea of what personal business that was. "I'm on my own until then?"

"Until then, try to stay close."

I nodded.

Warren returned several days later to inform me that Lisa's suitor would not be returning.

"So Lisa hates me?"

"And me. But mostly you."

"No surprises there. Mother?"

"Sent your things. I don't know that she's pleased, but she didn't say much concerning you." He blew out a sigh. "Did Lieutenant Marcell tell you that you were starting classes?"

"Whenever you got back."

"Meet me for breakfast tomorrow morning and I'll let you know." He rubbed his eyes tiredly. "I need to catch up tonight."

"Then go on. Nightfire needs oiling anyway."

He let out a yawn. "All right. Good night, sis."

The next morning, Warren, much more alert, laid out my schedule. He informed me it was light, but since I'd missed the beginning of these classes, nobody would mind. I figured no one really thought I could handle this schedule, much less a regular one.

We started out on staffwork. Nightfire watched from above. Having never trained with such a large class and having never trained with any male besides Raz, I hung back and watched for several minutes. When the instructor realized I wasn't participating, he paired me up with Maynard Lennox, who had gotten pudgier in two years. I couldn't have been more delighted. I still remembered his statements about how I was too stupid to understand what I was reading. We mutually scowled at each other, and then he attacked.

I moved to block, the wood clacking hard as our staffs met. I forced him back, returning the strike. He slid his staff aside, trying to catch my fingers, and I followed the movement, dropping my staff suddenly to slam into his foot. He let out a yelp and hopped on one foot for a moment, then quickly tried to throw up a block. I easily shoved that aside and whacked him hard on the shoulder, then used my staff to twist his staff out of his hands.

Maynard winced, anticipating the coming blow. I simply set my staff on one end, regarding him. "You don't defend very well. Smashing your opponent's fingers is child's play to anyone with some serious training."

The instructor looked astounded. Warren was beaming, the proud older brother.

"Let me see that again," the instructor ordered.

I hefted my staff. Maynard reluctantly retrieved his, seeming to realize he'd lose again and have it be publicly witnessed by his friends and classmates.

"I'll go against her, sir," Warren volunteered quickly.

"Fine. Recruit Madara, go against your sister."

I let my brother attack first, sliding my foot back to steady myself. Warren was clearly concentrating, trying to outmaneuver me. I kept searching for a weakness, and quickly found it on the side block. He managed the first block, the second one was desperate, and the third block broke, allowing me through his defenses. I whacked his side, his wrist, and then his leg. His leg gave out and he crumpled to one knee with a yelp. I put my staff down, signaling victory.

"I *told* you she was good," I heard someone mutter.

"Warren just got beat by a *girl*," someone mocked.

"She'll beat you too," Warren said, flashing a grin at me. "Geez, sis. You've got to teach me how you do that! It's like you could read my mind!"

"There's not much up there. It isn't hard," I teased.

The instructor narrowed his eyes at me. "Who's been training you?"

"Raz Greenclaw," I replied.

"Greenclaw?" He frowned. "I don't know him."

I just shrugged.

"Very well." He cleared his throat. "If you're done warming up, line up in pairs!"

We worked a few specific blocks and strikes, rotating who we fought against. I didn't find it boring, but it wasn't very exciting either since I already knew this.

After staff training, Warren guided me to class. He let me glance through his books on the way and pointed the seat beside him. I took my seat, watching as the others filed in. A few glared, some ignored me, but a handful nodded a greeting, even if it was discreet.

Professor Whelan breezed in, ignoring my presence as he went over the lecture on survival they'd previously had. After a twenty-minute review, he ordered us to get out paper and ink and write down what we needed to survive in the mountains. I hid my grin and took the paper Warren slid over to me, and the extra ink jar. While everyone else was scribbling things down, I quickly wrote down my six items and capped the ink jar. Then I listened to the others write, wondering what all they thought they could need. I looked down at my six items again, confirmed that was all I needed, then started thinking about the dragons in the mountains. I wondered if any were nearby. I was curious as to how Ironclaw was doing, and Embereyes, and all the other dragons.

"Quills down." The instructor's voice was sharp. "Lady Madara."

I looked up. "Yes?"

"Sir," Warren muttered.

"Sir," I added quickly.

He frowned at me. "Stand when I address you."

"Oh." I quickly gained my feet. "Yes, sir."

"How many items are on your list, Lady Madara?"

"Six, sir."

"Were you thinking, Lady Madara, or were you done?"

"I was done, sir."

"With six items?"

"Yes, sir."

There were soft snickers.

"And you can survive on those six items."

"Yes, sir. I can, and I have."

That stopped the snickers.

Professor Whelan looked at me over his glasses. "You've survived in the mountains on six items, Lady Madara?"

"Yes, sir." I felt annoyed at having to use all the formalities.

"Then please tell the class what those six items are."

I didn't even glance at my paper. "Shelter, a medicine pack, clothing, a knife, a bow with arrows, and blankets."

"What about something for a fire?"

"There are items in a medicine pack to start a fire."

"Access to running water and a food source?"

"There's no point in having shelter if it isn't near both those things, sir."

"You've taken no food supplies to live on."

"I didn't take food with me, sir. Just Nightfire."

"Most people don't have a dragon, Lady Madara."

I resisted rolling my eyes. "That's why I didn't put him on the list, sir."

"How long did you live in the mountains, Lady Madara?"

"Five months, sir."

"And you lived alone?"

"No, sir. I lived with Nightfire and the other dragons."

He took his glasses off completely. "Dragons? How many dragons?"

"About fifteen or so."

Stunned silence rang in the classroom a moment. "Fifteen dragons?" he repeated. "And you lived with them?"

"Yes, sir."

Professor Whelan was silent for a minute, studying me. "Explain your choices to me, Lady Madara."

I ticked off the reasons quickly. This was no different than the scenarios Raz had done with me on a nightly basis. "I need shelter to protect me from the weather. I need a medicine pack in case I get hurt. I need clothing for obvious reasons, and a knife for cutting food or whatever I need to cut. I need a bow and arrow to defend myself or hunt, and I need blankets to keep warm. Sir."

He put his glasses back on. "I might suggest you put water and at least some food on your list when you go to the mountains, Lady Madara, in case the weather is bad. You should also plan for anything that isn't in your basic medicine pack. Better to have excess than not enough."

I felt like I'd passed a test. "Yes, sir." And I took my seat.

We went through others in the room. Most had listed items I'd assumed would be in the medicine pack, such as soap and lye soap for washing clothing. Several had included a compass, maps, a generous food supply, and a small armory to defend themselves with. Professor Whelan mentioned they needed to be able to carry everything they took and suggested lightening their weapons supply to start with. My brother beamed throughout the class, his pride in his sister evident.

We broke for lunch, then I was taken outside to the stables for horseback riding. I wore pants underneath the loose skirt. The man there looked me over and said, "We don't have a sidesaddle."

"I don't ride sidesaddle," I replied, keeping his matter-of-fact tone.

"Have you ridden a horse recently?"

"Not really. Mostly a dragon."

"Do you wear pants?"

I nodded.

"Good. I'll get you a horse." He paused before walking inside, turning back to face me. "Do you use a saddle on a dragon?"

I shook my head. "I couldn't make one. I don't know that Nightfire would wear one."

"I'd consider it. It might give you more mobility."

"Yes, sir."

Horseback riding wasn't bad. I was rusty. As soon as the recruits quit squawking over the pants underneath the skirt, we started class. I didn't have the skill they did, but I wasn't new to this either. I managed to figure out what we were doing a beat or two behind everyone and ended up doing fine. The instructor didn't care that I was female or that I wore pants; he just wanted me to do what everyone else was doing and left me pretty much alone.

After horseback riding was my final class. I was distressed to learn that it was knives. Students were picked out one by one to throw at a target, trying to compensate for the fierce, autumn wind. The instructor passed me by the first time, but I didn't care. Nightfire was overhead, lying on a roof and watching. *"This is not a good idea,"* he warned as the instructor spotted me.

"Madara, female," he barked. "Your turn." He handed me a knife and gestured to the target.

I held the knife he gave me, studying it. Doing nothing more than that brought memories I'd worked so hard to forget. I dropped the knife to the ground. "I can't."

"You can't? What do you mean you can't?" he demanded.

I shook my head, not meeting his gaze. "I can't do it, sir."

I could feel his displeasure at my lack of even an attempt. "I was told about your... handicap. Have it your way. I teach two weapons; one is knives, one is swords. Pick one or the other, but you're going to have to do one of them."

It was a short internal debate. I'd killed with a knife, but swords represented killing, and I had vowed not to become a soldier who carried a weapon that was good for only killing. In the end, I silently pointed to a sword. That didn't have traumatizing memories. Yet.

"This is not a good idea," Nightfire said again.

"Surely I can handle this," I said unconvincingly as the professor chose another boy to spar against me.

I reluctantly picked up the sword. Dillon took his place by my brother, eyes intent on me. I didn't know when he'd appeared.

I was rusty, that was clear, but even more so, I was hesitant. The one time I made an attack, my opponent wasn't expecting it and was nearly too slow to defend. I had a flash of a picture, the shock and terror in Raphael's eyes right before my blade sank into his chest. The heat of fury and the dripping blood. The whimper.

I threw the sword on the ground between us, stepping back. "No. No, I can't do this. I'm not fighting anymore."

Dillon stepped in quickly and signaled my opponent to stop. He obediently lowered his sword, looking confused.

Before anyone could say anything, Nightfire came towards me. He touched his head gently to my cheek a moment while the recruits parted quickly for him. *"It was not a good idea,"* he reminded me.

"I guess you're right," I whispered. I clenched his head tightly and squeezed my eyes shut.

"I'm removing Kaylyn from this class," Dillon said.

"Sir, how is she supposed to learn if she doesn't train?" the man argued. "You informed us we would have to train her, and I admit I wasn't thrilled. But just because she's beaten our recruits in the competition is no reason for her to start slacking."

"My sister isn't slacking, sir." My brother came quickly to my defense. "She's not ready."

"And why, Corporal, would she not be ready for training?"

There was a moment's hesitation while my brother looked to Dillon for approval. Dillon nodded.

"A man tried to kill her and Nightfire, sir, and she killed him. It was her first kill, sir."

Tears slipped down my cheeks as the memory came back. *"I'll never be free of him."*

"You will," Nightfire promised, humming the soothing noise. *"You will."*

Chapter 30

After my meltdown, my schedule was quickly rearranged. Instead of going to training with knives or swords, I worked with Dillon every day. It gave me something to do, something to think about besides the memories that left me shaky. The instructor had stopped complaining about my apparent weakness in learning that it wasn't female swooning. It appeared that everyone remembered their first kill and that very few, if any, hadn't had trouble dealing with it afterward.

To my immense distress, the generals moved into the School for meetings while their new meeting-place was being built. Dillon told me they'd probably be here a month to conduct all their business. "You'll be joining us at the meetings," he said.

"Why?" I sputtered.

"Because you have nothing better to do, and because they suggested you join us."

"They asked that I join their meetings?" It was said with more than a touch of doubt.

"Of course. Why wouldn't they want their most powerful ally to see them make good changes to Centralia and proving they really had your best interests at heart?" he appealed.

"Because I'm female? And to quote them, a guttersnipe, barely more than a child, poor, irresponsible, and showing no consideration for convention?"

"You're a talented fighter and you have a connection with the most powerful creature in Centralia. And his being a dragon connects you to other dragons," he pointed out, now serious. "Whether or not you're female, they want to be on your good side, and they want to make up for their previous mistakes."

I shook my head. "So instead of ordering me to the front lines, they're going to sweet talk me now."

"It's at least a more pleasant tactic, isn't it?"

I sighed. "I suppose."

"I'll send someone for you when it's time to slip in. Until then, the time is yours."

My first meeting was filled with formalities as they greeted me. They inquired after Nightfire; I said he was doing fine. When they eventually wound their way to the threats of the Silons in the south, I decided to cut off their request before they gave it.

"Do you know what a mindlink is?" I asked General Amea. He annoyed me the least, and seemed the most reasonable. Even when I'd first dealt with them, his motivations had been more logical and less greedy. And he hadn't looked down on me for simply being female.

"I'm afraid I don't."

"When Nightfire hatched, he formed a mindlink with me. I feel his emotions, he feels mine. I can sense where he is and he knows where I am. If I get hurt, he feels it, and if he dies, I won't want to live."

This news shocked the generals. "You mean you'll die?" General Amea demanded, appalled and looking wary now, as if I would be suddenly overcome with the desire to cease living.

I shrugged. "I won't want to live," I repeated. "That's why no one who's ever killed a dragon has lived to tell the tale. The dying dragon forms a mindlink, and once the dragon dies, so does his killer. The dragons use it as a weapon. Nightfire and I don't use it as a weapon, but it's something we have to be cautious of. That's why you can't send him out there. First of all, I won't make him. Second of all, if he gets hurt, I'll feel every ounce of pain that he does. If you send me out and I die, you're going to lose Nightfire as well. We aren't invincible."

This took the wind out of their sails. After the much subdued meeting had ended, I returned to my spot outside Nightfire's and my little home. My time was spent carving. I was enjoying the sunshine, working on a piece when a shadow covered my carving. I already knew who it was; I'd heard the puffing all the way across the commons.

"Lady Madara," General Maddox said graciously.

"General Maddox," I replied.

"I have heard that your skill has improved since the recruit's competition. Would it be possible for a demonstration?"

"I don't fight anymore." I only fought with staffs, and I usually paired with my brother. He was improving quickly. His friends could only occasionally convince him to switch with one of them because he wanted more time against me.

This took the wind out of his sails a second time. "You don't fight?"

"No."

"All that talent going to waste," General Maddox grumbled.

"You didn't *want* me having this talent in the first place," I informed him. "You wanted me to be the proper woman whose one goal in life is to get married."

He blustered for a moment, and I cut him off. "Nightfire, do I speak the truth?"

"Yes," Nightfire said calmly. "I do not understand why he feels you are neglecting your duty but still thinks you are doing men's work."

I studied the block of wood in my hands, and started to carve the upper left corner. "I'd like him to tell a female Eagle she's doing men's work. Probably the best part about female Eagles is they have to keep secret, isn't that so, General?"

"You're putting words in my mouth," he grumbled, but without his usual anger.

"I'm speaking what you're thinking." I put the knife down and met his gaze squarely. "Why are you so afraid of what women can do, General?"

He didn't answer and puffed his way in another direction.

"Ironclaw is right," Nightfire commented. *"He sounds like a bellows to start a fire. If he were put in front of a flame, he could be put to better use."*

I laughed and went back to my carving.

"Excuse me, Lady Madara?" a woman's voice came timidly.

I looked up to see a frail woman, maybe eighteen, twisting her hands nervously. "Yes?" I asked, putting the block of wood in my lap again.

She curtseyed nervously. "I would like to speak to you a moment. If I may."

"Of course you may. Would you like to sit down?" I pointed to the other chair.

She took a seat, smoothing out her dress. "I don't mean to pry, Lady Madara…"

"Kaylyn," I interrupted. "It's just Kaylyn."

She nodded, her hands still twisting together. "My sister, she attends the university. She is engaged to marry a friend of Lord Devillier."

My eyes flashed. "I hope your friend has a better man than Devillier."

"Oh, yes, Lady…Kaylyn. He is a good man. He does not have much wealth to speak of, but he is very bright. Very smart."

I nodded, wondering where this was going.

"I heard what you did to protect your sister."

"So Oliver figured it out, did he?" I murmured.

She shook her head. "No, Lady…Kaylyn," she corrected herself again. "Nettie is my cousin."

"Is she? I didn't know that." There wasn't much family resemblance, except for maybe the same blond hair and a slight build.

She nodded shyly. "Nettie speaks very highly of you, and said I could come to you for help."

"How can I help?"

She looked down a moment. "I work for Lord Wannabee."

I couldn't help the twitch of my lips. "Wannabee, huh?"

Nightfire chuckled in my mind.

She gave a tiny smile. "Yes, ma'am. He goes by his first name, Lord Richard, and owns the Gable estate."

I nodded, recognizing the name. "A powerful and influential man."

"Yes, ma'am."

"Don't call me ma'am. Kaylyn."

She nodded and took a deep breath before continuing on. "Lord Richard has been…most abusive these past months. He says he will not let me leave. He threatens to have me arrested if I try, or make sure I can never work in a respectable household again." Tears filled her eyes.

"I do not like this Wannabee," Nightfire growled.

"I don't either. What do you think we should do?"

"Burn his house down," he suggested.

I laughed silently and spoke aloud. "The idea has merit."

She looked nervous. "What idea?"

"Nightfire would like to burn his house down," I said.

Her eyes widened in alarm and she hastily spoke. "Nettie says I should go before a judge. She said if *you* were on my side, I would have a chance."

"I suppose we could go in front of a judge," I said. "Do you have a judge in mind?"

"I would be under Lord Pennington." Her voice was despairing. "He is close friends with Lord Richard."

"I see. Well, I'll send someone to inform him he has a case to deal with." I got to my feet. "Do you have a place to stay?"

She shook her head.

"Then we'll find you a place." I let out a piercing whistle to get the attention of a lone recruit passing by. "Hey! You! Private, or whatever your rank is!"

He looked pained. "It's *Corporal*, miss. I have two stripes. The same as your brother."

"I thought my brother had three arrows."

"That's a sergeant, miss. And they're stripes, not arrows."

The woman beside me smiled.

"Right. Corporal, would you be so kind as to take this woman and find her lodgings for the night? She's under my protection."

"Yes, ma'am."

"They aren't so bad," I said to her. "Since I beat them all in their yearly competitions, they don't give any disrespect to women, at least not where I can hear. If you need me, ask someone to fetch me and tell them you're under my protection. They'll do what you ask. What's your name, by the way?"

She bobbed a shy curtsey. "It's Brooke, miss. Brook Havener."

"Sorry. I'm terrible with protocol. And don't call me miss. It's Kaylyn."

My mind churning, I barely heard her reply as I headed towards Dillon's office. Once there, I leaned against the doorframe. "Say I wanted a law changed. How would I do that?"

Dillon sat back in his chair to give me his full attention. "That would depend on what law you wanted to change and how much you wanted to change it."

"The law where nobles get to act like judges. I want it removed."

"You'd have to get the generals to pass that law."

"Any chance I could get this done in three days?"

"*Days?*" he asked incredulously.

I shrugged. "I'm not very patient."

"It takes longer than three *days*. Maybe three *weeks* if you're lucky."

"I don't have three weeks."

"Why do you need this law changed?"

I told him Brooke's story, and the upcoming problem.

He sighed. "I'm afraid there's no helping her. Unless Lord Pennington wants to pass it on to an actual judge."

"Right. Being good buddies, he'd do that." I sighed too. "I don't suppose my showing up at this trial will help anything, will it?"

"Not likely. Being good buddies and all, I don't see how anything less than a group of generals will make a difference."

I straightened. "The generals? They'd help?"

"They are the lawmakers."

"Do you suppose I could have them sit in at the trial?"

"I suppose you could ask. If you ask, you're going to need a good reason for asking them."

"Brooke isn't enough reason?"

"Brooke is one girl. You're going to need more than just Brooke to get the change you want."

"Then I need some help. I need a lot of people with this problem. And I need to find them in three days."

He studied me, then he got up and put on his jacket. "Come on. You should meet my wife. If she knows anything, it's about injustice. She'll get you all the connections you'll need."

Lady Marcell listened to my story with avid interest, her hands absently rubbing her belly. She was just starting to show and looked as put together as I'd expected. Her dark brown hair was curled and coiled and her outfit held what I'd somehow heard was the latest fashion, though there was no reference to her wealth or status. I liked her.

"Four months," she said absently, telling me she'd seen my glances. "That's how far along I am. At least, that's our guess. As for poor Brooke, of course we'll help! This law is just leftover from the days when the favored nobles got whatever they wanted from the king. It needs to go." She sipped her tea, then set it down. "How many do you need?" she asked.

"As many as we can get," I replied. "If we throw numbers at them, they'll have to at least think about it."

"Yes, I agree. It's the perfect thing to do with my time. I need a good cause. This pregnancy thing is wonderful, don't get me wrong, but I dislike being confined so much. Drat that doctor for saying pregnant women should be confined to bed rest to find tranquility. Tranquility, ha!" she said, causing me to smile. "Laying in bed doesn't keep me tranquil, it keeps me annoyed and bored. And neither are good things." She pushed herself out of the chair. "Maggie! Maggie, get my pen and paper! I know just who to write to," she said to me as she searched through a little book. "A very close friend of mine provides shelter for those who need it. She gives them work, and in exchange they get a doctor to tend to them when they're sick and a place to stay. They don't stay long, some of them, but others have made it their living running the place."

"She must be very rich."

"Oh, she is! She married General Amea's eldest son."

I felt my eyebrows raise. "Is that so?" I murmured.

"It is." She paused. "Are you going to present this to the generals?"

"I'm going to try. But I need someone to tell me what to say."

"Sit down, dear. We'll get you all set up. Tell me, what are you going to wear?"

Two days later, I stood in front of the generals, fighting nerves. I was dressed carefully, according to what Lady Marcell had directed me, and I carefully repeated the words she had told me to say.

"Generals, it has come to my attention that there is a law that requires your consideration," I said. "One that allows nobles to abuse their subjects."

"What law is this?" General Maddox demanded.

"That nobles may act as judges. In my opinion, sirs, some nobles know little about the law and judging, and I don't believe they should have the right to use this law to mistreat those who have the misfortune to not be noble." I itched to free my hair. It had been a while since I'd tied it back into some kind of fancy hairdo.

"How do you know these nobles are acting unfairly as judges?" General Amea asked.

I provided the papers. "I have letters. Complaints. Witnesses who will verify they were mistreated under this system. Some of them wrote to you. Many of them couldn't because they're women and never learned to write. One of them is due to go to court tomorrow. The man she works for is abusing her and has threatened her if she leaves. Under this law, she would present her problem to another noble, who happens to be a very close friend to the man who is abusing her."

"Perhaps this man will do his duty."

"Perhaps. But I would like you to come to the trial. If he does not do his duty, I would ask that you intervene on the behalf of this woman and those that have complained to you. Let matters for judges go to judges."

They exchanged glances, then General Amea spoke. "Perhaps we could consider this matter. When is the trial?"

Although I thought that had been far too easy, I felt a trickle of relief. "Tomorrow at noon, at Lord Richard Wannabee's estate."

"Very well. Tomorrow we'll go stand at the trial."

Brooke, as carefully dressed as I'd been, stood nervously next to me the next day. I'd arrived at the field half an hour before on Nightfire. Lord Pennington had arrived shortly after I had and I'd watched him greet Wannabee. It was obvious they were loyal to each other.

Lord Wannabee was an arrogant man. Nightfire could sense the arrogance. After two minutes, it became apparent. He spoke cordially to Pennington, and dismissively or rudely to anyone else. And he had no concerns for the pending trial.

"Don't worry," Pennington assured him quietly. "It'll be taken care of. Just like all the others."

Brooke clutched my hand. "I'm afraid," she confessed in a whisper.

"Don't be," I whispered back. "If he does exactly what we expect him to do, it's all going to turn out just fine."

She looked confused.

I squeezed her hand. *"Here goes,"* I said silently to Nightfire.

"He has no intention of being fair," Nightfire said silently. *"I want to light his home on fire as well."*

"I wish we could." I cut my eyes to the arriving crowd. Among them, in the back, stood several of the generals. I'd convinced them not to step forward. "How do you know how they usually act otherwise?" I'd asked. "No thief is going to steal if he knows the guards are watching him." I'd actually been quite proud of myself for that line. "If you want to know what he does when

you're not around, you can't let him know you're there." I wished I was standing in the back with them. Everyone was staring at me. It may not have helped that I was standing right next to Nightfire.

Pennington managed to get everyone's attention as he took his place on the wooden box that was also used for hangings, and we quieted. Brooke and I remained standing on his left, with Wannabee on the other side, also standing. Most people were standing, since this trial was held in a field outside the town itself, but a few children were seated near the front, seemingly entranced by the black dragon right in front of them.

Pennington seemed annoyed by all the formalities and raced through the statement on upholding the law and standing as the law, and that he would act fair and impartial. I kept my face straight, but Nightfire snorted in contempt, scaring a couple in attendance.

"Lord Richard," Pennington said, nodding to him. Wannabee nodded back.

Pennington then turned his gaze to me. "And you are?"

"Dragonrider Kaylyn Madara," I stated clearly. "I'm here on Brooke's behalf."

He scratched his head, then smoothed his light blond hair back. "Very well. Lady Madara…"

"Dragonrider," I interrupted, correcting him.

He merely included it. "Lady Dragonrider, are you familiar with the law?"

"Fairly well."

"Very well. You may go first."

With Emma Marcell's help, I'd written and memorized a statement that I found utterly compelling. Brooke seemed to relax more and more as I verified her claims. But when Pennington barely covered a yawn, I knew all the work had been ignored. That was fine with me. I'd said it for the benefit of the lawmakers hidden in the crowd behind me. They could evaluate what was given to them.

After I finished, Pennington asked Wannabee for his statement.

"It's all a lie," Wannabee said, feigning hurt. "I have never treated Brooke with anything less than the honor her station deserves."

I felt that to be the truth as he saw it.

"I have never abused my servants, or threatened them. If Brooke had wanted to find employment elsewhere, all she had to do was say so. A man of my station has no need to worry over one servant. There are plenty others out there who would do just as well, or better. The insult to my character is outrageous, and does more damage than she could ever understand."

Pennington nodded, his face serious. "There is no excuse for this kind of behavior." He frowned at Brooke. "I cannot believe anyone would be so ungrateful. I personally know Lord Richard to be kind and a man of honor. You have severely damaged his reputation, and such an offense will not be allowed. You are fined a year's wages, and you will serve with hard labor until you have repaid Lord Richard what you owe him for defamation."

Brooke started to weep. I crossed my arms. "All he said was that it was a lie, and you're going to take his word over everything I've shown you?"

"His proof was convincing, Lady Dragonrider."

"His proof of friendship and money, you mean. It must pay well to be a judge-for-hire. Do you only take noble clients, or do you auction your decision off to the highest bidder?"

"I won't take this insult from you, Lady Madara," he snapped at me. "Continue to speak, and I'll charge you next and you'll be working next to the servant girl."

I turned to the generals. "Is that proof enough, General Amea?"

To my delight, Pennington's face slowly paled.

"You bluff," Wannabee accused.

"Poker players bluff. I don't bluff, Wannabee," I informed him.

General Amea was the first to come forward, followed by the other five. His face was stern. "This behavior is unacceptable," he said, his voice like a whip, slicing both Wannabee and

Pennington. "And both of you will be punished for your behavior today."

Brooke was still silently weeping, but hope had entered her eyes. "The generals?" she whispered.

General Amea turned to her. "Miss Havener, I will remove your sentence and grant you repayment for your treatment. Lord Wannabee will be punished."

"He needs to be an example," General Maddox said. "An example to the others."

Nightfire had an idea. "Make him a commoner."

Wannabee looked too horrified over the suggestion to realize a dragon had spoken in his head. "Over a *servant*? You can't do that!"

"Unfortunately for you, Brooke was under my care," I told him. "And I happen to not only be in the military, but a noble."

"A *minor* noble, you wretch!"

"That's Lady Dragonrider to you," I said with dignity. "Nobility is nobility. I'm in full agreement with Nightfire, General Maddox. Strip him of his noble title. Pennington too." I gave a wicked smile at the color Pennington turned. "You'll handle it, Pennington? Just like all the rest?"

He didn't look like he could speak.

Nightfire wasn't surprised when Wannabee attacked. I hadn't been quite prepared for it, but Raz had trained me well. I evaded the knife that appeared in his hand and, despite the training that showed in his moves, laid him out before a minute was up. I somehow ended up with the knife in my hand and dropped it to the ground before glaring at Pennington. "Do you want to try me?" I asked, the threat evident.

He knelt on the ground, hands held out to show he wasn't going to attack and didn't have a weapon on him.

"That was...very impressive, Dragonrider." General Amea was impressed enough to use my self-given title.

I nearly shrugged, then remembered my manners. "Thank you. This is what I've been training for," I added.

"This?" General Amea sounded slightly amused.

I shrugged now. "Keeping peace. Preparing for battle." I looked at Brooke. "Helping those who need it."

Brooke knelt at my feet. "Thank you, Lady Dragonrider," she whispered magnanimously. "Thank you."

"Stop that," I said crossly. "I'm not some noble who thinks he's king. Stand on your feet and don't curtsey to me."

"But how can I thank you otherwise?" she protested, still on her knees.

"You can take whatever recompense given to you and go to my mother's estate and tell her she's hired you, if you need a job. If not, then go wherever you want and write a letter to my sister telling her that no man ever has the right to give abuse to those around him. Now get off your knees. For pity's sake."

She slowly rose to her feet. As she started to dip, I pointed my finger sternly at her. "And don't curtsey."

Brook finally smiled. "Yes, my lady."

I just sighed. "I knew you were going to use my title on me."

"You deserve it," she said sincerely. "You're what it means to be a lady."

I couldn't help but smile. "Be sure to include that to my sister. She'll be overjoyed to hear it."

Chapter 31

Women continued to show up at the School, begging my help. Led by Lady Marcell, Lady Amea, and assisted by me, we gave the generals plenty to do. Outside of going through every decision made by several nobles who were just like Wannabee, they had to strip Pennington and Wannabee of their titles and grant them elsewhere. Several nobles were glad to be rid of the duty of acting as judge and were more than eager to provide a place for a judge so they didn't have to deal with the law. Judges suddenly had a storm of cases to overlook, double check, and handle.

Aside from that law, I assisted in bringing six more laws that needed changing or removing to their attention. I knew very little about what I was doing, but I could easily see the wrong. It was Dillon who knew best how to fix it, and Lady Marcell and Lady Amea who told me best how to say it. However, I was the one with position and influence, so I was the one who had to point out the problems others showed me. The politics and law departments of the university were more than eager to help out. With the sudden upheaval of the system, the law department had nearly doubled in size.

When I wasn't pointing out the flaws of the government, I spent my time carving. It was relaxing. I had half a dozen shapes carved out. I was currently working on a figurine of the cat that had made its way inside and usually spent the day curled up and sleeping at my feet. The first two times Nightfire had come to investigate this creature he'd never seen before, the cat ran off. Disgusted, Nightfire informed me that cats were silly creatures and of no use and sulked for half a day. The next day, the cat crawled up on him while he took a nap and joined him in sleep. Nightfire quickly decided that cats weren't so bad.

While Nightfire had his fun with the cat, I was now dragged to just about every meeting held at the School. Until their new building had all furniture and whatever else moved in with the finishing touches, the generals used the School as their base. I did my best to fight my way through the meetings without saying anything. It was a difficult challenge some days. During my umpteenth meeting, someone mentioned the dragons that lived in the mountains and what, if anything, could be done about them. Their plans were along the lines of penning them like goats, or measures to keep them away like we did with wyverns. They didn't bother to consult me, and it took all I had not to scream at them for their ignorance. The instant break was called, I left the room, not sure I could go back and be polite.

"Kaylyn!" Dillon was trying to catch up to me. "Do you want to get something off your chest? You look...bothered."

I looked down and shook my head, knowing if I said anything it would spill out of control in my anger.

I felt him studying me, and said, "Come on. I have something in my office I need. We can take our break there."

The instant we reached his office, he closed the door. "All right, Kaylyn, what's going on? You've barely said a word since you got here. I'm not sure you've said a handful of words in that room, in *any* of the meetings, outside of what my wife or I tell you to say, and that's not like you. The Kaylyn I knew wasn't shy to give her opinion."

"So I grew up."

"Growing up doesn't mean talking less. You were the one who complained that we only seem to expect...what was it...silence and sewing out of women."

Anger threatened to crack through. "I'm sure most of them still do."

"You know the most about dragons of anyone in that room. Why aren't you sharing what you know?"

"Because I can't do it like I'm supposed to," I said, giving up. "I can't do the diplomatic stuff. I'm *trying* to be mature, but being in that room makes me want to scream! They know nothing about dragons! They think dragons are stupider than sheep, which couldn't be *further* from the truth! They've met Nightfire!"

"And doubtless they've forgotten much of what they learned two years ago. You're the only one that can speak for the dragons. You've been included in the meetings because they feel you deserve to be there. You have the right to give your opinion."

"They won't *listen* to me! They'll call me an immature child, and I'm sick and *tired* of being called that!"

"You won't reach adulthood if you keep everything bottled up like that," he pointed out with humor. "If what you say makes sense, they'll listen. If you can't manage to say it all with proper decorum, I'll help."

"You're just dying to be dishonorably discharged, aren't you?"

"It's my career to risk, isn't it now? And I think for the dragons, it's well worth the risk."

"I ought to let them soak in their own stupidity," I muttered, but I knew I was giving in.

"You're a better person than that, and we both know it."

I sighed, but just for formality. "All right. I'll try."

When we rejoined the generals, Dillon murmured something to Captain Durai, and then took his seat by me. I tucked the little journal with all my notes in my lap and wondered just how far they would go to pacify me.

"There are a few new ideas concerning dragons that could be shared," Captain Durai said calmly. "Before we move on."

"What new ideas?" General Olina inquired.

Dillon answered. "Dragonrider Kaylyn has lived with dragons for several months. She would know their habits as well as anyone."

"Dragons? How many dragons?" Hesperian was usually quiet, but if I'd caught his interest, I'd certainly caught everyone else's.

"Less than twenty." I took the ripped jacket I assumed belonged to General Maddox and slid it down the table. "Ironclaw belonged to that clan."

Eyes widened as the jacket was unfolded. Maddox looked stunned. "You lived with that beast?"

I held the irritation at bay. When being chased by a dragon like Ironclaw, I could forgive his description. "I did."

"Did you live with them, or near them?" Hesperian asked, looking for clarification.

"I lived with them."

He sat back, thinking quietly.

"Then you know their weaknesses," Olina said.

I only partially held my scowl. "I know *them*."

"How much information have you gathered?" Amea inquired.

I held up the journal so they could see. Eyes zeroed in on the many pages filled with information.

"You've managed to gather all that information by yourself? That's enough for a book, maybe even two," Maddox said to the others.

"This isn't so I can become the next Doctor McDragon," I informed them. "Most of this was given to me by the dragons, and they didn't say I could share."

"The dragons surely don't care."

"They absolutely care. They don't talk to people they don't trust. This is so I can take care of Nightfire, not for any other reason."

"What about our protection, Lady Madara?" General Amea asked, gesturing to the jacket still on the table.

"If you leave them alone and stay out of their territory, you don't need protection from them. They don't like you, and they don't want to deal with you."

"If they raze the town…"

"Wyverns raze towns. If you stay out of their mountains, the dragons will leave you alone."

"There's no guarantee of that."

"Dragons aren't stupid, you know. They're smarter than all of us put together. They know bothering you will bring more of you to their mountains, and they don't want that. Leave them alone, and you won't have a problem."

"And what if a problem arises?" Maddox pressed.

"Then you did something stupid, and I have no idea of how you'll fix it. You can't light a fire to scare them away like you can with wyverns. You have to make peace with them, as if they were another country."

Olina looked displeased. "Make peace with *dragons*?"

"You know, considering that they're smarter than you and you don't know the least useful thing about them, you ought to be grateful they haven't decided to be rid of the human race and flown down here to destroy you."

Dillon moved just slightly, signaling that I should stop now. "From what we have seen of the dragon race, it is very hard to defeat a dragon. I have seen evidence of their knowledge, and plenty of proof that they're more than capable of doing whatever they please. Things have always been strained between us. We live in fear of them. Perhaps now is the time to consider offering an olive branch."

"Is that the same as a treaty?" I whispered.

He sent me a smile. "That's the first step."

"A peace treaty with a dragon has never been done before!" Maddox protested.

"We've never had a Dragonrider before either," Dillon reminded them. "Kaylyn has disproved nearly all of Doctor McDragon's statements, showing there's quite a bit she can validate regarding dragons. If the dragons were willing to trust her with valuable information, we could use her to bring a treaty of peace into existence."

I figured that was a fancier and much more polite way of stating that now was the time to try instead of whining about how it had never been done.

To my severe disappointment, they did nothing but discuss how a treaty could be done, and whether or not it would be legal to create a treaty with a dragon. I repeated four times that dragons could understand a treaty, each with slightly more impatience. In

382

the end, they wrote a bill saying that if anyone broke a law concerning dragons, I would be called in. I didn't know what laws were in existence involving dragons, but I was pretty sure it just involved dragons attacking humans. When I left, I paced around the grounds once to cool my temper. Then I remembered Raz, and decided I'd write him a letter to let him know where I was and what I was doing. Nightfire said he'd take it to Raz as soon as I'd finished it. It didn't take long to write. I strapped a light pack over his middle and slipped the letter inside. "Tell Raz and Carmella I miss them," I said.

"You could come," he pointed out.

I shook my head. "It's probably better if I don't. Raz is training Carmella. She needs her training. And I'll only get jealous again."

He nuzzled gently.

I fingered the strap. Nightfire hadn't minded the strap, and the instructor in horseback riding had mentioned the saddle again. "Nightfire, would you mind wearing some kind of saddle to keep me on?"

"Saddles are heavy."

"What if it wasn't?"

"I am not a horse."

I held the smile. "I wasn't suggesting you were. I just wondered if you'd consider it. It might help if you didn't have to catch me so much."

Nightfire was silent, disapproval warring with consideration. *"I will think on it,"* he declared.

"That's all I want right now." I hugged him. "Safe flying, Nightfire."

Meetings went back to boring. The generals decided they'd have to think and consult on what to do about the dragons, and so moved on to different laws. I barely understood what they were talking about sometimes as I stared at the jumble of large words that made up a law. When Nightfire returned, I asked to go out one afternoon when there were no meetings. Dillon gave his approval and I didn't hesitate. I needed time away from politics, and I couldn't do it at the School. I was hoping I might see another dragon as well. They mentioned they moved every once in a while, and there were plenty of caves nearby. It didn't hurt my chances that the recruits had been talking about dragons they'd seen lately.

I wore pants without the skirt because I wasn't planning on seeing anyone else. I had a bow and arrows on my back because I'd been informed it wasn't safe to go out without a weapon.

"Who do I need protection from?" I asked. "Dragons? I've lived with them. And I have Nightfire."

"All the same," Dillon replied. "It can't hurt to be careful."

Nightfire and I headed north, towards the mountains. We'd wheeled over Crystal Lake when Nightfire's head whipped to the left. Immediately, he changed course and shot towards the mountains.

"Nightfire?" I asked, feeling his urgency.

"I hear cries. Dragon cries."

I listened hard. As we grew closer, I caught the faint sound of a roar. The closer we got, the more it sounded like sorrow, and agony.

Nightfire pushed himself faster. I flattened myself against him, trying to help him go faster by providing less wind-resistance. But the closer we got, the fainter the cries, and then they suddenly stopped. The silence frightened me.

We arrived minutes too late. Nightfire scaled a hill and saw a green dragon down below. He dove down, the wind screaming in our ears, but landed carefully. I stumbled off and ran to the dragon. It was covered in gashes, black blood on the wounds, and the eyes were white. I had never seen the eyes void of color before. And I was sickened to recognize this dragon. Embereyes. The first dragon who had accepted me into the clan.

"He is dead." Nightfire's tone was full of agony. *"Embereyes is dead!"* He let out a roar of fury and anger, the sound terrifying and simultaneously saddening. Then he spat flame at the discarded weapons on the ground. The broken spears. The half melted swords.

"Nightfire, stop! Nightfire, *stop* it!" I ran to him, grabbing his leg to prevent him from taking off, conscious of the claws digging into the rock. "Listen to me!"

He stopped flaming, breathing hard. His eyes were red as he dropped his head to meet my gaze. *"They must pay."*

I wrapped my arms around his muzzle quickly. "They'll pay. I promise it," I said. "They'll pay. But not like this. And not by you. Help me, and I promise they'll pay." My voice hitched. "I'm so sorry, Nightfire."

His eyes closed and anger reverted to sadness. A soft keening, almost like a whimper, voiced his distress.

"I know." My voice choked as tears ran down my face and onto his. "I know. I'm sorry we didn't get here in time. I'm sorry he's dead." I pulled back and wiped at my face. "Go find them. Tell me where they are and I'll help you bring them back. Don't hurt them, Nightfire. Not yet."

Nightfire closed his eyes and listened. *"They are traveling back to the School. They are recruits. They traveled in that direction."* He turned his head to the southwest, the most direct line back to the School.

"Fly. I'll follow."

Nightfire took flight. One look at Embereyes and I felt rage take me. I snatched up the bow I'd dropped and took off without hesitation. All I could think was that they weren't walking away from this. There wasn't a chance I was going to let them walk free and clear, and I'd do what it took to make them pay. Part of my mind was frightened by the rage, but the rest of my mind was contemplating how they would die.

It didn't take long to catch up. I was faster, I'd spent more time moving in the mountains, and they weren't thinking of escaping. I could hear sounds of celebration which only increased my temper. As I came over a large rock, I spotted them not too far below. There were seven or eight of them, recruits from the school, most of them dressed in uniform. *"I found them."*

"I will stop them." Nightfire spat a flame, drawing a line in front of them they couldn't pass.

I launched an arrow over them and into the ground in front as they scrambled around, some of them going for their weapons. "If you fire one arrow," I shouted, "I'll kill you!"

They turned to the voice, seeing me. "Lady Madara, it's a black dragon!" one shouted. "It'll kill us!"

"It wants to kill you all right, and so do I! You murdered a dragon! And you think you're going to slip back to the School?" My hands shook with fury. "Up the hill! Every single one of you! If you run, I'll make sure Nightfire goes after you. You can't outrun a dragon."

They hesitated, murmuring among themselves.

"Now!" I shouted at them. "Right *now*, or I'll have your friends drag your body back! I've killed once and I'm about to kill again!" My threat was accompanied by Nightfire's furious roar and a shot of flame behind them.

This motivated them. I let them all pass by me, grabbing the last recruit. "I thought better of you," I growled.

He flinched and had the sense not to answer.

"You're going to find Dillon Marcell. You're going to tell him that you have shamed the School and if he wants to witness the punishment handed out, then he had better get here. You're going to lead him and whoever he chooses to bring back here. And Recruit, if you don't do what I've commanded, I will spend every waking moment hunting you down, I will drag you to the mountains tied to the belly of a donkey, and I will deliver you to the dragons. And no general, noble, or officer of the Army will save you. Got that?"

He nodded, shaking in my grip.

I shoved him away. "Run."

He took off. I watched him enter the forest before I headed up the mountain after the rest.

I didn't allow talking, and smacked the offender with my bow when one or another tried. They quickly quieted, wheezing their way up the path again. I pushed them ruthlessly.

When we reached the dragon, I removed the ropes they'd used to hold Embereyes down and tied the recruits together facing

Embereyes. They sat on the ground silently. Only once I'd had them tied up did Nightfire leave to find the dragons.

The humans arrived first. The exhausted recruit was leading Dillon, Captain Durai, three generals, and a troop of officers. They gaped at what they saw. I rose from the ground near Embereyes, grabbed the boy by the back of his neck, and dragged him over to the rest where I tied him to the end of the line.

"Lady Madara, I really don't think that's necessary," General Maddox tried to protest.

"He's a murderer and a thief and he deserves to be treated like one. Do you see what he's done? What all of them have done?" I pointed to the ground in front of the recruit. "Everything you took. If I find one thing still on you that belongs to a dragon, I'll gut you like you gutted him."

The recruit hastily piled everything on the ground. There was a small pile for each of them. Mostly scales, one had a claw, and two of them had teeth. It sickened me.

"I don't think this is the best way," Captain Durai said. "Let the boys up. We'll go back and deal with this."

"No." My voice told them I wasn't backing down. "I knew this dragon. I have the right to punish them. And they'll get punished."

"You don't have the rank."

"What is my rank, Captain?"

"Kaylyn," Dillon tried to interrupt.

I ignored him. "What's my rank, Captain? Would you say I rank below a private?"

He hesitated. "No. I wouldn't say that."

"Then we've established I have a rank. We've also previously established that I deal with dragons. You approved that any broken laws concerning dragons was to be dealt with through me. And I don't know for certain, but I'm pretty sure killing a dragon applies. It's a good thing these recruits were trained to uphold the law." The contempt in my voice as I glared at the line of recruits on the ground had several of them flinching. "As the only Dragonrider, I have authority to hand out punishment. I'm the only one who gets to decide what that punishment is. You're going to witness it, and you're going to make sure this never happens again."

One of the boys started to whimper, to plead, and I stepped in front of him, an arrow nocked to my bow. "What did I say about speaking?" I asked in a dangerous voice.

He fell silent, his shoulders shaking with sobs.

"Captain, she's gone mad!" General Olina exclaimed. "Take her down!"

"I'm not crazy. I'm furious. I knew this dragon. He wasn't some monster. He hatched three eggs, did you know that? By our reckoning, he's a grandfather, maybe a great-grandfather. He has a dragon mate, somewhere. He was kind, and patient, and these recruits *murdered* him, for what? Trophies?" I kicked at a pile of scales and watched them flinch. "For pride? For bragging rights? He was a *friend*!" I was shaking again, grief clawing at my throat. "And they tied him down and they killed him! I can't even say they killed him painlessly! I heard his cries for *leagues*! They *tortured* him!"

"Surely it was not their intention..." General Maddox began.

"I don't *care* what their *intention* was! I *care* what they *did* and they're *going* to pay for it!"

General Olina drew himself up. "I forbid you," he said imperiously.

I could have laughed once at the utter imperiousness and how he expected me to crumple at his tone. "I don't care."

He looked astonished at my refusal. "Are you disobeying me?"

"If you think I'm going to let you sweep this under the rug, you're wrong. I know *exactly* what you think about dragons after the past week, and if you believe for a *second* I'm going to let you walk away and pretend this didn't happen, I'll call for satisfaction, as is a *noble's* right." I knew my eyes were bitter. "As is the *military's* right. And trust me, if you think I'm vengeful, you've got no idea what's coming from the dragons."

General Amea was smarter and tried to reason with me. "Lady Kaylyn, please," he coaxed. "Do you want to know that these boys are no longer alive because of you? Do you understand the toll it takes?"

"Yes. I do. And for Embereyes, I'll go through it again."

He tried a different tact. "Think of all we've done for the good of Centralia. The laws that have been changed. For us, as a personal favor, pardon them."

"I don't have to do anything for you! Why would I? You shouldn't side with them! You should be siding with me! These murderers have just *destroyed* any chance at peace with dragons that you ever had!" My voice choked once and I faced Embereyes in case I couldn't control the tears.

Dillon crossed to me, rested his hand on my arm. "Kaylyn, this isn't the right way," he said quietly. "Killing them won't bring him back."

"I know." I blinked back tears.

"Then let us take them back. We'll punish them."

"It's out of my hands, Dillon. Nightfire's on his way back with the dragons." The solidarity of him flashed into my mind as he came into range. "They'll deal with them."

One recruit gave a low, sickened moan. The first one started to scream. "Help me! Help me! The dragons are going to kill us! They'll rip us apart and eat us! They'll…"

I turned on him. "They could very well do to you what you've done to Embereyes!" I snapped. "And you'll deserve it. Unless a dragon is interested in hearing what you have to say, you aren't going to make another sound. If I let you walk off this mountain, the dragons will follow and destroy you all. And I won't stop them."

Dillon breathed a curse. "Kaylyn, listen to me. Kaylyn, *look* at me."

I turned my eyes to his so he could see the grief and the tears I was still trying to fight. Seeing that, his voice gentled. "Kaylyn, I know you're hurting. I'm sorry you lost a friend, but I need you to help us here. You don't owe the rest anything, but you owe me."

I could barely believe my ears. "Why would you call it in for them? For what they did?"

"Because I have a responsibility for these recruits. And because if you let the dragons kill them, their families and hundreds of others will come here and try to wipe the dragons out."

"They deserve to die!"

"Do the dragons? What about Nightfire? Angry people will be coming after you and Nightfire, and all that work you put in to help Brooke and all the rest will be reversed and destroyed. You're only fifteen so you don't see the ramifications. Kaylyn, you have to ask for their lives."

I was silent for a moment. When I spoke again, my voice wavered. "What if I can't?"

"You have to."

"I don't want to."

I could sense the sympathy. "That's the hardest part about duty. Sometimes you have to do what you don't want to. But you have to try."

I didn't want to try, but I knew what I owed Dillon. I knew what he'd sacrificed for me, and I knew he could see all too clearly what would happen if I failed him now. I dashed a tear away from my face and handed him my bow. "Lay your weapons down. All of them. If you don't, they'll see it as a threat."

"Throw your weapons away!" Dillon shouted. He laid my quiver on the ground and laid his own sword on top of it, and his dagger. I walked between Embereyes and the line of recruits that faced him and knelt down while the others hastily followed Dillon's example.

There were five dragons with Nightfire. He landed behind the rest. They nearly slammed to the ground, bouncing the rocks and shaking the earth beneath our feet a little. Seeing Embereyes dead and mutilated, they let out roars of agony and anger.

Ironclaw was the first to speak. "Who did this?" His eyes were red, nearly to flaming level. "Who has done this?" he demanded of me.

"Recruits from the School for Officers and Gentlemen," I answered. "They killed Embereyes."

"How do you know this?"

I pointed. "They held the proof. Nightfire and I heard the cries. We got here minutes too late. We brought them back and they all held something of Embereyes's. Their proof sits in front of each of them."

Ironclaw roared at them, watching them flinch back and weep in terror at the hostility from the black dragon. "They are cowards!" he hissed in derision. "Embereyes was an old dragon! He was not violent! They have no excuse for what they have done!"

"No, they don't," I answered. "I asked Nightfire to find you. I wanted you to see the ones who had killed Embereyes. I wanted you to know that it wasn't a secret and wouldn't be hidden from you. They will pay for what they've done."

Crystalscales hissed, the snake sound louder and fuller. "We will repay them. Blood for blood. They weep and whine as cowards do. We will not give mercy." Her light blue tail lashed angrily.

"What about his mate? Where is she?"

"She died. She became sick and could not be cured. There is no mate to avenge him, so we will do it. Take those who were not responsible and leave. You will not need to return for the bodies."

I closed my eyes. "I must ask you for their lives."

"What?" Crystalscales was astounded. "You who called us for justice, you who knew Embereyes and trusted him, seeing what they have done and knowing how they have tortured him, would ask for their lives?"

I took a deep breath. "Yes."

Ironclaw knocked me backwards, his eyes going a darker red. I could nearly feel the flames as his claws scraped over the rocks. "Why, human, would you ask for such a thing?" he growled.

I swallowed hard. It had been a long time since I'd been this afraid of what a dragon might do to me. On the rock behind the dragons, Nightfire tensed. I managed to find my voice and spoke. "I'm asking for you. Humans are vengeful creatures, just like

391

dragons. If you kill these people, guilty or not, their families will come after you."

"Let them come," Crystalscales hissed. "We can deal with them."

"You'll suffer," I countered. "You'll be hunted day and night. You'll never be safe. The more you kill, the more will come. You have young ones that would be in danger."

Ironclaw growled, impatience evident. "You do not wish for them to be pardoned. You want punishment, just as we do. Why will you plead for them?"

"Because someone I trusted asked me to. Because I owe him and he's doing his duty. Because I don't want to see you dead next, which is what will happen if you get what you want."

He pulled away, allowing me to sit up. "You ask for the impossible."

"I'm not either. You claimed you were smarter than humans. You know I'm telling the truth, and you know you can walk away if you choose to."

Ironclaw paced over to Embereyes's body, his eyes turning blue with grief, then looked at the people behind me. I hoped they were unarmed. I could almost feel Maddox shiver.

"You trust this human?" Blackstar demanded.

"With my life," I said immediately. "He has worked hard for me and Nightfire. He will protect you if I ask him to. But he has a duty that requires him to ask me that I stand for his people. I'm the only one who has the right to ask that you pardon them, and I'm asking for it."

"I do not like this," Ironclaw grumbled.

"I don't like it either!" I shouted at him. "Look, dragon, this isn't about like or don't like! You *owe* me!"

Ironclaw bristled at the reminder and growled softly.

"You said before that humans were not to be trusted." Nightfire spoke to everyone. "I have seen humans that can be trusted, and humans that cannot. Use this to prove that humans can be trusted."

"Give us a second chance," I pleaded. "They'll be punished. If they aren't, I swear to you that I'll tell you and you'll have your chance to seek revenge. I want peace between us, and if there's a chance of peace at all, then you have to take the blow this time. I promise I will fight with everything I have to make sure this won't happen again. There are three generals here who will work as hard as I will to make sure there's a law preventing anyone from harming a dragon."

"I have your word?" Ironclaw demanded, eyes on me.

"You have my word."

General Olina, possibly trying to help smooth things over, spoke quickly. "You have our word as well."

Ironclaw hissed at him, glaring balefully. "You are not a human we can trust. Your word is not worth having."

I gave a painful smile, knowing Olina would be indignant at such a refusal of his offer. "I'll have Nightfire tell you what punishment they get. I promise this won't be forgotten."

One of the recruits spoke, his voice quavering. "You aren't going to eat us?"

Six pairs of dragon eyes landed on him. "Humans taste terrible," Ironclaw declared. "But we will not rip out your heart and drop you from the sky. Today, we will pardon you, as Embereyes did. You may never return to the mountains. We know your voice. We know your smell. Return a second time, for any reason, and you will be killed." His eyes moved to me. "I swear to that."

"So be it," I replied. "You have my gratitude." I bowed to them. "I am sorry for your loss today. I am sorry for Embereyes and his mate and everyone they mattered to."

Blackstar crossed the distance and rested her nose against my cheek, startling those behind me. "He mattered to you. You suffer with us today." Her eyes closed. "Embereyes would approve of this. He would say you have grown in maturity and in strength of your will. You have grown wiser. You are a human we know we can trust."

"My debt is repaid, human," Ironclaw said, still unhappy about letting them go. "I owe you nothing."

I nodded silently.

"Leave, humans," Crystalscales ordered, lifting her blue wings in warning. "We will take care of our dead. Not until the smoke fades may you return to this mountain."

It was a silent retreat. Everyone left with their weapons. Nightfire remained on his rock. *"Are you coming?"* I asked.

"Not yet. I will stay. Go."

I nodded, slung my quiver over my shoulder, picked up my bow, the only weapon left, and headed down the mountain. Behind me, smoke drifted to the sky.

Chapter 32

Nightfire returned before darkness. I was waiting for him. I closed the roof and curled up against his neck, weeping softly until I fell asleep. My eyes were dry and gritty when I awoke and I scrubbed my face over the little sink until the reflection in the mirror looked more alive. I looked ill and felt sick at heart, not knowing if I'd done the right thing. I hoped I hadn't just allowed those in charge to cover up the murder of a dragon when humans and dragons were enemies. The dragons would never trust humans again. Right at the moment, I wasn't sure I could either.

I went inside the Great Hall and saw two guards who stayed with the generals on either side of a set of double doors. I walked up to them, noting how they shifted to block my way. "What's going on?" I demanded.

"The recruits are being questioned," one stated.

"Questioned, or interrogated?"

"I couldn't say, ma'am. I've been on duty."

"Can I go in?"

"No, ma'am. No one goes in."

"Fine. Then tell someone in there to let me in or tell me what's going on."

The guard rapped softly on the door, murmured my request to a guard on the other side. Dillon let himself out and quietly closed the door. "According to Doctor McDragon, dragon scales have tiny gemstones in them. Green dragons have emeralds. They were looking for riches," he said heavily to my questioning expression.

"The teeth? The claw?"

"Ivory claws and teeth."

"That's why?" Anger was building. "They killed Embereyes for *riches*? They were *poaching*?"

"Would you have preferred they killed for sport?" Dillon asked, voice still quiet.

I glared at the ground. "No," I answered tightly. "It makes it worse though. They were killing for riches that didn't exist."

"I'm sorry. If there's anything I can do…"

"There is. Get me Doctor McDragon."

"I'm afraid we don't know where he is," General Maddox said, letting himself out of the room as well. "After it came out that he…"

"Was a fraud?" I finished for him.

"That he falsified his records of dragons," General Maddox continued, "he left. We haven't seen him since."

"His *books* are still around. He's as responsible for this as anyone. I want him here."

"But we don't know where he is."

"Then *find* him!" I shouted. "Root him out of whatever *hole* he's living in and drag him here. I won't have the entire country thinking they can get rich off of killing dragons because of his *fiction*!"

Dillon rested a hand on my shoulder. "We'll find him," he promised. "Do you want to come inside?"

"No. Because I'll want to kill them." Despite my threat, my voice choked with tears.

"Go find my wife then. I sent her a message that I wouldn't be home for some time. If you'll make sure she knows why I can't come, I'd appreciate it. Maybe being there will make you feel better."

I nodded. As they went back inside, I called out, "Dillon."

He paused with his hand on the door to look back at me.

My voice was small, like a young child pleading for comfort. "Will you promise they'll be punished? I promised the dragons they would. Promise they won't be pardoned?"

"I promise," he said. "They'll be an example."

I nodded and watched them go in before I headed to the Marcell home.

Lady Marcell was already awake and dressed and answered the door herself. "Oh, Kaylyn! It's good to see you! I thought maybe you were Dillon."

"He's at the School. He's busy questioning the recruits."

"I managed to get a little information out of the messenger boy, but I didn't get much. Maybe you could explain what's going on?" she asked hopefully.

The explanation took an hour, three handkerchiefs, and four glasses of water, and I'd paced the room enough to have walked to the Esperion Mountains and back. By then, Emma and Maggie were in total sympathy with me and wholeheartedly agreed that the recruits should be punished. "My Dillon will make sure it happens," she assured me. "And if there were generals there, I'm sure they will too. Being faced with angry dragons is the biggest motivator you could have."

"What do you think they'll do?"

"Expel them from the School for starters. Beyond that, it depends on what they're arrested for. Poaching, at the very least. Poaching gets you two years."

"For a dragon, they could push that higher," Maggie pointed out. "At least to five, maybe even seven years since they are sentient creatures."

For the grief I felt, I didn't know if that would be enough.

"How about some nice tea?" Emma said brightly, reading my expression. "Honey with it?"

"Yeah. Sure." I sat down heavily.

It didn't take much coaxing for Emma to convince me to stay. I ate lunch and listened to Emma talk as she sewed. She talked with Maggie sometimes, and sometimes she just talked. She didn't usually require me to say anything, which was fine with me. Half the time I didn't even know what she was saying. By the time Dillon came home, as Maggie was setting the table for dinner, I was tired and had worked through most of my grief. I'd been through it with Raphael and my father and had an idea of where the end of the emotional turmoil was. Emma went to the front door to greet her husband.

Dillon gave a weary smile and kissed Emma's cheek. "Is Kaylyn still here?" he asked. Then he spotted me and murmured something to his wife before entering the sitting room and taking the seat across from me. "We're done," he said quietly.

"Were they punished?"

"They were."

"Does Nightfire know?"

"Knows and approves. He's gone to tell the other dragons."

"Okay." I got up.

"Don't you want to know what the punishment is?" he asked.

I shook my head. "No. If Nightfire approves, that's enough. The table's already set for three. I'm just going to...walk somewhere."

"Poor girl," I heard Emma murmur to Maggie as I opened the front door. "She doesn't know what to do."

I walked around the School, wondering why I felt so lost. I walked and walked, tired and still feeling as if there was an answer I was looking for but couldn't find. I couldn't figure out what I was wanting, and I felt too restless to be able to sit still long.

The answer came when the gate I was passing by creaked open. Warren stood in the opening. "Nightfire not back yet?" he asked awkwardly.

I shook my head, silent.

"You want to sit with me until he does? It's getting late."

"Dragons hate flying in the dark." It came out a whisper.

"Then he'll be back soon. You can sit with me until he gets here." He offered his hand.

I felt myself crumple as I walked to him. I didn't cry, but that was only because I didn't have any energy to. Suddenly, I wanted nothing more than to lie down somewhere and sink into oblivion. "I miss Embereyes," I whispered into Warren's shoulder. "I know he was a dragon, but it's like losing Dad all over again."

Warren held tight. "I'm sorry, Kaylyn. I'm sorry you're going through this at all. I wish I could help."

I sniffed hard, but didn't move. This moment, this human companionship, was what I missed. I needed not to be alone. I needed the human comfort of someone who wasn't hurting to tell me it was going to be all right again. Dillon had someone to go home to. The other dragons could deal with it in their own way in their clan. I didn't have anyone, not even Nightfire at the moment. When I left here, I'd go back to living alone. At the moment I envied Madelyn, because she had somebody to love. "Tell me it's going to be all right."

"It's going to be all right, Kaylyn," he promised. He kissed my temple. "It's going to be all right. You'll see."

I stayed with Nightfire when he returned. Food was delivered to us, and we stayed closed in our little home. The carelessness at Embereyes's death hurt, and I wasn't interested in dealing with the generals right now.

Three days after Embereyes's death, I'd gone back to carving, this time making a dragon curling over an egg, showing the parenting affection I'd always felt from Embereyes. I was carving out the base when Nightfire's head came up. *"I smell him. I hear him. Doctor McDragon is here."*

"Good." I got up. *"Let's roast him."*

"Literally?"

"Figuratively."

"It is always figuratively."

"Someday. I promise."

Dillon was waiting for me outside and followed me in the room where Doctor McDragon was. Doctor McDragon may have been disgraced, but he was still dressed well. I was disgusted by the wealth he wore.

I glared at him. "Remember me?"

He was already sweating. "My dear girl..."

"That would be Dragonrider or Lady Kaylyn to you," I snapped. "Don't patronize me."

"Kaylyn," Dillon murmured.

I pulled back on my anger. "How many books have you written?"

"My books? Why…five, I believe."

"You're going to get rid of them."

"What?" He was indignant and furious. "I will not!"

I poked him hard in the chest. "Let me spell it out for you, you fraud. Three days ago, a group of recruits went and killed a green dragon, Embereyes, because your book promised that there were emeralds in his scales and his teeth and claws were ivory. Everything you've put in those books was a lie, and thanks to you we nearly had a lot of angry dragons ready to kill every human they could find. Someone tried to kill Nightfire because he thought black dragons were dangerous and out of control and ready to kill anyone they saw. I wonder if he didn't think there was money to be had too. Their deaths are on your head. And you're going to fix it."

He backed away from me, struggling to maintain composure. "I…I suppose I can offer something to aid in repayment. How much money can I offer?"

The thought that he wanted to pay off the dead made me want to hurt him. So I decided to. "Money? You can donate every last cent you made on your books to the Dragonrider fund that's just been set up. Every cent you have."

"You'll beggar me!"

"It's better than the alternative. After you've turned over all the payment you received for your lies, you're going to go to give a speech telling everyone what you wrote was a fraud and that you know nothing about dragons. Every book you wrote is going to be destroyed. You're going to make sure of it."

"My books are international!"

"Then you have a lot of work to do, don't you?"

He puffed up. "I won't do it! These books are my life's work!"

"Your life's work nearly cost hundreds of lives!" I snarled at him. "If you don't do this, then Nightfire and I will find you, no matter where you go, no matter how safe you think you are. After we strip you of your title and your lands, we'll drag you up the mountain to see the dragons who live there. I'm sure they'll be pleased to meet the man who claimed to know everything about them. Crystalscales in particular will be interested to know she sometimes lives underwater."

He paled.

"Didn't think anyone would find out, did you? I have a couple male, white dragons who would love to greet you. Oh, and although I haven't seen them, I'm told there is a male bronze and a female bronze who might like to give you a close look at their scales before they incinerate you." I waited a moment. "Your choice. Are we visiting dragons, or are you going to recant?"

His hands were white as they clenched together. "You leave me no choice. I will recant."

"Good. Now, there are three things you need to make sure you say every time you give this speech. And there will be two members of the military who will be traveling with you and will make sure you say these three things. First, dragons do not hoard treasure. We do not need suicidal treasure hunters. Second, dragons do not have gemstones in their scales, and nothing about them is of any monetary value. I won't have people poaching dragons for riches that don't exist. Third, everything you wrote in your books was a lie. Now, you can spin the rest of your speech however you want. You can say you're sorry for the lies. You can say I'm an evil, little brat who doesn't know her place. You can say you were forced to write those things by a man who blackmailed you. I don't care. But you will say those three things every time. Got it?"

"Yes."

"Yes, what?" I challenged.

He swallowed hard. "Yes, Dragonrider, I understand."

"Good." I stepped back. "Go practice your speech right now to everyone in that room. And then you'd better get going. You have three days to turn over your funds and start your journey. There are two men who are very eager to start their travels and have been instructed to gag you and give you a night in the stocks if you try to bribe them."

"Stocks? Nobody uses stocks anymore," he said, with just a hint of his former derision.

I smiled evilly. "We found some. I knew there had to be some around here somewhere. They're transportable. They'll ride with you everywhere you go. They can also put you in the stocks if you try to escape, or if you don't do what I've ordered, or if you make them unhappy. Enjoy your trip." I headed for the door. I felt vindictive, but I didn't feel guilty for it.

Doctor McDragon was nothing if not a showman. He threw down his hat in anguish. "You might as well thrust a sword through me now," he proclaimed. "Dying would be easier than the shame I must bear!"

I came to a stop. Then, to even my own astonishment, I heard myself give a quiet, little laugh. "Do you think so?" I turned. "Do you know why you're alive? Do you know why those murderers who used to be recruits are alive? Because of Embereyes. The recruits should have been dead the instant Embereyes died. That's what happens with a mindlink. Embereyes could have created a mindlink and taken all those recruits with him. He didn't, and it was a choice for him. He was good, the kind of good I could never be. If I was being ripped apart and tortured to death, I'd do whatever I could to take whoever was doing it with me. Embereyes let them live. And you, Doctor McDragon, get to live because I hope to someday be as wise as Embereyes. Keep in mind, as you travel, that if it had been any other dragon, those recruits you're about to talk to would have been dead because of you."

I didn't bother to look back as I left the room, leaving Doctor McDragon taken aback and a little paler than when I'd entered.

Dillon found me in his office. I was staring out the window, looking at the recruits walking below. I couldn't help but wonder if more of them would have gone to kill a dragon. If they had tried to go and prove themselves, make themselves richer, and simply hadn't found a dragon.

"Here." Dillon cupped my hands around a warm glass with tea. "My wife says this will make you feel better."

Tears pooled in my eyes. "I don't want to be here, Dillon. But I don't know where to go. Everywhere I go, I see myself as a terrible person."

"How could you see yourself as a terrible person?" he asked. "You've done nothing but help others since you got here. I hardly think you're any different elsewhere."

"I don't love my sisters or mother. And I was too late to save Embereyes." A few tears plopped into the tea. "Dragons are known as these vicious, uncaring creatures, and Embereyes was more forgiving than I could ever be. He let them live, Dillon."

He sat down in his chair. "Why did he let them live?" he asked seriously.

I gave a watery laugh. "Because he probably thought they were hatchlings. We mature so slowly to them. He knew what they were looking for, and he let them walk away when he died. But he was wrong. They're evil. They *killed* him. And I can't see another person out there without wondering if they would do the same thing."

Dillon studied me a moment before he reached inside his desk and pulled out a long scroll. On it were hundreds of names, carefully printed. He laid the scroll on his desk and gestured to it. "This is a list of every graduate we've had from the School," he began. "Well, this is part of the list. We have several more scrolls. Some of these people were good people, and some of them were not so good. Some of them were later arrested. But some of them made changes to Centralia. Big ones, little ones, some better than others. Every recruit that passes through here has a shot at becoming someone better. Sometimes that lesson doesn't get learned. But sometimes, that lesson stays with them even through the highest rank of General."

I shook my head. "I don't understand whatever it is you're trying to say."

"Come here. Read this name." He tapped a spot on the scroll.

I set the tea down and moved to see what he was pointing at. My eyes blurred momentarily when I saw the name. "Thomas Madara," I whispered. "My father."

Dillon adjusted the scroll. "Now this one."

I smiled a little. "Dillon Marcell."

Dillon unrolled another scroll, laying it out for me to see. I read off Captain Durai's name, and five of the generals I dealt with, including General Amea and General Maddox.

"We have a long history of good and bad recruits," Dillon said, bringing out a third scroll. "What the others did was wrong. It was cruel and unjust. But it doesn't make them evil. And it doesn't make all the others evil. The laws didn't fully protect the dragons, and I didn't do as much as I could have to help protect them. I share in the blame." He laid out the scroll, and unrolled it until it became blank. "I also share in the victories," he said quietly. "Your brother is one of many hoping to have his name written on this scroll. He's one of the good recruits. It would do you good to see how staunchly he's defended you. How he's defended Nightfire, and all the dragons. It would make you proud to see the difference he's made to many recruits and even some of the professors here."

It made me feel a little better to know how much my brother loved me. I knew standing up for women, especially his youngest sister, couldn't have been easy.

Dillon tapped the blank space on the scroll. "You're also one of my recruits," he said, holding my gaze. "And I believe there's a spot for your name right here. My question to you is this; what kind of a difference are you going to make?"

Silence sat in the room for a minute. I stared at the blank spot on the scroll, noise from outside filtering in on this blustery, fall day.

"I'm not a good person," I said softly. "I wanted them to die."

"But you let them live. And more importantly, you let Doctor McDragon live despite how much you've always hated him. And that tells me more about you than you know." He retrieved the tea and placed it in my hands again. "You love your family. All of them. It's just hard to see some days. If you didn't love them, you wouldn't care so much what happens to them."

I looked up at him, tired, confused, and torn apart. "Do you think I'm a good person?"

I couldn't doubt the honesty in his tone. "I think you're more than a good person; I think you're a person who I could trust implicitly no matter what circumstance, no matter what your orders were, and no matter who or what was at stake. I, Kaylyn, would follow you into battle and step in front of your arrow of death to make sure the world was a better place for a little longer."

I couldn't have felt more humbled. And some of the weight left me. I took a sip of tea, feeling its warmth soothe me. "Thank you. But just so you know, sir, I'm supposed to follow you into battle. And I'm not sure what my rank is, but I'm pretty sure it's below yours."

Dillon grinned. "With you, Dragonrider, it's only a matter of time before you start your own war."

Despite what Dillon said, I couldn't rejoin classes. I couldn't concentrate enough, and Dillon silently pulled me out of everything but horseback riding. Nightfire didn't care how often I went riding, stating horses weren't *that* fast, and they weren't nearly as smart, and he wouldn't get jealous of something so easily frightened. The instructor there hadn't even fussed when I'd stopped wearing skirts when riding. He'd shown me a few plans for possible saddles for riding Nightfire, most of them promising to be light.

I spent some time inside with Dillon. I didn't always work; sometimes I just read through papers, or stared out the window at the mountains beyond. Dillon moved in and out of his office, with more things to deal with since the generals were still here but preparing to leave in the next week. I was just glad they were leaving and I wouldn't have to come up with excuses to avoid meetings over laws I no longer remotely cared about.

I was jerked out of my thoughts when Nightfire called urgently. *"Kaylyn, there are dragons approaching."*

I jerked to my feet and ran to the window. *"Dragons? How many? Where? Do we know them?"*

"They are coming from the north. They are not far. There are four of them, and led by Ironclaw."

I leapt over to the door and sprinted down the hallway, narrowly avoiding Captain Durai. "Don't sound the alarm!" I shouted. "Keep everyone inside! Oh, geez, they're going to get *massacred*!"

Recruits were milling about outside when I ran out the door. "Get inside!" I shouted. "Inside! Now!"

Hearing the urgency of my voice, reinforced by Captain Durai's bellowed order, they obeyed. Every single person quickly barricaded themselves inside, leaving me alone in the courtyard.

"That was not necessary," Ironclaw's voice said to me.

"Things aren't calm between us right now," I answered. *"And if you didn't want to kill them, they probably wanted to shoot you."*

Ironclaw appeared over a building and settled on the ground in front of me. Nightfire landed behind me, silent. Behind Ironclaw, one dragon was flying slowly and carefully, as if it was carrying something.

"What's this?" I asked, confused.

"This is your second chance, human." Ironclaw moved aside so Crystalscales could land. She gently deposited an egg on the ground and landed just behind it. The dragons on either side landed on the roof of a building.

My knees nearly went weak. "An egg?" I whispered.

"It belonged to Embereyes and his mate," Crystalscales informed me. *"We cannot care for it."*

"You want *me* to raise it?"

"Not you. You are already connected with Nightfire. You must find another. Another like you. Someone dragons can trust." Crystalscales nuzzled the egg gently. *"There were two eggs. The other one died inside the shell the day after Embereyes was killed. We do not know if this one will survive. If it does, it will be your chance to prove dragons can trust humans. Raise it. Make it like*

you. Make a...a Dragonrider," she said, hesitant with the unfamiliar term. *"You have a dragon with you and you have raised Nightfire. He will know who is like you. You will both know how to help raise this dragon."*

I felt staggered by this burden. This was our chance to make peace between dragons and humans. If I could pull this off, I might be able to create a truce that would protect both sides from mistrust and misunderstandings.

"Do we have your word you will do this?" Ironclaw asked sternly.

I nodded. "You have my word."

"It is yours now. Do well by it," Crystalscales ordered. I knew what it took for her to hand over an egg, to give it a human parent.

"How long?" I asked. "How long do I have until it hatches?"

"Two months. Nightfire will know when." Then they all took off, winging their way back to the north.

After the dragons were gone, recruits started to carefully exit, looking nervously around before creeping a little farther out. There was an awed hush at the sight of the egg in the middle of the courtyard. I knelt down in front of it, and touched my fingertips to the shell. From inside came a gurgling croak; the curious cry of a hatchling.

"Hello there, little one," I said softly. "Don't worry. We're going to find someone to take care of you."

Chapter 33

The egg was moved to the space Nightfire and I shared, making sure it would be warm enough for the egg at all times of the day. The generals were notified about the new egg. I allowed them to see it for five minutes, and then shooed them out.

"Have you had thoughts about who will become the next Dragonrider?" General Amea asked, looking thrilled.

"It's not my choice, General, not entirely," I replied, latching the door shut. "It's going to be up to the dragon."

"We have some suggestions," General Maddox began.

"It has to be someone young," I interrupted before he could start naming people off. Nightfire and I had already discussed some of the qualifications. "Someone between the ages of thirteen and nineteen. Nightfire and I will be screening every person who comes. Nightfire knows better who's right for a dragon and who isn't. And in the end, the dragon will choose someone for itself. We can't influence it one way or another. It will just know. It won't depend on status or wealth. Consider this a true test of the heart, Generals. It's going to depend on who the person is if they had nothing to their name."

"How long until the dragon hatches?"

"Two months. We'll have some time, but with everyone wanting to be the next Dragonrider, it's going to be hectic." I rubbed my forehead wearily. "I would appreciate some help. Someone to help screen applicants."

"We'll find the right people to assist you," General Amea promised.

"Nightfire and I get the final say," I informed them. "And anyone can try for this. Nobles, servants, men, and women."

"This is your area of expertise," Dillon said, earning a dirty look from Maddox.

"The dragon may not take anyone," I warned. "You can't force it."

"We remain optimistic, Lady Dragonrider," Hesperian said blandly.

"Hovering won't help," I added quickly. "It's better that the egg is left alone. No one gets to see the egg unless I allow it."

"This is your area of expertise," Hesperian said, repeating Dillon's words. "We follow your lead in these matters."

I felt relief. With Hesperian on my side, he'd convince the others to leave.

Four days later, the generals left, leaving Captain Durai in charge of finding people to help sort through those streaming to the School to fight for a dragon egg. Applicants were forced to remain outside the walls, and anyone who managed to sneak in, or any recruit or servant who dared approach the egg, left in a hurry. Nightfire guarded the egg, leaving only when I sat outside to guard it. Only threat of severe punishment from Dillon kept them from trying over and over again, or encouraging new ones to join in.

With Nightfire standing guard, I left the School of Officers and Gentleman, a letter in hand. I needed help and a full moon was tomorrow night. Following the directions, I slid my way through the crowds at Caspane until I found the glassblower's shop. I stepped inside, reveling in the warmth, and a man stepped through the back door, his eyes piercing. I only vaguely recognized him. He remembered me, however. "Lady Madara."

Raz had told me the questions to ask to confirm who was an Eagle and who wasn't. "Did you have the honor to stand for your country in the last war?"

His eyes flickered once. "I did."

"Do you know Raz Greenclaw?"

"I do. Through Pentra. I had his back in the last war."

I gave the proper response. "And he had yours." I offered the pendant.

He offered his in return, showing a set of staffs crossed in an X. "The tattoo isn't appropriate for a lady." He tucked his pendant away. "What can I do for you?"

I stared at the Eagle feather, then I tucked it in the letter and held it out. "I need you to find Raz," I said softly. "Tell him Kaylyn needs him."

ABOUT THE AUTHOR

Kristin Stecklein is an Oklahoma music teacher. She spends most of her free time writing or reading. She loves traveling and lives with her cats who are an almost constant source of amusement. She likes working on musical and literary works with her friend and fellow novelist/composer, Angela. Kristin graduated from East Central University with a Bachelor's in Music Education, but took creative writing classes for fun from East Central University and Oklahoma State University. She enjoys fantasy fiction, science fiction, hero-princess-dragon-magic fiction, and fairy tales. She also likes action movies, Disney movies, and singing along with any and every song she knows.

58811699R00249

Made in the USA
Charleston, SC
19 July 2016